SOLANGE

Solange

A Novel of Terror

Rodric Edward Cascio

Sense of Wonder Press
JAMES A. ROCK & COMPANY, PUBLISHERS
FLORENCE • SOUTH CAROLINA

Solange by Rodric Edward Cascio

SENSE OF WONDER PRESS
is an imprint of JAMES A. ROCK & CO., PUBLISHERS

Address comments and inquiries to:
SENSE OF WONDER PRESS
James A. Rock & Company, Publishers
900 South Irby Street, #508
Florence, SC 29501
E-mail:
jrock@rockpublishing.com   lrock@rockpublishing.com

Internet URL: www.rockpublishing.com

ISBN-13/EAN: 978-1-59663-678-1

Library of Congress Control Number: 2008925534

Printed in the United States of America

First Edition: 2010

This book is

dedicated to

my wife

Sue Ellen

Acknowledgments

This novel was definitely a collaborative effort. First, and foremost, I'd like to thank my wife for endless hours of proofreading and meticulous attention to detail. Secondly, I am forever grateful to my teacher and writing mentor, Donna Underwood. Extensive line-by-line editing and a thick coat of polish to an otherwise rough manuscript helped launch this project. In addition, I offer sincere, undying gratitude to my parents for their emphasis on education, work ethic, and perserverance. Finally, thank you, God, for the gift of words. I hope that this publication is my gift to you.

CHAPTER ONE

Sunday, March 20, 1932
I remember the crash

Herein lies my first journal entry. I've never written one before, as I'm not much of a writer by trade. My fiancé seems to think keeping a journal could be therapeutic for me. At this point, I'm willing to try almost anything. I guess the key word is almost. I'm rather afraid to put this story into words, because many who'll read it will think I'm a lunatic. I'm not crazy, although the fact remains that I cannot logically explain what has happened to me. I cannot even pinpoint when the delusions began, but I do remember that gradually, bits and pieces of a life with which I was totally unfamiliar began to infect my conscious mind. I've experienced cravings, longings and even affections totally foreign to my persona.

The best way I can describe all of this is to have one imagine a puzzle, whose pieces gradually come together to form an image. The image is foreign, and yet is a place that offers a lifetime of memories and life experiences. Figure that one out. One has never been there but has lived there his entire life. To be more accurate, one has never been there, but has lived there someone else's entire life.

Robert dropped the pen onto the desk and arose from it. "I can't do this."

With embroidery ring in hand, Ruby was sitting across the room on the sofa. "You haven't given it a fair try. Let me see what you've written."

"Come look."

As she arose and walked over to the desk, he reached for the notebook.

"You've written only two paragraphs."

"I told you that I cannot do this."

"Yes you can. You just have to put forth a little better effort. Maybe give yourself some time to think."

"You don't get it do you? Everyone will think I'm insane."

"Who's everyone? This is your own personal journal. No one else will read it."

"Well … you'll read it."

"I don't think you're insane …" Her voice trailed away as she said this. Rubbing her head in contemplation of what to say next, she took a few steps toward the center of the room.

"This is not a diary or a true confession, Robert. This is strictly a written chronology of events. It's a map that might give you some direction as to where all of this came from. Does that make any sense?"

"Yeah, it makes plenty of sense."

"You have to have some order if you're ever to get a clear picture of why this is happening to you."

"And then what, Ruby? We give this to the doc to analyze? We let a real professional confirm I'm a nut case? I don't need that. I know I have problems. I don't need this discussed with anyone else right now."

"Oh God …" Visibly trying to conceal her agitation, Ruby swallowed hard. "Did you just hear me a moment ago or was I wasting my breath? No one said anything about discussion, Robert. I'm just trying to help you. There is no way I can do that if you won't at least meet me halfway."

He looked at her and said nothing.

She held the pen out to him once again. "Try this. Sit down and write the details exactly as you've told me. Put into words why you feel that you've lived before in another lifetime."

"You weren't listening."

Ruby took a deep, ragged breath. "You're doing this on purpose. You are determined to turn this into a fight."

"I'm just saying that what I was referring to has not happened yet."

"In a manner of speaking, but you have memories, Robert. You have life experiences that are past."

"You know exactly what I meant by that. You're just dancing around the meaning of words, Rube."

That was it. There was no more patience. The understanding demeanor had evaporated. "All right, then, you figure out what to do. You sort out how we're supposed to deal with the fact that six days before our wedding, my future husband decides that he's been reincarnated, or so you're sure that I'm listening to you, going to be reincarnated. I'm all out of ideas. Maybe ask someone in your future life what you should do."

"That was mean as hell, Ruby."

"Well, I've had it, Robert! You're not the only one who needs answers. You must write this journal for both of us."

Releasing a long exaggerated sigh, he contemplated a return to the desk. Finally, he did so, taking pen in hand and beginning to write furiously.

The first memory I have is that of an automobile accident. Like no other automobile I've seen, a time machine or futuristic caricature would be the only modality of providing a means of accurate description of the vehicle. There was a crash. I was driving and looked down for only a moment. When my eyes returned to the road, a vehicle was in front of me at complete rest. There was no way I could avoid the collision.

Robert reread this paragraph as he dipped his pen into the well.

I remember being extremely fatigued. Looking back now, maybe that's why my reflexes were not what they should have been. Maybe that's why I was not able to stop in time.

He looked up from the journal once again. "How do I describe a fatal accident?"

"You know, I think I'll put the water on to boil. Maybe if I'm not in the room, you won't be so distracted. I'll bring you a cup of coffee when it's ready."

His eyes followed her as she left the room. "A little snack wouldn't hurt either. Sugar cookies taste pretty good with a fresh cup of strong coffee …"

The sound of the crash was deafening and the impact was horrible. It felt as if someone had taken a sledgehammer to my chest. The last thing I remember was seeing a crowd of people running toward my automobile. I looked up and thought, 'good, they'll help me out of here.' I blacked out after that.

The black that enveloped me was thick and oppressive. It wasn't normal darkness. I could see nothing and felt suffocated. As if I were suspended in a hopeless void or wasteland that stretched forever, this feeling of total black immersion brought about panic. I was all alone and terrified. Suddenly, much like someone flipping a switch, I opened my eyes and found myself in a Catholic church. Somehow, I knew the place. I was relieved to be in familiar surroundings, and yet, I knew that none of this was good. Perhaps I was relieved to be delivered from that horrible blackness, but in the back of my mind, I knew this church did not bring safety and comfort. I looked around and saw people that I hadn't seen in years. Dreamlike, the atmosphere was blurry, as if a haze of some sort had settled into the room. Something was missing, however; something did not quite make sense. It was then I realized that all of these people around me had passed on. They were dead. My heart began to race as I thought to myself, 'this is it … I'm deceased. This is the afterlife and these people are here to greet me.'

After this, memories of the experience degrade to bits and pieces. A shard of remembrance will come to me from time to time, but with no context or meaning, it only adds to my confusion.

He soon noticed the aroma of fresh coffee had begun to waft into the room. Robert looked up from his journal. "Why don't you come read this for me? Tell me what you think?"

With coffee-cup in hand, Ruby walked into the living room. Setting it down beside him, she began to read. After a bit she finally said, "How would you like me to answer this? What do you want me to say?"

"Well, Ruby, how about something like 'you understand' or 'that it makes no sense at all.' You know, an honest opinion here?"

"Oh, I understand perfectly. Apparently, from what you've written, in some other lifetime you were killed in an automobile accident."

He smiled after she said this. It wasn't a true smile, but one of bittersweet recollection.

"What do you think people around here will say when they hear I'm going to be reincarnated?"

"What people? And stop smiling, Robert. This is serious. We have some alarming issues here and I'm frightened. Outwardly I may act calm, but I am terrified."

"Too scared to hear anything else?"

"Oh God … There's more?"

"There's a little bit more. That Catholic church I referred to burned many years ago. Somewhere, in the back of my mind, I knew that it no longer existed. Clinging to every detail, I looked around that church and began to cry. Laden with an overwhelming sense of emptiness and loss, my heart felt heavy. Even though I was there, I knew it wasn't reality. How's that for crazy?"

Ruby breathed deeply and exhaled. "Well, for starters, no church around here has ever burned that I can remember. The Catholic church is still standing, Robert. We can ride over there if you like. Perhaps it will put your mind at ease."

"Perhaps it would put my mind at ease." He walked over to the window. "Damn, look at the wind. I think a storm is brewing."

Disrupting an eerie stillness that had settled into the atmosphere, the wind had begun to gust. Much like mini cyclones making their way across the brown grass, dry leaves were swept into a spiral, circular pattern. The air was heavy and thick. So moisture laden, it was almost hard to breathe.

"It's looking pretty rough out there, so maybe you should go ahead and leave. If you wait much longer, you may be spending the night here."

"In that case, I probably wouldn't get much sleep, either."

"Oh yes, that's exactly what I need now … Jed and Lorna finding us in bed together six days before we're to be married. I don't think so." She walked over to the door.

"Go home, Robert. Try to rest. We'll talk more about all of this tomorrow."

"It's a hell of a way to start a wedding, huh Rube?" He gave her a half smile after he'd said this.

"This is not the start of anything …"

"Oh, but it is." Robert then turned his attention toward the front stairway. As he began his descent, a gust of wind enveloped him. He grabbed his coat and held it closed as it passed. He then turned back toward her. "And I don't see any good coming out of it."

"Don't make your mind up too soon. You've already lost if you decide there is no good ahead of us."

"That's not what I said …"

She interrupted him. "No need to explain, I know what you meant. Now go on home, and we'll talk in the morning." Saying nothing else, Ruby shut the door behind him. Large rain droplets began to pelt the window in front of her as she watched him make his way to the car. *This is not the way anything is going to start.* She closed the drapes and left the living room. *I'll make sure of it.* Turning off the light, she made her way to the back of the house.

CHAPTER TWO

She was beautiful. Her skin was palest pink and smooth as a fine, soft silk. A wisp of blonde hair at the crown of her head shone so white it was luminous.

"Angel hair," he muttered. Brad looked at his wife and smiled. "The true embodiment of a miracle."

She returned the smile. "She is truly a miracle. Do you think her eyes will stay blue?"

"I think so."

She straightened herself in bed. She winced as she did this. There had been twenty-two hours of labor followed by a Caesarian section. "Oh God that hurts ..." The baby stirred a little but did not awaken.

"Here, let me help you with those pillows." In an effort to make her more comfortable, he patted and fluffed an army of down pillows. Looking about the room, he then exhaled a bit. Even the birthing process had become competitive. This 'suite' was decorated with expensive furnishings and wallpapers. Her hospital bed shared the room with an elaborately carved four-poster one, while coordinated bedding and throw pillows managed to complete the designer birthing room concept. "What the hell happened to stainless steel tables and a good slap on the butt?"

Jennifer turned to look at him as he said this. "What?"

"Who needs a hospital hotel room and soft music to have a baby? Whatever happened to the days of a doctor, rubber gloves and some hot water?"

"You're delirious. Maybe I'd better call my mother to stay with me tonight."

He laughed a little. "I am delirious."

"Then go home and rest. You can take some of these flowers with you."

"You know, I didn't know we had so many friends. I don't think I've ever seen this many flowers in one room. I feel more like a florist than a new dad."

"You know what else?"

"What?"

"I honestly didn't think you'd take to fatherhood so quickly."

"It's just a natural instinct, Jen. You don't miss what you never had. This little bugger has changed my life."

Jennifer smiled. "In a good way, she was a long time getting here …"

She paused for a moment as she said this. "We used to think we knew everything and planned with such meticulous detail. I remember pouring over fabric swatches and quarts of paint. I needed Ellen Colby shoes for my cocktail dress and a change of diamond in my engagement ring every birthday."

"Seems silly now …"

"We know nothing, Brad. This baby proves we have an insurmountable task ahead of us. All that crap—designer shoes and expensive watches—are meaningless now. How could we have been so naive?"

"Maybe ignorant is a better word. We just didn't know any better. This baby brings closure to a longing none of that stuff would ever satisfy. For some reason wisdom and youth cannot occupy the same existence. There's just no room for both."

"That isn't true for everyone. I believe there are old souls, and I've known people far wiser than their years."

"We'll do the best we can. We'll muddle through this parenting just like everyone else does. It will enrich our lives and our mistakes can guide us somewhat."

"That's what my parents have always said, but I never listened."

"Neither did I …" He looked away for a moment toward the hospital window. Breathing in deeply, he exhaled. "And so it begins again with Caroline." He began at that moment to cry. Emotions embraced a full, deep hurt, so raw it became almost unbearable. The noise was horrible. So abrasive, it was relentless and unforgiving.

As it should have, the rich, warm atmosphere receded. His subconscious then retreated to the submissive place intended for a lucid existence. Slowly, he opened his eyes and acclimated himself to his surroundings. Contemplating a fall, the alarm clock danced furiously about the edge of the nightstand. The time was half past six, and he'd had the dream again. Nighttime was fast becoming a dreaded event instead of a respite.

Robert reached over and pushed the *alarm off* button. "Damn," was all he said as he headed for the kitchen to start coffee. After he'd done so, he sat at the breakfast table and watched the rain fall beyond his window. *I'm on the other side of the looking glass … Where's Alice when you need her?*

CHAPTER THREE

Monday, March 21, 1932

A single day exists in history that forever marred the lives of an entire nation. The memory of this day still brings a shudder to those involved in the world of investments. Historically, October 24, 1929 is often referred to as "Black Thursday." Black Thursday unceremoniously precipitated a jagged, trenchant demise of the Roaring Twenties. Thousands of investors—many of them ordinary, working class folks—were financially ruined.

By the close of 1929, stock values had dropped as much as fifteen billion dollars. Many of the banks, which had speculated heavily with their deposits, failed as a result of the falling stock prices. Failed businesses, factories, banks and investors all contributed to the downward spiral that would signal the onslaught of the Great Depression.

Conway, much like the rest of the nation, was caught in the throes of this depression. Necessities were in short supply, while luxury items such as gowns, jewelry and couture accompaniments were virtually non-existent in the working-class family. Wedding dresses generally fell into the "opulence" category. Meticulously altered to suit current trends in fashion and style, bridal gowns were often inherited or passed down through generations.

As luck would have it, Ruby's mother—Lorna Carraway—had taken great pains to preserve her gown as well. She hoped that one day her daughter might have use of the dress for her own wedding ceremony. Although the years had softened its color from true white to creamy candlelight beige, the dress was lovely, nevertheless.

Ruby twirled a bit as she studied her reflection in the tri-fold mirror surrounding her. She smoothed the bodice as the seamstress straightened the train of the dress. Edna Barton was an excellent modiste; with no lack of self-confidence, she was also the self-appointed authority on wedding gown alterations throughout Faulkner County.

"Miss Edna, do you think it's still a bit full in the waist?"

"No, hon, I think it's fine. If we alter it anymore, it'll look scant. Besides, you want it a little full. That way, when you reach my age, it'll still fit. " Edna straightened the train again and began altering the skirt of the dress to the proper length. "This really is a beautiful gown … You don't see workmanship like this anymore. The detail in the veil alone would take a year to finish."

Ruby sighed. "Maybe we should just elope."

As Ruby said this, Edna refocused her concentration from the bodice of the dress upward.

"Elope? Don't be ridiculous. You're getting married Saturday."

"I think the stress of all of this is getting to everyone."

"Something troubling you, honey?"

"Well, as a matter of fact, something is troubling me. I had a conversation with Robert last night that was bizarre to say the least."

"About what?"

Ruby started to recant the story but then paused, her voice trailing to a mere whisper. "Oh, Edna, it's too complicated. We'll be here all night if I try to recall all that's transpired. If you don't mind, I'd like to see how the veil hangs down the back of the dress."

She turned around. "Could you rearrange the train one more time for me?"

"Sure, honey, give me just a moment to smooth it out."

After they'd straightened the dress once again, Edna presented her with a hand-held mirror. "Use this to see the back of the dress."

"It looks lovely. It's just what I'd envisioned."

"I'm so glad."

"If you don't mind, there is one thing I'd like to ask you."

"What's that?"

"Do men usually act a little strange before they get married?"

Edna laughed. "Not only before they get married but throughout their whole existence, Ruby. Their saving grace is that they're so very predictable. Men aren't that hard to figure out. A little pat on the head and a big, hot supper usually takes care of most dilemmas. Why on earth do you ask?"

"I'm asking because Robert has been acting peculiar lately. He's been saying odd things and remembering events that never happened."

Edna's look changed to one of concern and bewilderment. "Oh, honey … How long has this been going on?"

"About three days as well as I can remember. The change was sudden, almost from one day to the next. He sat me down and presented this long scenario of events and happenings he was convinced he'd experienced."

"What did you say?"

"I asked him not to tell anyone about it and that we'd work it out together."

Edna smiled. "Then why are you telling me all of this, Ruby? I think you already have the right idea."

"I don't know … I just had to talk to someone. It's overwhelming, Edna. I don't know what to say or do anymore."

She had turned and was facing the mirror once again. Affectionately, Edna put a hand on each of Ruby's shoulders as she looked at their reflections in the mirror. "Honey, let me remind you of something: this is a big step in life and everyone reacts differently. We'll get all of this 'fuss and bother' behind you two and things will settle down. Old Edna's seen many a nervous bride and groom in her day, so trust me. It'll be just fine."

"I hope you're right."

"I know I'm right." Edna knelt behind her as she said this. Beginning to hem the dress again, she seemed to be concentrating intently with a mouthful of straight pins protruding from her lips. "There … that looks pretty good. I think we're through. Off to change and put a smile on that face. Can't have a bride-to-be moping about."

CHAPTER FOUR

He didn't really know what drew him to St. Joseph's Church. Maybe it was the fact there was a Catholic church in his dream or maybe it was Ruby's suggestion to drive by there. She was right, though. It hadn't burned. Everything was intact.

St. Joseph's was an unassuming structure. Simple in architecture, tasteful landscaping surrounded the perimeter of the building. The parking lot in front of the church was gravel and extended toward the right of the sanctuary. Accommodating only a couple dozen cars, the lot was relatively small. It was adequate, however, and managed to well serve the church population.

Robert approached the front doors of the building and discovered the church was unlocked. As he stepped inside, he saw two rows of pews leading to the front of the sanctuary. Beyond the pews was a cushioned step-up. Separating an altar from the rest of the church, a wrought iron railing stood in front of this cushion. On the right, situated about ten feet past the railing, was a confessional. Three doorways concealed by curtains were built into the structure. A man was apparently sitting in the sequestered center section.

Robert walked up to the structure, drew the curtain to one side, and stepped into it. Making sure no one saw him, he closed the confessional drape and knelt on a small, rectangular wooden bench. As he knelt down, a light appeared beneath a window of frosted glass. The window immediately slid open to reveal an opaque screen, and a disembodied voice began to pray.

"How long has it been since your last confession?"

"About sixty-seven years."

The priest changed positions in the confessional, as the comment had obviously startled him. He put his face near the window and whispered, "Son, this is no place for jokes. The sacrament of absolution is to be taken seriously."

"I didn't mean to sound sacrilegious, Sir. I just hoped that maybe …" Robert didn't finish the sentence. "I don't know what I had hoped … I'm sorry to bother you." He stood and turned to leave.

Realizing that this was someone who may be in need of counseling instead of confession, Father Donovan stepped from the confessional and drew back the curtain behind which Robert was standing. He smiled. "It's four forty-five now. I should be through here in about fifteen minutes. If you like, maybe we could talk in my office."

Robert thought for a moment and replied, "If you have time, I could really use some help."

"It's the room at the end of the hall. Make yourself comfortable. I'm Father Donovan, by the way, the pastor here at St. Joseph's."

Robert smiled. "Robert Davis, Father. It's nice to meet you."

"Are you from around here? I don't believe I've seen you at Mass."

"I'm from Conway. My father is Ned Davis, and our family owns Davis Hardware Store. We're members of New Light Baptist Church."

"Ah, Brother Lawson's congregation."

"You know him?"

"I know him well. We have dinner together occasionally and discuss various scriptural issues. We don't always agree but usually end up heading in the same direction. Although a bit opinionated, he's a knowledgeable fellow." Father Donovan laughed. "I tend to be that way a little myself."

Robert smiled again. "I guess we all are, Father."

"I'm glad to meet you, Robert. I'll see you in about ten minutes. I need to remain in the confessional until five."

"Sure, I'll be waiting for you in your office." As he made his way toward the end of the hallway, he wondered how he would present this scenario to Father Donovan. More than that, how would Father Donovan react? *If he can just help me make sense of this ...* He took a seat in the office and waited for the priest.

Arriving a few minutes after five o'clock, Father Donovan smiled as he entered the room. He made his way around the desk and sat in the chair behind it. Looking Robert squarely in the face, he began. "Usually in a counseling session, I begin by getting to know the person a little better. Why don't we start with your telling me about your family, children, and profession? That'll give me a better perspective of your situation when we discuss your problems."

"Well, let's see. As I've told you, we own a hardware store downtown. I'm not married yet, although I am engaged to be married this Saturday. Obviously, I have no kids and live by myself." Robert paused for a moment and began again. "So as for the perspective of my situation, that's about it. As for the situation itself, it's really hard to figure out where to begin." He returned Father Donovan's intensive stare. "Honestly, I can't even tell you why I'm here."

"Perhaps God sent you here."

Robert looked down at his hands in his lap. "Do you really think so? I hope he did. I hope you still feel that way when you hear my story."

"Well let's hear your story. Start from the beginning."

He let out a long sigh. "OK, I'll do that."

He began to unveil his story in detail. Father Donovan listened intently without judgment or apparent bias. He simply sat, took notes, and asked questions in an attempt to construct a litany of events.

Finally, after long contemplation, Father Donovan looked at him and began to speak. "There are many things in life we don't understand, Robert. Perhaps you're having these dreams, delusions or whatever as a result of some traumatic incident in your life. You know, the Bible is full of miracles that can't be explained away by man ... they're just miracles we have to accept on faith. Do you believe in God?"

"Yes, of course I do."

"Then delusion, miracle or however you'd care to label this phenomenon, consider it a test from God. Perhaps the Lord needs you here for some reason. Maybe your life is in jeopardy and you're in some kind of limbo. Maybe your consciousness has retreated to the past for shelter or comfort … I don't know. All I can tell you is to pray and ask the Almighty for guidance." Father looked down at his Bible and opened to the middle of it. Handing Robert two cards with prayers written on each of them, he then looked up again. After he'd done so, he reached into his pocket and removed a string of beads with a crucifix attached to it.

"Here, take this."

"What is that?"

"It's a rosary. Here is a card with instructions on how to use it in prayer." He pointed to the second card. "This is a prayer entitled Act of Contrition."

"Well, thank you. Do I owe you anything for these?"

"No, no … of course not. However, I think it might be wise if we meet again soon."

"I'd like that." Robert stared at the beads and prayer cards for a moment. His face became scarlet as he suddenly arose. "Oh, my God, you have no idea …" Pausing mid-sentence, he swallowed hard.

"No idea about what?"

"How it helps to have someone listen to you who doesn't think you're crazy or losing your grip on reality."

Father Donovan was nonplused. *Here was a volatile, vulnerable man in desperate need of consolation. What he said next could save him or push him over the edge.*

He took a deep breath and began again. "I'll pray for you, but you must feel free to call me at any time if you need me." He then made the sign of the cross in the air. "Go with Jesus, Robert, and God bless you."

Robert turned to leave and began making his way toward the door. He stopped just short of it.

"You know, Father, I appreciate all of the prayers and beads, but you do remember that I'm not Catholic, don't you? We don't say the rosary."

"I know that, but say the prayers anyway. They'll do you some good. After all, you came to confession and most Baptists don't do that, either."

Robert smiled. "I guess you're right … they really don't."

"Remember, I'm always here if you need someone to listen."

"Thank you, Father. That means a lot. " With that, Robert opened the office door and left.

CHAPTER FIVE

The First National Bank of Conway was located downtown. In the thick of Conway city commerce, the stately brick building stood proud. Ornate Corinthian columns adorned the front of the structure, and a tremendous square clock hung suspended from its left corner. Many employees of the bank had been there for years, and all knew the customers on a first name basis. First National of Conway was a well-oiled machine that not only provided excellent service but also safe monetary investments. The Great Depression had taken its toll on the bank, but astute personnel and a wealth of business savvy kept it afloat during the runs. Even though there were some close moments, the bank remained sound and continued to grow.

Ralph Perkins was the bank manager. Known about town for silly antics and contagious laughter, he usually found himself much funnier than others seemed to. He was highly respected in the community, however, and known to be an honest banker.

As Ruby entered through the front doors of the bank, Ralph was standing near the tellers' station. "Well, Miss Ruby Carraway, what brings the bride-to-be to my establishment this fine morning?"

"Good Morning, Mr. Perkins. How are you?"

"Fine, fine, Ruby. What can I do for you?"

"I'm looking for a wedding gift for my fiancé."

"Here in the bank, Ruby? I guess cash is as good a present as any." Ralph then broke into a legendary fit of inappropriate laughter.

Nonplused, Ruby smiled. Given the circumstances before her, she really didn't know what else to do. When he finally managed to compose himself, she seized the opportunity to begin. "I'd like a twenty-dollar gold piece, Mr. Perkins."

His expression changed to one of righteousness. Suddenly, by throwing a fist across the air, he was validating her decision to buy a wedding gift at the bank. "Well, you know, Miss Carraway, I stand corrected ... that would make a fellow a lovely wedding gift. We don't stock those at the bank, but if you'd like, I can ask around and maybe find a source for one. Why don't you check with me in a day or so, and we'll see what we can come up with?"

"It'll have to be a day or so, Mr. Perkins. I'm getting married Saturday."

"I'll have my secretary get on the telephone right away. It shouldn't be too hard to find one. It's the least I can do for a couple of fine 'soon to be newlyweds' like you and Robert. We'll find him a nice piece."

"Thanks so much, Mr. Perkins."

"Oh by all means. Who knows? Maybe you're beginning a trend ... we'll start registering brides here!" Another avalanche ... face red, stomach shaking ...

"Oh God ..."

In an attempt to contain himself, he removed a handkerchief from his coat pocket and wiped his eyes.

Seeing this second outburst was coming to a close, she decided to make a break for the exit. A forced smile and wave good-bye brought a sigh of relief as the bank doors slammed shut behind her. She shook her head in exasperation. "Maybe I should have gotten him some new leather gloves ..."

* * *

Judging her mother's reaction to her wedding gift decision, leather gloves may not have been a bad idea. A tall woman with pale, smooth skin, Lorna Carraway was considered attractive by most that knew her. Resourceful in nature, Lorna wasted nothing. Hard work and frugal living were essential if one were to survive the Great Depression. As a rule, she and Jed were not preoccupied with frivolous matters, and this would explain her lackluster enthusiasm when Ruby presented her idea for Robert's wedding gift.

"A twenty-dollar gold-piece? Where on earth did you get that kind of money? Twenty dollars, Ruby? Did you have to be so extravagant?"

"I've been saving money from each paycheck for over a year and a half. I really wanted to get him something special that he could keep forever. It is legal tender, Momma ... If we ever get in a bind, we could always spend it."

"I ... I guess I see some logic in that. It is money and you really haven't spent it yet."

"And there is some romance attached to this gift as well. To me something gold signifies being pure of heart. It's corny I know, but sometimes corny is appropriate."

"Well, honey, I won't argue with you about it. One thing you may want to remember is we're in the middle of an economic depression. It wouldn't hurt to use that money for a little nest egg."

"It'll be fine, Momma ... I promise. Don't worry."

"I'll always worry I'm your mother. Now, that being said, I think I'm off to the garden for a bit. I'll see you in a while."

"I love you." She said nothing else as her mother made her way outside.

Maybe I'll save enough money to get you one as well, Momma. You deserve something special, too.

CHAPTER SIX

Wednesday, March 23, 1932

Robert walked outside onto the porch to enjoy the quiet perfection of morning time in spring. The air was cool, but the sun was shining with no trace of cloud to mar its brilliance.

He decided to take a seat and watch the bustle of people going about their business. Since he worked most Saturdays at the store, he usually took a day off in the middle of the week. Neighbors, cars, and the occasional carriage passed in front of him as he sat there; his train of thought was broken by the realization he was becoming rather hungry. *Time to take a walk toward the Carraway place ...* Ruby hadn't called this morning, so he had no idea if she was home or not. Getting breakfast wouldn't be much of a chore, though, as the Carraways were accustomed to his lurking about the kitchen around mealtime.

Up from the porch and on his way, he hadn't noticed much happening around him during the stroll. Hunger has a way of livening the pace and commandeering the mind, especially when the hunger emanates from a man who happens to be young as well as single. The Carraways lived on Ash Street, only a few blocks from his house. He was nearing there when he felt the hair on the back of his neck begin to bristle. *Strange feeling*, he thought to himself. He had no chance to react further, for only bits and pieces of an event, which would alter his existence forever, remained with him.

The pain began in his chest. Searing its way to the backbone, a tremendous explosion seemed to rend a sharp, ragged trench through the center of his body. His knees buckled as he convulsed and fell to the ground. A second wave engulfed him before there was any chance of recovery. Every neural synapse was activated after which every skeletal fiber contracted. Flailing in agony for what seemed eternity, Robert was left helpless. The sky was now a myriad of colors; with his body now wrenched into the fetal position, consciousness began to drift away.

As he approached, Ruby stood in front of the kitchen window slicing vegetables. Her smile turned to an expression of horror as she saw him fall to the street.

"Oh my God!" was all she could utter in those first given moments. Frozen with fear, the colander slipped from her hands and fell to the floor. Vegetables spilled everywhere. "Momma!" She screamed. "Please don't let him be dead! Please, dear God ..."

She ran out of the kitchen and raced across the yard toward him. Lorna followed closely behind. Making her way quickly to his side, she cradled his face in her hands to see if he was conscious. He was breathing. She watched his chest rise and fall several times to reassure herself of this fact. Gently, she stroked his face in an attempt to stimulate a response.

"Please wake up. You cannot die on me like this!"

Robert could hear her voice. He tried to respond but could not. His mind had created the image of a long, dark tunnel, and he seemed to be standing before the edge of it. He could hear a beckoning voice at the far end of the tunnel, but could not discern the face of the person calling him. A woman—someone he knew—was urging him to traverse the narrow, dim corridor. As he started to do so, his conscious awareness initiated a return. The tunnel then dissipated and his vision began to clear. A bit blurry at first, Ruby's face came to view.

Pacing behind her daughter, Lorna Carraway anxiously wrenched her apron in her hands. In an attempt to give Ruby time to assess the situation, she remained quiet as long as she could. She could stand the suspense no longer. "Is he all right? Is he alive?"

Ruby looked upward. "He's alive, Momma, but I have no idea what has happened. I'll need a cool rag for his head. He's beginning to stir."

"I'll … I'll get it. I'll be right back …" Hurrying toward the house for the rag, she left them.

As she watched the silhouette disappear, Ruby thought to herself, *Mother could never handle a crisis.* Her attention then focused back to Robert. *What on earth could have caused this? This has to be more than pre-wedding jitters.*

Lost in thought, she wasn't aware that her mother was again approaching.

"Here you go, hon. This should help. I had some good, cool water in the icebox."

"Thank you, Momma." Still stroking his face, she draped the rag across his forehead. Upon doing so, he began to stir.

"Welcome back," she whispered. "We thought we might have lost you."

Robert opened his eyes to blinding sunlight beaming its way into them. "Damn. What happened?"

"I was about to ask you the same question."

Looking bewildered, he sat up. "I don't know, Rube. I think I was struck by lightning. I felt an electric shock burn its way through every inch of my body."

"It wasn't lightning, darling … there's not a cloud in the sky. You fainted. You must have had some sort of seizure."

"That was no seizure. Something just shocked the hell out of me and damned near killed me."

"Look around you, Robert. There are no clouds, and the weather is beautiful. Why don't we wait awhile and let you recover somewhat before we decide what has happened to you. You've experienced a lot of peculiar happenings here of late."

"You know, I really don't appreciate your condescending attitude …"

"Wait a minute. Condescending what?"

"I'm not hallucinating, Ruby, imagining electrical storms and such."

"I didn't say you were. You took that totally wrong." She took a deep breath and exhaled. "Look, you've been under a great deal of stress lately and …"

"It was lightning, goddammit!"

Lorna Carraway wheeled about in amazement. "What did you just say?"

"You heard me."

"Yes, I heard you alright. I was hoping I was wrong. Before you get any further into this family, young man, there is a lesson you very much need to learn."

Her mouth was open and her finger pointed at Robert.

"You seem to think that you can act any way you please around us, but I assure you that is not the case. I did not appreciate the way you talked to my daughter a moment ago and want to make it clear that we are not the favored recipients of your temper tantrums. The Davises may have to put up with that behavior, but the Carraways do not. Above all, understand that you will not take the Lord's name in vain in front of me ever again. If you do, I will wash my hands of you for good. Be certain that you understand that. I don't care if you did pass out."

As she said this, Robert managed to stand. Dusting himself off, he readied himself to return fire.

Ruby saw the situation rapidly getting out of hand. "I need a minute alone here, Momma."

Lorna's gaze did not falter.

Gently, she placed her hand on Lorna's shoulder. "Please."

Lorna's voice was quiet and deliberate. "I'll be in the kitchen if you need anything else. I suggest you straighten this out, Ruby, or rest assured, I will."

With that, she left.

Taking a deep breath, Ruby brushed her hair from her face.

"Well done, my darling. You have totally offended my mother."

"Well, how would you feel, Ruby? I was struck and rendered unconscious by God only knows what. I awaken on the ground—in your front yard, nonetheless—only to be reassured by the two of you that nothing happened. It was all a figment of my imagination."

"We never said you imagined anything, Robert. " She felt the tears begin to rise. "You were not struck. You fainted. I saw what happened and so did my mother."

She took her handkerchief from her pocket and wiped her eyes. She hated herself for crying at that moment. "Come inside and lie down. I'm calling Dr. Belton to see if he can make a house call. Maybe among the three of us, we can make some sense of this ordeal."

"I think I'd rather lie down at home." Looking shaken and unsteady, he attempted to walk around a bit. "Will you bring me some lunch?"

"Lunch? You want lunch? How can you think of food at a time like this?"

"It's the main reason I came over here in the first place …"

She ignored the lack of tact, which accompanied the comment. "You'd better come inside. We need to make sure that you're alright and not going to have another attack."

"I'm alright … I'm just a little shaky, that's all."

"I don't think it's a good idea for you to be alone right now."

"I said I'm fine."

"Dad can drive you home, and I'll bring some lunch around in a bit. In the meantime, lie down and rest." Her expression changed. "When you feel better, you may apologize to my mother."

The unflinching gaze left no doubt that she meant business. "Looks like I don't have any choice on that one. I'll make amends this evening … but she sure got every bit of her say in. I didn't get a chance to defend myself at all."

Ruby interrupted. "Just make this right, Robert."

"I said I would do it."

She hesitated once again. "Are you sure that …"

"I'm leaving now. Don't bother your dad; I don't need a ride."

She exhaled in defeat. "As you wish …" Still wiping her eyes, she turned and made her way back to the kitchen to help with the noon meal. Lorna was standing at the sink washing vegetables once again.

"Well, where's Robert? Is he all right?"

"I don't know." She returned her gaze to the window. Looking across the yard where he'd fallen, she simply repeated, "I really don't know."

CHAPTER SEVEN

Still feeling guilty for his outburst, Robert attempted cordiality. "Evening, Lorna, and Jed, how are you tonight?"

"Hi, honey." Crossing the room, Ruby lightly planted a kiss on his cheek. "Feeling better?"

"Much. I think I was just shaken up. Probably why I was so irritable."

A poor guise for an apology ... "What did Dr. Belton have to offer?"

"Not much, actually, he just examined me, then hummed and grunted a bit. He scheduled me another appointment in a week."

"Did he give you any medicine?"

"No, he drew some blood and said to come see him if it happened again. He thought it might be tension from the wedding activities and everything."

Lorna interrupted, "Ruby and I have cooked all afternoon. Dinner will be served shortly. Ruby, if you'll please help me put the food on the table, and Robert, make yourself comfortable in the living room. We'll call when we're ready."

"Sounds like a plan to me." Robert deposited himself on the sofa. The incident today had left him tired and listless, so taking a load off felt pretty good right now. *Lorna's never shoveled me off to the living room before dinner. This must be a little scheme to get Jed and me alone together. God, I'm not in the mood for any of his bullshit tonight* ... He realized his eyelids had begun to grow heavy. *I need to rest for a moment ...*

"Ready for Saturday night, boy?"

The comment startled him. His thoughts quickly returned to the present. "More than ready, Sir, wish it was already said and done. I almost wish this was a family only ceremony."

"Know what you mean. I hate weddings too, putting on the monkey suit and all ..."

"It's not just that. It's all of the added stress that goes along with it ... the extra financial expense, the cooking and cleaning ... all for just an hour or two."

"Son, what you're saying is true, but realize that in hard times like these, folks also got to have something to look forward to. They need a reason to celebrate and socialize. They need a reason to lift their spirits. It's not like when you lived at the turn of the century as a rich dentist. Things are more difficult here."

Robert shook his head in disbelief. "What did you just say?"

"Times are going to be good ... Prosperous. This market crash will be no more than a historical event."

Jed's words began to echo. *I'm losing my mind ...* He felt the fine line between reality and insanity distorting much the same way salt is poured from a shaker.

"Darling?" Ruby gently patted his shoulder. "You dozed off. Dinner's ready and smells wonderful, I might add."

In a daze from being awakened, his mind took a moment to clear. Attempting to get his bearings, he looked about the room. He saw that Jed was also dozing in the chair adjacent to the couch.

"Damn," was all he said as he managed to stand. He then yawned and wiped the back of his hand across his mouth.

"Rube?"

"Yes?"

"I need you to call Father Donovan for me."

A look of concern washed across her face. "It's a bit late, don't you think?"

"He said anytime."

"Alright, I'll call him, but in the mean time, you go ahead and eat. I think you'll feel better after you've had some food."

If that were only true, he thought to himself. *Food wasn't going to make anything any better. In fact, dinner or no dinner, things were soon going to be a whole lot worse.*

CHAPTER EIGHT

Thursday, March 24, 1932

New Light Baptist church was a relatively small structure. Fashioned in typical Southern Baptist style, a lovely heptagonal steeple adorned the front gable. Painted white, the clapboard siding served as an ideal backdrop for the four gothic stained-glass windows built into the side walls of the church.

The New Light congregation was abuzz about proper church decorum for the Carraway wedding this weekend. Early in the spring season, not much was available in the way of fresh flowers.

Some neighbors had blooming quince and daffodils, but most of the tulips were already spent. Those who had the later blooming tulip varieties promised to snip them and bring them to the church just before the ceremony.

Enter Hilda Bergoine, the Events Committee chair. Hilda strongly objected to this outpouring of tulip generosity, for in order to use them, the stem of each flower had to be stuffed with wet cotton. Boisterously announcing that tulips are nothing more than weeds and would be minimally utilized in the altar bouquets, the general consensus was that much greenery would have to be employed since Miss Carraway insisted on such an early spring wedding.

With hour by hour scheduling of fresh flower arrangements, all décor would look professional and fresh. Final flower placement would occur shortly before commencement of ceremonies, ensuring that even the most delicate of flowers would last throughout the entire event.

Amazed at all of the fuss, Ruby stood watching. She knew that none of these women were professionals, and most were not even familiar with the word décor, but she was keenly aware that all of the pomp and circumstance gave them a purpose and made them feel important. She laughed to herself. *Oh well, as long as it makes them feel important.*

"Ruby? Ruby!"

Her train of thought interrupted, Ruby realized her name had been called from the back of the church. She turned to discover Heloise Pullman waving furiously in her direction. An active member of New Light Baptist Church Ladies' Circle, Heloise also happened to be Hilda Bergoine's younger sister.

Making her way through the crowd toward her, Ruby smiled and returned the wave.

"Ruby, Mabel Agnew rang a call through for you a little while ago."

"From whom?"

"She put a call through from Dr. Belton. He asked that you ring him back, as he had something he'd like to discuss with you. Is everything all right?"

"Fine, Heloise, just fine. Instead of returning the call, I think I'll stop by his office on the way home."

"OK, dear, as you wish. We'll finish up here, so you can go ahead and leave. I think most of the details have been covered, but if there's anything else, I'll drop by Lorna's later."

"Thank you, thank you so much. Everything looks just beautiful."

"It's only because we love you."

Affectionately patting her back, Ruby embraced Heloise tightly. "And I love you too, Heloise Pullman. I don't know what I would do without you."

Heloise awkwardly returned the pat. A spinster by trade, she wasn't used to such generous displays of affection. "Well, we were glad to do it, darling. Now you hurry along and don't keep Dr. Belton waiting."

"Thank you all again." As she made her way toward the door, she took one last look at the church. *It's perfect . . .*

"Bye, dear."

Heloise, Hilda and the rest of the Ladies' Circle gave frozen smiles as she departed.

Hilda turned to Heloise and whispered from the corner of her mouth, "I wonder what that's all about. I never had to see the doctor right before I got married. So secretive, you know, and she has put on a bit of weight here lately ..."

"And that's not all, Hilda; I've heard her fiancé has gotten rather daft ... been seeing things and all."

"Such a pity ... Ruby seems to be such a sensible girl. Why would she get herself into such a mess?"

"I know, Hilda; it's a shame, isn't it?"

CHAPTER NINE

As Ruby opened the door to Dr. Belton's office, his receptionist greeted her with a pleasant smile.

"Hello, Miss Carraway, what can we do for you?"

"I need to see Dr. Belton."

"I don't think we have you scheduled today."

"You don't; he called earlier at the church and asked that I return his call. I thought I'd drop by and see him in person, instead."

"Oh dear, his schedule is full. Let me see if he can spare a few minutes."

The receptionist returned and gestured for Ruby to come to the back.

"Miss Carraway, the doctor will see you. This way, please."

Despite his often grouchy demeanor, Dr. Charles Allen Belton had a lovable quality about him. Short in stature, he was a heavy-set man. A thick shock of mostly brown hair sat in odd contrast against a ruddy complexion and white mustache.

"Hello," he growled as he entered the room.

"Thank you for seeing me on such short notice."

"Ruby, we need to talk about Robert."

"We do, Dr. Belton; I'm worried about him."

"I didn't find much clinically except for two circumscribed bruises on his chest. Very peculiar lesions, they almost looked like burns."

"Burns? Robert hasn't been burned that I know of. He swears lightning struck him yesterday, but I told him it was nonsense."

"It is nonsense. A massive shock like that would kill a fellow, and there's nothing I or anybody else could do for him. To be honest, I don't know what could have caused those circular burns. Your fiancé has no idea what happened, either. The whole damn thing is a mystery. We'll watch those lesions, and I told him to come see me if anything like this happened again."

"And what will you do then?"

"We'll cross that bridge when we come to it. In the meantime, try to keep that man of yours calm. His nerves seem a bit frazzled."

Ruby sighed. "That's easier said than done." She turned to leave. "Do I owe you anything?"

"I'll send you a bill. Better than that, tell Lorna I'm ready for one of her home cooked meals. That should square us up. Jed Carraway's the best-fed man in the county, and I want to share the wealth."

"Tell you what, I'll cook for you myself when we get moved."

"That'll work. You've got a deal. Have Mabel call me when dinner's ready."

Ruby smiled. "You just plan on bringing a big appetite next week ... you'll need it."

CHAPTER TEN

Robert walked onto the porch. Turning his face into the wind, he breathed in deeply. His lungs filled with balmy air. Hanging low and deep, the sky revealed an unusual blackness. Emanating a sense of doom, thick, oppressive fog had begun to blanket the atmosphere. There were no reassuring stars or hints of moonlight anywhere, just an electrically charged atmosphere of anticipation that usually signals an imminent storm.

His train of thought was interrupted when the phone rang. He turned and walked back into the house to answer it.

"Hello?"

"*Mr. Davis?*"

"Yes?"

"*I have a call for you from Father Donovan*"

"Thank you, Mabel, could you put it through?"

"*Certainly, have a nice evening.*"

"Robert, Father Donovan here. Your fiancée called the rectory last night, but unfortunately, I wasn't in town. She left a message with Mabel stating that you needed to reach me. She also said it was urgent."

"Thank God you called, Father."

"Yes, Robert, that's appropriate."

Robert was not sure that he appreciated the play on words. "Do you think we could meet tomorrow?"

"Of course we can. Is everything all right?"

"Everything is OK. I just had ..." Scratching his head, he paused for a moment. "Well, to be honest, I had a disturbing dream, Father."

"I see."

"It's ... It'll sound silly if I try to explain this over the phone. In order to put this into proper context, I need to discuss it in person. What time tomorrow?"

"Well, let's see. I have to make rounds at the hospital at noon, so I can see you either midmorning or early afternoon."

"How about I come to the rectory tomorrow afternoon around 3:30?"

"Perfect. I'll look forward to seeing you then."

"Until then. Take care, Father." Robert returned the phone to its cradle. He felt comforted. The mere fact he'd have an unbiased opinion allayed much of the anxiety these recent episodes had brought forth. At least now, there was an avenue of stability and reassurance.

As the storm intensified, the wind began blowing harder. Shortly thereafter, electricity was lost. Robert lit the gas lanterns in response. *Hmm, I guess there are a few advantages in owning an older home.* He lay down on the couch and turned on the gramophone. Wishing Ruby were here beside him, he closed his eyes and became lost in the melodic bliss of the love song.

His attention diverted by a flash of lightning, he turned toward the window. Violent electrical flashes illuminated the room. Claps of thunder then shook the old wooden house. The scene was much like that of a motion picture ... there was something exciting, almost sexual, about an electrical storm. Maybe it was the anticipation of a dangerous event.

As the rain began to fall, the smell of ozone infiltrated the room. He turned his head to the left and saw her.

"I knew you'd come."

"I've been searching for you everywhere," she replied.

"I wondered how you'd be able to find me. I've lain awake night after night wishing you would come."

As she removed her cloak, it slid softly from her shoulders to the floor. Robert's gaze met hers; the longing was mutual. Roughly unfastening her silken blouse, he pulled her to him. Grasping the back of her head, he kissed the soft lining of her lower lip. Thunder continued to rumble in the background. As if narrating the ominous, passionate arousal careening beyond any boundaries of self-control, there was nothing left but surrender to the sympathetic delirium.

Eyes closed as he undressed her, she threw her head back. Their naked bodies in full contact, she moaned as he slid on top of her. Lightly, she rubbed his back in a circular motion. She ached as she felt him making his way inside of her. Gently biting her shoulder as he entered her, Robert caressed her thighs. She arched her back in ecstasy and cried out as she brought her face next to his. He made love to her, thrusting again and again until he could hold back no more. Their bodies as well as their souls had become one. Releasing all his passion deep inside of her, he screamed as he came in a shudder of orgasmic rapture. His heart beating wildly, he lay on top of her, brushing the side of her face with his.

"Oh God, I love you! I love you so much!"

Breathing the scent of her perfume, he kissed her again. He then rolled off beside her. Wet with perspiration and lust, he embraced her tightly once more. As consciousness drifted away from them, it was soon replaced by a satisfied, peaceful sleep.

She kissed his sleeping face and whispered into his ear, "I love you, too. Please come back to me."

CHAPTER ELEVEN

Friday, March 25, 1932

Robert awoke to the morning news on the radio. He looked around and realized he was alone. Moving to the opposite side of the bed, he buried his face in the pillow. *No perfume … Damn these dreams! I can't tell what's real or imagined anymore.* He wiped his eyes and looked about the room. *I don't think I've ever had a dream that vivid.* Slowly, he slid out of bed and made his way toward the kitchen. *Did it happen?* Pausing for a moment, he scratched the bearded stubble on his neck. *Maybe … Hell, I can't tell anymore.* Walking into the kitchen, he put the kettle onto the stove. *I know I'm not describing this one in detail to the good Father.*

* * *

Ruby made her way into the First Bank of Conway. Greeting customers as they entered the establishment, Ralph Perkins was standing by the entrance. He smiled as she walked through the door, energetically waving that fist through the air once again.

"Good morning, Mr. Perkins."

"And the top of the morning to you, Ruby Carraway. I have your fiancé's wedding gift ready for you to pick up. It's a lovely one too, I might add. Come have a look."

"Did you have any trouble finding one?"

"Not much, Ruby, it's a 1907 Liberty twenty-dollar gold piece. Since it's not too old, we didn't have to pay extra for it. It's in mint condition, though. I think you'll like it."

He handed her a leather box.

Immediately, she opened it.

"Oh, it's perfect, Mr. Perkins, it's just perfect. This is exactly what I had in mind." *A wedding gift Robert can keep forever ...*

"One that'll keep its value, too," Mr. Perkins chuckled. "Sorry we don't have it wrapped." After this, of course came the laughter. Ruby knew it was only a matter of time before he broke down. Once again, there were no surprises.

"That's quite all right, Mr. Perkins." Gritting her teeth, she waited for the episode to pass. It finally did, at which time she quickly interjected, "I'll pay you and be on my way."

"I'll see you tomorrow, Ruby. Best of luck to you and Raymond."

"Robert."

"Him, too," was audible in between belly laughs.

Determined not to acknowledge old man Perkin's laughter, she made her way to the car. *Most assuredly, leather gloves next time ...*

On their wedding night, she would give him the gift. To hold off—even for that short time—would be agony. She would wait, though, at least a little longer. Already, the coin had forged a bond between them. It was tangible, and they'd always have the memories attached to it.

In hopes of retrieving her wedding dress, she decided to make her way toward Edna's. She stared long into the horizon that enveloped her. Breathtaking, a semi-circular arc of azure perfection radiated around the small town of Conway. The rage of a ferocious storm, pummeling the area with wind and rain, was difficult to imagine. Some fallen branches and the occasional puddle were the only telltale signs of its existence. *Everything is going to be beautiful. Tomorrow will be a most perfect day.*

* * *

Azaleas and wisteria, those were his favorites. Beautiful and precious, their brilliant colors seem to last but a moment. Signaling the demise of yet another spring season, this rich, vivid palate would soon disappear. Robert found himself staring at them, absorbing their beauty before the blooms were spent.

How bittersweet that spring's beauty is breathtaking, and yet so very short-lived. Then again, everything seems to be short-lived, lately. Much of the hurt, despair, and confusion appeared to be gone this morning. Tomorrow, he and Ruby would marry and put this turmoil behind them once and for all. To dwell on all of the confusion and mayhem would inevitably drive him crazy; today brought a feeling of closure and resolution.

"I'm here to stay. At least for now that's what I'll tell myself."

"What will you tell yourself?"

"Oh, Father Donovan … You startled me. I was coming to see you this afternoon."

"I'm out for a walk, Robert. Care to join me?"

"I'd like that. I'd like to talk as well, if you don't mind."

"Not a bit. Besides the fact you've managed to confiscate one of the most beautiful girls in Conway, what's on your mind?"

"Do you remember all that I told you the other day?"

"A story like that would be hard to forget."

"Well, the story continues to unfold. Several strange things have happened to me since we talked in your office."

"Do you want to tell me about them?"

Robert answered with a heavy sigh.

"You can start by telling me how you are feeling."

"How am I feeling …" In deep contemplation, he paused for a moment. He looked downward, as if something below could provide a means of expressing his sentiments. "You really want to know this?"

"I asked, didn't I?"

"I feel like a lost soul."

"So you feel you need absolution?"

"No, Father Donovan, not like that. I'm talking in a literal sense. Do you remember when you mentioned to me that you couldn't explain why I was going through all of this? There may have been some truth in what you told me."

"If that is so, then you must find your purpose for being here."

"I'd be a lot better off if I had some idea what that was. You know, Father Donovan, maybe I just need to let go of this nagging de JA vu and be content here in this time and place."

"Would that be so bad?"

"Of course not, I have a good life. I have a beautiful fiancée, a nice family and I'm getting married tomorrow … I could be happy here. It's just that …"

"What?"

"I'm tired of feeling I'm at the edge of a cliff about to fall over it."

"Then let your faith guide you. Let God guide you through this. One day you'll understand everything, but for now, take one small step at a time. Don't look too far ahead."

Robert walked a few paces in silence. "I … I guess I could try to do that." After a moment, he looked up and smiled. "You know, Father, you're here for a reason as well …"

"And what might that reason be?"

"You're my guardian angel."

"Believe me, I'm no angel. I'm a man, just like you." Father Donovan put an arm around Robert's shoulder. "You have much to do today young fellow, so you'd better be on your way. Oh, and Robert?"

"Yes, Father?"

"I wasn't invited to your wedding, but I'm coming anyway."

"You're invited now."

"I'll be there with a big appetite. I want to be well fed at that reception. I heard tell instead of the usual cake and punch reception, they're having a covered dish supper. I'm coming to uncover a few of those dishes."

Robert chuckled. "I hear Heloise Pullman's in charge of the reception. Better tread lightly, Padre. She's pretty fierce with that protocol."

"Miss Pullman can never resist a man of the cloth, no matter what denomination. I'll have her piling my plate in no time."

"Bye, Father."

"God be with you, Robert."

CHAPTER TWELVE

Saturday, March 26, 1932

Mrs. Blanche Harrington
232 Orange Grove Blvd.
Hollywood, California

Dearest Blanche:
Just as I promised, I am writing with all of the details of our wedding. I so wished you had been there, and know that you would have if it were possible.

I hope all is well out west. Maybe one day, in our wildest dreams, Robert and I will make the sojourn to California. Also, I hope your future career in the motion picture industry is successful. The talkies have indeed revolutionized the industry, as they are now a global phenomenon. Who would have thought?

Blanche, we truly had a picture perfect ceremony. I know you remember the Pullman sisters, Hilda Bergoine and Heloise Pullman. They did a beautiful job with the flowers, as well as organizing the food for the reception. Hilda even spent several hours preparing tulips for the altar bouquet—something she swore she absolutely would not do. I appreciated all of their effort. Although those two can be overbearing, they mean well.

Robert looked handsome in his gray tweed suit. It was my father's suit and had hardly been worn. A couple of years ago, Edna Barton tailored Father a new suit for Grand's funeral. As luck would have it, he and Dad happened to wear the same size. Call it serendipity if you wish, but we had beautiful wedding attire for the groom.

I am sure you remember the Barrow sisters, Dinah being the oldest. Blanche, there were four girls, all about two years apart in age. Mrs. Barrow called Mother and offered Dinah's bridesmaids' dresses for the wedding. Even though they did look a bit dated, we decided to use them anyway. If you'll think back a little, Dinah was married in 1928. Since I was wearing Mother's wedding dress for the ceremony, I decided this would be a wedding with a vintage theme. I was thrilled to receive the dresses, and again, 'Edna to the rescue.'

Their color was a pale, Alice blue, which looked stunning against the pink background of tulips and quince. The whole scenario was fresh and spring like.

We held the reception at the church hall. Our Ladies' Circle organized a covered dish supper, so of course there was plenty to eat for everyone. Some of Robert's friends provided musical entertainment. Naturally, there was no dancing, but the music provided a nice backdrop for conversation.

During the celebration, I met Conway's Catholic priest, Father Donovan. He has a church north of downtown Conway, and has apparently befriended my husband. I don't know why Robert feels he cannot confide in Brother Lawson anymore, but if this newfound acquaintance helps him contend with stress, I won't argue. I just find it curious as to why he turned to a Catholic priest for comfort. We don't even have any Catholic friends.

Laura Barmore caught the bridal bouquet. (Lord knows she needs all the help she can get). She was thrilled.

For my wedding gift, Robert reserved a room at the Rosalind hotel. It's from here that I'm writing this letter. We have the honeymoon suite, and it's lovely, Blanche. Such a shameful indulgence, but one only marries once in this life. Maybe that will justify the splurge.

The Thompsons insisted we use their carriage to leave the
church. What a quaint, sweet idea that was! Old Mr. Thompson
likes to gad about town in a buggy once in a while. They had the
whole rig spit and polished for the ceremony. I loved it.

Please come home soon, Blanche. I do miss you. I check on
your Aunt Ina when I have a chance, and she misses you terribly
as well. All my love goes to you in Hollywood! I look forward to
the day you and I can visit, and cannot wait for you and Robert
to become reacquainted.

Yours truly,
Ruby

Ruby was furiously writing at the roll top desk when Robert
entered the room. Elaborately clad in antique furniture, feather mat-
tresses and, soft, white linens, the honeymoon suite was beautiful.
With hard wood floors meticulously polished to a high luster, the
pungent smell of beeswax filled the air. Decorated in deep shades of
pink and burgundy, furnishings were richly appointed. The room was
paneled, with recessed beamed ceilings stained cherry in color. The
squares made by the beams were wallpapered in a small print with the
background of the wallpaper coordinating perfectly with the colors
of the room.

An indoor bath was a luxury to which Robert was not accustomed. Having an older home, the usual bath included a teakettle
and a number-three tub in the kitchen. The honeymoon suite at The
Rosalind Hotel, however, not only had its own bathroom but also a
water heater. A gloriously hot bath was an amenity Robert and Ruby
would truly miss at home.

As she was composing her letter, Robert walked up behind her.
"Writing me a little love note?"

Startled, Ruby jumped from her chair. "Oh my God, Robert, I
thought you were in the bathroom. You scared me half to death!"

"You don't have a secret pen pal, now do you?"

"Don't be silly. I'm writing my cousin Blanche. She couldn't make it
home for our wedding, so I promised I'd write and tell her all about it."

"Well, story time is over, my dear. The honeymoon is now to commence."

He bent down and kissed her. The touch of her soft fragrant skin caused a stirring deep in his groin.

Breathing in his essence, she wrapped her arms around him. She held him tightly. As he kissed her neck, she threw back her head. "Ooh," she moaned. "Oh, Robert, I've waited so long for this moment."

With one swift motion, Robert dropped her robe to the floor. As his manhood pressed urgently against her, he pulled her to him and kissed her forcefully. He disrobed, standing naked and erect in front of her.

She rubbed her fingers across his hairy chest. Lightly brushing his nipples, she kissed him just below his shoulder. She caressed his back and kissed him again as she rested her hands on his buttocks. Able to anticipate no longer, Robert lifted her onto the bed and began to make love to her. Closing his eyes, he concentrated on the entire length of her body beneath him. She cried out in a mixture of agony and pleasure when he entered her.

As they lay spent, Robert drifted into a dreamy state of semi-consciousness. He envisioned a pink haze beginning to surround them as the atmosphere seemed to grow misty and thick. Suspended in air, he now felt as if he were floating. It was a wonderful sensation. He then saw her about four paces from him. Waiting patiently for him to come to her, she smiled.

He approached. "Now I understand. It was you the night of the storm, wasn't it?"

"It's just a remnant, you know. It's past."

"I know. I've known that all along."

"Will you come back?"

"I don't know."

"You can. You don't have to stay."

As she spoke, her words echoed. Sounds distorted and perspectives skewed. *This must be some altered state of awareness ...*

"I don't know how to leave, and no one can seem to help me. There has to be a link ... I can feel it. The window is not yet closed."

"True, the window is not yet closed, but you must realize this is a vestige. You cannot hide here forever. It won't sustain you."

"I'm not hiding! I don't even know how I got here."

"Sometimes a bridge like this helps to ease the transition. In your case, it's not necessary. I can tell you this much: you'll find a portal. Then you must decide whether or not you want to use it. Either way, you must realize this is only a moment."

* * *

Tracing the outline of his lips with her finger, she managed to awaken him.

"Well hello again, sleepyhead, you were napping so peacefully that I hated to bother you."

"I'm glad you did." He sat up in bed.

Ruby looked deeply into his brown eyes. Kissing him lightly she said, "I love you, Mr. Davis. You've made me the happiest girl alive. I wouldn't trade places with anyone, anywhere."

Robert looked down and exhaled. "Someday, you may have no choice but to do just that."

There was a moment of silence. "I hope I never have to make that choice."

"I hope you don't either, Ruby. A choice like that tears the heart right out of you but leaves all of the fear and anguish behind."

"Well, since fear and anguish are not my favorite colors, maybe I can lighten this sudden influx of darkness."

She handed him a small, wrapped box.

"What do you have there?"

"A wedding gift."

"For me? I thought you were my wedding gift."

Ruby laughed. "I am, but here's a little something extra. It's something you can keep forever. It'll bond us together always. I would have given it to you last night, but I was distracted. Anyway, I hope you like it."

"Damn … A twenty-dollar gold-piece. A bit extravagant, Carraway, am I worth all this?"

"You're worth every penny. Nothing's too extravagant for you."

"We may should have bankrolled this money … We don't have much."

"Oh, Robert, you sound just like my mother. I've waited forever for this moment and here comes my second lecture. If that laughing hyena at the bank thought it was a good idea, then it couldn't be too bad of an investment. But no … all I get from you and Lorna is a barrage of financial advice—none of which I asked for. This is a gift. The least you could do is …"

"Wait, wait, you are right. I'm sorry."

"I mean, I've scrimped and saved …"

"I'm sorry, honey … I really am. I shouldn't have said that. I love it."

"I thought it could be something like a symbol of our undying love. You could show it to our children and grandchildren …"

"OK, Ruby, enough. I've apologized twice and admitted I was wrong. Why don't we start again."

"Starting again may be a good idea. Why don't we? I just gave you a gift and got a not so nice little lecture, so let's do try this one more time."

"Let's make a pact. From this day forward, this gift will represent our everlasting devotion to each other. We'll begin with a kiss and then proceed to make sure our pact is well sealed. There are plenty of good ways to do that, you know …"

"Well, that being said, I guess I should have given it to you last night. It would have been really sealed, then."

"Oh, not to worry, we'll seal it up really tight." He took her into his arms. "Might take all day."

CHAPTER THIRTEEN

Thursday, March 31, 1932

The intimacy of repetition often eliminates the element of surprise. Many find this vague definition of familiarity somewhat comforting, although it may also elicit feelings of resentment. A love of the arts, liberalism, and things bohemian are often stifled by those afraid of change. In small, rural communities, there is seldom room for such nonconformity, and those who insist on such practice are deemed outcasts. Some adapt, others rebel, and many escape, seeking sanctuary from the ideals of uniform thinking that tend to ensnare creative natures and forever hold them captive.

Blanche Harrington was one such escapee. She'd made the break from Conway long ago, never regretting a decision made at an age many felt too young to do so. Long, tall, and olive complexioned, most would describe her as striking. Framed by eyebrows plucked to semicircular perfection, her eyes were dark brown. She had big hands, big feet, and strong Mediterranean features. She had perfected the art of drawing a "cupid-bow" mouth on her lush, full lips, and all of this dark, exotic beauty was starkly contrasted by a shock of platinum blonde hair.

Her flat was within walking distance of the studio. Originally a house, the elderly owner had divided the home into two small apartments. In order to generate some extra income, she rented one side of the duplex. Eclectically furnished with odds and ends Blanche had managed to acquire over the years, the apartment was neat and clean. Although the fashion statement was somewhat lost amidst the heavy influence of the occult about the place, she tried her best to be fashionable on her modest budget.

Ruby's letter came to mind. She knew if Ruby were to visit, all of the relics would have to be put away. They'd lived a great part of their lives together, but thought differently when broaching this subject. How unlike they actually were! Content with her life in Conway, Ruby had always been a kind, gentle soul. Blanche, on the other hand, dreamed of fame and fortune. In her youthful days, a gypsy enlightened her as to her gift of spiritual communication, and also warned that one day she'd no longer be able to resist the calling of the arts. Maybe that calling is what led her in pursuit of a movie career.

Returning Blanche to the present moment, the daydream ended. Looking about the room, the reminiscing inspired her to make her way to the bureau and gather her tarot cards. *A little peek of what's in store for the newlyweds might be nice.* After dealing a Celtic cross pattern on the coffee table, she sat back and contemplated what was in front of her.

This can't be right.

In an attempt to comprehend the magnitude of what the cards had revealed to her, she lightly ran her fingers across the pattern.

Oh my God …

CHAPTER FOURTEEN

There was a knock on the door.

Standing in front of it, banging furiously as Robert approached, was Heloise Pullman. Unlike his wife, Robert had never liked the Pullman sisters. They were always spreading gossip or stirring up trouble among poor, unsuspecting folks. In fact, Robert had learned to dislike them so much he no longer felt the need to be cordial.

I wonder what she wants. He opened the door. As if the mere mention of her name required great effort, he exhaled, "Heloise. What a surprise ..."

"Please try to contain your enthusiasm, Robert. I'd like to speak to Mrs. Davis if you please."

"Won't you come in, sweet Heloise."

Marching past him, Heloise harrumphed in. Serving no purpose other than to accentuate all three of her chins, she removed an outrageous feathered hat. "I assume Mrs. Davis is available?"

"Why of course. So you can dish out all of the latest dirt around town, let me let her know you're here." As he said this, he could barely contain his laughter.

"Well, I never! Robert Davis, I have a good mind to call ..."

"Everyone you know?"

Mouth agape, Heloise simply stared at him. After a moment, she began again. "Your lack of tact is not surprising at all, but much to your disappointment, I'll not stand here and be made a fool of any longer. If your wife is not available, I'll be on my ..."

49

"Oh by all means, Heloise, wait here. I'll get her for you."

* * *

Having no clue of the previous conversation, Ruby entered the living room smiling.

"Heloise, darling."

Still scowling, she turned her back to Robert. Making a conscious effort to clear her throat, she began.

"Hello Ruby, dear, so nice to see you."

She turned her head slightly to see Robert still mischievously grinning. "I'll get right to the point. I've come on behalf of the Ladies' Circle at church."

"In what capacity, Heloise?"

"Well dear, the Ladies' Circle has nominated you as co-event chairwoman for the coming year. Since you are such an efficient thing, we can think of no better person to be in charge."

"I thought you said co-chairwoman."

"Hilda, of course, will stay on one more year to kind of guide you through. You'll be an understudy of sorts, and with Hilda there you won't be so overwhelmed."

"I see."

The fiendish smile returned to Robert's face. "Actually, we have some news, Heloise."

With a bewildered look, Ruby turned to Robert.

"And what is this news?"

"Ruby will have to decline your generous, honorable nomination, as we've decided to join the Catholic church. Father Donovan and I have discussed it at length."

"ROBERT! What on earth!"

"Well this is certainly news to me," Heloise replied. "And just what does Lila Davis think about all of this?"

Lila Davis, Robert thought to himself. *Lila Davis?*

"And have you told your mother this news, Robert?" Ruby glared at him without so much as a blink.

Robert realized there was a huge piece of this puzzle missing. As he sank into a chair, he said, "I don't remember."

Ruby turned to Heloise. "I have no idea where this is coming from, but I'll get to the bottom of it."

"Of course you will, dear. Think about what I've told you and give me a call when the two of you get this worked out."

"I will. And Heloise?"

She interrupted. "I know he's just trying to get my goat. I'm not paying any attention to all of that nonsense. I'll be in touch." Assuring her departure, she slammed the screen door loudly behind her.

Ruby walked across the room to the telephone.

"This is the operator. Number, please."

"Hello Mabel? It's Ruby. Could you please ring Lila Davis for me?"

"Of course, please hold."

"Lila? Hi dear, It's Ruby. Well, not too good. Lila, if you two are not busy, I think we'd like to come for a visit. No, no … don't worry about dinner. And Lila, I'm not sure exactly what is going on, but it's not turning out to be a very good day. I just thought I'd better warn you. Yes ma'am, OK. We'll see you at seven."

Robert was still sitting in the chair. "I've called your parents and informed them we like to visit around 7:00 P.M."

"Great. I'll look forward to meeting them."

"You need to grow up. You're feeling neglected? We just saw your parents Saturday."

Robert didn't acknowledge the comment. "I got a call from Morten's today."

"The telegraph office?"

"Yes. They said they have a message for you."

"I can't imagine from whom. The only person I can think that would send me a telegraph is Blanche."

"Hmm … maybe she got her big break. Maybe she finally got that starring role, and wants to invite us to the premiere. Maybe she wants to be sure we see that name up in lights."

Ruby was not amused. "Robert, you don't even know my cousin Blanche, and you're making fun of her. I'd appreciate it if you'd keep those snide little remarks to yourself. You have no reason to be so cynical."

As he took the number three tub off its hanger, Robert grinned to himself once again. "Would you put the kettle on? I think I'll have a bath and clean up a bit before we leave."

"No need for the kettle, you need to cool off a little."

CHAPTER FIFTEEN

It had begun with a realization. Nagging de JA vu, familiarity with places he'd never seen before, and sporadic amnesia would ambush the day-to-day living. Unbridled stress would then manifest. Things he should have known and people with whom he should be familiar were virtual strangers. It was a random ailment, obliterating the familiarity of important people in his life and making them the equivalent of large blank canvasses. This frightened him, as he could find no reason for it.

Ruby was right. He should remember his family better than this. He had just seen them at his wedding on Saturday.

As they neared the Davis farm, Ruby noticed Robert was becoming increasingly agitated. "Honestly, Robert, I've never known you to be so fidgety and nervous about visiting your folks before. Usually, you love coming here to devour your mother's home cooked meals. I asked her not to cook, by the way, but I have a feeling she's baked one of her famous chess pies."

"I hate chess pie."

"Since when? You almost ate a whole one last week." Ruby looked away in disgust. "You've been in such a dark mood lately. I wish there were some way I could help you snap out of this … this phase you are going through. You've always loved chess pies, Robert. When did that change?"

"I hate fucking chess pie."

She did not address the declaration immediately. She simply turned off the highway and made her way down the dusty drive toward the house. When she'd reached the garage, she pulled alongside Ned Davis' old T-model Ford pickup and brought the Dodge to a complete stop. "Since you feel so strongly about this, Rob, why don't you tell your mother how much you like her pies? It'll make her feel good. Shall we go in?"

* * *

His mother, Lila Davis, was a kind soul. Tall and thin, with a head full of silver hair, she was what most would describe as stately. She wasn't beautiful, but had a way about her that made her seem that way. Rearing her children across the pasture from the old home place, she had lived in Conway most of her sixty-five years.

"Lila, darling! How are you dear?"

"I'm fine, Hon, and I'm so glad you two made it. This is such a surprise. What's wrong, son? Missin' your Mama?"

Hiding his clueless status behind a big, knowing smile, he replied, "Missing my Mama? I'd plumb forgotten what you looked like. Let me look at you. You haven't changed a bit."

Behind this conversational ruse, Robert studied her carefully. Her timeworn face was that of a kind person, but he really wasn't able to tell if he looked like her or not. Maybe he'd know more when he saw his father.

"Mama, do you have that family photo album?"

Lila let out a little laugh. "Whatever are you talking about? I'd love to have a family photo album, but who has the money to hire a photographer for pictures on a regular basis?"

"I just wanted to see all of the family."

"Come to think of it, I think we did have a Davis family photo taken here in Conway a few years ago."

"May I see it?"

"Oh, I'll have to find it for you. I have it put away somewhere."

"What about the family Bible, Mama, the one with our family tree?"

"What's gotten into you, boy?"

"Just curious, that's all. Most of the older folks are gone, and if I don't start writing some of this down, I may never be able to chart my family tree."

Trying to discern if he was indeed serious or just playing a prank on her, Lila stared at him intently. She could not remember a time in his entire life that he had a care about his ancestry. *Suddenly, he's ready to write a book?*

Robert waited for an answer. He raised his eyebrows in anticipation, but still she stared at him. "Well, Mama, you there?"

"I'm here, and I must say I'm floored by this sudden interest in family genealogy."

She paused for a moment and began again. "I'll find it ... I'll find everything. I'll just have to look for it. You might want to discuss some of this with your father; he loves talking about his Irish lineage."

"Where is he, by the way?"

"He went to Pringle's. I needed some Octagon Soap for the wash."

"Did he know we were coming?"

"Not to worry, he'll be right back."

Then I can see which one of them I look like.

He perused the living room to see if anything sparked a memory. Nothing came to him. He did, however, notice a huge collection of homemade wooden knickknacks.

Lila smiled. "Used to be your favorite pastime back when Momma was still your number one girl."

This broke his train of thought. "I can't believe you've kept all of this."

"I wouldn't part with a single one of them. You were quite the little woodcarver."

Before he could reply, Ruby interrupted their conversation. "Here, darling, your mother made your very favorite."

"Mmm, I love flakin' chess pie."

"Why do you think I made it?" As she finished, the front door opened to reveal the second half of the mystery. "Oh, here he is; I think that's your father now ..."

He wheeled around to face the door and smiled.

"Afternoon, boy," the man said.

"Dad," Robert answered expectantly.

CHAPTER SIXTEEN

ComingtoConwayTuesdayStopveryimportant
stoparrivaltime6:30pmCSTstoploveBlanchestop

Ruby read the telegram. Pausing for a moment to digest its meaning, she took a breath. "Something is wrong. Something is terribly wrong."

"Nothing's wrong," Robert snapped. His upper lip curled into a snarl as he said this.

Ruby persisted. "Robert, to get Blanche Harrington on a train back to Conway would take nothing short of a disaster. Something horrible has happened."

"Now how do you know that?"

"Think about it. She didn't have the money to come home for our wedding. Blanche would have never missed that if there were any way possible for her to get back here. She'd have been my maid of honor. That should give you a clue that good news is not the reason she's beating a path home."

"Maybe it's that she just didn't want to come home. She's a lot older than you are and still single ... it's kind of a slap in the face that you're the one getting married first."

"That's not it."

"I'll bet it is, and now she's feeling guilty for missing the wedding."

"I know what I'm talking about here. There's something bad attached to this telegram."

"Goddamn, Ruby! Does everything have to be such a 'prophesy of doom' with you?"

A still silence fell over the room. Even though there was no conversation, the silence spoke volumes. Waiting for a reply, Robert stared expectantly.

Finally, she began. "You know … I've had about enough of your foul mouth."

"Well, hell, you make such a big deal over every little thing …"

"I think you'd better leave me alone. It may be wise if you don't talk to me anymore tonight. I'm going to the bedroom."

Yeah, her ole' whore cousin couldn't even afford to come home for our wedding, and now suddenly is on the first available train to Conway? How does she afford that? He walked into the bedroom. "Here's your apology. Sorry I snapped at you."

"You're not sorry about anything. You meant every word you said."

"I still think Blanche is just feeling guilty. I don't think this telegram is some "foreboding omen of doom." She just acted like a piece of shit and now wants to make amends."

"She doesn't have to make amends, because I'm not mad at her. I'm mad at you. You're the one acting like a piece of … Oh, I will not even stoop to your level. Tell you what, instead of me, why don't you tell God you're sorry? You've broken that commandment again, and it's getting to be a habit."

"Like you've never broken one, Rube?"

"Maybe I have, but not like that. You need to get a handle on that big mouth of yours. It's not very becoming."

Robert closed his eyes and puckered his lips. "I said I was sorry."

"Stop it."

He puckered even harder. "I really am."

To no avail, Ruby shook her head for a moment and waited for him to curb the theatrics. Finally, she had to smile.

"There, that's better."

"OK, Robert, if acting like an idiot is better, then I guess it is. Now go. Get out of here. Give me a few minutes to get over this latest ambush."

"Have you figured what could possibly bring 'The Academy Award Winning Blanche Harrington' back to Conway?"

"Suddenly my forgiveness is fading."

Robert held his hands up in surrender. "Wasn't thinking …"

"That happens a lot. To answer your question, I still have no idea why she's coming here."

"Do you know what time she arrives Tuesday?"

"The telegram said 6:30 P.M. I don't even know what Blanche's connections are that day, but surely there won't be too many trains arriving in Conway on Tuesday."

"Probably only one, Rube, and Blanche will be on it."

"In the mean time I'm off to Pringle's. I've invited Dr. Belton for dinner tonight."

"This is the first I've heard of dinner guests."

"I invited him a couple days before our wedding. I think it was the day after you had that attack in front of the house. Poor man, I feel sorry for him. Since Liza died, he probably doesn't have too many home cooked meals."

"Are you kidding? Belton is the most eligible bachelor over sixty in the county. Every widow in town makes sure he has a home-cooked meal. He probably eats better than we do."

"As you wish, darling. I've had my fill of your sarcastic wit for the morning. No … actually, that's not right. In reality I've had my fill of your sarcasm for the whole day. So, being that I'd rather go grocery shopping than to put up with it any longer, I'll say goodbye until later this afternoon." *And let's hope you'll have that big mouth of yours shut by then …*

* * *

Tuesday, April 5, 1932

She would have rather taken a beating than return to Conway, Arkansas. No one liked her there, but the feeling was plenty mutual. The trip was arduous as well as expensive, and Blanche really didn't have the money to make the journey. *Ruby is the only one I'd return for.*

The wind blowing in from the train window was neither cool nor refreshing. She'd grown accustomed to the mountains and the ocean breezes. The West Coast was both beautiful and untamed, while Arkansas felt humid and stifling—no matter what the season. The self-righteous, close-minded people of Conway had never really accepted her; she was tolerated there because of her well-respected aunt. Even though the Carraways had always loved her as one of their own, she never felt she truly belonged.

As the train pulled into the station, her thoughts returned to the present. *It hasn't changed. It still looks the same. No growth, no progression, just the same deadbeat town I left seven years ago ... A self-contained little nothing in the middle of nowhere.* People stared as she stepped down in her white, form-fitting dress and heels. Her platinum blonde hair was finger-waved closely to her scalp and she probably had more red pomade on her lips than necessary.

"Blanche? Blanche Harrington? Is that you?"

With eyes closed, she grimaced. *How could she possibly have known when I was to arrive? How fitting that the person I hate the most serves as my welcoming committee.* She forced a smile. Heloise Pullman, darling. Why am I not surprised you'd be the first to know exactly when I arrived in town? Just a coincidence I'm sure ..."

Heloise returned the smile. "Yes, I'm sure. I see you haven't changed a bit, Blanche—at least on the inside, that is. I'm also certain that is proper attire for the likes of Hollywood, California." She paused and looked at Blanche again. "Here in Conway, we're still much less flamboyant ... I guess that's what you'd call it."

Blanche maintained her frozen smile. "I don't mean to be rude, Heloise, but I really must run. I'm in town only for a short time and have things to tend right away."

"Things? What things, Blanche dear?"

"Oh Heloise, you'll have to defame someone else's character at your Ladies' Circle meeting. I'd love to arm you with lots of juicy gossip, but as I just said, I must hurry. Ciao, Darling."

With that, she grabbed her bags and left.

In disgust, Heloise watched the tall, slender silhouette disappear. *What a whore. I should have invited her to church on Sunday ... maybe we could have helped her.*

＊＊＊

The bags were heavy, but fortunately, the hotel was close to the station. As she made her way through the hotel door, the clerk rushed from behind the desk to assist her. With eyes firmly fixed on her cleavage, he smiled. Without looking up, he asked, "May I help you?"

"I need a room, please."

He smiled again. "Well, it just so happens we have a vacancy. We have a bunch of them in fact."

"That's so kind of you, but I only need one—with a bath if possible."

"You are in luck. We do have a room with a bath. Say, don't I know you?"

"Would it really matter if you did?"

"Blanche? Blanche Harris?"

"Harrington."

"Is that you?"

"It is I. And you are?"

"Floyd Robertson. We went to school together. I remember you; only ... You weren't gray-headed back then."

Taking a deep breath, she paused for a moment. "I'll bet you're still single aren't you?"

"I sure am, and I'm free tonight, too." Eyes wide with anticipation, he was still smiling.

"It's blonde, Floyd, not gray."

"What?"

"The hair ... It's blonde."

"Well, why don't you let me run my hands through that blonde hair over dinner? I'd love to catch up, and after that, maybe we can find out ..." He finished the sentence with a knowing wink. "Well, you can probably figure out the rest."

"Oh no ... no, no, no, I don't think I can. After we've caught," Blanche hesitated in mocking search of exactly how to phrase the next statement. "After we've caught whatever you've deemed necessary, and those hands have made inroads into my scalp, what exactly do we need to ascertain the nature of? Please, Mr. Robertson, do not leave me in suspense any longer. If you do, I'll surely die of curiosity."

Speaking in almost a whisper, Floyd leaned across the counter. "Maybe we need to find out how blonde you really are, Miss Harrington."

This brought forth a laugh. She put her hand to her mouth as she did so. She leaned into him a little closer. "I don't think so, Mr. Robertson. Let me make a few things perfectly clear to you. Even if I was a true blonde, I can assure you that you'd never, ever find out for sure. And as for dinner, if I was hungry a few moments ago, the appetite is now so very gone. So why don't you be a nice boy and show me to my room. If you can't handle that, maybe there's somewhere else I might stay?"

The smile vanished from his face. Resenting the ridicule he just been handed, he dropped Blanche's bags right in front of her. "Well now, Miss Harrington, that's about what I deserve for being neighborly to trash like you. Not to worry, though … I had plans for tonight anyway." He then handed her a key. "Your room is on the second floor, that way. Room 205. Take the elevator in the hall. I guess you can come to the front desk and pay after you get settled in."

"That's very kind of you, Floyd. I'll do that."

She retrieved her bags and began to walk toward the lift. Floyd watched as she made her way down the hall.

"And Blanche?"

Blanche again turned toward him. "Yes, darling?"

"Fuck you."

She smiled, turned around, and continued toward the elevator. After she'd gotten on, she peeked her head out of the opening. "You know, Floyd, you're probably the only guy in high school that didn't." Floyd saw her burst into laughter again as the doors closed in front of her.

Still laughing, she made her way down the hallway to her hotel room. It would be a relief to simply get in and settled. The Rosalind actually seemed like a nice place. With the exception of the moron at the front desk, it was quite comfortable. Blanche unpacked her suitcase, making sure she was fresh in anticipation of the Davis household. Trying in earnest to brush out any wrinkles, she straightened her dress. Finally, after all was done, she looked into the mirror and said, "Well … here goes nothing."

* * *

There was a ring of the doorbell. Ruby approached the door from the back of the living room. She began to smile when she saw Blanche standing there. "Oh Blanche, my sweet, sweet Blanche, I'm so glad to see you."

Caught off balance, Blanche stumbled into the embrace. She thought to herself, *this is probably one of the few people in this world that really loves me.*

"Hi, honey. I'm glad to see you, too."

"Come in, dear. I have dinner all ready."

Blanche took a moment to look at her surroundings. The house was definitely old and had been added onto at least twice. The living room was wrapped in beautiful, floral wallpaper and gas lanterns adorned most of the doorways. The ceilings were beaded board with thick dental molding framing them. No doubt, a woman's touch had been added to this pristine, immaculate place.

"Where's Robert?"

"He's here. I'll get him for you. I'm so excited two people who are most dear to me in this world are about to meet."

"Darling, you forget I remember you two as love-struck teenagers running around the house all starry-eyed …"

"I know that, but now you'll finally get to know him. He's such a good man; I think you will really like him."

I just hope he still likes me after he hears what I have to say.

Robert walked out smiling. "Well hello there, stranger …"

As Blanche watched him enter the room, the smile vanished from her face.

"It's nice to see you again."

The air became thick. Something was wrong.

"You remember me?"

Cocking her head to the side a bit, she tried to discern what did not seem right about him. Carefully, as he walked toward her, she studied him. It then came to her. His aura was wrong.

Emanating feelings of who we are, as well as our level of comfort in our present surroundings, auras surround each one of us. They give clues as to a person's essence and the energy the persona might expend. Auras can be felt, and sometimes even seen by those with enhanced psychic perception. When they appear wrong or in conflict, they usually signify the person is in some kind of trouble.

"Blanche?"

Her deep hypnotic train of thought was broken. "Forgive me, Robert. I was a million miles away. Of course, I remember you. It's so nice to see you again as well."

CHAPTER SEVENTEEN

Ruby and Blanche stood at the sink washing dishes.

"Wherever did you learn to cook like that?"

"Are you kidding? Lorna Carraway reared me with a rolling pin in one hand and a wire spoon in the other. Oh Blanche, I've rolled enough pastry to forge a trail back to California for you. It's fun cooking for a spouse, although I'm sure one day the new will wear off."

"Speaking of spouses how is Robert?"

"Funny you should ask that …"

"What's so funny about it?"

"Robert's not doing too well these days."

"He does seem out of sorts, doesn't he?"

"That, and he's been acting strange."

"I sensed some unrest. He's nervous and fidgety. Any idea what's going on?"

"We've all been worried sick about him but can't seem to help him. He's unbearable at times. Sometimes my patience wears so thin … I keep reminding myself he's going through something I don't understand. God, I hope it will pass soon."

"Ruby, there is a reason I've come."

"I knew there was, Blanche. I just didn't want to pry. I knew you'd get around to your reasons when the time was right. Is everything OK?"

"As far as my life goes, everything is fine. I'm not exactly sure I can say the same about yours."

Ruby sighed. "I'll be fine. I hope I'll be fine …"

"Ruby, you will find this disconcerting and you'll not approve of my means, but before you chastise me, hear me out. The other day, in order to get some insight as to how your new life was progressing, I dealt a hand of tarot cards."

"Blanche Harrington!"

"Please, let me finish. After I had dealt the cards, several troubling things appeared."

"Like what? What did you find amidst all of your occult nonsense?"

"If you'll stop interrupting, maybe you'll find there is no nonsense. Maybe you'll find I have some answers for you. Do you want me to continue?"

"I don't know if I want you to or not."

"Your husband is in a deplorable state of spiritual transition."

"What on earth are you talking about?"

"His spirit or his essence, if you will, is at extreme unrest. Something has interrupted the time-line continuum and sent his life force careening across God knows how many spiritual planes of existence. For whatever reason, his consciousness has managed to land here in this time, in this place. The aura which surrounds him is completely inappropriate for this era and I fear he cannot continue this progression much longer."

Ruby looked away. Now two people in her life were saying inane, crazy things. Her bottom lip quivered. "OK, Blanche, you've succeeded in frightening me. I have no idea what you're talking about, but now I'm more terrified than ever."

"There's no room for that."

"What?"

"You have to be strong."

Looking down, she swallowed hard. "I don't have much strong left in me …"

"I feel a sense of desperation emanating from him, and his time with us is short. There's no margin for error, Ruby. If we can't help him soon, we may lose him forever."

Ruby took a couple of steps forward and sat down in a daze. "Lose him forever? As in going mad?"

"I've dabbled in many things over the years, but these feelings are intense and decisive. Some force is urging me to provide a link, which will enable your husband to find peace."

"A link?" Both women wheeled around to see that Robert had entered the room.

"Darling … we just were …"

"Blanche, you used the word link. You said it."

"And you have a problem with that?"

"Ruby, leave the room. Blanche and I need a minute alone here."

"What?"

"Get out."

"I will not …"

"Get out! Now!"

Taking a deep breath, Ruby cupped her hands around her mouth and nose. She exhaled. Speaking quietly and deliberately, she began. "Let me make one thing perfectly clear. You don't order me to do anything. You have just humiliated me in front of my cousin and that won't happen again, either." She placed the dishtowel she was holding into the sink. "Now, you may apologize to Blanche for this latest bizarre, random outburst, and then if you value any harmony in this relationship in the foreseeable future I suggest you find yet another way to make amends to me as well." Ruby stared at him for a moment longer and then diverted her glance to Blanche. She said nothing else and quietly left the room.

* * *

"You didn't have to be so rude to her."

"That's none of your business. I want to know who you are and why you're here."

This curt, abrupt interrogation briefly caught Blanche off guard. Launching an offensive attack, she quickly recovered. "I am who I say, Robert. I think more importantly we need to ask, do you know who you are and why you're really here?"

"I told the girl in my dreams I felt there was a link. I used that word, Blanche, and you used that word as well."

"I think we've already established that."

"Well then, why don't we cut through the bullshit and you just tell me what you know."

"First of all, it's not bullshit as you so crudely put it. Secondly, it's not so much what I know, Robert, it's what I feel. I can feel the turbulence of your spirit. That's why I'm here."

"I can't believe you came all of this way because you were worried about my turbulent spirit."

Blanche's eyes narrowed. "It wasn't you I came to protect, Robert. It was my cousin. Personally, I don't give a damn what happens to you, but if I have to solve your problems to protect her, then so be it."

Robert raised his eyebrows in anticipation of an answer. "So how do you propose to help us, Blanche?"

Blanche looked him dead in the eye. Without flinching she said, "We have to find a portal."

CHAPTER EIGHTEEN

"A what?" Robert exclaimed. "Well, Blanche, why don't we just conjure up old Lucifer right here in our living room? It'll save a lot of time and trouble. There's no sense in beating around the bush."

"I should have known not to expect much from you. I won't even dignify that last statement with an answer."

"Stop it, you two," Ruby said as she re-entered the room. "It's hard enough to deal with all of these mood swings, Robert. I don't need you and Blanche getting into a fistfight."

"I wasn't going to punch her, Rube, just slap her around a little."

"I'd like to see you try ..."

"Please, you two ... enough! Robert, I think now I'd like to be the one to talk to Blanche alone. Can you give us a couple of moments?"

"Sure, I've said all I have to say." He mumbled something else as he left the room that neither Ruby nor Blanche could make out. Perhaps it was better that they were not able to do so.

"I overheard the word séance, Blanche. A séance? Whatever do you hope to accomplish with something so ..."

She interrupted. "Hear me out, Ruby. I'm not trying to conjure up a ghost or a demon. I'll attempt to tap into the spiritual world for some answers. The veil between this world and the next is pretty thin sometimes, so hopefully this will work."

"And maybe we'll be wasting a lot of time and energy playing spooky campfire tales."

"Darling, I wouldn't be here if I didn't think I could help. Lord knows I hate this place … but I've read the tarot and I know what I saw. At least we owe it to ourselves to give this a try."

Ruby exhaled. "OK, what exactly do you have in mind? And remember, this is a gossipy little town, so if you have something macabre in mind, it won't work here."

"Nothing macabre, Ruby, just bringing forth enough energy to discover what fuels Robert's situation."

"Why don't you be a little more specific?"

"I'll try to explain. If Robert's spirit is displaced, or to put it plainly, from somewhere else, there will be an energy signature accompanying it. If we can follow the signature back to its source, we'll know where it came from. Maybe we'll even learn how we can resolve the situation. Naturally, you and I cannot do this alone. We'll need a link of sorts. The link would be able to 'read' the trail for us, giving us a clue as to why he is really here."

"Blanche, we're talking about my husband, not some displaced spirit. He's been acting strangely, that's all. If his spirit is displaced, it's been that way for the last twenty-eight years. Why would all of this manifest now?"

Carefully attempting to construct a plausible reply, Blanche closed her eyes for a moment. Without looking up she said, "OK, I'll try. I'm not sure you'll understand. I'm not even sure you'll want to, but I'll try."

"Try what?"

"To explain the sequence of events …"

"Please, Blanche, enough with the drama, already. Just tell me what you think you know."

Blanche looked at Ruby. "It's a replay."

"A what?"

"We're characters in a replay. It's a film term, which means to play again after it's filmed. In other words, we're simply replaying events that have already transpired. This is sort of like an imprint in time or a memory that has lingered. We are part of the imprint so we perceive it as reality."

"This is insane! I can't believe I'm listening to this nonsense. Maybe all three of us need to bed down at the asylum."

"Maybe so."

Ruby swallowed hard. "Assuming what you're saying is true—and I'm going out on a limb here—is there any way to do this other than a séance?"

"Oh ... My ... God!"

Startled, Blanche and Ruby turned to see that Hilda Bergoine was now standing in the doorway.

"What did you just say?"

"Oh, Hilda, darling, how delightful! You must have come by to pick up where your nosey sister left off. I heard she and Robert got along fabulously."

"I thought I heard someone say séance."

"You did, Hilda, but we were just ..."

"Talking about how this old witch could cast some ruthless spell on you and your sister to make your lives—what's left of them—pure unadulterated hell. After all, it's more than you deserve."

"That is enough, Blanche! Hilda, dear, please come and sit. I'll explain all that I can. Blanche has returned to Conway to help me with Robert. You see he's been having ..."

"Too much company from that intrusive, overbearing Ladies' Circle. No need to explain, Ruby. I'm sure Hilda has much to do and is on her way out." Blanche was standing behind Ruby, arms folded, with her weight on one foot.

"I certainly am on both of those accounts."

"Please, Hilda, wait just a moment. Give me a chance to explain ..."

Hilda interrupted her. "It's all right, honey, so don't worry about any of this. We all know Blanche and don't expect anything different from her. We'll talk when she leaves. Hopefully that will be sooner rather than later." She then turned to Blanche. "Conway was a better place when it got rid of the likes of you, and I hope to God you're not here to stay."

"No reason to bring God into this, Hilda. I'm not here to stay. Actually, even three thousand miles is not far enough away from you."

She took a step closer. "Just so you know, you're not significant enough to warrant another insult, so why don't you be on your merry way. Go harass some other family. We've had enough for one day."

"You're trash, Blanche. You always were, and always will be. Even those fancy clothes and dyed hair don't camouflage what you really are. You wreak havoc wherever you go, but I guess that doesn't matter in a place like Hollywood. It seems to be a home for wayward trash."

With all of the self-control she could muster, Blanche tried hard not to burst into a fit of laughter. She was not successful. She began laughing so hard she had to hold her side. While attempting to regain her composure, she walked over to the screen door. Finally doing so, she opened it, saying, "Get out, you narrow-minded, self-righteous bitch." She began to laugh again, but cleared her throat to stifle it.

For the first time in her life, Hilda was speechless.

"GET OUT!"

Turning to leave, Hilda said nothing else. She looked at Ruby and quietly said, "I'll call you, dear."

Blanched yelled, "Tell Fat Mabel I said happy gossip! You got what you came after!" She laughed again for a moment and turned to Ruby. "I'll bet the phone lines are going to be hot tonight!"

Ruby half smiled. It was not a happy smile, but one of resignation and defeat. "OK ... that went well, don't you think?"

Blanche was still smiling. "Amazingly well."

"The way things have gone lately, there will be no one in town speaking to me before the end of the week. I look forward to an icy reception at church. I have to ask, who's next?"

"Robert, I hope, and time is drawing near. Let's get to work."

Ruby wondered if Blanche's coming was in reality a blessing or a curse. Judging from the volatility of recent encounters, it was anyone's guess.

"I need a few things, Ruby. I'll need some candles, and we'll need to move the dining room table to the middle of the room. Also, I need something of great significance to both of you."

"I'll get the candles," Ruby said as she left the room. *I cannot believe I'm allowing Blanche to go through with this.*

The séance went against every grain of her moral fiber. *Something of great significance to the two of us ...* The gold coin immediately flashed into her mind. She went to the top drawer of the bureau to retrieve it. Once the table was moved, they were ready to begin. Ruby handed her the candles and the coin. "Here, Blanche, I gave this to Robert as a wedding gift."

"Thank you, dear." Focusing on it as she held it in the palm of her hands, Blanche looked at the coin. Her eyes widened. Immediately, she grew pale.

"Blanche, what is it? What's wrong?"

Blanche diverted her glance from the coin back to Ruby. "I ... I don't think we'll need a séance after all."

CHAPTER NINETEEN

Wednesday, April 6, 1932

"But Blanche, you just got here!"

"I know, honey, but there are a few things—a few items—I have to get my hands on if we're to get to the bottom of this."

"New Orleans, Blanche? Why must you go so far?"

"Ruby, the things I need to put me in touch with the spiritual world are considered 'black magic' around here. No one would even consider having them. I'd probably be burned at the stake if I were to inquire as to their whereabouts."

"You can't go there by yourself. I'm going with you."

"Honey, you forget I live in Hollywood, California. Blanche can take care of herself."

"I'm going."

Blanche placed a hand on Ruby's shoulder. "You'd surely die aghast at what you'd see in New Orleans. You'd better stay here and look after Robert."

"For the last time, I'm going."

Making sure they made eye contact, Blanche turned to face Ruby. "OK ... I don't seem to be getting through to you. I have a specific agenda in mind in New Orleans. I'm going to a voodoo store, Ruby. I'm also consulting a medium by the name of Madame Solange DeShotel about all of this, and I plan to ask for her assistance in contacting the spirit world. She's considered an evil woman. Many are deathly afraid of her and believe she's capable of eliciting curses on those who cross her. Have I made myself clear? You're out of your element. Stay home."

"Apparently that hair color has affected your brain. I'm going, Blanche. It concerns my life and you are part of it—a big part, I might add. If you won't let me go with you, I'll just make my way down there alone. You're not from there and something could happen to you in that godforsaken city. Apparently, you'll be dealing with some dangerous people involved in sinister, perverse practices. How could you expect me just to happily send you on your way?"

"I don't expect that. I just need you to let me handle this and understand I'll be back in a few days. Don't make this difficult, Ruby. The means to an end you won't approve of, but the end result may be the key to this whole nightmare."

"Get this through your head, cousin. I'm going to New Orleans. I'll have Mabel place a call to the train station and see how soon we can get ticketed. I guess we'll hope for a hotel when we arrive; if not we'll find a church to sleep in. I'll pack a lunch and get some money. I have a few dollars in my hatbox; we'll need that for the trip." She turned to leave the room. "Now I'm going to gather my things and explain to my husband why I'm leaving him twelve days after I've married him. He'll be the one to die aghast when he finds out what we're up to."

With her shoulders slumped in defeat, Blanche sighed loudly. "Maybe it's better if he doesn't know what we're up to. If this is to work, you have to go along with it. You have to keep your mouth shut and do as I say."

"That depends on what you say." Not bothering to look back, Ruby walked out of the room. "I'm calling Mabel, Blanche. My hatbox is on the top shelf of the hall closet. I think I have about sixteen dollars in there. That should help."

"I'll gather my things as well." Ruby had already left the room. Blanche was now talking to an empty doorway. She walked over to the closet, got the hatbox from the top shelf, and then paused for a moment. *Don't say I didn't warn you, Ruby Davis. I tried, but you would not take no for an answer. You may have just gotten more than you bargained for this time.*

CHAPTER TWENTY

Thursday, April 7, 1932

    As I write this entry into my journal, it is still hard for me to believe I have made this sojourn. Passing from Arkansas into Louisiana, I saw nothing but timber and swampland. As we made our way through Baton Rouge, it became evident that the city of New Orleans is virtually sequestered from the mainland by waterways. I am in amazement the city is habitable at all. Already quite warm, the quantity of mosquitoes is horrid.

    We're staying in a part of the city named The French Quarter. The architecture is unlike any I have seen. Most buildings have balconies with beautiful, elaborate wrought iron railings. During carnival, people line up on these balconies to throw beads and trinkets to the crowds below.

    Narrow houses line the back of the French Quarter. Most have immense ceilings and tall windows. I've learned the tall ceilings, along with fans help to provide comfort during the sweltering summer months. Furniture as well as beds are low-slung and situated in front of the large windows in hopes of catching breezes. Interesting to note, the houses also have working shutters, which can be closed to conceal the windows. These shutters help to protect the homes from wind-driven rain and flying debris when monstrous storms invade from the gulf.

    In the center of some of these homes are charming courtyards. Beautifully landscaped, they're filled with tropical plants from many different ports of call. Frost is uncertain here, therefore the flora is vastly different from that of home.

If I were to write a history of the cultural melding of this place, I'd need several volumes to complete the task. Historically, this city has been a port for immigration. As a result of these immigrations, certain segments of the city have a heavy Italian concentration, while others are predominately German. Papa would be thrilled to learn that there is an area of the city referred to as the Irish Channel. I wonder if any of our relatives immigrated into the United States through the port of New Orleans?

Before closing tonight, I must make mention of Saint Charles Avenue. The Avenue houses mansions representing many different architectural schemes. Tremendous in size, and so very beautiful, I can only imagine what type of southern gentility lives in them.

"What could possibly be so fascinating about that journal?"

"Nothing fascinating, just a way to put my thoughts in order. I like to read my journal from time to time and reflect upon my life. I've encouraged Robert to write one as well. I was hoping in doing so, he may be able to make some sense of this emotional trauma he seems to be experiencing."

"Well, put it away. Here comes the bellhop. You'll need to hand him your bags."

Ruby closed the journal and carefully slid it into the top sleeve of her luggage.

"Here you go. " Smiling, she handed him the suitcase. She turned to Blanche and whispered, "Floyd just hands you the key to your room. I've never stayed in such a grandiose place. Are you sure we can afford this?"

"Of course not, who can afford the Monteleone Hotel? I raided a little stash I'd put back for a rainy day. I guess this is our storm."

She looked around the lobby. "More like a hurricane."

* * *

"Zip me up, Ruby, will you?"

"You're going out? At this hour?"

"This is New Orleans. There is no 'this hour' and yes, I'm going out. I'm to meet Madame DeShotel shortly."

"Why can't it wait until morning?"

"There are certain elements in this life that do not materialize in the morning." Blanche turned toward the door to leave.

"I'm going with you."

Blanche abruptly turned around. "No, you're not."

"Oh yes, I'm going with you."

"If I have to tie you physically to the bed, so help me God, you are not going with me. You were so overbearing that I had no choice but to bring you down here, but now I'm drawing the line. I won't take no for an answer. Get it straight: you are staying here."

"No."

Blanche's face suddenly turned scarlet. Forcefully she shoved Ruby against the wall. Through gritted teeth she muttered, "I'm not kidding, Ruby. You are staying put right here."

"Take your hands off of me. I'm a grown woman and I'll do as I please. I'm not afraid of you, Blanche Harrington, so don't tell me where to stay put."

Blanche let her go and made an exaggerated attempt to smooth her hair. Breathing hard, a large blood vessel pulsated across her forehead. "Look, if something happened to you, I'd never forgive myself. That's why I don't want you with me. You could be in great danger."

Ruby's expression became cold. This took Blanche by surprise, because she rarely experienced a reaction like that from Ruby. Ruby stared at Blanche for what seemed an eternity and finally said, "Then go. I don't know if I'll ever forgive you for this, but have it your way." She said nothing else. She then went into the bathroom to change her clothing. When she returned, Blanche was gone.

* * *

The night air was thick. Obscuring any hopes of a starry horizon, clouds filled the sky. This obscurity made the French Quarter seem even darker than usual. Blanche had Madame DeShotel's address crumpled tightly in her hand as she made her way to the back of the Quarter. Late, and the streets deserted, she suddenly felt vulnerable and alone. When she reached St. Ann Street, she turned left and began to walk toward Rampart. Finally, just a block from Rampart Street, she'd reached Madame DeShotel's flat. On the door was a large, ornate brass knocker; she used the knocker to announce her presence. Several moments passed before anyone answered the door.

A voice demanded, "Who's there?"

"My name is Blanche Harrington. I'm here to see Madame De-Shotel; I'm expected."

"A moment, please."

Blanche heard heavy footsteps move away from the door and then back again. The massive wooden door opened and Blanche found herself standing face to face with a light-skinned woman of color. Blanche wondered if she was mulatto. She'd read about the mulattos, quadroons and octoroons of New Orleans. Although a bit overweight, the woman was pretty. Her eyes were amber in color and her hair fell in soft curls about her face.

"Madame DeShotel I presume?"

"No, who would you be?"

"I'm Blanche Harrington, and I believe Madame is expecting me. She said she'd see me at half past twelve."

"She is expecting you. If you'll follow me, I'll fetch Madame. Would you care for tea?"

"No, no thank you. I'm fine."

"Have a seat in the parlor, Mrs. Harrington, and I'll return shortly." The lady then disappeared down a long, narrow hallway.

"It's Miss Harrington …"

As she took a seat, she had a look about the flat. The furnishings were elaborate, ornate, and beautiful. With all of the macabre rumors floating around, she had halfway expected to make acquaintance with Madame in some sort of dungeon. She never expected to meet this person in a beautifully furnished flat on the edge of the French Quarter.

Her train of thought was abruptly broken.

"Blanche?"

"Madame DeShotel, I presume?"

"What can I do for you, Blanche?"

She, like her flat, was not at all what Blanche had expected. Standing no more than five feet two inches tall, Madame DeShotel was a petite woman. Her thick, auburn hair was neatly tucked into a chignon at the nape of her neck. Her emerald green eyes accentuated her flawless, fair skin. It was hard to imagine this dainty, soft-spoken beauty cursed an entire existence if one wrong word was spoken. This small presence was the evil, imposing Madame who struck fear throughout the world of the occult.

"I have a problem—a matter I don't know quite how to deal with."

"Go on."

Proceeding to tell the whole scenario, Blanche explained Robert's predicament and its effect on Ruby. She elaborated on the relationship she and Ruby shared and the reasons why Ruby's happiness and emotional well-being were so important to her. She also told Madame DeShotel of the gold coin and the power she believed it possessed.

"Did you bring the coin with you?"

"I did."

"Let me see it … in fact, let me hold the coin."

Blanche removed the coin from her purse and handed it to Madame. As Solange took the coin from Blanche's hand, she gripped it tightly and closed her eyes. "There is a definite energy signature attached to this piece."

"Can you help me?"

"Your definition of this paradox is correct. However, you've grossly underestimated the magnitude of the powers associated with the situation."

"Then tell me."

"I cannot tell you. I can only show you."

"You are my only hope in this, Madame. I must understand in order to help my cousin. Will you show me?"

"Do you really want me to?"

"Of course I do. Right away, if possible."

"As you wish, but keep in mind that knowledge of forces this powerful comes with a price."

"I'm prepared to pay any amount needed. If you'll help me, I'll get the money, somehow."

Madame arose from her seat and made her way across the room toward an armoire. Opening its two top doors, she removed a small leather pouch from the upper compartment. She called for Angelique, who promptly arrived with two steaming demitasse cups.

"Tea for me, Angelique." She then turned to Blanche. "There are herbs in this pouch which will open your eyes to everything you desire to know."

"By all means …"

She proceeded to pour the herbs into Blanche's cup. Much like the color of strong coffee, the resulting liquid was a rich, dark brown.

"Thank you, Madame, thank you so much." As she drank the herbal concoction, she noticed its odor was musty, like that of cooked mushrooms. It was sweet enough to be palatable, but finished harsh and bitter.

"How long before I know?"

"You will know before morning, Blanche. In the meantime, perhaps you could leave the coin here tonight so that I may further study the energy signature. I may be able to understand more fully its power and capabilities."

"I don't know, Madame. It was a wedding gift from my cousin to her husband. I wouldn't feel comfortable leaving it with a stranger."

"But of course, Blanche, I understand. I will just have to make do with the limited knowledge I've gathered in this short time. I truly hope I can be of service to you and your cousin. Maybe this small bit will be enough."

"You … You think you'll be able to do more?"

"If I fully understand the magnitude of the powers of this piece, I can give you an accurate map of correcting events. That knowledge will be invaluable."

"Then perhaps I can pick up the piece in the morning after all. If you really feel more time could provide greater knowledge, I'll make some sort of excuse as to why I have to leave for a while. If it will straighten this situation out, it's well worth the risk …"

Doing her best to convince herself this was a wise decision, she babbled on for a moment. Her gut instinct, however, predicted a much different outcome.

"Blanche," Madame interrupted, "you must not tell anyone of this place."

"I will say nothing, Madame, for you are my only hope in this matter. You mentioned price a few moments ago, how much do I owe you for your help?"

Madame simply replied, "You must go now."

Angelique led Blanche to the front door.

She began to leave but stopped shortly before crossing the threshold. She turned back to Madame once more. "Thank you, Solange. Thank you so very much." As she said this, she took Madame's hand and squeezed tightly.

Solange released the grip and simply replied, "Goodnight, Blanche."

∗ ∗ ∗

Walking down the dark, narrow streets of the Quarter, Blanche began to reflect on what had transpired. Creating doubt as to whether Madame was truly legitimate, a nagging skepticism followed her. After all, the only thing that she'd gained from the recent encounter was a prediction: *You'll know the answers by morning.* That sounded weak to her, resembling a swindle rather than a solution. Like a fool, she'd left the coin with her. Acting on impulse rather than sound judgment, she realized now she'd made a mistake in doing so. If she were wrong, Madame would have some answers when she returned to retrieve the gold dollar. If not, they'd made a long, expensive trip for nothing.

As she rounded the last corner and approached the hotel, she realized she was also feeling a bit defeated. She felt a lump arise in her throat. *I've done the best that I could. This is all beyond my capabilities.*

Her train of thought was broken as she passed the clerk seated behind the front desk. She returned the smile and made her way across the lobby.

Giving full audience to a replay of the hotel room altercation, the elevator doors closed in front of her. *Poor darling, she must have thought I was a raving lunatic. I'll make amends tomorrow, somehow. Hopefully she'll understand I overreacted out of concern for her safety.*

The elevator doors then opened onto the fourth floor hallway. She walked into it, making her way toward the hotel room. *God, I'm tired. Some rest will help to clear my head.*

She found Ruby inside the room asleep. Perhaps she'd lie down beside her for a moment and rest as well, for suddenly she felt it impossible to manage another step. The bed felt warm and comfortable. So inviting, she'd wait a bit to undress. She laid her head on the soft, down pillow, and her eyes began to close. She was tired now, so very, very tired.

Dissipating much like shards of glass falling away from an impact, her conscious mind began to splinter. Behind this wall of cerebral logic was an alternate presence. More abstract in nature, this presence was governed by a patient, lurking subconscious. As bits and pieces of reality rapidly fell away, the pink swirls and hazy atmosphere described in Robert's dreams began to materialize. How odd this seemed to her! As this wonderful feeling grew exponentially, she felt at peace. Quickly consumed by a vortex of sorts, her cognitive reasoning continued its disintegration. Spiraling away from her toward an infinite oblivion, all logic and reasoning finally surrendered to a deeper, more powerful sleep.

Everything made sense now. The pieces of the puzzle had fallen into place, and Madame DeShotel was right after all. She had indeed gained the understanding she sought to achieve before morning. As the last bit of her conscious mind decided to make its retreat, she envisioned a long, dark tunnel before her. A light, ever increasing in brilliance, shined at the end of it. Behind her, a woman much like the one Robert had detailed in his experience stood smiling. Gracefully, her presence billowed in a warm, seeming wind. She was indeed beautiful. The woman began to walk toward her, pausing as she reached the place Blanche was standing. Blanche turned to look at the woman. She then turned toward the light once more. *How unfortunate,* she thought to herself, *that I will not be able to help them after all. I'm sorry, Ruby, so very sorry.*

CHAPTER TWENTY-ONE

Friday morning, April 8, 1932

"These eggs are swell."

"It ain't Wednesday so you came sniffin' around here for breakfast, huh boy?"

"Tastes good, too."

"Had any more of them spells?"

"No, Dad, I've been OK."

"Ever figure out what caused 'em?"

"No, sir."

"Word has it around town you've been acting really strange, like you've kinda' flipped your wig. Folks are talkin'. They think you're losin' your mind. What's ailin' you, boy?"

"You'd never understand. In fact, if I explained it, you'd think I was crazy as well. I'd just as soon keep you and Mother out of this."

"There's something else I don't understand."

"What's that, Dad?"

"Why you and Ruby just got married and she up and ran off with that fortune-teller cousin of hers to New Orleans. Damn, boy, you know what kind of place that is? What the hell is going on? What kind of man lets his wife take off like that right after the honeymoon? I just don't get it."

"I didn't want her to go any more than you did, Dad. I could have made her stay and she would have. She probably would have never forgiven me but she'd have stayed. The reason she went to New Orleans was she was afraid for Blanche to go down there alone."

"That slut would've fit right in down there, Robert. She'd have been fine. I just hope she doesn't corrupt your wife and drag her down the same road to Hell she's on. Conway was a lot better off when that piece of trash left here for Hollywood. She should've stayed there. You should've heard those Pullman sisters talking, Robert. It's all over town."

"Dad, Conway would be a lot better off without those Pullman sisters."

"I don't know what's happened to you son. I thought you had better sense than this."

"Look. If those old biddies would just stay out of our business, everything would be OK. We're not bothering anybody. Why they find the need to constantly pry into our lives is beyond me. Maybe it's because they don't have lives of their own. Hell, I can sure see why, too."

"When's Ruby gettin' back?"

"I should get a telegram today. Their return ticket was issued for tomorrow."

"There's something else, Robert."

Robert let out a long exaggerated sigh. "What now, Dad?"

"I hear you've been hangin' around them Catholics at St. Joseph's Church."

Mabel Agnew, Robert thought to himself, *the Ma Bell Blabbermouth of the South.* "I haven't been hangin' around them Catholics, Dad. I've cultivated a friendship with the priest there. His name is Father Donovan and we've talked several times. He's been a great help to me. He's given me a lot of much needed support, too."

"You could've talked to Brother Lawson, Robert. He's always available to help the congregation. There is no reason why you had to haul off and march across town to that Catholic church for comfort. You could have found it right here in your own Baptist church. What are you trying to prove anyway, boy? Your mother and I are too old for all of this fuss and bother. Why can't you get yourself straight?"

"Look, Dad, with all due respect, I haven't asked you and Mother for anything. I'm sorry if I've upset either of you with any of this and I'll try my best to get it all worked-out soon. I will tell you that I don't

give a damn what the folks of Conway say about my friendship with
Father Donovan or what they think about my marriage. I don't care.
I'd appreciate it if you'd tell those Pullman sisters to steer clear of my
house for a while. Lord only knows what will be said if they confront
me again."

"You'll respect your elders, boy. You won't embarrass us anymore
around town, either. Get your things and get to work. I think it's time
for the visit to be over."

* * *

As Ned Davis settled into reading his newspaper once again, Lila
entered the living room. She was pale, almost ashen. "Where's Robert?
I thought you two were in here talking."

"I sent him on to the store. We had words."

"Oh God …"

"What on earth is it, Lila? Why are you white as a ghost?"

"I have to talk to Robert immediately."

"About what for God's sake?"

"That was Mabel with a long distance call from New Orleans.
Something has happened, Ned; something horrible has happened."

CHAPTER TWENTY-TWO

Friday, April 8, 1932

"They think she might have been poisoned. There was a funny color around her lips, and she had vomited all over the bed."

"Yeah, you're right. I thought the same thing."

"Who else was here with her last night ... in the room?"

"That girl over there. I asked her what she saw or heard but she didn't hear nothin.' She's just been crying and mumblin' it's all her fault. She's a real mess."

"Poor thing, somebody needs to call her folks."

"I've called them."

"She's wearin' a ring. Must have a husband somewhere."

"I've left word for him with my in-laws."

"Wonder what these two broads were doin' down here by themselves anyway?"

Ruby had been listlessly staring out the hotel window. Here, in her bedroom, were two strange police officers talking about her as if she were not there. She felt numb inside. She felt so alone. Her beloved cousin was dead and her newlywed husband was four hundred miles away. Four hundred miles ... it may as well have been a million. Mabel had promised to track Robert down immediately. God, she hoped so. She needed his strong arms around her to assure her she'd get through this ... Her life had become so complicated these past few months.

The officers were still talking. She heard them refer to her repeatedly. No longer able to tolerate the non-person status, she said, "Not that you've heard me, but I've answered you twice. If you want to know what us two 'broads' were doing here, why don't you try asking me? I'm not deaf! You men carry on as if I don't hear a word you are saying."

"Just didn't want to disturb, Ma'am. This lady was a friend of yours I assume?"

"More than that, she was my first cousin."

"So if I might ask, Miss …"

"Mrs. Davis. My name is Ruby Davis."

"So if I might ask, Mrs. Davis, what were you and Miss Harris doing down here in New Orleans, anyway?"

Ruby sighed. "Miss Harrington. Blanche Harrington and it's an extremely long story, officers."

"Mrs. Davis, looks like there may have been a murder here. Our job is to find out who, where and why 'dis happened, so if it's a long story maybe you better get started on it."

"Have you ever heard of a lady by the name of Solange DeShotel?"

One of the officers choked and sputtered the minute she uttered the name. Trying to compose himself, he managed to rasp, "How would a classy lady like you possibly be associated with the likes of Solange DeShotel?"

Ruby sprang to her feet. "You know her?"

The other officer replied, "Let's just say we know of her. The real question is what does Solange DeShotel have to do with any of this?"

Ruby sighed again. "Have a seat, officers, and let me order you some coffee. We're going to be here awhile."

* * *

"We were just about to have lunch. Sr. Alexandra has prepared homemade soup. Would you like to join us?"

"I'd love to, Father. I'm a bachelor these days."

"What? What do you mean a bachelor?"

"Not what you are thinking. Ruby and her cousin Blanche have gone to New Orleans."

"For what, Robert? Why didn't you go with them?"

"They didn't ask me to. Blanche felt she could obtain the help she needed in New Orleans and Ruby insisted on going with her. Blanche didn't want her to, but Ruby would see no other way. Father Donovan, there is something sinister about that cousin of hers."

"Sinister? That's a pretty serious word."

"Blanche is obsessed with the spirit world and the afterlife. She's always dealing those tarot cards or having a premonition. I don't like Ruby being around her at all, but they've grown up together. They are like sisters and my wife is very protective of her."

"What about her own parents?"

"Let's see. Her father apparently deserted them when Blanche was very young. Blanche was the youngest and had two older brothers. If my memory serves me correctly, one of them went back to Ireland while the other moved out west to California."

"I thought that's where Miss Harrington is living."

"She is living in Hollywood. I don't know where exactly in California Eustis lives, but it's not Hollywood."

"So what happened to Mrs. Harrington?"

"She died of appendicitis when Blanche was about eleven. Blanche went to live with her aunt—my mother-in-law—Lorna Carraway. Blanche is five years older than Ruby, so they more or less grew up together."

"Where did Hollywood and the occult come into play?"

"I'm not exactly sure. Ruby said Blanche had a weird perception of things. She always saw people who weren't there. She'd describe their clothing and what they were doing. She swore she saw them. I remember Ruby telling a story of how Blanche ..."Robert paused for a moment. "Father, do you remember the old Tanner place?"

"You are going back about thirty-five years, Robert. Yes, I remember it, but it burned somewhere around '96 or '97. Why do you ask?"

Their attention was diverted when Sister Alexandra brought in two heaping bowls of vegetable soup. They smelled wonderful. Robert's mouth immediately began to water. She set the bowls down, and beside them, she also set down a plate of crusty French bread. Fresh butter and two glasses of iced lemonade accompanied the meal.

She smiled and said *"Bon appétit"* as she left the room.

"Dig in," Father Donovan said. "And please continue. We were taking about the Tanner place."

"Well," Robert started, "the story goes that Blanche was telling Lorna of a beautiful house she'd seen down the road. She described it in meticulous detail and talked of the nice lady who smiled and waved at her. She described the woman as tall and thin, with long red hair up in braids. She was wearing a floor-length lavender satin dress."

"That had to be Irma Tanner. I vaguely remember Irma, and Blanche's description fits."

"Apparently, this story unnerved Lorna because Blanche's account was so accurate. Anyway, as Blanche got older, she would hang around those transient gypsies on the edge of town. That was the beginning of her bad reputation. One of the women gave Blanche a deck of tarot cards in trade for some of her nicer clothing. I think the gypsy even taught her how to read them. She foretold fame and fortune for Blanche in the western part of this country. Blanche must never have forgotten because she moved out west after her eighteenth birthday. She says she's gotten bit parts in movies and is on the edge of her 'big break.' She has an agent and everything." Robert paused for a moment. "I don't know ... I just have this bad feeling about Blanche. I don't feel comfortable around her and I really don't want her hanging around too much, either. She has great influence over my wife."

"I'm so sorry to interrupt, Father."

"What is it, Sister?"

"I feel it is of paramount importance that you take this call immediately."

"Robert, excuse me please. I'll be back shortly."

"Of course."

As he ate in the rectory alone, thoughts of Ruby and Blanche in New Orleans filled his mind. *Things will be better when Blanche leaves for California.* Pondering the situation, he savored the hot, delicious soup. *His life would de-tangle soon ... hell, it had to. Get that bitch back on the train to where she belongs ...*

Father Donovan re-entered the room. "Perhaps your bad feelings about Blanche were justified. That was the New Orleans police on the telephone."

"The New Orleans Police?"

"I'm afraid I have some rather disturbing news."

* * *

"I can't believe I let those two go down to that God forsaken place," Lorna said as she wept into her handkerchief.

"Now, now, Lorna ... There is no way you could have known what was going to befall those girls."

"Jed, I knew New Orleans was a bad idea, two small town girls in a place like that."

"I wouldn't exactly call Blanche a small town girl ..."

"I heard that," Lorna snapped. "She's dead, Robert, so it really doesn't matter what you call her anymore. She can't defend herself, so why don't you let her rest in peace?"

"I'm sorry, Lorna. That was uncalled for."

"Damn right it was."

Jed wheeled around in amazement. He'd never heard Lorna talk like that, much less swear. "We have to get down there, Lorna. Our daughter's in that hellhole all alone."

Lorna wiped her eyes again. She took a deep breath and began. "It's all been arranged, Jed. Brother Lawson called, and apparently, the congregation has raised enough funds for three train tickets to New Orleans. They have some sort of emergency booking clause and we were able to get reservations immediately. Brother Lawson knows a Baptist missionary minister down there who has invited us to stay overnight at the parsonage. We have a way to get there and a place to stay."

"How soon can we get down there?"

"Tomorrow evening's the soonest," Robert interjected.

"She'll have to go it alone tonight, oh my poor baby." Lorna began to cry again.

"Oh God, Lorna, I'm so sorry." Jed put his arms around her. "We'll get through this ... we have to for Ruby's sake. Let's try to keep busy in the meantime. We'll need to pack and get some food."

"None of us have eaten. I'll make some sandwiches and prepare extra for the trip."

Jed turned to Robert. "Why don't you go home and pack. We have a long day ahead of us tomorrow. I hate to ask this, Lorna, but what about the body?"

"They said something about an autopsy, and then the body has to be embalmed before it's brought across the state line."

"I don't mean to interrupt," Robert said, "but Blanche hated this place."

Jed looked at him intently. "What's your point?"

Robert swallowed hard. "Have you ever considered … Maybe cremating her?"

"You mean burning her up?"

Robert could feel Jed's intimidating stare burning a hole through him. "Forget it, just a thought."

Lorna took a long look at Robert. She'd known him all of his life, but at this moment, he may as well have been a stranger. "We'll make a decision about arrangements when we know more. Robert, would you like a sandwich?"

"No thanks, Lorna, I ate just awhile ago."

"Across town, huh Rob. They feed you well?"

Robert turned to answer and then realized the point was mute. The judgmental sneer said everything. "Just fine, Sir. I'll see you folks in the morning. Call me early."

CHAPTER TWENTY-THREE

Still in shock, Ruby went through the motions of dressing. To keep from going mad, she had to leave the hotel—even for a momentary diversion. The reality of Blanche's murder was hard to accept. She kept hoping it was some horrible dream from which she'd soon awaken.

She made her way through the hotel lobby and then outside onto the streets of the French Quarter. She'd walk for a while, hopefully losing herself in the ambience of the surroundings. It seemed sad that such a unique, exciting place would now hold captive the memories of Blanche's murder; and for Ruby, that would never change. Perusing the shops and enjoying some of the architecture, she'd decided to make her way down the sidewalks of the Quarter. Maybe this would provide a brief respite from the situation at hand. Walking as far as Esplanade Avenue, she decided to turn back toward the hotel. She had no idea how far she'd walked or how long she'd been gone, when she came upon several beautiful oil paintings clad in elaborate gold leaf frames. Displayed in the front window of an art gallery, they were sitting on easels.

"So very lovely," she mumbled to herself.

"Yes, they are."

Abruptly, Ruby's dreamlike state was interrupted. "Oh, I'm sorry, I was just looking."

"Please don't let me interrupt." Standing in front of Ruby was a beautifully chiseled man. Tall, lithe and perfectly proportioned, his pale skin served as the ideal backdrop for his clear, blue eyes. Tousled about his face, a thick shock of black hair completed the picture.

"They're stunning."

"I'll consider that a compliment from a lovely lady such as yourself."

Realizing she was thinking aloud, she blushed. "Please forgive me, Sir. I wasn't being forward. I must go."

"Forward was never an issue. I don't have many visitors expressing a genuine appreciation of art as you just did, especially visitors as lovely as you. If you have a moment, I'd like your opinion on some of the other works in the gallery. It would be a treat to hear your thoughts on them."

"There are so many beautiful things here."

"My name is Rupert Staten."

"Such a formal name, Mr. Staten. Mine is Ruby Davis."

"Mrs. Davis, I presume?"

"Yes, Mrs. Ruby Davis."

"Actually, it wasn't a presumption at all, Mrs. Ruby Davis. The ring gives you away. It's lovely."

Her glance was diverted to her engagement ring. "It is lovely, thank-you. I believe this to be an heirloom piece from my husband's family."

His gaze unflinching, he answered with only a smile.

Ruby could feel her face becoming hot. She broke his gaze and walked toward the back of the gallery. There, on the back wall, was a framed painting entitled La Paraseusse.

"Oh, this is exquisite! It's an Erté."

"You're familiar with Erté?"

"I have always enjoyed his covers of *Harper's Bazaar*. I'm not a huge fan of Art Deco, but like everything else, it has its place. His name is actually Romain de Tirtoff."

"Parlez-vous Français?"

"Oh no, I've just read about him. His initials are pronounced err—tay in French." Ruby laughed to herself. "I must sound pretty ridiculous to an art connoisseur."

"Actually, you just sound pretty. Have a look at the detail here. Erté used a wide array of colors in this one, not to mention incorporating a lot of detail into 'The Lazy Woman.' The white background kind of sets her apart from the rest of the painting." He stared at the artwork for a moment. "This particular Erté is one of my favorites." Rupert had Ruby's hand in his and both were pointing to the upper left corner of the painting. Bending his head toward her, he breathed in deeply the aroma of her perfume.

Ruby felt his breath upon the back of her neck. Feeling the weight of her body slowly sinking into his strong massive frame, she perceived an emergence of comfort and safety. It was blissful. Suddenly, she no longer felt alone.

Reality reemerged, bringing with it ugly thoughts of impropriety. Aware of her vulnerability, she broke the embrace and turned to leave.

"I must go."

"You'll come back and see the rest, Ruby?"

"I don't think so. My husband is on his way and ... I have to leave." Ruby abruptly turned and left the gallery. Her eyes filling quickly with tears, she could hardly catch her breath. *It must be the stress of all that has happened ...*

She made her way about a block toward the hotel and then stopped. She could walk no further. The nurturing, protective cushion of shock was now spent. The long expected post-traumatic emotions had begun to surface. Leaning against the corner of a building, she could no longer stop the tears. At this point, she wasn't really sure if she wanted to. The world began to spin as she slid to the ground; overwhelmed, she could handle nothing else. Suddenly, she felt two strong hands grab her and sweep her into a strong, secure embrace. "Hey, hey ... There now. It's OK. Nothing can be this bad. What could possibly have upset you like this?"

Irrational may be the word to best describe the next moment. There was no more strength, no more reserve, only surrender to the consuming grief. She could no longer distinguish fantasy from reality. "I knew you'd come. I knew you'd find me." Feeling such relief her husband was here to comfort her, Ruby fell into his arms sobbing. Everything was all right now. Everything would be OK.

* * *

"Where are you staying?"

"The Montelone Hotel."

"We're almost there. It's only a few blocks away."

In an attempt to steady herself, she took a deep breath. She then wiped her eyes with her handkerchief. "I'm a little embarrassed by this whole thing. I'm so sorry. I've been in such a state. You'll have to forgive me."

"Nothing to forgive, I'm just glad I could help."

Shortly thereafter, they arrived at the hotel. Walking through the lobby, Rupert stopped short of the elevators.

"I trust you can get to your room?"

Ruby managed a smile. "I'm fine now. I'll be OK."

Rupert returned the smile. "I'll be off then." With that made his way toward the door.

"Rupert?"

He turned toward her after she'd said this.

"Thank you again."

"You're welcome." He gave a small nod of farewell. "Perhaps we'll meet again someday."

"Perhaps … Someday."

He turned to leave once more. *We'll meet again, Mrs. Davis. I'll make sure of it.*

* * *

"She is dead I tell you."

"Oh, Heloise, you and all of your ridiculous notions."

The New Light Baptist church Ladies' Circle had gathered in the church hall for the weekly quilting bee. The Ladies' Circle would quilt blankets, coverlets, and sew garments for an anticipated arrival. No quilting bee was complete without a covered dish supper and the latest gossip.

"Well, I don't care if you believe me or not, Hilda, but Mabel spoke with Lorna Carraway yesterday."

"Let's translate that: Mabel eavesdropped on Lorna Carraway yesterday."

"All I know is Blanche Harrington is dead. They think she was murdered."

"Who are *they*, Heloise?"

"Why the New Orleans police, of course. They're investigating right now."

There was an excited mumble amongst the ladies in the circle. "Murdered? But how? Who would want to kill Blanche? What about Ruby? Was she alright?" The atmosphere was charged with excitement.

"I'll just bet Blanche Harrington was on those streets making a living before she met her maker."

A few women gasped. This was one of those instances in which everyone may have been thinking the same thing, but no one dared say it aloud—no one except Heloise Pullman, that is.

"Heloise," Hilda exhaled, "this is neither the time nor the place."

"I'm only speaking the truth. That Blanche Harrington was never any good, always telling fortunes, reading those cards, and doing the devil's bidding. You should have seen how she was dressed the other day. The world's a better place without her."

Hilda looked around at the Ladies' Circle. Some mouths were agape; some had gathered their coats, while others had simply ignored Heloise and kept quilting.

"I'll tell you something else."

"No, nothing else." She turned her attention to the crowd. "Ladies, I think it's time for our dinner break."

Heloise ignored her and continued. "That Blanche was preying on Robert Davis' mental illness. She was giving him all kinds of crazy notions. She lured our poor, sweet Ruby to that … that sinful place and then got herself killed working those French Quarter streets. The good Lord knew what he was doing. She was well on her way to dragging both Ruby and Robert down the path of doom and destruction, right along with her. Everyone in this town feels sorry for Lorna Carraway. Blanche has put such a burden on her since her mother died. Fine way she repays Lorna, walking those streets at night. I hope she rots in Hell."

Ushering her to a corner of the room, Hilda tugged on the sleeve of Heloise's dress. "And Lorna Carraway will not appreciate the fact that you're airing her business in front of the Ladies' Circle. You have gone too far."

"Hilda, you know I'm telling the truth."

"I know you're telling the truth. They know you're telling the truth, but the real truth of the matter is there are human emotions involved. The woman was murdered for Christ's sake! Think of her family. You hope she rots in Hell? They loved her, Heloise. They will be devastated when they hear what you've said about them." Contemplating what to say next, she stared at her sister for a moment. "Sister, I think it's time for you to leave. You've done enough damage for one night." She then left Heloise in the corner of the room and returned to the group. "Ladies, why don't we discuss something less controversial over this evening meal?" The atmosphere had grown tense in the hall. Several of the women were mumbling their disdain for Heloise's outburst. "Why don't we all retire to the cafeteria?"

Still in the corner of the room, Heloise interrupted. "Since I've obviously offended many of you tonight by speaking the truth, I've been asked to leave. I will do so, but not without leaving you with food for thought."

Most of the women didn't bother to acknowledge her parting comments. There were a few, however, who stopped to listen. "At one time or another, everyone in this room has conveyed to me what a whore Blanche Harrington was. I, for one, am not afraid to admit it just because her life is over. The fact that she's dead now does nothing to moralize her reputation. Call me what you like, but one thing you will not call me is a hypocrite."

The lingering crowd waited for her to say something else. There was nothing. Slamming the hall door to accentuate her exit, she merely turned and left. Hilda walked over to the remaining women and ushered them through the breezeway. "Let's not use her parting comments as food for thought."

CHAPTER TWENTY-FOUR

Lorna, Jed, and Robert arrived in the Crescent City around 6:00 P.M.

As they stepped from the train, they were overwhelmed by the bustle of activity about the station. Looking around, Lorna took a handkerchief out of her pocket and wiped her brow. She was amazed how thick and muggy the air felt. Searching for the man with whom Brother Lawson had made arrangements on their behalf, she scanned the crowd. Finally, toward the back of the mass, she spotted a sign reading Carraway.

"There it is."

Jed and Lorna began making their way through the crowded platform. Carrying most of the luggage, Robert followed closely behind. As they approached the man holding the sign, she said, "Hello, I'm Lorna Carraway. I believe you to be the man who is to help us?"

The man returned the smile. "I'm Brother William Faust, Lorna. I wish I could welcome you to New Orleans under happier circumstances. I've talked to Brother Lawson and am well aware of the situation facing all of you. Why don't we get your things loaded into the car and work on getting all of you settled for the evening?"

At this point Robert set the baggage down and stepped forward to join Jed, Lorna, and William in conversation.

"This is my husband Jed Carraway and my son-in-law Robert Davis. We all appreciate your gracious hospitality, but if it were all the same to you, we'd rather get to our daughter first."

William smiled apologetically. "Of course, I understand. She's staying at the Monteleone Hotel in the French Quarter. We'll check her out of the hotel and then retire to the parsonage for the evening. My wife Vera has prepared supper for all of us."

Jed replied, "We'll try not to impose, Reverend. Our return ticket is for tomorrow."

"Don't be ridiculous. We're glad to be able to help you. Vera has sleeping arrangements for everyone. It will be cozy but I think we'll be comfortable."

Robert turned to Brother Faust. "I don't care if we sleep on the kitchen floor. We just appreciate your hospitality."

"We can do better than the kitchen floor, Robert. Right now, we need to concentrate on getting that child back into the bosom of her family. If we're all ready, I think it's time to head for the hotel."

"Amen to that," Jed replied. "Let's go."

* * *

"I can't believe it."

"Can't believe what, Madame? "

"All of my life, in vain I've searched for this. I've looked everywhere and finally it falls right into my lap."

"What exactly have you found, Madame?"

"A portal. I've found a breach through time and space. I've finally found the thing that will allow entry into another dimension, Angelique." Madame rubbed the gold dollar between her fingers. "The energy signature on this piece is phenomenal. Used correctly, there is no limit as to what I can attain with this."

"That's the piece the woman gave you night before last?"

Madame threw her head back in laughter. "Stupid fool, she came to me for 'spiritual guidance.' She needed help on how to proceed with her problem. She had no idea what she was confronting." A sneer made its way across her face. "I gave her all the answers she needed; it just cost her life." Again, she laughed tauntingly. "Ironic, isn't it? Our tarot card reader was too ignorant to realize that she held the key to her 'mystery' in her hand the whole time. This is an icon, Angelique, a window past the veil which separates this world from the next one."

"If you rip that veil, Madame, you may find you can no longer control the power you hold in your hands. You are dealing with forces more powerful than you."

"Shut up, fool. How dare you talk to me like that? Apparently you have no clue as to the powers you are dealing with in this very room."

"I meant no disrespect, Madame, but I have practiced much in the arts of Voodoo."

"The powers I now possess will make your Voodoo rituals look like nursery rhymes. Don't you realize what I have here? It's a virtual beacon across the ages, a beacon that I don't have to share with anyone. It's all mine."

"Does the power belong to you or are you now the subservient one?"

Madame's eyes narrowed to slits. She hissed, "You know nothing. You are nothing. You are but a slave girl to me, so how can you speak of my subservience?"

"I'm no slave, Madame; my people were freed more than sixty years ago."

"If you persist, I'll throw you out into the streets with nothing." Solange closed the distance between them. "How dare you question my vast knowledge? How dare you have an opinion? You're ignorant and illiterate. How could you possibly know the magnitude of this occurrence?"

"My apologies, Madame."

Saying nothing, Solange stared at the piece in her hand. The room was silent for a moment. Finally, she looked up and said, "I'll take tea in the living room."

"Yes, Madame."

Walking toward the front of the house, she left the room. After a few steps, she stopped and turned to face Angelique once more. "I give you fair warning not to ever speak in the manner you spoke to me tonight, Angelique. I'll not tolerate it again and you will wish you'd never been born. Are we understood?"

"We're understood, Madame." She stood there waiting for Solange to continue; there was nothing else.

"Will that be all?"

Madame nodded yes. She returned the gesture with a tacit nod and quietly left the room.

* * *

Oh God, there he was. She wouldn't cry. She would be strong. The tears came anyway. She'd tried to hold them at bay when she saw him, but was overwrought with emotion. As Robert, Jed and Lorna walked toward her, she broke down. She approached them, arms outstretched. "Oh Momma, Daddy ..." Her head came to rest on Jed's shoulder.

"It's OK, Baby, we're here now. Everything will be alright."

"It'll never be OK, Daddy. Blanche is dead. She died right beside me and there was nothing I could do to help her."

Robert walked over and gently took her arm. "Let's sit down, Ruby. Let's all have a seat."

She sat down and began wiping her eyes with a handkerchief. Taking a few deep breaths, she struggled to compose herself. After a moment, she realized there was a man she didn't recognize standing amongst them. Wiping her eyes once more, she said, "Hello, I'm Ruby Davis."

The man smiled sympathetically. "I'm William Faust, Ruby. Brother Lawson is a close, personal friend of mine and asked that I tend to all of you while you're in town. Why don't we gather your luggage and head over to the parsonage. You can all relax after such a hard journey."

"That's very kind." Ruby managed a smile and turned to her father. "In light of the circumstances, the hotel has made provisions for me until tomorrow. I told them I'd be returning to Conway then."

"You want to stay here in the hotel, Ruby?"

"I'm just saying they have a room reserved for Robert and me if we want it. They've offered it at the hotel's expense."

Brother Faust listened intently to the conversation. "We certainly don't mind having all of you for the evening, but this might make everyone a little more comfortable. Ruby, why don't you come to supper with us, and I'll see you and Robert back to the hotel for the night. In the morning, I'll take you all to the train station."

Ruby turned to Robert. "OK with you?"

"Ruby, I don't want to stay in the room Blanche died in."

"Oh, no, that room has been sealed by the New Orleans Police, darling. The hotel has offered us a room on the sixth floor. If you'd rather stay at Brother Faust's, I'll go pack. It's entirely up to you."

"No, no, that's fine. We can stay here, but why don't we take him up on his dinner plans? I'll get my luggage from the car and head up to the room. Then we can leave."

Ruby felt her eyes begin to tear again. "Oh Robert, I'm so glad you're here."

Robert took Ruby into his arms and kissed her. "I'm here, Ruby, and I'm not going anywhere without you. Stay with Jed and Lorna. I'll be right back with my things."

As Robert made his way toward Brother Faust's automobile, Ruby realized how utterly alone she'd felt. A sense of relief washed over her as she realized that she no longer had to cope with this situation alone. "Thank you, God," she prayed.

✻ ✻ ✻

The night was spent in long conversations, tears, and making love. Kissing and caressing, they laid in each other's arms. "I guess I haven't been a very good husband."

"Why on earth would you say that?"

"A good husband would have never allowed you to come down here and fall into this situation. I should have said no."

Ruby sat up in bed. "Pardon me, Robert, but that wasn't your decision to make. Rest assured I did not ask you whether I could come or not."

"I'm just saying I should have persuaded you to stay in Conway. Ruby, we are barely married. The timing was not exactly appropriate for you to foray into the bowels of the New Orleans underworld—alone, nonetheless."

"I wasn't alone, Robert. I was with Blanche. I couldn't let her come here alone. I was terrified of what might happen to her. The saddest part of all of this is my fears were justified. If you thought this so inappropriate, why didn't you come with me? You could have come with us … Perhaps things would have turned out differently."

He sat up in bed as well. "This is not my fault, Ruby Davis. You didn't ask me to go to New Orleans."

"I should not have had to ask."

"You and Blanche made it pretty clear that was not an option. Sure, it's easy to look back and cast blame, but that's not the way it was, Ruby. That's not the way it was at all and you know it."

Ruby's lip began to quiver. "I just keep hoping I'll awaken from all of this; it's too much."

The anger between them faded. In an attempt to reassure her, Robert kissed her tenderly. "We'll get through this. I promise. It'll just take time."

As he said this, there was a knock on the door. Startled, Robert and Ruby sat straight up in bed. "Who on earth could that be at this hour?"

"I have no idea. Stay put." Robert got out of bed and put on his robe. He went to his suitcase and pulled from it a revolver. He then went to the door. "Who's there?"

"Mr. Davis?"

"It's late and I don't talk through a door."

"I suggest you open it then."

"Let me first tell you I have a gun and won't hesitate to kill you if need be. I've just called the police. I suggest you get out of here while you still can."

"I'm Angelique Gravois, housekeeper for Madame Solange De-Shotel. I have something that belongs to you, something I think you may want returned to you this evening."

"Don't, Robert!" Ruby implored. "Get away from the door! It's a trap!"

In an attempt to call the hotel operator, Ruby ran to the phone. Her hands were shaking so badly that it fell to the floor in a mass of tangled black cord and receiver. She fell to the floor after it, desperately trying to untangle the mess and call.

"Wait," Robert whispered, "just wait. Don't call." He turned his attention to the door. "How do I know you are who you say?"

"It's a 1907 twenty-dollar gold piece, Mr. Davis. That's how you know."

As he slowly opened the hotel room door, he pulled the hammer of the revolver toward him and cocked the gun.

Standing in the hallway was a beautiful woman of color. She could not have been more than twenty years of age.

"Where's the piece?"

"I have it, Mr. Davis, but before I return it to you, I must talk to you. It's a matter of life and death—yours as a matter of fact. Much hangs in the balance of what I have to say."

CHAPTER TWENTY-FIVE

"She treated me like a servant. No, it was worse than that ... she treated me like a slave. She didn't think I could read or write. Madame was sure I was totally illiterate. She needed someone like that working for her. She needed someone too ignorant to catch on to her evil ways and be aware of what she was doing. I knew just how evil she really was. Solange DeShotel poisoned your cousin Blanche, ma'am. She murdered her. I served them in the living room and Madame gave her a poisoned tea. I'm sure of it."

"Then why in the hell haven't you gone to the police?"

"Both of you are in grave danger, Sir; my life is as much as over as soon as Madame discovers I've told you all of this."

"All of what?" Ruby asked.

"Unfortunately, Blanche Harrington believed Madame could help her with your problem. She was no match for someone like Solange. Blanche may have gained some trivial knowledge through the tarot and folklore she'd collected throughout the years, but the lady she went to for help is a sleeve of Satan's cloak. You see, Mr. and Mrs. Davis, Madame DeShotel has as much as sold her soul to him. In return, I guess she's received certain supernatural gifts. She's not omniscient, mind you, but she is very powerful. I don't know what has transpired to bring about your situation but Madame has recognized the fact it has torn a rift in the time-space continuum. She recognized this piece immediately as a portal."

Robert looked at Angelique. "I remember Blanche telling me we had to find a portal. What exactly is a portal, anyway?"

"It is a key or entryway into the spiritual world. One can utilize a portal to leave this dimension and enter another. The piece you possess has the ability to lift the thin veil between our world and the spiritual one, allowing passage from one to the next. Unfortunately, Madame knows this and is well aware of how to use it. God himself only knows what havoc she might wreak upon the ages if she were to have access to this portal. It was not meant for her hands. I firmly believe it was meant to aid you in your journey home."

"He is home," Ruby snapped.

Angelique did not acknowledge the comment. She continued. "In other words, this piece is the solution to your problems. It did not appear in your life by accident. You must guard it with your life because your very existence depends on it."

Ruby yanked her robe around and stepped forward. Her demeanor was that of agitated as well as offended. "I'll have you know that it was my idea to buy this coin for my husband. It was not an accident, Angelique. It was my idea. It is not mystical, and it is not a portal. It is a wedding gift."

"Enhanced by the Voodoo religion, my catholic roots run deep. I have myself learned you are on a time ribbon fast approaching end. Guard your energy signature with your life and leave this place as soon as you can. You and your wife must stay safe until this time paradox is resolved. Your spirit, Robert Davis, could be lost for the ages if Solange gains this piece. I'm done and now I must go."

Ruby grabbed Angelique by the arm. "You can't go back there, Angelique. She'll kill you."

"No ma'am, I'm not going back. I'm leaving, never to return. With God's help she'll never find me, and I will stay safe as well."

"Before you go, Angelique, where is she staying?"

"She has a flat one block from the corner of St. Ann and Rampart."

"I'm giving the address to the police," Robert said as he walked over to the telephone. Maybe they'll find her there. Maybe they can stop her once and for all." Waiting for an answer, Robert stared into the transparent brown eyes.

"Be warned: as I told you before, she possesses many powers. She may not know why she must run, but she will follow her instincts. If those instincts have already manifested, she may very well be gone. I must go now as well. Godspeed to both of you."

* * *

Sunday Morning, April 10, 1932

The night offered only fitful sleep. Around 4:00 A.M. Robert abandoned the notion of rest. Arising to gather their things, he checked the armoire. Making sure no clothing was left behind, he then rechecked the pouch in their suitcase. The coin was still there. There was nothing more to do than to return to bed and wait for morning; amazed his wife had not yet awakened, he did so.

Around seven, Ruby did awaken. Rubbing her eyes, she blinked repeatedly in an attempt to clear her vision. "You're already dressed. Did you sleep in your clothes?"

"Didn't sleep much last night. I finally got dressed around four. I've packed, too, so we're ready to go."

"Then I'd better hurry." She arose from bed and made her way toward the bathroom.

He followed her into it. "Not to worry, I've called the front desk. We have the room until noon."

"Perhaps you'd better call the parsonage and let them know what time we'll be ready."

"You know, we have a long trip in front of us, Rube, and I feel like I've been run over by a train. If it's all right with you, I need a hot bath. Maybe it'll make me feel better."

"You go ahead and do that, honey. I'll call Brother Faust. She walked over to the window of the hotel room. "I've never been so glad to leave a place in all of my life. If I never come here again, it'll be too soon."

"No reason for you to come back here, Ruby. We just need to go home and get our lives back to normal." After he'd said this, he paused for a moment. Leaning back into the large, claw-foot tub, he closed his eyes. "Damn this feels good; I think every bone in my body aches right now."

"Did you pack my print dress? I want to wear it home today."

"I left your hanging clothes on the door. Are you hungry?"

"A little, I still have to put my makeup on. I should be ready in a few minutes, though. We'll go down to eat when you're done with your bath."

"Since you're almost ready, why don't you go on down to the hotel restaurant and order us some breakfast. There's money in my wallet."

"I don't know if I want to do that or not."

"What's wrong?"

"I'm not particularly fond of going anywhere without you right now. If that lunatic suspects we have this coin, she may be waiting for us."

"We can't let her rule our lives, Rube. At this very moment, there are police manning the doors of the hotel lobby. I'll call the New Orleans Police for an update. Maybe that'll put your mind at ease."

"Nothing will put my mind at ease until they catch Blanche's killer."

"Order us some food, and I'll come down and fill you in on everything."

"Well, it will probably be cold by the time you get there. How long do you plan to soak?"

"I'll be down in a few minutes."

For a long moment she hesitated. "OK ... I guess that'll be alright. I'll just finish dressing after we eat. What do you want? For breakfast I mean."

"Eggs, bacon and coffee. See if you can get me some freshly squeezed orange juice as well."

Ruby turned toward the door to leave but stopped. Tucking a tendril of hair behind her ear, she looked back at Robert. "For an independent woman, I don't feel very independent right now. I hate that ... Hurry up, OK?"

"Ten minutes tops."

"Oh, and I never did call Brother Faust. You need to do that. Don't forget."

"I won't." Ruby closed the door behind her and made her way toward the lift.

✳ ✳ ✳

The elevator doors opened, revealing the rich, beautiful lobby. She'd almost made her way across it, when she heard a familiar voice. "I hoped I'd run into you."

This sudden accosting startled her. "Rupert! Oh, my goodness. What a surprise …"

"A good one, I hope."

"Of course it is." Feeling herself blush, she half-smiled. "I just didn't expect …"

"I have something for you."

"For me?"

"Here. Hopefully with this you won't forget me and my little gallery in the quarter."

"La Parasseuse? Oh Rupert, I couldn't. This is much too expensive."

"Not too expensive, Ruby. Consider it a wedding gift. Where is your husband, anyway?"

"He's on his way. He's not yet dressed, so I came ahead to order breakfast. Would you like to join us?"

"No, no, I have to return to the gallery. Ruby, I say goodbye now and want you to know if I'd …" Rupert looked down and paused. He began again. "Well, perhaps your presence will grace my gallery again someday."

"New Orleans doesn't leave much in the way of happiness for me, Rupert. All I've felt here is fear, sadness and anxiety. How did you know I was leaving this morning, anyway?"

"Actually this is not as big a place as you might think. Even here, word does get around. Where are you off to—as in where is home?"

"Conway, Arkansas."

Rupert's expression changed from smiling to one of deep concern. "Beware of Solange, Ruby; I've heard she's dangerous. The further away from her you stay the better."

"Good advice from a stranger. Who are you?"

"Oh my stars!" She turned to face him. "Robert … now you've startled me as well."

"As well? You sound as if you've already had a bit of a jolt, my darling."

She swallowed hard "I'd like you to meet a friend of mine. This is Rupert …"

"Staten, Rupert Staten." Stepping forward toward Robert's approach, Rupert extended his hand. "And you must be Robert Davis?"

Robert shook his hand, replying only, "I am."

"You're a very lucky man, Robert."

"That I am as well." Robert turned to Ruby and then back to Rupert. "How did you two make acquaintance, by the way?" As he said this, he waved two fingers between them as if there was some bond or alliance he didn't quite understand.

"He's a gallery owner here in the quarter."

"I met your wife a couple days ago. She was perusing some impressionistic oils in the front of my shop." He held the painting forward. "I've brought you two a wedding present."

"Mr. Staten, pardon me if I appear ignorant, but that looks nothing like impressionistic oil."

"It's an"

"Erté, I know. Did some covers for *Harper's Bazaar*. Funny, you learn something new about your spouse every day. Ruby, I've never heard you mention Erté."

"Since we have such a busy day ahead of us, I think we best get to the restaurant. If you care to further discuss Romain de Tirtoff, we can do so then." She turned to Rupert and extended her hand. "Thank you for the gift."

"My pleasure. Nice to meet you, Robert. Be careful traveling home." Rupert headed toward the door.

Robert turned to Ruby. "Maybe you've left something out here?"

"I've left nothing out. I'm as surprised by this gift as you are."

Walking away from him, she said nothing else.

Cocking his head a little to one side, he watched her silhouette fade into the restaurant doorway.

I'll just bet you are … so pleasantly surprised …

✳ ✳ ✳

Ruby wiped her face with her napkin. "I'll have to admit that breakfast in a beautiful hotel is something I could easily get used to."

"Would you like anything else?"

"No, no, I'm fine, thank you."

"Here comes your Mother, Jed, and Brother Faust, right on time."

As the three of them approached, two men followed closely behind them.

"Good morning," Ruby said as she turned toward them.

Lorna bent down and gave Ruby a kiss. "Good Morning, darling. Were you able to sleep last night?"

"I did sleep last night. Having all of you here with me …" She didn't finish. It was too painful. She breathed in deeply and exhaled. "Are we all ready to head back to Conway?"

"Ruby," Jed began, "This is Officer Richard Esperanza and Officer Schuyler Smith."

Looking a little puzzled, she answered, "Very nice to meet you, officers." She then turned back to Jed and Lorna. "So, are we ready?"

Jed continued. "Ruby, the police have a hunch this DeShotel woman might be aboard our train. They're sending a team of officers posing as us on our train to Conway."

"Then how will we get home?"

"I'll drive you," Brother Faust interjected.

"Oh, no! There is no reason to endanger your life as well. We don't need to involve you any further in all of this. And besides that, it's a two to three day drive to Conway."

"The way I figure it, honey, between William, myself and Robert, we don't have to stop much. I'll admit it's not the luxury of a train, but if it's for our own safety …"

"It is for your own safety," Officer Esperanza added. We've arranged for a return ticket and hopefully will apprehend this suspect aboard the train. All proper personnel have been notified, and should the need arise, we've arranged extradition with Arkansas."

"Couldn't we just take a later train or use an alias or something?"

"Mrs. Davis, there is something else. There was a fire in the French quarter last night near the corner of St. Ann and Rampart."

"Oh my God … Solange. Was anyone … did anyone perish?"

"No, the place was empty. Evidently, whoever had been living there was gone, and apparently, had left in a hurry. Mrs. Davis, the sooner you slip out of town, the better. I ask that you leave this morning and let this man drive you. The arrangements have been made."

"I'm becoming aware of that. Well, nothing else to be said, so let's get this trip behind us."

"Here, Rube," Robert said as he reached for her luggage. "Let me load those."

William walked over to Robert to help him with the suitcases. "I have a luggage rack of sorts on top of my car, Robert. We should be able to put most of this up there." He then gathered a rope from the trunk and began to fasten the baggage to the rack. "I've never been to Arkansas, but I've heard it's beautiful."

"It is," Robert answered. "It's a different beauty than this with its own unique charm."

Lorna, Jed, Robert, and William all settled into the automobile. Ruby was the last to get in. Her back was to them, but Lorna could see her eyes brimming with tears once again. She turned to the others and said, "I'll just be a moment." She then got out of the car and gently put her hand on Ruby's shoulder. "Come on, honey, it's time to go." Softly, she took her arm and guided her toward the sedan.

Ruby turned for one last look. "Goodbye, New Orleans, and goodbye to my Blanche …" She wasn't able to finish the sentence. A lump arose in her throat. Covering her face with a handkerchief, she began to cry.

With tears in her eyes as well, Lorna tried her best to console her. As they pulled away from the hotel garage, she put her arm around her daughter and held her close.

From the hotel lobby window, Rupert watched the sedan's silhouette rapidly fade away.

* * *

Monday, April 11, 1932

"And so that's it. We ended up driving home from New Orleans. Poor Ruby vomited all of the way. She gets carsick so easily."

"Well, I do vow." Lila cut her eyes toward Ned, who returned the glance.

"So, Robert," Lila began, "is this DeShotel woman still at large?"

"They really don't know where she is."

"Well, it's not a very settling feeling. Have you contacted the police here in Conway?"

"They are aware of everything."

Ned interjected. "Lotta good that's going to do if that crazy woman comes at you with a gun. I suggest you get one yourself and keep it handy. Learn to use it, boy."

"I've already done that."

"You got a shotgun?"

"No, I bought a pistol."

"You need a shotgun ... and some shells, too. I'll call Dick Carson and tell him you're going to stop by his store. You can do that on your way to work. He'll get you all set up."

"Yes sir."

"We've been short-handed at the store, so don't dawdle. I'm going to get dressed. See you in a while, boy."

I can hardly wait.

CHAPTER TWENTY-SIX

Just as she desired, the room was dark. Casting an ominous, evil ambience, candles were set about the floor in a peculiar geometric pattern. A sickly-sweet pyramid of incense glowed from the center of the candle configuration.

Shadows produced by the flames flickered about her face. The dim shards of light accentuated frozen images of bizarre facial expressions made as she recited black magic incantations aloud.

"I'm so close … so close to penetrating the veil that I can almost see it. My opportunity for escape from this time has finally arrived. I must get the portal and leave before this imprint dissipates. I shan't be trapped in this short matrix for all time. Soon, I'll be free to roam across the ages, amassing great wealth and power."

"Once the man is dead, his soul will leave. His woman has no purpose here either. She may as well die, too. I have no power over their souls, but can eliminate their physical presence with great satisfaction. I can leave an imprint on history by providing them with a violent demise, one that is physically repulsive."

She pulled the hairpin from her hair. Encircling her delicate, chiseled features, her auburn tresses cascaded downward. Reaching for the crystal stem in front of her, she drank deeply. Her eyes closed as she ingested its contents. Her lips grew crimson from the residual. She laughed aloud. "They are so stupid to think they can ever find me. They'll all die as a result of their noble ambitions." She laughed again. "They have no clue they are all doomed …" She then burst into evil, horrific hysterics. As she gazed into the mirror in front of her, the laughter abruptly ceased. Her eyes widened as if she were actually talking to the person behind the glass. "The real question is where must I kill them?"

* * *

Wednesday, April 13, 1932

"Look at it, all white with bright red and blue tulips all over it. Looks like Heloise is wearing her new 'Spring Fat Dress.'"

In a corner of the fellowship hall, Beverly Martin and Eva Nell Alexander critiqued the Ladies' Circle attire.

"She looks like a greenhouse explosion," Eva Nell snickered, "and that feathered hat ..."

"Must be Hilda's ..."

"And to think Hilda was actually married. Who would want to ... ?"

"You both make me sick," Ruby interrupted.

"I don't remember inviting you to join our conversation," Beverly snapped back. "And I'm not the one making you sick these days, Mrs. Davis. Let's just hope the real reason doesn't happen to be a little early?"

Ruby knew exactly what Beverly was thinking, and in reality, the thought of pregnancy had crossed her mind. However, at this moment, Hell would freeze over before she gave these two the satisfaction of acknowledgment. Her eyes narrowed. "So, Bev, will you deliver yours or do pit vipers hatch from eggs?"

Beverly laughed. "How cute."

"Tell you what. Why don't both of you hypocrites get out of here? Just go home and stop pretending to be decent. At least Heloise is genuinely ..."

"Genuinely what?" Ruby looked around to discover that Heloise Pullman had joined the threesome.

"Heloise," Beverly began, "we were just commenting on your new Spring F ..."

"Fiesta Dress," Ruby finished.

"That's not exactly what I was about to say, Ruby."

"What on earth is a 'Spring Fiesta Dress'? Is that good or bad? Is it some new style I inadvertently ran across?"

"Oh no, Heloise; you've been working on that style for years," Eva interjected.

"Come along, dear," Ruby said as she took Heloise's arm. "I have some questions about the Events Committee. I thought that perhaps you, Hilda and I might have a cup of coffee and brainstorm a little."

"Oh and Ruby?" Ruby turned around without a word. "You look ever so pale, dear. Perhaps a bit of fresh air would do you good."

"Beverly, there has to be some redeemable quality about you, although right now I can't think of a single one. You might go home and sharpen your fangs a bit. You seem to be losing your touch."

"Oh I'm not losing anything. I'm not exactly sure I can say the same about your household?"

Heloise's mouth dropped open in total amazement.

"Come, Heloise, let's find Hilda."

As they left the room, Heloise gently wrapped her arm in Ruby's. Patting her hand, she said, "Don't pay any attention to her. She's trash. I will have a talk with Brother Lawson about that Beverly Martin ... You can be sure of that!"

"Don't bother, Heloise. He already knows."

"Oh really? I wasn't at all aware."

"Let's just say he ..."

She paused for a moment. "Never mind, it's not worth repeating."

"Well, now you have to tell me or I'll wonder about this all night. I won't sleep a wink."

She began again. "Let's just say they reacquaint in a 'biblical sense' every Thursday night, if you know what I mean ..."

Heloise grabbed her handkerchief and began to fan the air rapidly with it. "I ... I think I'm about to faint."

Ruby sighed in defeat. "I knew shouldn't have said anything. Heloise, I think I've had enough of this for today. Why don't you and Hilda drop by the house one day this week and we can have a nice long talk then? Right now I really need a change of scenery."

"Here, let me sit down for a moment and catch my breath." She continued fanning until her breathing slowed. "I don't know how welcome we'll be there, Ruby. Perhaps that's not such a good idea, either."

"Don't pay any attention to Robert, darling. I'll cook for you both. Let's make a date."

"You're such a sweet dear, Ruby. I'll be sure to discuss it with Hilda this evening."

"Then you'll come?"

"If you have a handle on Robert, I don't foresee a problem."

"I'll handle Robert, Heloise."

"I guess we'll be on our way, then." Heloise arose to leave. As if she'd forgotten something, she suddenly stopped.

"Oh, and Ruby?"

"Yes, Heloise?"

"Mabel said they usually meet on Tuesday nights …"

* * *

Returning home was always associated with a pang of nostalgia. The kitchen in which she'd been raised was well worn to say the least. Badly needing a paint job, it was, nevertheless, filled with wonderful memories. To spend time at home and embrace some semblance of the life she'd always known brought comfort and security. Now, more than ever, she needed that stability.

Even though she appeared fearless in front of Beverly and Eva Nell, the thought of being pregnant weighed heavily on her mind. Usually, when faced with something of this magnitude, she went to Momma for advice. This time was no exception.

"Well, there's my girl. This is a nice surprise. How are you?"

Without changing expression, Ruby replied, "I think I'm pregnant."

Lorna poured herself a cup of coffee and turned to sit at the kitchen table. "So soon, my darling. You didn't waste much time." She took another sip. "Do you know for sure?"

"Not for sure, Momma, but morning sickness is my new best friend."

"Have you missed a cycle?"

Ruby's face turned scarlet. "Oh, Mother, don't embarrass me."

"I'm not trying to be rude, honey, but that is a sure way to tell. Have you?"

"Not yet. I'll know soon."

Lorna smiled. "A restoring essence to all of us ... It'll be wonderful having a baby around here."

Ruby sighed. "I guess so."

"You guess so?"

"Well, let's see, Mother ... My husband's in a state. Someone I love dearly was murdered, and that same psychotic killer may be trying to harm me as well. Don't forget we're newlyweds who now have a baby on the way. It's too much ... way too much, Momma. I can't handle anymore."

"This is not something to handle, Ruby. This is a blessing from God. This baby has been sent to heal all of those emotional wounds and to mend your life."

"Solange DeShotel is not an emotional wound, Mother. She's a nightmare! Almost every night I awaken in a sweat."

"Well, you have someone else to think about now, Ruby. You have to take care of yourself and this baby."

"Oh, Momma ..." Ruby began to cry.

"Baby, I'll help you. Everything will be all right. I remember having this same conversation with my mother when I was pregnant. It's a new mother thing."

"I didn't realize someone murdered your cousin, too."

Lorna winced. "I'm only trying to help."

Wiping her eyes, Ruby smiled apologetically. "I think right now I'd like to change the subject."

"Why don't you sit down and have a cup of coffee with me."

"Do you think I might have one of those fried apple pies, too?"

Lorna shook her head no. "I'm afraid that might not agree with you, honey. They're awfully rich. Why don't you let me fix you some toast? Have you told Robert?"

She sighed. "I don't plan to just yet. He has issues to resolve first. I don't want to spring anything else on him now."

"It's his baby too, Ruby. He has a right to know."

"In due time, but for now let's keep this between us, OK?"

"Sure, honey, but sooner or later he's going to ask me why I can't stop smiling."

CHAPTER TWENTY-SEVEN

"Who is that, anyway?"

"Doesn't matter."

"It must matter. Her painting is in the window and now you've started again."

"She is beautiful, isn't she?"

"Yes, she is. Do you know her?"

Rupert sighed. "Ever heard the term star crossed lovers?"

"Yeah, I've heard the term, but I've never seen this woman before. She must be a well-kept secret."

"No secret, Caris, just a burning passion. Our paths will cross again, and until they do, I'll have to settle for her portrait." Rupert continued painting.

"Have you heard about the murder here in the Quarter?"

"No, I haven't."

"Gruesome. Woman was decapitated and her body was completely drained."

"How horrible. When did this happen?"

"I just heard about it last night."

"Do the police have any leads on the murderer?"

"Rupert ... Do you know who the woman was?"

"No, who was she?"

"The housekeeper for Madame Solange DeShotel."

Rupert's face paled. "Oh my God ... Have you heard talk of DeShotel lately?"

"Heard she left. Murderous bitch, a good riddance to her."

"Supposedly she murdered this woman's cousin." Rupert pointed to the canvas with his brush.

"The woman you're painting?"

"Yes. They left in haste. The New Orleans police asked they leave immediately. I barely had time to tell her goodbye."

"Tell her goodbye? What do you mean tell her goodbye? And what does this have to do with the housekeeper?"

"I don't know, exactly. I do know she warned them. She warned them of something and Solange killed her for doing so."

"How do you know that, Rupert? How do you know she warned them?"

Rupert turned with a cold, indifferent stare. "Word gets around here, Caris. How it gets around is none of your business." Descending deep into thought, he paused for a moment. He began again. "I'll bet they have no idea this woman is dead."

"Probably not." Wondering how and when his best friend had become so deeply entrenched in these foreign lives, he stared at Rupert as he said this.

"I need to tell her."

"Her?"

"Them. I need to tell them of this murder."

"Let go of her, Rupert. She's not for you. Find someone in your own world."

Rupert stared at the canvas. *She will be in my world ...* "Maybe the hotel can give me some information as to their whereabouts."

"You'd probably have better luck at the police station. Don't you think the police have already contacted them?"

"I have to find out. Nothing can happen to her, Caris. I have to make sure of that."

Looking down, Caris shook his head. "Pity, Rupert, to waste such passionate emotion on a distant land. She belongs to someone else."

"For now." He grabbed his coat and put the closed sign in the door. "Coming with me?"

Caris sighed in defeat. "I guess."

* * *

Thursday evening, April 14, 1932

"Ashes to ashes, dust to dust, may her soul rest with God, Amen." Father Donovan made the sign of the cross over the urn. "All we can do now is pray for her."

"So be it," Ruby said. She looked around the chapel. An intimate setting, only Robert, herself, and the priest stood before Blanche's remains. Ironically, now she had turned to the Catholic church for solace. She couldn't face hypocritical condolences and whispers as she walked by. At least here, Blanche could have a solemn remembrance. She could bid farewell to her beloved cousin without the added pressure of defending her memory. She was grateful for that. Lorna and Jed weren't interested in participating. They'd deal with the loss in their own way and in their own time. A different church, an urn full of ashes and a Catholic service was too much, too overwhelming for them.

"I still can't believe your folks let her be cremated, Rube."

"You were right. She hated it here, Robert. If somehow she knew her remains had to spend eternity here, she'd never rest. It would be a travesty to bury her here."

"So what now?"

"I will take these ashes to the sea, somehow. I'll spread them over the ocean."

"Which ocean?"

"Which ocean? Why would you ask me that? The Pacific Ocean, of course. It's where she belongs. It's what she would want. I'm keeping the urn here until I can one day do this. It's a promise I've made to myself. It's not an unattainable goal, Robert, and I'll do it, somehow."

"I'll help you do it."

Robert grinned. It was not a happy smile, but one of irony and pain. "I can only imagine what's racing though the Baptist church right now."

"I don't really care. My cousin deserves some peace."

"As do you."

"I sometimes wonder if I'll ever know the meaning of that word again."

"You will. You'll know peace … I can promise you that much."

As if laden with weights, her heart felt heavy. At that moment, somehow she knew there would be no peace in their futures. In a devastating way, their lives were about to change, and nothing she or anyone else could do would prevent its onslaught.

"I need something to eat."

"Let's go home then."

Father Donovan turned to Ruby. "I will tell you the same thing I tell your husband. If you need me, do not hesitate to call."

Ruby smiled. "You're very kind. I see why Robert is so fond of you. Would you care to join us for lunch? It's just leftovers, but I have plenty."

"Well … As a matter of fact, I do feel a little hungry. I'd love to join you two if you can handle a Catholic at the dinner table."

Ruby smiled. "We'll manage, somehow. Shall we go?"

Robert turned to Ruby. "Don't forget Blanche."

Ruby sighed and looked toward the urn. Silvery white with a thin black line around the top, the urn sparked a familiar sentiment.

"Who picked this out, anyway?"

Robert smiled. "I did. It reminded me of Blanche. I can't quite put my finger on it, but something about that white contrasted with that black line …"

"Shame on you, Robert Davis." Ruby looked at Robert with her brows together. Calling a pile of dust a bleached blonde."

"Me?"

Father Donovan smiled in amazement. How these two managed to find a little humor amidst all of this was beyond him. *Oh well, if it works …* He turned out the light in the rectory as they left.

CHAPTER TWENTY-EIGHT

Tom had spent the day in the woods downing timber. He was tired and his shoulders hurt. A constant reminder that this business was for a much younger man, the aches and pains signaled that he'd soon have to start delegating some of the manual labor. It was hell getting old.

He pulled his old Ford truck alongside Brinson's Diner and parked. As he walked though the screen doors, Eb Brinson looked up from behind the grill. "Evening, Tom."

"Evening, Eb. It's been a long day. Think I need to wash up a little before I order something to eat."

"Tired?"

"I'm beat."

"Use the sink behind the kitchen."

Tom walked past the counter at which several folks were eating. While Hattie Brinson kept everyone's coffee cup filled, Eb kept at least two pots boiling and dripping at all times.

Walking past a pair of swinging double doors, Tom made his way to the kitchen. He turned left. In front of him, a small hallway led to a bathroom. Shutting the door quietly, he walked into the bath.

He'd been this route several times and knew the procedure by heart. He turned to his right and opened the linen closet door. He knocked on the wall behind the shelves, two knocks and then three more. The wall swung open, and Tom entered the speakeasy.

He felt sure the sheriff knew about the speakeasy, but the Brinsons probably padded his income enough for him to leave it alone. Hell, he probably stopped by for a drink on his own way home.

Tom needed whiskey and plenty of it. Before heading to the house, he usually drank the fatigue away. Sometimes it helped, and sometimes it gave way to irritability and a bar room brawl. He had a bottle gash scar across his right cheek to prove it.

Nick Brinson set a glass in front of him and said, "What'll it be, Tom?"

"You know what it'll be, Nick. Whiskey, and leave the bottle."

Nick slammed a bottle of bourbon onto the counter in front of him.

Tom poured himself a drink and downed it. He gulped and took a deep breath. *First step to unwinding* … He poured himself another one.

He wasn't sure what made him look to his right, but as he did so, he caught sight of her. She was so beautiful! Obviously, she did not belong here, as most of the women in the speakeasy had been around. They usually came to drink and then go home with whoever bought them enough liquor to merit their company. She smiled at him.

This wasn't a broad or a dame; this woman had class. He took his glass and bottle and walked over to her. "I haven't seen you in here before. What's a classy lady like you doing in a speakeasy alone?"

"I guess appearances can be deceiving."

Tom raised his eyebrows and looked back at his bottle. "Can I pour you a drink?"

"You may." Brushing her chestnut hair away from her face, she smiled.

"Where are you from?"

"New Orleans."

"Schoolteacher?"

"No, I'm a Madame."

Spitting his whiskey across the bar, Tom choked after she'd said this.

Nick wheeled around. "Hey! Do that again, and I'll throw your ass out!"

"Sorry, Nick."

Clearing his throat, he turned his attention back to her. "You're a what?"

"A Madame. A whore. What do you not understand?"

"It's just that I've never seen a whore who looks like you."

"What do most whores usually look like, Mr.?"

"Tom. Tom Banks."

"You have a preconceived notion of what whores should look like, Mr. Banks?"

"No ... Uh ... Well, it's just they ... You ... I mean you're so beautiful."

"Thank you."

"Starting a new business here in town?" *Shit ... that sounded really stupid.* He poured himself another drink and downed it.

"No, as a matter a fact, I'm just passing through. I'm en route to Conway, Arkansas."

"What's in Conway?"

"You ask a lot of questions, Mr. Banks. Let me ask you one. Are you interested in going to Conway?"

Tom pulled a cigarette out of his pack and lit it. He inhaled deeply and blew out the smoke. "I might be. It's a pretty good little piece up to Conway. Depends on if you make it worth my while or not."

"Ah, a bargainer. I assure you, it will be an experience you will never forget."

Tom took another drink and refilled Solange's glass. *Looks like I got lucky tonight.* "What's your name, anyway?"

Solange slid her hand under his untucked shirt and ran it up the entire length of his chest. Her fingers tangled into the hair at the base of his neck. "I'm whoever you want me to be tonight, Tom."

* * *

Early Friday morning, April 15, 1932

As he walked toward her, she rested the baby on her hip. He was smiling. Revealing teeth both white and perfectly aligned, the smile was beautiful.

Beckoning him to come, her right arm stretched toward him. He moved toward her in seemingly slow motion. Suddenly, the smile left his face. His expression turned to one of anxiety and horror. Spreading across his belly, a line of crimson appeared on his white shirt. As he began his descent in front of her, she opened her mouth to scream. The words seemed to distort as she said them. He fell to the ground before she could reach him. It was too late.

"No," She screamed, "No, No, No!" As the words left her, they echoed repeatedly. She reached down to touch him, but as she did so, she found her hand covered in blood. She turned to run. She had to save the baby.

Ruby opened her eyes. Replaced by the quiet darkness of the wee morning hours, the scene had mercifully disappeared. This time she was having the nightmare.

What a dream! She turned toward her husband who seemed to be sleeping peacefully. Wiping her face with the sheet, she took another breath. She would wait for daylight. Sleep was out of the question.

CHAPTER TWENTY-NINE

Robert looked around the room. "Looks like we bought out Pringles. There's enough food here to feed Conway. Who died?"

Saying nothing, Ruby cut her eyes toward Robert.

"Maybe I'd better rephrase that."

"It would be nice, but nothing you say surprises me anymore."

"What's the occasion?"

"The occasion is an agenda meeting for the Events Committee. I'm having your two favorite people over for lunch tomorrow. You know, the ones you insulted so much that they left? It's a wonder they'd even consider coming over again."

"Considering how I feel about them, it's a wonder you'd even consider having them over. What is it with you and those two anyway? Nobody else in town likes them. Surely, you don't think they don't talk about you just like everybody else? They are vicious, old, two-faced busybodies. Why do you mess with them?"

"I mess with them because I love them, and I've known them all of my life. Some people you love in spite of their obvious flaws, Robert."

"Not those piranha flaws."

"They do mean well. You could use a little more patience where Heloise and Hilda are concerned. Anyway, it may be best if you find something else to do while they are here. It might make things a little less tense."

"More relaxing would be if you all met somewhere else. Why don't you go over to one of their houses?"

"Because I invited them here. Don't worry about it. I'll feed you and then you can make yourself scarce for a couple of hours. You'll never know the difference." Placing her left hand across her stomach, she abruptly stopped. "Oh God ... the smell of this bacon is making me sick. It must be bad. I'm going to throw up." Ruby covered her mouth and ran to the back door of the kitchen. He could hear her vomiting.

"Smells alright to me ... tastes pretty good, too." He walked to the back door. "Are you OK?"

Ruby was wiping her mouth and eyes with her apron. In an attempt to compose herself, she cleared her throat. "Well, other than just having thrown my guts up, I'm fine." She breathed in deeply and exhaled. "That horrible bacon has to go. I've never smelled anything that bad in my entire life."

"Ruby, you must have some sort of sickness. That bacon is fine. I ate some."

"Maybe so. I do feel a little under the weather. I think I'll lie down for awhile. Would you put the rest of the groceries away?"

"Sure, honey." Ruby walked past him to the bedroom. Robert watched her pass and followed her as far as the kitchen. *That bacon tasted all right to me ...* He walked down the hall to the bedroom. With a wet rag across her forehead, Ruby was lying in bed. "When are those Pullman sisters supposed to come over, anyway?"

"The day after tomorrow. I need to rest now; we can talk about this later."

"Hope you feel better." Robert lingered in the doorway for a moment. *Sure came on suddenly ...*

The phone rang. "Hello?"

"Mr. Davis?"

"Yes, Mabel."

"I have a call from Morten's Telegraph Service for you."

"Thank-you, Mabel."

"Hold please and I'll connect."

"I'm holding ..."

"Robert?"

"Yes?"

"Bob Morten here."

"What can I do for you, Bob?"

"Your wife has a telegram here from New Orleans, Louisiana."

"Who would be sending my wife a wire from New Orleans? Is it from the New Orleans police?"

"I don't know. The sender is a Mr. Rupert Staten."

Silence on Robert's end of the conversation.

"Robert, it's here waiting on you whenever you or Ruby can get down here. By the way, it's marked *urgent.* "

"Ruby's not feeling well, Bob. I'll be there shortly, and thanks for calling."

"Sure thing, be seeing you soon."

Robert returned the receiver to the telephone base. *Why would that art dealer be sending my wife an urgent telegram? I might have to plan a little trip to New Orleans to settle this. His art career may be ending real soon. I wonder how well he'll paint with a broken face.* He grabbed his coat and hat and headed for the door.

"Robert?"

"Yes, Rube."

"Who was on the phone?"

"Wrong number."

"Mabel rang you through a wrong number, Robert? I don't think so. Who was on the phone?"

"Bob Morten."

"And ... ?"

"And I have a telegram down there."

"Then why didn't you tell me that in the first place?"

"Didn't want to worry you, since you are not feeling well. Go back to sleep. I'll be back shortly."

"I'm feeling better now. Hurry back?"

"I won't be long. Love you."

"Love you, too."

* * *

As long as Robert could remember, the Mortons have lived in Conway, Arkansas. Bob Morten was known about town as thrifty, to say the least, but had built a good, solid business throughout the years. The first and only telegram they had received from Mortens announced Blanche's arrival in Conway. Apparently, the second was from Rupert Staten. *If this Rupert Staten planned a little reunion of sorts, Ruby was not the one who would be meeting him at the train station. If he was not coming to Conway, what was so urgent?*

"Hello, Bob."

"Robert. Didn't take you long to get over here. Give me just a minute, and I'll get your telegram."

Robert smiled as Bob walked to the honeycomb of shelves behind the counter. He looked about the place. The old, dark room had been finished in stained pine beaded-board, while overhead, beautiful, stamped tin adorned the ceiling. The front windows hadn't been dusted in awhile, and the Mortens' name painted on the window had begun to peel. *I guess an old established monopoly doesn't need too much image ...*

"Here you go."

"Thanks, Bob." The door jingled as he walked outside onto the sidewalk.

He looked at the envelope. *Might just be an invasion of privacy if I open this, but what concerns her concerns me. This is correspondence from another man. I don't owe anyone a fucking apology for anything.*

He began to open the envelope.

She'll never know about it, anyway ...

"More news from Hollywood?"

Obviously startled, Robert looked up. Standing in front of him was Beverly Martin

"No ... It's not."

She craned her neck slightly and smiled. "Tsk, tsk, darling; not nice to open others' mail."

"Anything else I can do for you, Beverly?"

"Why don't we take a peek? I won't tell if you won't."

Robert glared at her with a mixture of disbelief and disgust. "You really are some kind of bitch."

"Why thank-you, darling. Tell you what, why don't you let me buy you a cup of coffee, and we'll further cultivate this passionate little undercurrent we have here."

"How can I put this ... I think I'd rather fuck a rattlesnake?"

"Now there's a thought, and you might like it, too. Lots of men get turned on by the hisssss."

"Well, slither back into your den and think of someone else for prey. I'm done with this conversation."

"Feel free to call the snake pit if you need help with a credible lie, Robert. Somehow I think you're not very good at it."

"Good to see you, Bev."

She blew him a kiss and turned to leave. "Needs work, but good for a first try."

"Damn," was all that he muttered. He stuffed the telegram into his pocket and headed home.

* * *

The E&B café was a popular spot for lunch. The air was usually thick with the smell of fried foods; delectable fares, such as chicken and hot water cornbread, were served alongside fresh garden vegetables. There was always a full house, as owners Elizabeth and Bruce Anding made sure lunch was worth the wait. Most weekdays, in the wee hours of the morning, a group of downtown folks met at the E&B for coffee. They did their best to solve world's problems before seven. What was not resolved by work time was generally tabled for the next morning's agenda. Typically drawing a less volatile nighttime clientele, the café was open for dinner as well. Sunday night was an exception to this rule, as New Light Baptist church's congregation tended to migrate toward the cafe after evening services.

Passing through the double doors of the restaurant, Robert spied an empty back-corner booth. As he took a seat, Mary Burfield approached the table.

"What'll you have, honey?"

"Just coffee."

"Got a good blue plate special today, Rob. You ought to give it a try."

Rob? Where the hell did she get Rob? "No lunch today. I just need a quick cup and I'm headed home."

"Got a fresh baked lemon cake back there. I'm going to bring you a piece my treat and I won't take no for an answer."

Robert looked up and replied, "Thanks, Mare." A cocky grin traipsed across his face.

Alas, his retribution victory was to be short-lived, though. The nickname retaliation apparently sailed right over her head. With no reaction, she simply replied, "Sure thing, hon. I'll be back with your cake and coffee."

Robert watched her walk away.

He reached into his pocket and removed the telegram. *I'm opening this.* Sliding his finger under the flap, he ran it across the entire length of the envelope.

DeShotel housekeeper murdered/Stop/DeShotel wanted for questioning/Stop/whereabouts unknown/Stop/please be careful/Stop/Rupert

Robert felt the blood drain from his face. *Angelique had warned them, and apparently she was right. This thing, this evil manifestation was most likely trying to find them. He had to think of what to do. Should he go home? Should he get Ruby to pack them up and disappear? Would that be enough to steer clear of Solange's intuitive powers? Maybe she wouldn't come here, but who was he trying to kid? Solange really believed they possessed a dimensional portal and would stop at nothing to get it.* Robert put his face in his hands. He had no idea of what to do next.

Mary sat his coffee and lemon cake on the booth table.

"You OK, honey? You look like you've seen a ghost."

"Oh no, Mare … a ghost would be entirely too easy."

CHAPTER THIRTY

All he'd planned to do last night was to stop by the speakeasy, have some whiskey and get drunk. Instead, he'd ended up on the road with a woman that scared the ever-living hell out of him. He felt a hot, sharp sting on his chest. He looked down; just below the nipple, Solange had dragged a long red fingernail across his chest. He began to bleed. Gently, she began to clean the wound with her tongue. She looked at him lustfully as she slid on top of him. Taking him inside of her, she began gently rocking back and forth. Tom closed his eyes in physical ecstasy.

He rolled his hips toward her as she began gyrating more forcefully. Softly, she began to moan. The sound became guttural as she took him inside of her again and again. She smeared the blood of his still weeping wound across his pectorals, and as orgasm came in a rush, she held him deep inside her. Tom could no longer distinguish the fine line between pleasure and pain. He'd do anything for her right now ... even kill for her if he had to.

"I'll take you to places you've never imagined."

"Right now, I don't want to go anywhere."

"Do as I say and you'll see a hundred lifetimes."

"Baby, you keep this up, and I'll do as you say right here in this one."

"You have no idea what you're getting yourself into."

"I don't care."

Solange laid on him and kissed his chin. She took her index finger and scratched again, this time just under his jaw line.

Tom winced. "Solange, if you keep this up, I'll bleed to death before you get through with me. I look like I've been in a catfight. No more claws, ok?"

She rubbed her face against the bleeding wound. "I'll have you as mine inside and out before I'm through with you."

"You already have that, baby ... right here, right now."

As he rolled on top of her, she kissed him deeply. "Soon we'll get the portal and begin our quest for power and wealth. Stay with me, Tom, and I'll make you rich beyond your dreams. Cross me, and you'll beg for a place in Hell."

"In that case, looks like I'd better stay put." Caressing her body lustfully, he kissed her again. Feeling as if he'd fallen into an abyss, he devoured the euphoric intoxication her body brought him. Somewhere, though, somewhere deep inside, he felt the need to feel frightened.

* * *

"This is the operator, your number please."

"Hi Mabel, it's Robert Davis. Could you please ring 4476?"

"Certainly, one moment."

"Hello?"

"Hi, honey, it's me."

"Where are you?"

"I'm at the E&B café."

"What?"

"I just dropped in to grab a cup of coffee."

"Robert, I've been worried to death. You've been gone a long time. After I vomited my guts up and discovered we have yet another mysterious telegram, you decide to grab a cup of coffee?"

"I did."

"You beat anything I've ever seen. Did you at least get your telegram?"

"No."

"What? What do you mean 'no?' "

"There is no telegram."

"I can't believe this ..."

"It would probably be easier if I explained this at home."

"No, you explain it now."

"Unless you want the 'Agnew Express' to catapult this through the entire town, you'd better wait until I get home."

"Well, if Mabel is listening, she's probably gotten her feathers ruffled by now. Maybe you need to watch what you say as well."

"And maybe Mabel needs to quit eavesdropping."

"I don't believe for one minute there is no telegram. If that is true, Robert Davis, then you've lied to me for the third time."

"I have not."

"You haven't? First, you say Mabel rang through a 'wrong number.' When I don't believe that ridiculous story, you proceed to tell me that we have a mysterious telegram awaiting us. I ask you to read it to me and suddenly there is no telegram after all. That makes three lies, Robert. So come clean. What was that phone call about? Rest assured that if you don't tell me, I'll bet there's an eavesdropping someone who would be happy to bring me up to date on every detail."

"That fucking bitch …"

"Oh, that was nice …"

"Look, I have one more stop on my way home, and then I'll explain everything."

"Don't bother. I don't want to talk about this anymore. Whatever's going on has you scheming and deceitful. I wouldn't believe any of your explanations, anyway. Apparently, you cannot tell the truth about this."

"Ruby, I …"

She didn't bother to let him finish; she simply slammed the phone onto the receiver.

Taken aback, Robert looked at his receiver for a moment before he returned it to the cradle. *I'm almost tempted to call that Martin trash … boy oh boy do I need a good lie …*

* * *

"Hello, Sister, is Father Donovan around?"

"He is in counseling right now, Mr. Davis. He should be through within the next twenty minutes. Would you care to come in and wait?"

"As a matter of fact, we are through." Father Donovan, along with another woman, entered the room. The woman's puffy eyes gave clue that she'd been crying. As she walked toward the side door, she managed a weak smile. "I'll see you next week, Father."

Smiling sympathetically, Father Donovan nodded.

"Poor child …" Sister Alexandra also returned a sympathetic smile. As the door shut behind her, Sister decided to leave as well. In a vain attempt to keep up with the exit, her starched black habit billowed and flowed behind her as she left the room.

"What's wrong with her?"

"Anything discussed in counseling or confession is confidential."

Somewhat embarrassed, Robert looked down. "My apologies, Father, that did sound pretty nosey." *I'm usually a little more discreet …*

"What can I do for you today?"

"I could use some advice."

"Feel like discussing it over a cup of coffee? I was headed for the drip pot."

"Sounds swell."

"Mrs. Grayson brought over a freshly baked lemon cake, too."

"Damn, they're contagious."

"Sorry?" Obviously, he'd missed the gist of the comment.

Robert smiled sheepishly. "I just had a piece of lemon cake at the café; coffee, too."

"I'll brew some tea. Let's make our way to the kitchen."

* * *

Surprisingly well equipped, the rectory kitchen was clean and functional. All of the necessary amenities were there. A Hoosier cabinet provided much needed cabinet space, while the nice, new icebox kept perishables cool and fresh. Although a bit austere, the space actually worked well.

"Mr. Dawson has graciously offered to buy the rectory a refrigerator. Can you imagine that?"

"Nice gift," Robert replied. "You should be able keep plenty of food in here. That ice box looks brand new, though. Do you really need both?"

"Well, whether we need both of them or not, we'll have them. Ironically, the ice company just bought this box for us. They must have heard about Dawson's generosity. We can use the room, though, for often times the Ladies' Circle prepares food here for various functions." As he measured tea into the cloth, Father Donovan looked on intently. He tied it with a string and waited for the water to boil. "So what's on your mind?"

"This." Robert pulled the telegram from his pocket.

"It's a telegram." He craned his neck to get a little better look. "It's an opened telegram with Ruby's name on it."

"She hasn't seen it yet. I read it at the café."

"And what prompted you to do that?"

"I met this fellow—the one who sent this—in New Orleans. He's an art dealer of sorts, and seemed a little too familiar with my wife. I didn't have a good feeling about it, so I thought I'd see what he wanted."

"And in doing so you totally invaded Ruby's privacy. You should not have read this, and I don't think I should read it either. Neither of our names is on it, so perhaps it would be wise to let your wife have a look at her telegram before you decide on a course of action."

"Consider this a confession."

"That's fine, but I'm not reading the telegram."

"Please, Father; I beg of you. I'll never tell anyone you've read it. I need you to help me with this."

Father Donovan looked at Robert for a long time. Finally, with a deep sigh, he read it. When finished he said, "Robert, this is a matter for the police. They need to be aware of this. I would have thought the New Orleans police would have been contacted about this as well."

"Seems that way."

"You have some explaining to do to your wife."

"Seems that way, too."

"Level with her and tell her the truth. Tell her why you lied. Tell her why you felt you had to open the telegram. You'll suffer some repercussions, so take your medicine. Apologize and assure her that you will not pull a stunt like this again. You must convince her you're sincere." Father Donovan poured him a cup of tea. "Do you take lemon or sugar?"

"Squeeze a little lemon in there. I'm wondering if we need to get away from here until they apprehend that lunatic."

"Do you feel you are in danger?"

"I really do."

"Where would you go?"

"I don't know … somewhere safe. I have no idea where to go."

"I may be able to help you with that one."

"How? What could you do?"

"There's a possibility I could get you lodging in a seminary some-where … at least until this woman is caught."

"Hmmm." Deep in thought, he stared straight-ahead. "It wouldn't be easy, but at least we'd be safe." He was quiet for a moment and began again. "Father, I may take you up on that idea. I'm going home and present it to Ruby. I'm not really sure how she'll react, but maybe after she's had time to digest the plan, she'll see it's the best thing for both of us." He set his teacup down and stood to leave. "I'll be in touch soon; I'm headed home to drop the bombshell."

"And I'll do some checking and see what I can do, Robert. I'm not promising anything, but I'll see what I can find out."

"She bought me the wedding gift straight from Hell, you know."

"On the other hand, it may be your link to salvation."

"Salvation does come at a price, doesn't it, Father?"

"The price is well worth it. I'll be praying for you."

Robert left the rectory. *What a life … two lives, actually, and it seems both of them are pretty doomed.* The irony of all of this brought a smile across Robert's face. The smile turned to a look of conviction. *I belong somewhere, damn it all …*

CHAPTER THIRTY-ONE

Saturday, April 16, 1932

"You want me to kill her?"

"Of course, I want you to kill her, you fool. I want you to kill them both. How else can we be assured the portal will belong to us forever?"

"Solange, I've never killed anyone before. I don't know if I can."

"It's hard at first, but you'll get used to it. In fact, you may grow to like it. It's the ultimate power." Solange's eyes were dancing with excitement.

Tom studied her closely. He wiped his hand across his face. Bristly and bearded, he realized he hadn't shaved in a couple of days. "What if we get caught? We'll be hanged. Then what good is a portal?"

Solange laughed. "We won't even be here. We'll be dimensions away; there is no need to worry."

"When do you want me to do it?"

"So now you need a time line to kill?"

"We have to have a plan, Solange."

"Just do it, Tom. We have no time to waste. You want a plan? Ok, I'll spell it out for you. Here's what I want you to do ..."

CHAPTER THIRTY-TWO

Heloise studied herself in the mirror and then turned sideways for another good, long look. "I guess this really is a 'Spring Fat Dress.'"

"A Spring, Fat what?"

"Oh, Hilda, I overheard Beverly and Eva Nell making fun of me. Ruby tried to cover up, but I heard them. Do you like this dress?"

"Well, it is a bit ... botanical for my tastes."

"It's just a big, fat tent-dress old women my age have to wear."

"Heloise, whatever has gotten into you?"

"They were so mean, Hilda, so vicious."

"How can you let a couple of hypocritical harlots upset you like that? They only hope they'll look half as good as we do when they're our age."

"My age? You are two years older."

"Snap out of it. We've have to leave for Ruby's in short order for the meeting."

"Well, fat or not, I'm wearing this."

"You look fine."

"Maybe I'll have Edna make me something red next time."

"Red ... yes, darling, that would be nice. Now, I'm off to change, so why don't you have a soda and listen to the radio? I'll only be a few minutes."

"As you wish. I'll just take a Spring Fat Rest in my big Spring Fat Dress."

"Jesus, Mary and Joseph," was all that Hilda mumbled as she left the room.

* * *

"Smells delicious."

"Thank you. It's for my meeting, but I've prepared a plate of food for you as well. It's in the warming drawer above the stove top."

"And you baked a chess pie ... How nice." With a disgusted look on his face, Robert stood staring at the pie safe.

"I didn't have any fresh fruit on hand and no time to go to the market. If you don't like it, then don't eat it. Unlike Lila, I didn't bake that pie for you."

"Mmm ... I haven't had beef stew in ages."

"I've also baked some biscuits. They are in the pie safe by that 'you know what' chess pie." Robert wheeled around so abruptly he almost lost his balance. "Ruby! Such language ..."

"Sounds crude, doesn't it? Makes you want to think twice about using terrible language like that."

He laughed. "Better leave off the descriptive when the 'Pullman pigs' arrive."

"You know, it is possible to joke around without the brunt of the joke always being at someone else's expense. That wasn't funny at all."

"OK, OK, that was pretty cruel. I'm sorry."

"The thing about it is that you're really not. You say horrible things like that and think a token 'I'm sorry' makes everything OK. It doesn't."

Robert lay on the floor face down with his arms outstretched in front of him. Raising his hands toward Ruby in earnest, he began. "Please, oh please forgive me ... PLEASE!"

"Go ahead and keep making fun. One day you'll be sorry." She walked toward the dining room table. Instead of stepping over him, she walked right on top of him. Her heel dug into his back.

"Ouch! Damn! That hurt, Ruby!"

"Pretend that was one of your cruel remarks. They do hurt, don't they?" Ruby couldn't contain the satisfied smile that popped across her face. Why don't you get up and eat. The girls will be here in about an hour; I want you to make yourself scarce."

"I'll just take it outside. I'm headed to the church, anyway." *That hurt …*

"For what?"

"Brother Lawson asked me to check the wiring in the fellowship hall. It keeps dimming and then gets really bright."

"I have noticed that." She paused for a moment. "God, I hope there's no fire hazard. Be careful, Rob, and try to get that fixed. Maybe St. Joseph's wasn't the church you saw burning in your dreams after all. You'd better be on your way. I'll see you this evening."

With dinner plate in hand, Robert walked out of the room. Gingerly, he rubbed his lower back with the other.

"Shit … that hurt," he mumbled again.

CHAPTER THIRTY-THREE

Robert walked halfway across the front yard and stopped. He turned around and made his way back to the house. "Hey, Rubes, come here."

Ruby walked to the door. "What did you forget?"

"Do you really think those fat-ass Pullmans need a chess pie?"

Hopeless ... absolutely hopeless ... "First of all, I don't know anybody by that name. As far as need goes, they probably don't need a pie at all; I just thought they might enjoy one. If you'll think back a few moments, I told you I didn't have time to go to the market. What would you have preferred that I make?"

"Well, maybe something like a fresh fruit salad."

"A fresh fruit ... what? So now, you're planning menus? *All of a sudden, I'm supposed to whip up a fresh fruit salad?* She turned away from him and walked over to the phone.

"Hi, Mabel, could you please ring my mother?"

"One moment please ... "

"Hi Momma, could you meet me at Pringles? I will need some help after all. Love you too, bye." Ruby removed her apron and set it atop the Hoosier cabinet. *Well, now I have to hurry ...* She turned off the stove and grabbed her purse.

"Any other requests?"

"I didn't mean for you to leave now, Rube."

"That's exactly what you meant. You need to get going as well." Hurriedly walking past him, she climbed into the car.

145

Watching the car speed away, he yelled after her. "I can just walk! I didn't need a ride ... I'm fine ... JUST FINE!" He laughed a bit as nothing more than a cloud of dust remained where the car had been. *There ain't enough fruit in Arkansas for their big, fat asses ...*

* * *

"Hello, Heloise. What can I do for you?"

"Well, I'm having lunch at Ruby Davis' house this afternoon. I thought I might pick up a few soft drinks to bring with me."

"Ella just baked a couple of chocolate cakes. How about one of those, too?"

"No, no, no ... I've taken care of dessert."

Heloise turned around in surprise to see that Ruby was standing behind her.

"Darling, what on earth are you doing here? And there's Lorna. Is something wrong?"

"No, of course not, Heloise, Robert insisted that I serve fruit salad. Otherwise, everything is ready. Mother's on her way to my house to slice the fruit while I prepare a little glaze. Did Ella make any strawberry jam, Mr. Pringle?"

"She sure did. Here you go, hon."

Heloise watched and then turned to Ruby. "Ruby, I'm all dressed and ready. Since you'll be a few minutes, why don't I go over to your house and start things while you and Lorna finish up here."

"I wouldn't hear of it. You're my guest."

"Really, I don't mind. In fact I insist, and I'm leaving now." Heloise took the bag of drinks from the counter.

"Oh ..." Ruby was taken aback at Heloise's insistence. She gathered her thoughts for a moment and began again. "Well ... OK then. You'll find my apron on the Hoosier. All of the food has been prepared and is ready to serve. Everything just needs to be warmed, Heloise. The table is set, and I have fresh lemonade in the icebox."

"I'm on my way."

"I left the back door open, so just let yourself in."

"Ruby, dear, call Robert and tell him I'm coming. I don't want to startle him."

"Nobody is there. Robert and Brother Lawson are working on some of the church wiring."

"How nice; it's about time he became interested in his own church." Heloise began to walk toward the door. "I'll see you two shortly ... goodbye, everyone."

Everyone nodded his or her good-byes as she made her way through the doorway.

* * *

Heloise let herself into Ruby's house through the back door. The aroma that wafted toward her was wonderful. She spied Ruby's apron on the Hoosier. Walking over to the cabinet, she put it on. *How lovely. It has her name embroidered on it.* She began to lift the lids of the various pots sitting on the stove. *Looks delicious.*

She returned the lids to the pots, after which she brushed her hands together in an attempt to rid them of any imaginary residue gained from handling the cookware. Deciding to look around a bit, she turned her attention toward the living room. *A little pre-party peruse wouldn't hurt a thing ...* As she did so, she noticed tasteful accessories and detailed color decor had been added in all of the right spots. So feminine and lovely, she found it hard to believe this was once a bachelor's residence. Crocheted doilies adorned the end tables, and vases throughout the room were tastefully filled with fresh flowers and greenery. All was immaculate. *How does she do it? So efficient, she'll be perfect for the Events Committee.*

The dining room table was set for lunch, with fine china and sterling silver flatware resting upon a crisp, white linen tablecloth. Seating was delegated by carefully positioned place cards centered in each plate.

Heloise looked at the table again. *Wait a minute, I recognize this dining room furniture. This is Lorna's dining room table and chairs.* She raised her eyebrows in resignation. *She must have decided to give them to Ruby while she was young and could really use them.* Heloise smiled. *Ruby has a good start in life; she'll do just fine.*

While deep in thought, she caught a fleeting glimpse of a dark shadow lunging toward her. The arm that roughly encircled her neck was strong and muscular. Hot and trenchant, much like the sound of a string instrument stroked hard, she felt a stinging sensation across her neck. The stroke was shrill, unpleasant, and painful. Naturally, her hands grabbed at her throat the moment the arm released its hold. There was no breath. Her fingertips quickly became aware of flowing warmth cascading down the front of her dress. She had to sit down. She had to rest right there and decide what to do. She'd rest a moment and then contend with this. The footsteps moved rapidly away from her as the screen door repeatedly slammed in echo. She closed her eyes. *I have to find help,* she thought to herself. *I have to find help soon.*

* * *

As Ruby approached the back screen door, she noticed it ajar. *That's strange, why would Heloise leave this door open? Now we'll have a house full of flies.* Visibly agitated, Ruby forcefully slammed the door and fastened the latch.

"Mind if I come in, too?" Ruby had just slammed the screen door in Lorna's face. "Oh, I'm sorry, Momma. I was a little put out at this door being open. Where is Heloise, anyway? Heloise? HELOISE!"

"Maybe she's in the back."

"Would you look? I need to prepare this glaze and wash the fruit for the salad. We're running out of time."

"I'll be right back to cut up the fruit, hon. Cut the tops off of the strawberries and wash them well." Lorna passed through the swinging door of the kitchen. As she began washing the berries, she heard a scream describing nothing short of horror. Her blood ran cold as she threw the berries into the sink and made her way into the dining room. Standing with her hands over her mouth, was Lorna. She was looking at the body of Heloise Pullman slumped in a corner of the dining room. Her throat had been brutally slashed, and her body lay encircled in a pool of crimson. There was no color to her skin, making her appearance a ghoulish, unnatural white.

Ruby stared as well, taking several deep breaths before saying anything.

Struggling to maintain her composure, she began. "Mother, call the police."

Lorna didn't flinch.

"Call them!" Still nothing.

Realizing that Lorna could not face the situation, she walked over to the telephone and made the call.

"Mabel, I need the police."

Ruby spoke calmly and quietly as she recalled the sequence of events to the police. She was instructed not to touch anything and to leave the house immediately. No one was to enter and nothing was to be altered until the police had completed their investigation.

Sitting on the back steps, she stared toward the pasture. *So much was repetitive ... so much was familiar. She'd dropped the colander when Robert collapsed in her front yard. She threw the strawberries into the sink to witness Heloise's demise. She'd been prodded and questioned about all events leading up to the death of Blanche. Now, here was a policeman standing in front of her, wanting to know all of the details she knew leading up to the death of her dear friend Heloise.*

She looked up to the police officer and said, "How much is one individual supposed to endure? How many more of my loved ones do I have to see ... dead?"

The officer looked at her and replied, "I think this time it was supposed to be you, Ma'am."

CHAPTER THIRTY-FOUR

In Hilda's living room, Ruby and Robert stood in front of two wingback chairs. Hilda was seated in one of them, and beside them stood Brother Lawson, Lorna, Jed, Lila and Ned Davis.

Hilda was wiping her face with a wet, tear-stained handkerchief. Finally, she gave up the futile attempt to keep her composure.

"Why would someone do this to my sister? She never hurt a soul in her entire life."

"You must be kidding ..." Robert mumbled to himself. The comment was met with an elbow from Jed.

Ruby bent down and quietly said, "They were trying to murder me, Hilda. Heloise was wearing my apron." Her voice began to quiver. "I told her to put that apron on." She turned her face into Robert and began to cry.

With a look of bewilderment, she turned to Ruby. "I don't understand."

Robert stepped forward toward her. "The apron had Ruby's name embroidered on it. That's why the perpetrator ..." He paused for a moment. *Be tactful* ... He took a breath and began again. "He thought she was Ruby."

Looking through both of them, she stared ahead. "The murderer doesn't know who you are. That sick, demented killer is a stranger. The question remains as to why someone would want to kill you."

"Oh, Hilda, it's very complicated."

"Then you'll have to work that much harder to make me understand. I deserve to know. I have a right to know why my sister fell into the path of a ruthless, psychotic murderer."

Ruby looked at the floor and uttered, "Money and power, Hilda."

Hilda looked at her in amazement. "Money and power? Whose? This makes no sense."

"It doesn't, and when I'm through explaining, it still won't. You deserve to know the truth. Almost all of us know it here, and now you've been unwillingly drawn into this nightmare. We're going to tell you the truth as well."

* * *

Fervently praying, Father Donovan sat on the fourth row of the small Catholic church. For the most part, things were going well in his parish. Although small, the church membership was a cohesive, well-involved group.

As he heard footsteps approaching from behind, his train of thought was broken. He turned to find a lovely, fair-haired woman standing a few paces from his pew. As if the shadows cast by the church lights had beclouded it somewhat, her face seemed a bit obscured. When he turned to greet her, she smiled. As he introduced himself, he returned the smile.

"Hello, I'm Father Donovan. I don't believe we've met."

She simply replied, "I've heard of you, Father. You are a kind man."

"Why thank you! I consider that a compliment."

"With much turbulence, the next few days will pass quickly. It is then the remnant will have passed, for it can support no more emotional significance."

"I don't quite understand what you mean. Why don't you have a seat?"

She remained standing beside his pew. "You are essential in preparation for the return. Please pray that the realization of what must be will be accepted and understood."

"How can I do this when I don't understand myself?"

"It will be difficult and questioned. Usually, this helps in acceptance for passage, but in this instance the time has not yet come."

"What time?"

"Make preparations so the answers to questions and reservations can easily be found. You must do this to insure peace of mind and tranquility for all involved."

"I have no idea how to do this."

"Soon you will understand."

"Who are you? You've never told me your name?"

"You must get up now; it's time for Mass."

"Why won't you tell me who you are?"

"Please Father, parishioners will be here soon. You must find your vestments."

"I insist you tell me. I want to understand."

She took her hand and shook his shoulder. "Please awaken, Father."

Father Donovan opened his eyes and looked around the church. In a bit of a daze, he blinked several times and wiped his eyes. Before him was standing Sister Alexandra.

"We have to hurry, Father. Mass starts in a few minutes."

"I must have dozed off, and I had the strangest dream. I was sitting here and this woman ..."

"I don't mean to be rude, Sir, but we'll have some tea and discuss this after Mass. Up now and let's hurry. I'll light the candles while you don your vestments. As soon as I've prepared the altar, I'll start the Rosary."

"Thank you, Sister ..." He turned to leave and then paused. "I hope I don't seem distracted during services, Alexandra, for I haven't prepared a sermon, either."

"Speak from the heart, Father, as you always do."

"I'll speak of 'Preparation for the Return' just as I was instructed."

With a puzzled expression, she replied, "I'm sorry?"

"Sorry, Sister, just thinking aloud."

* * *

"You fool! You stupid fool!"

"I didn't know it wasn't Ruby! She was wearing an apron with her name on it."

Solange looked at Tom with seething contempt. "Did that old lady look twenty-four, Tom? If she did, it's a spell I very much need to learn."

"She had a hat on, Solange. I approached her from behind and looked over her shoulder. I saw the name! It was all over so quickly. I … I ran out the back door. I didn't know it wasn't her, dammit."

"I have no use for you."

"You have no use for me? You've turned me into a cold-blooded murderer, and now you have no use for me? For God's sake, Solange, I killed for you. Isn't that enough?"

"You certainly didn't do that for God's sake, Tom. I haven't much time and I have no room for mistakes. Where's the coin? Why didn't you get me the coin? We could have been out of here, far, far away. Your stupid bumbling wouldn't have even mattered if you would have done the one thing you were supposed to do."

"I got scared! She didn't die right away. I didn't want her to see me, so I ran."

Solange turned away from Tom. She walked across the room. "I see I'll have to handle this myself."

"I'll take care of it, Solange. I swear."

"You'll do nothing. You will do nothing but what I tell you to do. We have no margin for error. I can feel the end of this time paradox approaching, and I won't be trapped in it. Rarely is there a chance to change destiny and I'm altering mine. You, on the other hand, have become dead weight. You are a hindrance, not an asset."

"Just tell me how I can make it better. Just tell me what to do. I need you, Solange."

Solange turned around and stared at him. "Perhaps there is something you can do; only this time if you fail, I'll kill you. Are we understood?"

"Baby, I love you. I'll do anything for you."

"You will, Tom. You will do just that … all in due time."

CHAPTER THIRTY-FIVE

"Good evening, ladies. I'm sure my calling this meeting to order comes as no surprise to anyone in this room. I was asked by ..." Ruby abruptly paused and looked down at the floor. A tear began to track down her cheek. She wiped it away with her hand and attempted to begin again. "I was asked some time ago by my dear friend Heloise Pullman to co-chair this committee. I was to co-chair it with her sister Hilda Bergoine, but circumstances are such that it is not possible for her to function in that capacity right now. I'm sure all of you understand." Ruby took another deep breath. "Although I may have to rely on intuition in some isolated incidences, I feel confident I can handle matters adequately." Realizing she was inadvertently rubbing her hand across her belly, she added, "At least for a while. What has happened to our sister in Jesus is heinous. I will spend the rest of my life trying to understand why she was taken from us in such a violent, undignified manner. I can only take solace in the fact that God gives man free will and free reign here on earth. I'll never believe her vicious demise was any part of God's plan for anything. I take comfort in the fact she is in his presence and not suffering any longer. I welcome your suggestions and your comments, and I also welcome any help you have to offer. Veteran knowledge and expertise will only help me to become proficient at my job. Our meeting time will be Wednesday nights after evening services. We'll try to meet at least once a month, but if this is not suitable for some of you, please contact me and we'll try to get a general consensus on a favorable meeting time for everyone. That's all I have for now. Our next function is a memorial service for the late Heloise Pullman. Tentatively scheduled for Tuesday morning, the service will begin at ten. We opted for Tuesday morning in hopes of giving out of town family time to arrive. Brother Lawson will deliver a sermon for this event, and the food and beverage committee should prepare lunch for all who attend to be served afterwards. I have a list of hymns for the music director and would appreciate his meeting with the choir as soon as possible. Thank you all for coming. Please see me after the meeting if there are any questions."

"May I see you after the meeting?"

"Of course, darling. You can see me anytime you want." Ruby put her arms around Robert and laid her head against his chest. "I'm so sad."

"I know."

"There was no forewarning, Robert. We had no clue that we were being stalked. This whole thing struck right out of the blue."

"Can we go somewhere and talk?"

"We can talk right here."

"Please. Let's walk out to the courtyard. I have something I want to tell you."

Ruby thought for a moment. *Now was the time.* "And I have some news for you as well." She smiled.

"It's been awhile since I've seen a smile on that face. What's going on?"

By now they had reached the courtyard garden. A beautifully landscaped respite positioned between the two wings of the church, the garden was shielded from most of the damaging winds of winter and the pounding midsummer sun. Because of this configuration, the annual flowers lasted well into early winter. It was a protected, tranquil spot—a favorite of many church members.

"Well, there's something I need to tell you."

As Ruby opened her mouth to continue, Robert interrupted her. "There's something I need you to know as well." He pulled the telegram from his pocket.

"What is this?"

"I think you'd better read it." Robert's face was ashen. His hands were trembling as he handed it to her.

Ruby pulled the telegram from the opened envelope and read it. She then flipped the envelope over and saw that it was addressed to her. "Oh my God … This was for me and you didn't give it to me. You opened it and read it." Covering her mouth and nose with the envelope, she turned her back to Robert. Not knowing what to say or do next, she remained there for a moment.

"Ruby, I'm so sorry."

"You lied to me. You knew about this, and you deliberately deceived me. You knew exactly what you were doing when you went to pick it up. That's why you said 'wrong number.' You wanted to read it first." Ruby put the knuckle of her index finger in her mouth and bit down. She was looking straight ahead in deep thought. After a moment, she took her hand from her mouth and began to speak slowly and deliberately. "This could have saved her. If the police had known about this telegram, Heloise might be alive today."

Robert went to embrace her. When she felt his arms begin to encircle her, she became enraged. "Don't touch me! Don't you dare touch me!" She lashed out and began hitting him with all her might. She wasn't strong and wasn't particularly adept at fighting, so Robert was able to quickly subdue the attack.

"Why, Robert? Why? Why did you do this, you … you liar, you coward!" She began to cry. "You didn't even trust me enough to read my own telegram. You invaded my privacy, which probably contributed to the murder of an innocent old lady."

He'd had enough. He pushed her away from him. The anger he'd felt about the telegram was beginning to resurface. "I'm not a coward, Ruby. I wasn't afraid to read that telegram at all. *Why* you ask? Why did I do it? Think about it. The telegram was from another man, a man I saw look at you with love in his eyes. Do you think I'm stupid? Don't you think I wondered what the hell was going on? This 'pretty boy' appears out of nowhere and suddenly is on a first name basis with my wife. He gives you an expensive gift …"

"Us. He gave that to both of us."

"Bullshit!" Robert felt the muscles in his jaw begin to tense. "The next thing I know, the son of a bitch is writing a telegram to my wife. How you would react if the situation were reversed? How would you react if I'd received a telegram from some strange woman?" He swallowed hard. "You need to understand where I'm coming from on this."

Saying nothing, Ruby stared at him for a moment. Finally, deciding to break the pregnant silence, she spoke. "You disgust me." She then jerked her arm free and left, walking toward the meeting room of the church.

Still reeling from the row they'd just had, he watched her leave.

"She's feistier than I thought."

In a mixture of pain and aggravation, Robert closed his eyes. "Beverly, get the hell away from me."

"You should have let me give you a few lessons on lying, big boy. The truth really does hurt, doesn't it?"

"You're the one that's about to get hurt if you don't leave me alone."

"When will you realize that you need what I have to offer? It seems 'Mother Superior' in there just isn't quite cutting it these days."

Robert took a deep breath and walked over to Beverly. Grabbing her by the throat with his right hand, he snatched her toward him. Through gritted teeth he muttered, "I'm telling you to leave me the fuck alone. If you push me too far, I might just snap. Neither one of us would want to see that, now would we?" He released her and roughly shoved her away from him.

Beverly stumbled two or three steps backward. She smiled. "Damn ... You play rough. That's OK, lover. I like it that way."

Robert's eyes narrowed. "One day your whoring will get you into trouble, Bev. To be honest, I really don't give a shit, but maybe you'd better heed my warning. Use your brain instead of your cunt for a change."

"You're welcome to both anytime you want, big boy." Beverly gave him a wink. "See you around, I hope." With that she turned and left.

"I hate that bitch," he mumbled aloud as she walked away from him. As if the confrontation with Ruby was not enough, he had to deal with trash like her. He decided to make his way back to the meeting room. When he reached it, he found there were still about eight women lingering after the meeting. They were laughing and talking, but their attention diverted to him as he entered the room. "Has anyone seen Ruby?"

"I did. Looks like you two had a little lover's quarrel." Looking slightly amused at Robert's dismay, Eva Nell Alexander perched against the window.

Robert exhaled in disgust as he walked past her. He made sure he slammed the door loudly as he left.

Still smiling, Eva Nell watched him exit. Raising her eyebrows, she muttered, "Trouble in paradise?" She took a long sip of her iced tea and watched his silhouette disappear into the night.

* * *

When he reached home, he bolted through the door yelling, "Ruby? Ruby!" Looking in every room of the house, he realized she wasn't there. He went to the phone.

"Give me Jed Carraway's residence."

The phone rang several times.

"Hello."

"Jed?"

"Hi, Robert."

"Is my wife there?"

"She's here, where are you?"

"May I speak to her?"

"Perhaps you'd better get over here; she's pretty upset about something …"

Robert sighed. "It's something I've done, Jed. My coming over there might not be a very good idea."

"You two aren't kids anymore; you're married and grown. We can't fix everything like we used to, so get yourself over here and work it out with your wife."

"Yes, sir. I'll be there in a few minutes."

* * *

When he arrived at the Carraway's, Jed answered the door. Upon entering the house, he found Ruby and Lorna sitting in the living room together. They both looked up as he walked into the room.

"Hi."

Ruby's eyes were swollen from crying. She simply replied, "Hi" and looked down at her lap.

"Jed and Lorna, do you think we might have a few minutes alone?"

Ruby stood up. "There's no need for that, Robert. It's time we went home."

"We'll get past this, Ruby, I promise."

"We have to ... we have no choice."

Lorna cut her eyes over to Ruby who caught her glance. "You go home and get a good night's sleep, daughter. Everything will be better in the morning."

Ruby turned around abruptly. "No, it won't."

"Try and rest, honey, it's not good for you in your cond ..."

"It's not going to be any better tomorrow. What are you thinking? There is a killer after me. My husband over there is a liar and a thief. Then, just when my life is at the acme of despair, I find out I'm pregnant. What's a few hours of sleep going to do, Mother? Tell me, because I'd really like to know."

"What?" Robert yelled.

Lorna's bottom lip began to quiver.

Jed stood up and interrupted. "Apologize for that outburst right now and don't you ever talk to your mother like that again. She was only trying to be supportive." He walked to the center of the room. "We are all in this mess together, kids, and with God's help we'll get out of it. In the meantime, understand this: You will not lash out at either of us again. I assume I've made myself clear?"

Ruby said nothing and simply nodded *yes*.

"I'm sorry to tell you this, but it's not our job to be the favored recipients of your frustrations and hostilities." He turned and walked back to Lorna who was still sitting on the couch. "I'm really disappointed in you, Ruby Carraway."

"Davis," Robert interjected.

Without saying a word, Jed turned and glared at Robert.

He then turned back to Ruby. "If you two don't want to go home, you are both welcome to stay here. We have plenty of room, but I want this worked out. I don't know what caused all of this, but now is not the time for family strife. We have a murderer out there and a baby on the way to protect."

"Ruby, why didn't you tell me?"

"I was waiting for the right time. I wanted it to be a happy, joyful time we could both celebrate. Not like this, not like this at all."

Robert sat down on the couch in amazement. "Have you told my parents?"

"No, I haven't."

"I'm calling them. It's not too late, and they'll be thrilled."

Jed smiled. *Things may have not been perfect, but here was the silver lining. At least there was a silver lining …*

CHAPTER THIRTY-SIX

"I have a feeling I'm going to be up awhile. I'm wide-awake. Do you feel sleepy?"

"No, especially not now. Ruby, we need to talk."

"I think I'm talked out, and I'm really not up for another discussion tonight. No more drama. I just want to lie here and rest."

"We have to get out of here. We have to leave Conway. There's too much at stake, now."

"Oh God, Robert, please. Please, please, please. Let's tackle that subject in the morning ... I'm physically and emotionally drained."

"Father Donovan has offered to help us. He said he'd hide us at a seminary or something until all of this is resolved."

"Well, that's all well and good, but I have to have doctor's care, too. I don't think those priests deliver too many babies." Her back toward him, she'd turned over in bed after she'd said this.

"I didn't say I had all the answers, but for our own protection, we have to leave."

"I won't even get to have a normal pregnancy."

"No, you won't. And you can thank your cousin Blanche for that. If it weren't for her and her 'race to your rescue,' none of this would be happening. But it is, and we have to deal with it. I can't change anything now, so stop feeling sorry for yourself and help me try to figure things out."

"I'll thank you not to mention my cousin Blanche again."

"You know, at the church you as much as blamed me for Heloise's death. That is a lie, and I won't take the blame for it. You called me a liar and a thief in front of your parents and now you say don't mention St. Blanche? Well, uncloud your mind, Rube. Blanche brought that Solange demon into our lives. Her help and her tarot revelation are also what brought Rupert Staten, three murders and now our imminent sequestration about. So now maybe you have a clearer picture of why you won't have a normal pregnancy."

Ruby swallowed hard. For the first time, she realized that maybe Robert was right. She'd been blaming him for so much, and Blanche did bring all of the things he'd mentioned into their lives.

"What about all of your strange memories of another life? Was that Blanche's fault, too?"

"I didn't make that up. You know I didn't. Those feelings are not my fault, either. Damn, Ruby, I am not the enemy here. I am your husband and the father of our child." Robert then rolled over in bed as well, turning his back to her.

Ruby sighed in defeat as she began to stare toward the wall. "So when do we leave?"

Robert turned back around. "You'll go?"

"I'll go."

"I'll call Father Donovan in the morning."

"Maybe you'd better go over there. You know, Mabel?"

"God, you're right! Leave it to Mabel to get us killed before week's end." He sat up in bed as he said this. "Father and I will make the necessary arrangements tomorrow. Hopefully, we'll be out of Conway by nightfall. You'll need to pack for us while I'm gone and plan to bring that coin along as well."

"We can't leave tomorrow night. I have the memorial service on Tuesday."

"We'll leave Tuesday night, then."

"I wish I'd never seen that coin."

"Well, that's neither here nor there, Ruby. What's done is done now. We need Solange to believe, that like us, the coin has disappeared as well."

"To protect our families."

"I don't want her thinking our family knows the whereabouts of that coin. She'd just as soon kill them as look at them."

"Ask Father Donovan if he might locate a midwife, Robert. Who knows how long we may be gone and we have to plan ahead."

"Let's try to rest for a while, Ruby. We have a lot to tend to."

Robert felt under his pillow to reassure himself the pistol was there. He then turned off the lamp. *Much to do*, he thought to himself.

* * *

Early Monday Morning, April 18, 1932

It was not much of a night for sleeping. Ruby finally fell asleep in the wee hours of the morning only to be abruptly awakened by the rude, unforgiving ring of the telephone. She looked at the clock. 5:16 A.M. ... *Who on earth could be calling at this hour?*

Robert stirred and looked at the phone as well.

"Hello?"

"Ruby? It's Hilda."

"Hi darling."

"I'm sorry to call so early but I've made a decision."

"A decision? What kind of decision?"

"I've decided to leave town."

"Where are you going?"

"Abilene, Texas. I have a brother there and three nephews of which I'm very fond. They've been urging me to come stay with them, and ... Well, now that Heloise is gone, there is really no good reason not to."

"I think that is a wonderful idea."

"Ruby, the reason I've called is I'm leaving after the service tomorrow afternoon."

"So soon, Hilda? Isn't this rather sudden?"

"No, no, not sudden ... As you know, my family is coming to town for the service tomorrow. I told them I might like to accompany them to Abilene and stay for a while. Maybe there I'll be able gather my thoughts. They all thought it was a good idea. I think they are worried about my state of mind, and frankly, I am as well. I need a change of scenery, Ruby. I may just move there."

"Oh Hilda." Ruby sat up in bed trying to digest all of this. "Please don't do anything rash. You are in an emotional state right now. You're

probably still in shock. Give it some time before you decide anything
as drastic as a move. You have friends here, your church, your home;
you have a whole life here. See if you like Abilene before you decide
to relocate there."

"I guess this news leads to the other reason I've called you."

"There's more?"

"This decision affects my co-chairing the Events Committee for
the upcoming year, Ruby."

"Don't worry, dear. I've already told them I'll be handling things
alone for a while."

"That's not what I'm saying. You're going to have to handle this alone
for the year, as I don't think I will be here to assist you in any way."

"Not at all?"

"I think I'm beyond that capacity now. I just cannot think in terms
of administration at the church anymore. The hurt is too deep and
the wounds are too fresh. Will you be OK?"

"I don't know, Hilda. Judging from my predicament, I don't know
what the future holds."

"The church is depending on you."

"Hilda, I'll have to find some backup as well. I believe the monster
that murdered Heloise intended to kill me. To make matters more
complicated, I've just found out I'm pregnant."

"Again?"

"What do you mean again?"

"Oh, nothing dear, I meant nothing by that. I just thought your
seeing Dr. Belton before the wedding and all ..."

Ruby sighed. "We explained everything to you, Hilda. I know
it sounds incredible but it's all true. I wasn't pregnant. I was worried
about the episode Robert had in my front yard."

"Forgive me, women can be so ruthless. I'm sorry dear, and con-
gratulations. I also hope you have luck tending to the Events Committee."

"I'll find someone, Hilda."

"Well, I need to finish packing ... You know I love you, don't
you?"

"I know, Hilda."

"Then I'll say goodbye for now. I will be in touch and let you know what I've decided one way or the other. I'll be praying for you, Ruby, and I'll be praying they bring my sister's killer to justice."

"I love you, Hilda."

"Goodbye, dear, and take care."

CHAPTER THIRTY-SEVEN

Tom walked into the room. He found Solange sitting in the middle of the floor in a trance-like state.

"Solange?"

"I see the arc. We're approaching the beginning of this loop. Things will start again, and events will begin to repeat. It's all meaningless. I can't do it again."

"Do what?"

"I can't do it again. It's a form of punishment. It's a version of Hell."

"Wake up muffin, Tom-boy is here." He shook her.

"I'm awake, *Tom-boy*," She mocked. "I'm fully aware of what's going on. We're running out of time. We must get the portal at once. I feel the dimensions closing, Tom. We have to escape this time."

"We'll do it, baby."

Solange looked at him and stroked his face. "We'll get out of this matrix and have everything we've ever wanted." She reached up and kissed him.

He grabbed the back of her gown with both hands and ripped it open. "Let's celebrate."

* * *

"How's it going, old boy?"

"Can't seem to paint anything."

"Still thinking about that woman?"

Rupert sighed. "Yes."

"Rupert, this is merely a fantasy. You've seen this woman twice in your lifetime, and she's married for God's sake. Where is all of this coming from?"

"It's just a feeling I have. I can't explain it, Caris, but it's overwhelming."

"You're simply distracted and using this as an excuse."

"You're wrong."

"OK, I'm wrong, Rupert. So how do you make sense of this? How do you put it behind you?"

"I'm not sure I want to; I'm not sure I will have to."

"Don't be ridiculous. You mean nothing to her. You are probably no more than a distant memory. If you persist with this bizarre behavior, people will think your mind is going."

"People love eccentricity. I'll be famous. Here, take this." Rupert handed Caris a knife. "Cut off my ear. I want to send her a present."

Caris burst out laughing. "You are a crazy bastard, you know that?"

Rupert looked at him smiling. "I know."

"Anyway, you have to be original. That's already been done."

"You know, I'd love to see where she lives. I'd love to see the place she calls home and the people surrounding her."

"Well, I can assure you they are not bohemian artists ready to cut off body parts for birthday and Christmas presents."

"Caris, I wasn't going to cut off everything, just an ear or maybe an eyebrow."

"They are probably straight-laced and proper. They have respectable jobs and attend church on Sunday and Wednesday nights. They do not frequent the speakeasy for entertainment as we do. It's more along the line of quilting bees and church picnics. Also, I imagine the women stay in groups, while the men bond in a group of their own—discussing politics and the present economic disaster."

"I'm sure they are a little different …"

"Different? Rupert, you are an artist. You are a whoremonger and have a mulatto girlfriend. You live in what they refer to as 'Sin City' and probably have never seen the inside of a church. Furthermore, you get drunk every weekend and awaken in the bed of a stranger whose gender we may never be quite sure. Face facts. You're a slut and have no morals. Now, you have this 'vision of purity' you must possess and think that you are so infatuated that you must act as some present-day Van Gogh. Not going to happen, big boy, those Arkansas Protestants would refer to you as a sinner and white trash. You are socially beneath them, and I'll just bet that woman's mother would die before she'd see her daughter with the likes of you. The icing on the cake, my good man, is that you'd make her a divorced woman—an adulteress headed straight for Hell. It would do in the entire family unit. It is best that you stay here in the 'quagmire of the damned.' To venture where you fantasize will bring you only mayhem. Heed my words, Rupert, you know I'm right."

"Well, I might lack a little in the way of traditional ethics, but women find me attractive as well as charming."

"Many men do, too, but that's not the point. The truth of the matter is you are out of your element, so believe what I say. She is not for you. She is not of your world." Caris sighed. "I'm repeating myself now so it's time for me to leave. I'll stop in tomorrow and hopefully hear you've come to your senses."

"I may be on my way to Conway."

Caris turned around and picked up the knife. "OK, I give up. Lean over and turn your head toward me."

Rupert paled. "I think I'll just send her a painting. I've decided I want both ears."

"Now you are making sense. Forget her, forget Conway, and concentrate on your own life. It's a big enough mess already. You have plenty to sort out here. I'll see you tomorrow."

Rupert watched his best friend leave. He knew Caris was right but didn't care. He could change. Fate was on his side this time. The whores, the men, the women he lived with could all be classified under "wild oats." His wild side was the element that made his work so enchanting. Here was a beautiful flower in bloom, and somehow, some way he would possess it. Maybe he would have a look around at Conway to know what he was up against—the sooner, the better. Yes, that's right, the sooner the better.

* * *

As Sister Alexandra proceeded down the hallway, she heard a knock on the door. While the many yards of fabric in her habit continued to complete the one hundred eighty-degree turn she'd just made, she answered the door.

"Robert, What a nice surprise. I assume you are here to see Father?"

"I am. Please forgive me, but I opted to drop by instead of call."

"You probably would have saved yourself a wait if you had called."

"Sister, let's just say I opted to call in person for specific reasons who shall remain nameless."

"Well there's only one 'nameless name' I can think of, so point well taken. I'll see when Father will be able to meet with you. Please have a seat and make yourself comfortable. There is fresh coffee in the drip pot and a delicious pound cake on the table. Mary Burfield brought it last night, so by all means help yourself."

As she left the room, Robert licked his lips.

I think I'll do just that. I didn't get a chance for breakfast this morning, so a nice, big hunk of pound cake might tide me over.

As he poured himself a cup of coffee, he heard a familiar voice behind him.

"Good morning."

He turned to address the voice. "Good morning, Father. How are you?"

"I'm doing well, thank you. I assume you've considered my offer, and that's why you're here?"

"You assume correctly. The plot thickens."

"How in the holy name of Jesus could it get any thicker?"

"Ruby is pregnant."

"Oh dear. But how wonderful as well! How far along is she?"

"I don't really know. Believe it or not, I didn't ask. She can't be too far along. That being said, along with this sequestration, we're going to need a midwife."

"That shouldn't be hard. I have already talked to a seminary priest in Memphis, Tennessee, and he's arranging things for us as we speak. I'll ask that he find a suitable physician or midwife to tend to Ruby while you two are there."

"Why Memphis?"

"Well, first of all, Memphis has a seminary. Secondly, it's not terribly far from here, and the trip shouldn't be too difficult. Many of the nuns there tend to the poor and the sick, so I have no doubt there is a midwife amongst them."

"Wow." He took a deep breath. "Looks like it's all falling into place."

"Maybe they'll catch this horrible murderer and none of this will be necessary. Hopefully as soon as all of this is resolved, you both can return home to your lives."

"I guess now we need find a way up there. I could probably have someone in the family drive us."

"Not necessary. Sister Alexandra and I will accompany you in the church automobile. We'll leave at night. It won't be too hot and we'll have less chance of being detected."

"I agree."

"Tell no one, and I mean no one of your whereabouts."

"We'll call our parents when we've arrived safely. Hopefully having no idea of our whereabouts will keep them out of danger."

"That will be our prayer, Robert. Perhaps the Conway police should be patrolling the Davis and Carraway households."

"If we can get them to do that. The next question is when do we leave?"

"We'll leave tomorrow night if you can ready everything. The sooner we have you two settled, the easier it will be on both of you—especially with this pregnancy adding another variable to the situation."

How many more variables could possibly be crammed into this mess? Robert turned toward Father Donovan. "Before I go …"

"Yes, Robert?"

"I was going to cut myself a big piece of that pound cake."

CHAPTER THIRTY-EIGHT

Wednesday, April 20, 1932

Lorna Carraway had just finished putting the suppertime dishes away when she was startled by a figure at the back door. Standing in front of the screen, with a smile across his face, was Brother Lawson. When he saw he had gotten Lorna's attention, he raised his eyebrows in anticipation. Lorna smiled. Still a little surprised by the interruption, she walked toward the screen door.

"Good evening, Brother Lawson. Please come in. You're a bit late for supper but just in time for dessert."

"And I'll just take you up on that." It was no secret Brother Lawson loved sweets. A rather rotund man with an infectious smile, his charming manner brought a lift to even the most irritable situations. He was dearly loved by the congregation and made it his business to know all of them well.

"I'm so glad." Lorna turned to cut a chocolate pie she'd made earlier in the day. "I'd be really flattered if the reason you came to see us was to enjoy my baking expertise, but somehow I don't feel that's the case."

"This chocolate pie would certainly stand alone as reason enough to call, Lorna, but there is something else."

"Have a seat." Lorna set a piece of pie in front of him at the kitchen table and poured him a glass of freshly brewed tea. "I'm serving this iced since it's already so warm outside."

"Lorna, why don't you ask Jed to join us. I think both of you might need to be in on this discussion."

"Well here I am ready to discuss," Jed bellowed as he threw the kitchen door open.

Lorna's head snapped in his direction. "Good God Almighty, Jed, you startled me! You men are going to have to be a little less dramatic about your entrances. That's twice in ten minutes my heart has nearly jumped out of my chest."

"I sure am sorry, honey. I wasn't trying to startle anyone. I just heard my name mentioned and thought I'd see what it was all about."

Lorna was still looking at Jed when Brother Lawson began. "Jed and Lorna, I don't know if you are aware that Hilda Bergoine is now in Abilene, Texas."

"Ruby told me something to that effect a day or so ago. What on earth is in Abilene?"

"Apparently, she has family there that came for her in hopes of helping her cope with the death of her sister. I received a letter from her saying she's seriously considering a move, and if she decides to do so, her nephew will take care of the arrangements here in Conway. She went further as to say she didn't know if she'd be able to return for her things. Now that she's away, it may be too painful to do so until she's healed somewhat from her sister's murder."

Lorna poured Brother Lawson another glass of tea. "Poor Hilda. Ruby told me the church is buying Heloise a tombstone as a gesture of remembrance."

"As far as I know, that's being take care of, which brings me to the reason for my visit."

Jed said, "Go on ..."

"The tombstone detail falls under the duties of the Events Committee."

"How do you figure?"

"Well, it seems appropriate since Heloise was one of the Events Committee co-chairs. Those ladies worked most closely with Heloise, and all felt it would be something they could do as an act of memoriam."

Lorna smiled. "How nice."

"I need to get in touch with your daughter since she now chairs this committee, but I can't seem to get hold of her anywhere."

Lorna furrowed her brow in thought. "Come to think of it, I haven't heard from her either. She's usually called by now ... I wonder what's kept her so occupied?"

Brother Lawson finished his tea and scraped his last bite of pie together. "When you do hear from her, tell her to give me a call. I'd like this detail tended to right away. Also, Ruby and I need to discuss some possibilities for co-chair, as I've heard she's expecting." As he finished this sentence, the big smile and dimples returned once more.

"We're all excited, Brother Lawson. We can't wait for that little rascal's arrival. How about another piece of pie?"

"No, no, that's plenty. Got to watch my figure, you know."

Lorna burst out laughing. "Well, whenever I do manage to catch up with her, I'll give Ruby your message. Stop by if your sweet tooth kicks in again. There's plenty more pie."

"You two have a good evening, you hear?"

Lorna and Jed smiled as he left.

Jed scratched his head in curiosity. "Where do you suppose those two younguns are, anyway?"

"Probably at Lila's; I'll ring her a little later on." Lorna turned to the sink and began to wash Brother Lawson's glass, saucer, and utensils. She looked up and focused her gaze beyond the kitchen window. Something didn't feel right. For some reason, a reason she couldn't yet put a finger on, things weren't adding up. Maybe it was just a feeling. She hoped that's all it was.

* * *

"What'll you have, hon?"

"Just coffee."

"Want cream?"

"Black."

Tom lit a cigarette. He sat in the booth alone and watched as townsfolk trickled into the diner for a late supper. A few faces looked vaguely familiar; probably folks he'd seen on the sidewalks.

"Here you go. Sure you don't want anything to eat?"

"Yeah, go ahead and bring me a chicken-fried steak with milk gravy."

"Two vegetables, honey."

"Field peas and rice."

"Comin' right up."

Tom wasn't hungry but figured he shouldn't sit in a diner at meal-time and order coffee. He took another smoke of his cigarette, blowing rings, which twisted and contorted into oblivion above his head. He turned his head to the left and saw her staring at him. She was smiling. He gave her a half-crooked smile and looked back down at his booth. When he looked up again, she was standing in front of him.

"Don't believe I've seen the likes of you around here before."

"Why don't you believe it?"

"Seems like you're a stranger to our little town." Beverly Martin was never one for subtlety.

"Appearances can be deceiving."

"Dining alone?"

"Not yet."

"Handsome, rugged man like you ought to have a lot to offer in the way of conversation. Those deep lines and sun tanned skin usually show up on the sort of man that's been around."

"Around what?"

"Oh … People, places and situations."

Tom stubbed out his cigarette. "I guess if I wanted you to join me, the polite thing to do would be to offer you a seat."

"Something you haven't done yet."

"No, I haven't."

Beverly smoothed a hand down the back of her skirt as she slid into the booth. "So nice of you to ask. I'd love to join you."

Not saying a word, Tom stared at her.

Beverly smiled. "Maybe on the other hand, you're the strong silent type."

"I guess that's both hands, then."

Beverly reached over and took a cigarette from his pack. Willadene Parker's eyes widened as she gasped from the booth in front of them.

She was furiously prodding and poking her husband about this as Beverly lit it. She heard old, deaf Jake Parker saying, "Nothing that slut does would surprise me." Focusing her attention back to Tom, she introduced herself. "I'm Beverly Martin."

"OK ... anything else?"

"Well, you could tell me your name."

"Beverly Martin, you need to be careful. You have no idea what you might get yourself into. Why don't you hit on one of the locals?"

"Oh, they're all such boors. I've been with most ..." Beverly stopped herself.

She began again. "Well, let's just say I've been around."

"Sounds like you need a change of scenery."

"Might be fun for both of us."

"So, Beverly Martin, now that you've finally peaked my interests, tell me where you fit in here in Conway. What do you do?"

"Clerical. I work in the office down at the phone company."

"Oh, an operator."

"God no. If you knew how nosey our resident operators here are, you'd never pick up the phone again. Jesus ..." Beverly paused for a moment as she looked at her hands. There was a look of utter disgust on her face. "Nothing is sacred."

"Nothing as in ... ?"

"What's your name again?"

"I didn't tell you."

"Well, mystery man, if you want to keep your identity a secret around here, stay off the telephone. We have an operator that eavesdrops on everything said in Conway. Everyone knows if you need any dirt on someone, take fat-ass Mabel a chocolate cake and she'll fill you in."

"Fat-ass Mabel?"

"Sorry. Mabel Agnew, senior telephone operator in Conway. The sight of her makes me sick."

"That ugly, huh?"

"No, Stranger, that's not it. I hate the fact that she acts so pious and devout at church and then invites all of her old biddy friends

over for coffee and gossip afterwards. They beat a path to her house
to hear whose conversation she's listened in on lately. Then they gasp
and fan themselves and pass judgment like they are pure as the driven
snow." Beverly stubbed out the cigarette. "They think I'm a wanton
woman headed straight for Hell, but at least I'm not hypocritical. I'm
sure I'll have plenty of company down there if they are right." Beverly
exhaled and then looked at Tom. "Now that we've covered that topic,
which is of absolutely no interest to you, how about talking about
you and me."

"There is no you and me."

She raised her eyebrows. "There could be."

"I'm going to save you a lot of trouble and get out of here. Here's
some money, so why don't you have supper on me. Hope you like
fried steak." Tom got up from the booth and left without looking
back. He'd found a speakeasy on the outskirts of town and headed that
direction for a bottle of whiskey. He smiled to himself. "She might
have been a lot of fun."

✳ ✳ ✳

Thursday, April 21, 1932

   "This is the operator, number please."

"Good morning, Mabel. It's Lorna Carraway. Could you please
ring Lila for me?"

   "Of course, Lorna, please hold."

Something was definitely not right. She did not hear from Ruby
yesterday and now was beginning to worry. "Hello, Lila?"

"Morning, Lorna. What can I do for you?"

"Lila, I'm sorry to call so early, but I need to know if you've heard
from the kids. Ruby didn't call me yesterday and I find that somewhat
odd. We usually talk every day."

"More like inconsiderate, Lorna. I haven't heard from them either,
but who knows what those two are up to these days. They have a lot
going on."

"I'm just a bit paranoid, I guess. I'm still shaken from Heloise's
murder, and with Ruby being pregnant, well … My nerves are
shot."

"Such a horrible thing that happened to Heloise." Telephone in hand, Lila stood in the hallway contemplating what she should do. Finally, she said, "Tell you what, I have some marketing to do in a bit. What do you say I check on the kids on my way home?"

"I should probably do that since you live so far out …"

"Lorna, I'll pass right by there. Don't give it another thought. I'll take care of everything."

"Oh dear," Lorna sighed. "With all that's happened, it's easy to overreact these days. I'd hate for you to put yourself out, but I'd appreciate a call if you do hear anything."

"Give my love to Jed and the rest of the family. Try to relax, Lorna. All of this worry is not good for you."

"I will, take care." She exhaled in a mixture of exasperation and defeat as she returned the receiver to its cradle. She wouldn't rest easy until she got that phone call from Lila. As she turned to leave the room, the phone rang. "Surely it couldn't be …"

"Hello?"

"Mother?"

"Well I do vow. I just got off the phone with your mother-in-law. Neither one of us have heard from you two. She's on her way over there as we speak."

"Mother, I …"

"Ruby, I was starting worry. Is everything all right?"

"Mother, I need you to listen to me. We're not in Conway."

"What? Wait a minute."

"In light of the circumstances, Robert and I decided to leave town until the police can apprehend that woman. Now that this baby is on the way, I couldn't justify risking everyone's life simply hoping for the best."

"Where on earth are you?"

"We're in Memphis."

"Memphis? What in the name of Jesus …"

"It's a long story, but Father Donovan and Sister Alexandra have arranged for us to stay at a seminary here."

Stunned, Lorna held the phone to her ear. "Well ... well all right, if that's what you have to do. I ... I don't know what to tell you, Ruby. What about a doctor?"

"We're looking for a midwife, Momma."

"This is all so sudden. I had no idea this was happening. Ruby, are you sure? You may need us. You're up there all alone."

"I'll be alright. We're pretty sequestered here."

Lorna paused for a moment. Letting out a long sigh, she began again. "Well, I guess I'd better get in touch with Lila and let her know what has happened. She will not know what to think, either."

"I know, Momma."

"Will we hear from you again anytime soon?" Tears began to well in her eyes.

"I hope so. I'm not going to call so much in case word might get around as to our whereabouts. That could be disastrous. Robert would be furious if he knew I was calling you, but I couldn't let you worry."

"I'm not really worried about Robert being furious. In fact, I don't really care. When this baby comes, let his child disappear without a trace and see how he feels."

"I shouldn't have said that."

"No, you shouldn't have. But that's not the point right now. Stay safe, darling. If you have a chance, at least keep in touch and let us know you're alright."

"I love you, Momma."

"I love you too, Ruby. Take care of yourself, and call if you need me. I'll be on the first train out." Lorna grabbed a kitchen dishtowel and began dabbing her eyes. *It's not supposed to be like this ...*

* * *

Lorna fixed herself a restoring cup of coffee and made her way to the living room. The coffee smelled wonderful. Filling the room with reassuring comfort, the aroma wafted past her. She inhaled deeply. Taking a long sip, she took a seat by the fireplace. She had to think. *The kids are gone, at least for a while. I'll have to stop their mail or pick it up for them at the post office. Who will pay their bills? The yard has to be maintained and ...* Suddenly, she thought about Brother Lawson's visit a few nights ago. *Now there is no one to chair the Events Committee. Who's going to take care of Heloise's tombstone?*

She picked up the receiver again. "Mabel, I need the parsonage, please."

"I'll connect you, Lorna, but I know for a fact Brother Lawson will be in Searcy until tomorrow."

The small town of Searcy is situated approximately fifty miles north of Conway. A bit of a drive, it was doubtful that Brother Lawson would return to Conway before morning.

"It's important that I talk to him, Mabel. Maybe you'd better ring me through to leave a message."

"Of course, Lorna, please hold."

"Hello, Dot? Hi, it's Lorna."

"Lorna, how are you?"

"Well, Dot, to be candidly honest, I've been better."

"I'm so sorry. I assume you've called to talk to Ben, but he's not here right now. He's out of town until tomorrow. Is there anything I might be able to do for you?"

Lorna paused for a moment. "Well, could you please have Brother Lawson give me a ring when he gets in tomorrow? It doesn't matter what time. I have something rather urgent to discuss with him, a matter that we must attend to immediately."

"I will give him the message, Lorna." Dot hedged for a moment and then asked, "Is everything all right?"

"No, Dot; everything is not all right. In fact, it's all a mess. I really don't want to discuss this over the phone. Tell you what, are you busy right now?"

"I'm just doing a little sewing, why?"

"I've just made a pot of coffee. Do you think you might come by for a bit?"

Dot realized this must be important. Lorna was by nature a detail-oriented individual, and spontaneity was never one of her attributes. This was one of those times when she felt she'd better drop everything and make her way over there to see how she might be of help. She may be no more than a sympathetic ear, but sometimes that was the best medicine of all. "I'll see you in ten minutes, Lorna."

Lorna breathed a sigh of relief. "Oh thank you, Dot. See you soon."

As she hung up the receiver, Dot heard the familiar two clicks. A look of disgust manifested on her face. *One day her curiosity will get the best of her. She may get more than she bargained for.* Bound for Lorna's, she then grabbed her purse and headed out the door.

CHAPTER THIRTY-NINE

Gazing into it as if it were a crystal ball, he cupped his hands around his drink. Engrossed in the conversation, she sat at the bar beside him. She was both intrigued and a bit amused at his candor. As if he believed what he was saying with all of his heart, the look on his face reflected true sincerity.

"Sometimes memories are the only comfort I have. They elicit good feelings and bring back happy times. You know what else? Songs do the same thing; I often associate them with the memories." He smiled and paused for a bit. "I must admit that once in awhile they may even bring forth a tear or two. It can be overwhelming but does provide a great deal of solace as well. They are the only things no man can strip me of, and they are mine to keep forever."

She laughed aloud. "The past can't do a damn thing to help you. It's dead and gone. You should take consolation in the fact that you have control over your present situation. It's real, it's tangible, and the outcome is what you decide to make of it."

Rupert brushed a lock of black hair from his face. "That's a rather gloomy outlook from someone as beautiful as you."

Solange finished her whiskey and inhaled deeply. "Not gloomy, just the truth. Your memories are nothing more than cerebral ghosts. They are empty, unfulfilling and act as constant reminders of under-achievement and failure. I have no time for dreamers or fools. The only ones who survive in this existence are those who are nothing short of relentless."

Rupert poured them both another whiskey. "Nevertheless, relentless can be pretty lonely."

"It can be," Solange began, "but doesn't have to be."

Rupert rested his chin on the palms of his hands. Accentuating his boyish good looks, his hair once again fell onto his forehead. He smiled at her. "You look so familiar. I know I've seen you somewhere."

"I guess anything's possible," she replied, "but not probable. I'm from far away." She had begun to bore of him. She looked about the room and saw Tom working through the crowd toward the bar. "Perhaps that's where you should find yourself momentarily. My insanely jealous lover is making his way back to us as we speak, and now is no time for a row."

Rupert looked up and saw the big, burly stranger headed in their direction. "Perhaps you're right. I don't think an artist such as myself is fit to take on the lumberjack sort. He noticed the scar across his face. Looks as if he's already had a row or two." He finished the last of his whiskey and arose to leave. As he started to walk away from the bar, he turned back and said, "It's been a curious pleasure sharing my feelings with you." He held his gaze as a puzzled look appeared on his face. "You're sure we've never met?"

Solange nodded in confirmation. As his silhouette disappeared into the crowd, she said nothing else.

Tom turned to see who was monopolizing her gaze. "Who was that?"

She took another drink of her whiskey. "A fool. I cannot pinpoint how this imbecile fits into the scheme of things, but our paths are destined to cross again. I detect yet another energy signature."

"Speaking of energy … whatever the hell you just said, things have been quiet around the Davis place. It's totally dark over there and no one has been coming or going for the past two days."

"Now that you mention it, I haven't felt the presence of the portal either. I felt the loop climax approaching the other day, but our exit ticket to freedom is silent. I can't detect a signature anymore."

"Do you think they've skipped town?"

"It's highly possible." She thought for a moment and said, "They probably have the coin with them."

As she finished the statement, she drank the last of her whiskey. Enjoying the burn as she swallowed, she relished the oncoming intoxication. Slowly, it surrounded her in a blanket of warm, drunken haze. Staring at her reflection in the mirrored bar, she motioned to the bartender for another drink. He set the entire bottle in front of them.

"Tom, we have to locate them quickly."

As she said this, he realized there was a way to find the portal's whereabouts.

"I know how to find them."

Solange smiled. "You have a plan?"

"Give me a day and I'll know where they are."

He poured himself a whiskey and held his glass up to toast. "Thank Ma Bell, honey; she's about to connect us."

* * *

Sunday, April 24, 1932

Waiting for her, he sat parked across the street from the church. Cleaning up for the occasion, he'd managed to shower, shave, and even don a bit of aftershave for effect. Subconsciously he wiped his brow and realized he was getting a bit warm as the sun approached the noon position overhead. Tom flicked his cigarette from the window and attempted to scrutinize a mass exodus of hats, dresses, and suits that had suddenly emerged from the church doorway. It was then that he spotted her. As she began her descent down the front stairway toward the street, he quickly left his car and approached her.

"Hi."

She smiled. "Well, hi! Don't tell me you were in services. I'd just never believe it."

"No, I'm not that hypocritical. What were you doing in there, by the way?"

"Oh, old habits are hard to break, I guess. I figure I can atone for at least some of my misgivings during the week, don't you think?"

He paused for a moment after she'd said this. Still looking down, he kicked some gravel onto the road. "Want to misgive?"

Knowing exactly what he had in mind, Beverly cut her eyes at him. A grin crept across her face. No matter whom he belonged to, she could never resist a proposition from a good-looking man. Tongue in cheek she replied, "What do you have in mind?"

"Hop in and I'll show you."

"Looks like I might have to attend evening services too, stranger. Remember, I don't even know your name."

"Tom."

"Well, Tom, your place or mine."

"Yours."

"Want to follow me?"

"No, get in. We'll come back for the car later."

"Now won't that give the congregation something to talk about? I'll really be considered a slut then."

"At least you won't be putting on airs like the rest of them. They are just like you, Beverly Martin, just more discreet. Shall we go?"

Tom was standing beside the opened passenger's door. She smiled at him as she climbed into the car. While the pending encounter excited her to no end, it also frightened her a bit as well. Most of her romantic trysts, married or unmarried, were with men she knew. She'd been around, but this encounter was a bit of a stretch even for her.

After she'd gotten in, he shut the door to the automobile. Suddenly, a voice leapt into the car from the passenger's side window. "Darling, you simply must tell me who this delicious man is sitting next to you."

Tom turned toward the intruder.

"This is my friend Eva Nell Alexander."

Eva Nell smiled and extended her hand. "And you are?"

"Ready to leave." His glance returned to Beverly. "Where do you live?"

Turning her face toward her friend, she shifted uncomfortably in the car seat. "Evie, I guess he's ready to go ... I'll call you later? Maybe can we grab a cup of coffee or something?"

"Bev ..."

Tom sneered at her, signaling she'd better get the hell out of the way.

Moving her arm from the window of the car, she took a step back. Changing to a look of concern, the smile on her face had vanished. "Be sure to call, Bev ..."

Tom gunned the car and abruptly pulled away before Beverly had a chance to respond.

Still standing beside the road, Eva managed one last look at him as they drove off. She couldn't help but wonder if this time Beverly may have put herself in harm's way.

"So where do you live?"

Beverly pointed straight ahead. "This way."

* * *

"Want a drink?"

"You drink on Sunday?"

"Tom, I drink whenever I feel like it. Want one?"

"Sure."

Beverly poured two whiskeys and brought them to the sofa. She sat down beside him.

"This was a nice surprise."

"Glad you think so. Hope I didn't interrupt your Sunday meeting."

"What Sunday meeting?"

"I thought all you telephone gals met after church to dish the dirt. You did say that, didn't you?"

"At Mabel Agnew's? God, no! For one thing, Tom, I'd be the youngest one there by about thirty years. In the second place, those old women think I'm trash, and half the time I'm the one they are over there talking about. I hate Mabel. The sight of her makes me sick. You, on the other hand, strike a different chord." Beverly began to unbutton his shirt.

Tom could feel a stirring in his groin. "Does she live close to you? She might've seen us come here after church."

Beverly had unbuttoned his shirt completely and slid her arms around him. "She lives on Elizabeth Street, about three blocks from here. She'd have to make an effort to drive by, as it's not on her way to anything. Besides, who cares what that old battleaxe thinks? Kiss me."

Tom kissed her and in one swift motion rolled her under him. He reached under her skirt and roughly pulled down her panties, stockings still attached. "Want me to take them off?"

"I want everything off."

CHAPTER FORTY

Tom left Beverly's house after dark. She was stranded there as her car was still parked in front of the church. He didn't care, though, he had other matters to attend to. Remembering that Mabel lived about three blocks from Beverly, he drove around until he found Elizabeth Street.

Near the middle of the street, in front of an unassuming white-framed house, stood a mailbox labeled *Agnew*. Judging from the number of cars parked in the front yard, it looked as if many of the Sunday soiree ladies were still visiting Mabel. Apparently, she was quite the church social butterfly.

Making his way to the end of the dark, isolated street, he drove on. He would park the car and wait. Once all of them were gone, he'd pay Mabel a little visit—a visit he felt sure she'd remember. He wondered if he ought to give her a little thrill before he killed her. *Probably the only time she'll ever have it …* He smiled and then shook his head a bit to clear it. *Only if time allows.*

Time was of the essence. They either found the coin and got the hell out of there or soon faced a hanging trial. Things would have been a lot less complicated if that bitch hadn't stuck her head in the car window tonight. Along with Mabel, he'd planned to kill Beverly. Now, since he had a witness, that would be impossible. He would simply have to disappear before anyone discovered that Mabel had suffered foul play. Finally, sometime after eleven o'clock, he saw the last of the cars leaving Mabel's house. Letting himself in just like the rest of Mabel's friends, Tom made his way around the back of the dark house. *Stupid fool,* he thought to himself, *she even left the door open for me.*

Giving his eyes time to adjust to the surroundings, he hesitated for a moment. He could then see there was light. Probably emanating from a bedroom at the end of the hallway, he stopped just short of the illuminated bedroom door. As he crept down the hall, he could hear Mabel stirring about the room.

Inside, arranging covers and pillows for the evening, Mabel busied herself turning down the bed. The day had been long and arduous, but paled in comparison to the early week activities ahead. The beginning of the week was almost always met with an explosive bustle of activity. She'd decided to retire early in anticipation of the furious onslaught of Monday morning frenzy.

Hearing a creak in the hallway outside her bedroom door, she froze. Anticipating any additional bumps or creaks that may have been lurking in the space beyond the entrance to her bedroom, she stood still for a moment. "Old houses are always settling," she said aloud as climbed into bed and turned off the light.

In no hurry, Tom waited awhile in the hallway. A half hour passed before he was assured that Mabel was asleep. Heavy breathing, accompanied by a loud snore, prompted him to ease into her bedroom. He reached into his pocket, removed his pistol, and then felt for the light switch.

Pushing it to the *on* position, he said, "Surprise, Mabel."

Her eyes immediately flashed open. She sat up in bed and screamed to the top of her lungs. No sound emerged, for she was paralyzed with fear. She tried to scream but couldn't move a muscle.

"I'm glad you didn't scream, Mabel." He walked over to the bed. "See this? It's a pistol. Pretty powerful little gun, Mabel ... Comes complete with a silencer, too. It can take off a hand, your head. ..." He paused for a moment and began again. "Shit ... I can blow off your whole fucking face. But you know, Mabel, I sure would hate to do that." Tom looked at Mabel with a look that mocked genuine concern. "I'd hate to have to put the barrel of this little ole' pistol in your big, fat face and pull the trigger." He smiled. "I do have some good news for you, though. If I do, we won't disturb the neighbors. As I just told you, this little baby has a silencer. So all's well … Understand, Mabel?"

Mabel's eyes were wide and unblinking. She instinctively pulled the covers to her neck. "What do you want?" Her raspy utterance delivered the magnitude of fright she felt at that moment.

Holding the gun steadily at Mabel's face, he walked a little closer. He grabbed a cigarette from the pack in his front shirt pocket, put it to his mouth, and reached for his lighter. He then flipped it open with one hand and flicked it on. He lit his cigarette, took a drag, and blew it out without ever removing it from his mouth. He slid his lighter back into his shirt pocket. "What do I want, Mabel? Hmm … Let's see. Money? It would be nice but not really what I'm here for." His facial expression became one of evil intent. "I could make your ass feel like you just sat on a red-hot poker, Mabel."

Mabel stared at him unflinching. She didn't move.

"But what I really want is some information, Mabel."

"I … I don't understand."

"You see, Mabel, you and I are really not that different. We're more alike than you realize. We both take advantage of those who are …" He paused for a moment in mocking thought. He began again. "Let's just say a little on the unfortunate side. In other words, we're vultures, Mabel."

Mabel was unconsciously shaking her head "no" without reply.

"You listen in on disadvantaged, poor fools who have no idea their conversations include an eavesdropper. You further defile them after church, nonetheless, at one of your Sunday soirees. In case you're wondering about that last word, Mabel, I learned it from my lady friend. The whole town eventually knows their private business and personal problems. You're a disease, Mabel, and you need to be eradicated."

Mabel began to shiver. All she was able to utter was, "Please!"

"Maybe for me, Mabel, something useful can come of your destructive fetish. I need some vital knowledge from you."

"Wh … What could I possibly tell you?"

"Where are the Davises? Suddenly, they've vanished. They are not at home, and I don't believe they are even in town. I know you probably know by now, so tell me."

"I have no idea."

Tom walked a step closer and cocked the trigger. "I'm going to ask one more time, Mabel, and then I'm going to shoot off a foot." He grabbed the corner of the linens and threw them off her legs. He then pointed the pistol at her right foot. "Now where are they?"

Tears were flowing down Mabel's cheeks. Shaking and pale, she was a pitiful sight. "I swear I don't know."

Tom pulled the trigger and fired a blast into the heel of her right foot. Mabel screamed in agony and began wailing aloud hysterically. Sobbing and moaning, her hands became bloody as she grasped her foot. "Thigh's next, Mabel, and then I'm going to fire a bullet right up your fat ass. Now where are they?"

Rocking back and forth, Mabel continued crying. She moaned, "Oh God, Oh God, help me." She looked at him. "Please don't do this."

He cocked the trigger. "Maybe I'll blow off a titty, Mabel. That should let you know I'm serious." He fired the gun into the thigh of her right leg.

She screamed. "Please, please!"

"Where are they, Mabel? Tit's next."

He cocked the gun.

Mabel screamed, "Memphis! Oh God, Memphis! They are staying in a seminary. That Catholic priest got them provisions there."

"Memphis ..." Tom uttered to himself. "Damn. Well, I guess the plans have changed." He looked back at Mabel. "Want me to kill you now or would you rather bleed to death?"

Mabel was staring at him as he said this. She let go of her bloody leg and slowly leaned back against the headboard.

"I'm waiting, Mabel. Least I could do is put your old ass out of its misery."

Mabel didn't reply.

"Mabel?"

Mabel's mouth fell open. He looked at her chest and saw no movement. He leaned over close to her and felt no breath coming from her. Her eyes were fixed and pupils beginning to dilate. "Fuck … She's dead …" He stood there a moment and let out a long sigh. "And I didn't even get to have any fun." He looked around the room and shrugged his shoulders. "Oh well, maybe next time."

As he made his way out of the back of the house, he looked around to be sure he wasn't seen. He needed to think. *First order of business is to get back to Solange and let her know I've found the coin. Then, I need to get to Memphis. I'll take the slut with me to help cover my tracks. If she didn't discuss the operator with her friend, the police shouldn't link me to the murder—for awhile, anyway. Maybe I need to kill her friend before we leave …* He contemplated for a moment and then shook his head. *It's gettin' too complicated. I'd better just get the hell out of here.*

* * *

Robert walked into the Seminary Cathedral. Elaborately clad in rich, ornate woods and intricate frescos, the Cathedral was beautiful.

Moved by the beauty of the Gregorian chants, he decided to sit for a moment and enjoy the music. Built into a loft above the last seven pews of the church, the pipe organ was unlike anything he'd seen. Obviously weighing hundreds of pounds, some of the pipes were tremendous. Sound emanating from the organ seemed to rumble forward, engulfing everything in its path. All was consumed by this glorious tribute to God.

As services ended, Robert decided to remain in the pew and meditate. Pondering his family's uncertain future, he realized even though sequestration was somewhat claustrophobic, it was reassuring as well. True, they had little privacy, but at least here, they would not have to worry about their safety. His wife and unborn baby were protected. His father would continue to run the store, and the neighbors had agreed to watch the house. In the near future, he planned to arrange a secret meeting with both parents. It was bittersweet irony that he'd managed to protect his wife and child, and because of it, his family would have no part in the baby's birth. There would be no church celebration welcoming its newest member, and Ruby would have no baby shower to help prepare for a newborn. Nevertheless, when compared to the possible outcome of remaining in Conway, all of this was inconsequential.

His train of thought was broken as a warm wind engulfed him from behind. He turned to see if the Cathedral doors had blown open, but found them to be closed. He turned back around and saw her standing beside his pew.

"It's time to leave, isn't it?"

"Almost." She paused for a moment. "You will have a cross to bear as a result of the events which have transpired."

"This is no cross? How much more am I expected to endure?"

"You will not be given the gift of non-remembrance. You will carry this with you always. It will be a burden, but you will learn to use it for guidance and strength in times of challenge."

"How cruel! This is beyond my scope of comprehension. You should know that."

"It is your destiny. If you were given non-remembrance, your thoughts would appear to be at rest, but your soul would remain tortured. There would be no closure. In this way, you will now look for closure and eventually find it. You'll find a means to go on and make peace with that which has gone before you."

"I don't want to. I didn't ask to be here, but I am of this place now. How can you say it is my destiny to rip me from yet another existence? Am I destined to hop from lifetime to lifetime living in eternal limbo? Is this Catholic purgatory?"

"You are not deceased."

"Then what the hell am I? I'm not sure how much longer I'm supposed to go on in either lifetime. One has evaporated, and in the other, some crazed killer is after my family." Robert sighed. He looked at her again. "All I want is a sense of normalcy."

"It will come."

"When?"

"Remember to use non-remembrance for strength and courage."

Looking down, his eyes began to fill with tears. Shaking his head *no,* he put his face into his hands and wept.

I can't take any more …

At that moment, he felt a hand on his shoulder. As he looked up, he saw Monsignor Sebastian standing beside him.

"How can I help you, Robert?"

"There is nothing you can do but pray for me, Monsignor. The world is on my shoulders."

"I will pray. We will all pray for you and your family."

Now able to compose himself, Robert arose. He drew a heavy breath and then sighed. "I'm sorry for that. Thank you for the kind words; I needed them." Removing a handkerchief from his pocket, he managed to wipe his eyes. Turning to leave, he bid the Monsignor farewell. "Have a good day, Monsignor."

"God Bless you, Son, and remember, God won't give us more than we can handle."

Stopping abruptly, he turned to face the priest once more. "He's already done that." He said nothing else as he turned back around and left the Cathedral.

CHAPTER FORTY-ONE

After the encounter, Robert wandered aimlessly through the seminary gardens. Ruby found him sitting alone in the conservatory.

"I needed vibrancy, color, and beauty around me. My mood has been a bit lacking today."

She smiled. "Really? I hadn't noticed. I thought that was an expectant privilege to be moody and sullen."

"How about sympathy moods?"

"Well, I guess I can give you that one. Feeling better?"

"No, not really ... actually, I feel kind of numb."

"That's your body's way of coping with stress. I've been feeling that way myself here lately."

As he turned toward her, his expression changed to one of concern. "Whatever happens to me, Ruby, always remember I love you more than anything."

"I know that, and nothing is going to happen to you. We'll get through this."

"We will, just without the results we may wish for."

"What an odd thing to say! Result is a ridiculous word to use. This is not an experiment. This is real life. The 'results' I want are a normal life, a healthy baby and a happy husband. I want to live in my own home in Conway, Arkansas. So how's that for results? Unrealistic?"

"No ..." He paused and began again. "I just hope we can have all of that."

"Robert Davis, I cannot be the sole pillar of strength for every person in this family. I have needs and vulnerabilities just like everyone else. It will take both of us to get through this, so if you give up now, we're all sunk."

He smiled at her. "I feel chastised."

"Well then consider yourself chastised or whatever it takes to recharge those batteries."

Robert laughed. "Batteries … Hell, I'll bet our old Dodge won't even start now."

"Not to worry, we'll send Ned over there to get her running for us. Why don't we go back to our room and have some supper?"

"I think tonight's menu is beans and rice."

"Maybe we'll just skip supper."

"Sounds good to me. I could use a night of just radio and Ruby."

Ruby gave him a kiss and a reassuring hug. "Well, that's just what happens to be on the menu tonight, Robert Davis. So, sharpen your appetite … C'mon, let's go."

Arm in arm, they walked back to the living quarters.

* * *

Rupert stood outside enjoying the warmth and the sunshine. He inhaled deeply. *Even the air smells different here.* He'd lived his life accustomed to the stench of stale swamp air, but here the woods and surrounding farmland contributed an earthy, fragrant scent. At the edge of downtown, he looked down the street. The good people of Conway were going about their business shopping, working, and socializing. They seemed friendly enough … "It's amazing," he mumbled aloud. "Conway is not so terribly far from New Orleans but culturally may as well be across the world." He looked around again. "I wonder if I could belong here? I wonder if I already belong here?"

Feeling thirsty, he decided to head toward the pharmacy. Hopefully, he'd discover a nice, cool soda fountain or perhaps even a restaurant in the back of the store. As he approached the building, he noticed pharmacological bottles of various colors, shapes, and sizes all neatly displayed in the storefront window. A cigarette ad dangled in the top part of the glass door while a welcoming "We're Open" advertisement hung underneath from the door handle. As he made his way inside, the pharmacist smiled and said, "What can I do for you?"

He was in luck. There was a full service fountain. "Phosphate, please."

"What flavor?"

"Grape."

As the pharmacist prepared the phosphate, he looked up and said, "Don't believe I've seen you around these parts before."

"I'm sorry, I should have introduced myself. I'm Rupert Staten."

"I'm Ben Foster. "Where ya' from, Rupert?"

"New Orleans"

"New Orleans? What brings you up here to our neck of the woods?" As he said this, he handed Rupert the phosphate in a chilled fountain glass.

"I'm looking for the Davis place."

"Ned Davis' place?"

"That must be Mrs. Ruby Davis' husband?" Rupert began to rub his temple as he said this. He remembered a Ned Davis mentioned somewhere, but it didn't seem to fit the bill when he thought of Ruby's husband.

The pharmacist laughed. "You must not know them very well."

"It's been awhile."

"Then let me refresh your memory. If you're looking for Ned Davis, you'll need to get on the highway and head north of town about five miles. Be on the lookout for a dirt road on your right. You'll have to pay attention because there's nothing marking it. Ned's farmhouse is down that road about a quarter mile."

"Actually I'm looking for Ruby Davis."

Replaced by a look of suspicion, Ben Foster's smile faded. "You're looking for Ruby Davis ... Who'd you say you were?"

"Rupert Staten."

"Mr. Staten, if you don't mind my asking, what would you be wantin' with Mrs. Davis?"

"It's personal, Sir. I'd rather not discuss it if it's all the same to you. If you can steer me in the right direction, I'll be on my way. How much do I owe you for the soda?"

"Fifteen cents."

Rupert paid the man with three nickels. He stared at Ben waiting for an answer.

Ben stared back at him in silence.

After a long pause, Rupert raised his eyebrows and said, "Well, are you going to tell me or not?"

"Mr. Staten, you being a stranger and all, I suggest you get your ass out of town while you still can. I'll give you the benefit of the doubt and say you obviously don't know what's going on around here. On the other hand, maybe I'd better call the sheriff."

"Well then maybe you'd better, Mr. Foster. I have some information I think may prove to be useful."

Not breaking his glance, Ben replied, "Hang on."

As the pharmacist was calling, Rupert wondered if he'd just gotten himself into a lot of trouble. *This could be one of those nightmare scenarios in which a small town swallows up a stranger, never to be heard from again. On the other hand, if by some outlandish reason the Conway Police did not know Solange DeShotel might be in the area, the Davises could be in real danger.* His train of thought was interrupted.

"Sheriff's on his way."

Rupert didn't acknowledge the pharmacist. *What could that crazy woman be after? Ruby is obviously a woman of ordinary means, so what in God's name could she have worth killing for?*

"Did you hear me?"

Rupert was once again brought back to the pharmacy. He shook his head a little and focused on Ben. "Yes, I heard you." Fiddling with his empty glass, he wondered if calling the sheriff might have been a mistake. His gut instincts told him it was a big mistake … Unfortunately, his gut instincts were usually right.

* * *

The sheriff looked nothing like Rupert imagined. He halfway expected some tall, heavyset man to lumber through the door and slap handcuffs on his wrists as he spit his plug of tobacco onto the pharmacy floor. Instead, a young, wiry man of about twenty, with blonde hair, bright blue eyes, and a ruddy complexion made his way into the room. Carrying a notepad and pencil, he hardly looked old enough to be out of school, much less be the town sheriff.

"You may as well wipe that smirk off your face. I'm a hell of a lot more seasoned than I look."

"You don't look seasoned at all. You look like a kid."

"Sir, I'm not here to discuss my personal attributes. I want to know what you were doing the night of Sunday, April 24, 1932."

"Why?"

"Just answer the question."

"Sheriff, I have some important information I think you need to know. That's the reason I had the pharmacist over there ..."

"Name's Ben in case you forgot."

Rupert sighed. "That's the reason I had Ben give you a call."

"Name, please?"

"Rupert Staten."

"Mr. Staten, what were you doing the night of April 24, 1932?"

"I was ... I was out with friends."

"Where?"

"Downtown."

"Who can substantiate your story and the hours you were there?"

"I can't really give you any names."

"So you can't account for your whereabouts last Sunday night."

"I can, but it can get a lot of folks in trouble."

"Where were you, Mr. Staten?"

"This could cause you some trouble, Mr. Sheriff. I've heard you're subsidized by this establishment."

"Maybe you are not understanding me. I'll ask this one more time. Where were you?"

"I was at the speakeasy behind that abandoned warehouse downtown. Satisfied, Mr. Sheriff?"

"There is no speakeasy downtown, Sir."

"The hell there's not. I can take you there."

The sheriff set his pad and pencil down on the counter. He walked up to Rupert and bent over so that his face was very close. He then spoke quietly and deliberately. "This used to be a friendly little town, Mr. Staten. Lately, since we've had a generous influx of strangers, we have innocent folks being murdered, disappearing and run out of town. I don't like that, Mr. Staten, and right now I want to know if you're associated with the cause of it. Now, I'm going to ask you one more time, where were you the night of April 24, 1932?"

"I just told you."

The sheriff turned to the officer standing beside him and mumbled something that Rupert could not understand. The man left the room only to return with two additional officers. There were now four men standing in front of Rupert Staten. *This wasn't good ...*

"Sheriff, there is no need for reinforcements. I'm not here to cause trouble. I just need to talk to you. I have some vitally important information I need to share with you about a deranged killer that might be in your ..."

"Take him to the station. I'll be there in about an hour."

"Wait! You don't understand! I'm not the problem! It's a deranged woman named Solange ..."

Three officers brusquely escorted Rupert from the pharmacy. A bit dazed, Rupert realized his worst fears were about to come true. *She's going to kill her. She's going to kill her, and they're going to hang me for it.*

CHAPTER FORTY-TWO

Tuesday, April 26, 1932

The phone rang, but again there was no answer. Eva Nell had a horrible feeling about her friend Beverly. She'd not seen or heard from her since the encounter with the stranger. Although handsome in a rough-hewn sort of way, there was an air about him that worried her. She didn't know if he seemed volatile or dangerous. Maybe it was both. Beverly had always been attracted to danger; she loved liaisons with men who were married or in some kind of trouble. Her last affair was that of an ex-con who almost strangled her one night out of jealousy and rage. Nevertheless, the encounter didn't stop Beverly from playing mind games, which drove him to the brink of insanity. Her life was probably saved by the fact that he was re-incarcerated after beating a man senseless with a baseball bat.

She decided to make her way to Beverly's house to see if she was at home. If the reason Beverly wasn't answering her phone were this latest sexual tryst, Eva would be furious as well as relieved.

There were no lights, no sign of activity, and no car in the garage; she lingered a moment longer in front of the house hoping for some clue as to her whereabouts. *Where was she?* The nagging feeling that something was wrong would not leave her.

What options did she have now? Had Beverly been missing long enough to warrant a search? She decided that maybe talking to the sheriff and explaining what had transpired would put her fears at ease. God, she hoped it would … in reality, it could also confirm her worst suspicions.

There was a stop sign in front of her. She found herself sitting in front of it replaying that sneer—that hateful look of intrusion—in her mind. *He's evil,* she thought to herself; *he's going to kill her if I don't get help.*

Upon returning to the house, she walked into the living room and picked up the phone.

"*This is the operator, number please.*"

"Hello, Mabel. I need the sheriff's office. This isn't Mabel? Well where is she? What do you mean you guess I haven't heard?"

* * *

"Looks like you're in a heap of trouble, pretty-boy."

Rupert looked the deputy squarely in the eye and replied, "Looks that way."

"What you doing in these parts anyway? What'd you say you were? An artist?"

"That's right."

"Come to Conway to paint a picture?"

"No, Deputy Hubbard, I came to alert the Conway Police that a murderer may very well be in this area."

"That so ... and just how did you run across this valuable infor-mation, Mr. ... What'd you say your name was again?"

"I didn't."

"Oh, a smart-ass. You'll learn real quick, pretty boy, you ain't from these parts and will do a hell of a lot better if you keep your smart-ass comments to yourself. I'd hate to see that baby face get all ... well, you get the idea."

As the deputy said this, he leaned into Rupert and put his face about an inch in front of him. The sweet pungent smell of tobacco combined with acrid, neglected breath overwhelmed Rupert as he closed his eyes in disgust. "I get the idea."

"So ..."

"So what?"

"You gonna tell me what brings you to Conway or not?"

Rupert decided he'd better avoid trouble on this one. The sheriff was nowhere to be found, and he was basically at the mercy of this ignorant deputy.

"My gallery is in the French Quarter of New Orleans."

"And what does that have to do with your being here?"

"The Quarter is a very closed community. Much like this community."

"How the hell you know we're closed around here ... Whatever that means?"

"There is a woman who lived in the Quarter named Solange De-Shotel, a clairvoyant of sorts."

"A what?"

Rupert closed his eyes in an attempt to hide his aggravation. "A fortune-teller."

"Hey Valentino, are you fucking nuts or are you just tryin' to get me angry?"

"She's believed to be responsible for the murder of Blanche ... He paused for a moment. "Oh hell, I can't remember her last name."

"Harrington?"

"Yes that's right, the Blanche Harrington who was poisoned by this woman while she and Ruby Davis were in New Orleans."

"You know Ruby Davis?"

"Yes, I know her."

"Tell me something, pretty-boy. How would the likes of you come to know a married woman such as Ruby Davis?"

"She came into my studio looking at impressionistic art."

"I see."

Rupert knew the deputy had no idea what he meant by impressionistic art. He tried hard to stifle a smirk. "Deputy, I don't know what Ruby Davis has in her possession, but it is something Solange DeShotel wants badly. This woman is pure evil, Sir, and will stop at nothing to find it. It must be pretty powerful for her to come all of this way after it."

"You got you a real theory going there, don't you, Detective? I feel real safe knowin' you're all on top of this situation."

"Look, Ruby's life is in danger. Actually, anyone associated with Ruby might be in danger. This woman has no regard for human life. In fact, she delights in the brutal annihilation of it."

"Must be pretty close friends with the Davises, Mr. Staten?"

"No, Sir, more of an acquaintance." Rupert changed positions as he tried again to make a point. "Try to understand, this is a matter of life and death, Deputy. A woman's life is at stake. In fact, a whole family's life may be at stake. This monster must be stopped. Do you now understand my motivation for coming here?"

"Oh I understand alright ... Smooth talkin' city-boy artist flingin' all them big fancy words around. Better save your breath for now, Rupe. You're goin' to need to tell all these lies to the sheriff after while."

The deputy laughed a little and turned to leave the room. As he approached the doorway, he looked at Rupert again. "By the way, pretty-boy, you ain't got a chance with the likes of Mrs. Davis. She's a righteous woman."

* * *

"I like this one."

"I think it's nice."

"How would you describe it?"

"Oh, I don't know ... Maybe understated elegance?"

"For a tombstone?"

Dot Lawson and Lorna Carraway stood in front of several granite slabs in hopes of finding a marker for Heloise Pullman's grave.

"Some tombstones can be quite beautiful."

"I've just never thought of a grave as elegant. This one seems to be appropriate. It's not too big and the family can move it to the foot of the grave if they choose to do something else."

"Good point. You know, we've not even asked Hilda if she may want to take care of this herself. Do you think the church is overstepping its bounds?"

"I don't think so. It's only a commemorative gesture. The family is free to do whatever it pleases with this should they decide to do something different."

"I just don't want them to feel embarrassed they didn't take care of this detail themselves."

"Nonsense. Hilda fully expects the church to do something in remembrance of Heloise. We have to take care of this, Dot; there's really no one else to do it." Staring at the blank headstone, Lorna paused for a moment.

Dot instinctively knew Lorna was thinking about Ruby. "She'll be back."

"I hope so …"

The wind had begun to blow. Lorna and Dot huddled together as the gust swirled around them. "With Blanche gone and now Ruby … It's lonely, Dot."

"I know."

Lorna felt a need to change the subject. "I say we choose this one. The engraver said he needs about four weeks to complete everything."

"Do you have the correct birth date and scripture verse?"

"I have what Hilda sent me."

"Why don't we make our way inside and finish up. Then, maybe we can have a bite of lunch at the café."

"I'd really like that, Dotsie."

"My treat."

"That's not necessary. If Mary has something special for dessert, I may skip lunch. I'm feeling like I could use an indulgence."

"Let's go and see."

As the women walked inside to complete the task, Lorna hoped she wouldn't have to do this again for a long time. In the back of her mind, she didn't believe she'd get her wish.

* * *

Just as Cecil Ullman had finished a tombstone for the Ambrose family, Otis walked into the room.

"Looks nice."

"Thanks. Took a lot of work to fit that inscription there. People want a life history on these things but don't want to spend the money for a stone big enough. Really gets my goat."

"Lorna Carraway was just here with Dot Lawson."

"They picked somethin' out?"

"Yeah, you're not gonna like it. They want this scripture verse on a footstone."

"Son of a bitch. I guess I'm supposed to work miracles here."

"If you don't think it'll fit, call 'em. Hell, the church is pickin' up the tab."

"I am. I'm not gonna waste a slab of good granite and days—make that weeks of my time for something that ain't gonna work. Let's go out back and have a look. I have a stone out there that'll fit this inscription."

Exiting through the rear doorway, Cecil and Otis walked to the back of the shop. Most of the inventory was stored in an enclosed yard behind the business.

"Where is it?"

"I was thinking the heart-shaped rose granite would work. It's back on the third row."

Otis had walked ahead of Cecil to look for the stone. When he found it, he froze. He stood there and stared. As Cecil approached, he finally said, "This some kind of joke?"

"What?"

"That. What the hell is that? Do you know how much that stone cost us?"

"My God ..." Cecil muttered.

The two of them stood in the wind and read an epitaph engraved on the stone.

Here Lies Robert Allen Davis
Beloved son and husband
Born: January 26, 1904
Died: May 8, 1932
The remnant is done

Finally, after what seemed an eternity, Cecil said, "Get the tractor, Otis."

"What are you goin' to do?"

"Get the tractor and drag that stone out to the scrap pile."

"Who did this?"

"I don't care who did it. I don't care and I don't want to understand. I want this the hell out of here and not made mention of again. You got it?"

"No argument from me. I'll be back."

Otis returned to the shop. Cecil continued to stare at the monument. No one else in town had the capacity to engrave the stone, and he'd helped the driver unload all of the stones off of the truck. They were blank, every single one of them. This was a sign. It was some kind of omen. Neither he nor Otis was going to help it come to pass. Cecil walked back to the shop to find his sledgehammer. He would take care of this himself.

* * *

The historic city of Memphis, Tennessee is perched upon the Mississippi River. Situated at the apex of the Mississippi delta, the city is skewed into a corner of the state of Tennessee.

Tom and Beverly had made their way to Memphis. Upon arrival, they'd managed to secure a hotel room overlooking the river; a second story room provided a beautiful view.

"I should have come here years ago. There's so much action. I'm dying on the vine in that Conway hell hole." Beverly gazed out the window as a barge made its way down river.

"Don't go back." Wearing a tank style undershirt and boxer shorts, Tom was lying in bed. He lit a cigarette. "If you hate it that much there, stay in Memphis."

Beverly smiled. "I'd love to, but all of my things are there." She walked over to him and took the cigarette from his fingers. She began to smoke it as she walked back to the window. She exhaled against the window glass and continued to stare at the river.

"I need to find a job here."

"You've got one. Get me in to see those people."

"Well, I can tell you I didn't come all the way to Memphis to see Ruby Davis. I can't stand the sight of her in Conway, so why would I want to strike out and find her here?"

In one swift motion, Tom got out of bed and approached Beverly from behind. Sensing him, as he approached, she leaned into him. Suddenly, he grabbed a handful of her hair and yanked her head around so that she was facing him. There was a gasp. She wasn't sure if she'd gasped because he'd managed to pull out half of her hair or because she was frightened.

"You'll do whatever I tell you to, Bitch. Get that straight."

Beverly didn't speak. She knew to say nothing. There was a look of anger and belligerence in his eyes she'd not seen before. Suddenly, she realized she was far from home with a man she really didn't know. He let go in a motion that almost threw her against the window. Her cigarette smashed against the windowpane, as fire embers fell from it onto the floor. Looking from the window, she stood there a moment longer. Finally, she cleared her throat and began. "When do you want to see them?" She also wanted to know why but didn't dare ask. She had no intention of evoking a rage response again.

"Just find the seminary."

Beverly managed a look at him. "I'll find it."

"I need you to get me something else, too."

"What?"

"I need a large suitcase, the biggest one you can find. There are some department stores here downtown, so fix yourself up and go shopping."

Walking toward the bathroom, she said nothing else. She shut the door behind her and locked it. She knew that in reality the locked door would do no good, as he could easily break it down if he wished. For now, she'd better play along. She'd better keep quiet and do as he said. Rubbing her scalp where he'd grabbed her, she felt a throb. It felt swollen. Suddenly, Memphis had lost some of its shine. Maybe it was time to return to Conway after all. Maybe she'd better find a way to get there ... alone.

CHAPTER FORTY-THREE

Eva crossed the street and approached the sheriff's office. Situated at the edge of downtown Conway, the tall, narrow building was actually quite beautiful. Ornate and symmetrical, the front of the structure housed two elaborate mahogany doors. Leaded glass panes and massive brass handles further enhanced the splendor of the building.

As she entered the office, she noticed the deputy-sheriff concentrating intently on a document folded before him. He looked up as she approached. "Morning, Eva."

"You seem really involved in that newspaper, Luke; what did I miss?"

"Nothing … not much of anything." He folded the paper once again and stuffed it into a drawer behind the desktop. "What can I do for you?"

"I'd like to report a missing person."

Shaking his head, Luke let out a long sigh. "Damn, Eva; what the hell is going on around here? Who's missing now?"

"Beverly Martin."

Luke put his face in his hands and rubbed his eyes. "She ain't missing. She just hasn't wandered home yet. How long has she been gone?"

"Since Sunday, I think."

"You think? What do you mean, *you think?*"

"I *mean* I haven't seen her since Sunday. She left after services with this stranger—a man I've never seen around these parts before—and I haven't heard from her since."

"She left her car in the church parking lot, Eva. We finally had to impound it and have it pushed over here to the station. Do you reckon it's been there since last Sunday?"

"I know it has. She left in his car. As we left services, I remember him parked in front of the church."

"We?"

"Oh God, Luke, let me think. Several of us walked from the church together; I remember seeing Beverly ahead of me making her way out of the vestibule. I tried to get her attention, but she never looked up. I think she was talking to Lera Helmquist. Anyway, by the time I reached the front steps of the building, she was hurrying toward a parked car across the street. There was a good-looking man standing beside it, and he seemed to be waiting for her."

"Think you'd recognize him again?"

"A man like that would be hard to forget. I followed her to the car to find out who he was. I stuck my head in the passenger's window just to say hi ..." Eva Nell stopped. She swallowed hard and stared straight ahead as if deep in thought.

"And ... ?"

She turned to look at Luke. "Have you ever gotten a look that gave you chills? Ever gotten a look you knew meant trouble? When that man looked at me, I felt like he wanted to kill me then and there. He could have shot me between the eyes and never blinked. I'll never forget the look of hate in his eyes and the bulge in his jaw from clenching his teeth." Eva Nell's eyes became liquid. "She's in trouble, Luke, and I don't know if she'll get out of this one."

"What did he look like, Eva?"

Eva had removed a handkerchief from her purse. Making sure she didn't look like one of those helpless females who dabbed their eyes at the slightest hint of despair, she wiped her eyes in a quick sweeping motion. "He was really handsome. He had curly brown hair and blue eyes. Beautiful eyes, actually, but ..." Her voice trailed off as she said this.

"But what?"

"They were totally devoid of human emotion. They were empty, Luke, like the person inside was dead."

Luke returned to his notepad. "Anything else?"

"He was tall, muscular ... well built. That's about all I can remember."

"Shit." Luke stood up and shuffled some papers on his desk. "I think we may have a suspect. I'm going to get in touch with Sheriff Bagwell this afternoon and arrange a lineup. Do you think you might be able to come back later today?"

"I could arrange it. What time?"

"I should know within the hour. If I can't get in touch with you, call me before noon. If we can identify this man, we may get some answers as to Beverly's whereabouts."

"God, I hope so. I appreciate all your help, Luke. I know Beverly isn't too well thought of around here, but she's my best friend. I have to try to help her." Tears formed in her eyes again. "If we can still help her ..."

"Call me before noon, Eva. In the meantime, let's keep this information between us."

As she reluctantly turned toward the door, she shook her head in agreement. She left the sheriff's office feeling she was about to close a chapter in her life with no happy ending. Was she justified in feeling this way? She'd find out soon enough.

* * *

Most afternoons Robert had begun helping with accounting in the seminary's administration office. He was no accountant, but with no job here, he felt he must do something productive or else go crazy.

"Monsignor, it's about one o'clock. I think I'll take a lunch break and try to catch up with my wife."

"As you wish, Robert. I can expect you about two, then?"

"I won't be gone more than an hour."

In search of Ruby, Robert made his way through the halls of the seminary. He found her in one of the classrooms. She was sitting in front of an easel, holding a palette of various oil paints.

"You never cease to amaze me. When did we become interested in art?"

"I've always been interested. I've just never have had much opportunity to pursue it."

"May I look?"

"It's not much. Go ahead and have a look."

Robert walked around the easel and glanced upon the canvas. She'd painted a still life depicting the edge of a meadow. Centered around a trail, there were trees at the back of it. Disappearing into the forest, the trail made its way down the side of the meadow. On the right side of the meadow, a beautiful wisteria climbed the largest of the painted trees, while pink and crimson azaleas dotted the back of the landscape. Robert smiled. "Do I see a little 'Robert Davis tribute' in there?"

"There is one and I knew you'd notice. I'm thinking of painting dogwood trees on the other side; I think they'd look beautiful surrounded by green forest and azaleas.

"You need a bunny in this meadow."

"Feel free to paint a bunny in your meadow. This one is strictly a tribute to nature."

"Brrrr. It suddenly got a little colder in here."

Ruby stood away from the easel and walked toward him. When she'd reached him, she put her arms around him. "Here, this will warm you up."

"Mmm. That's better."

"Now that you're here, I have a surprise for you."

Robert sighed. "I've really had my share of surprises lately, Rube. If it's bad news, I think I'll wait."

"Father Donovan is coming to Memphis to see us."

The news seemed to energize Robert a bit. "Well now, that is a good surprise. When?"

Ruby looked at her watch. "It's a little after one. Actually, I think he's supposed to be here by now."

I'm on lunch break from Monsignor; why don't we go to the front and have a look."

Walking toward a formal living room located at the front of the building, they left the classroom. Painted golden yellow, the living room was adorned with crystal chandeliers and ancient wall tapestries. Usually, this was the only public room in the seminary; being guests of the establishment, the Davises had bit more freedom to roam.

Still conversing as they approached the living room, Ruby saw Father Donovan standing in the doorway. She smiled. As she opened her mouth to speak, Lorna Carraway emerged from the doorway as well. A lump rapidly forming in her throat, she closed her mouth again. She broke away from the conversation and ran toward her mother.

Eyes both liquid and closed, they embraced. "This was the best surprise of all. I had no idea you were coming."

"Neither did I. Father Donovan didn't tell anyone for fear of being followed. I don't even think Jed realized I was leaving until he'd found my note."

"Oh Mother, how will he feel about this—your coming without him?"

"He won't like it a bit, Ruby. But it's not about how Jed, myself or anybody else feels right now. It's about keeping everyone safe."

"Maybe he can come soon."

"He'd like that. He really misses his family." Lorna smiled. "Probably won't speak to me for a week when I get home. I'll have to fix all of his favorite meals and wait on him hand and foot to keep his feelings from staying hurt."

"Well for now, let's just concentrate on this visit. I'm worth it, aren't I?"

"Let me look at you." Lorna shook her head. "That girl of mine is starting to show. No doubt we have a baby on the way."

"No doubt, Momma."

"Ruby, I have something I need to discuss with you."

"What is it?"

Robert had not made his way to Lorna as of yet. He'd been engrossed in conversation with Father Donovan. "It would probably be best if we talked alone."

"Why don't we join the men for a moment and then make our way to the garden. We can talk in private there."

Robert and Lorna exchanged hugs and greetings. There were smiles and questions of goings on in Conway before Lorna and Ruby were able to excuse themselves to the garden. "I know you girls have some catching up to do, so Father and I are off to have a look at the vegetable garden behind the library. We'll meet up with you in a little while."

They started to leave. "Oh damn," Robert said.

"What's wrong?" Father Donovan replied.

"I told the Monsignor I'd be back at two to help with accounting."

"We'll go to the office first and make our plans from there."

"We'll be in the Meditation Garden, darling."

"Well, you two girls meditate on what you're cooking me for supper tonight."

"And you two meditate on the hunger pangs you'll have from skipping supper tonight. As I just said, we'll be in the garden."

* * *

As Ruby and Lorna entered the garden, Lorna spied a bench. Tucked beneath a beautiful wooden arbor, lavender blooms of Clematis covered the structure.

"This is lovely. Why don't we stop here for awhile?"

"Ok, let's." Ruby smoothed her skirt as she sat on the bench. "Now, what did you have to tell me, Momma? I'm dying of curiosity."

"First of all, you can think of some other way to express yourself."

"Sorry."

"There is a stranger in town, Ruby."

Expectantly waiting for Lorna to continue, her expression was one of anticipation. "And?"

"Apparently he's been asking questions about us."

"What kind of questions?"

"He's been asking folks around Conway do they know us and whereabouts we live."

"What does this stranger look like?"

"Abigail Albright got a look at him. To use her words, he was 'breathtakingly handsome.' The man was tall, with dark, curly hair and sapphire eyes."

"That could only be one person …"

"You know him?"

"But what on earth would he be doing in Conway? It makes no sense."

"What in Heaven's name are you talking about? Better yet, Ruby, who in Heaven's name are you talking about?"

"Mother, do you remember me telling you of an art dealer I befriended while I was in New Orleans? I wondered into his gallery after Blanche had been murdered. I was in a state, and he was very kind to me."

"No, I don't recall anything about an art dealer. Refresh my memory."

"I can't imagine I didn't tell you."

"Oh, I can imagine that."

"I'm sorry?"

"Well, let's see. I'm imagining a beautiful woman all alone in the big city of New Orleans. Obviously grief-stricken over the death of her beloved cousin, this beautiful woman exudes an air of vulnerability. How fortunate, in her time of need, that this kind, handsome man comes to her rescue. I can only imagine exactly how 'kind' this handsome man really was."

"So what *exactly* are you implying?"

"I'm not implying anything. You are from a small town and a sheltered existence. I have no doubt naiveté was written right across your pretty face. This man meant to take advantage of you. He still does."

"I'm not as naive as you think, Mother. And secondly, you're being ridiculous. He wasn't trying to take advantage of anything. He was just a kind man, that's all."

"Then what's he doing in Conway? It's not a short trip, Ruby. You and I know it is quite a journey. Does he know you are a married woman?"

"Actually, he does. He and Robert met at the hotel."

Lorna turned her head away and swallowed hard. She tried to put the notion out of her mind. "So … what was he doing at your hotel?"

"Not what you think. He brought me …" As she realized what she was saying, she began again. "Let me clarify that. He brought us a wedding gift from his gallery."

"How nice." Lorna had a smile on her face that didn't have to move much to be a sneer. It wasn't a smile as much as an expression of disapproval.

"Mother, you know me. You know I'd never …"

Lorna interrupted her. "You're right. I know you'd never, but as I said, you were extremely vulnerable at the time. You were alone and traumatized. A lot of men would take advantage of that. And now he's come all the way from New Orleans …"

"Well, there's no way he'll find me now, so put your mind at rest."

"I may have to pay this man a visit. I want to know what his business is with us."

"I think that's a good idea, Momma."

This response surprised Lorna.

"When you do find out, you must get in touch with me. I have to know."

"There is no good in this association, Ruby. Remove yourself from it, and I mean remove yourself from it in every way. There is temptation here. I can feel it."

"The only thing you can feel is an overactive imagination. In case you haven't noticed, I'm married and very pregnant."

"I did notice if you'll remember, and I'll thank you to use the word expecting in a public place."

"We're alone, Momma, and don't change the subject. Talk to Rupert Staten—if that's who it is—and find out why he's in Conway. He's from New Orleans and knows well of Solange DeShotel. He may have information he is trying to give us. It has to be important if he's come all of this way."

"I hadn't thought of it like that."

"Well, think about it."

"And you don't think about it until I sort out things. I'm not completely convinced of his ulterior motives. He sounds like a mature man, Ruby, one that's been around."

"Who needs to be dealt with by a seasoned veteran like you?"

"Don't be disrespectful. You know what I mean."

"I know what you mean, but before you jump to conclusions, get the facts. Your 'Mother's Intuition' may have missed the mark this time."

"I haven't missed the mark, young lady, and I know what I'm talking about. You play with fire, Ruby Davis, and you'll get burned. Rupert Staten is fire. Remember that."

"I'll remember." She said nothing else. There would be no changing her mother's mind, as she simply did not understand. *As for getting burned? There are other ways to be burned, Lorna. Sometimes you don't even have to play with fire.*

CHAPTER FORTY-FOUR

"I can't tell you how glad I am to see you. I know Ruby feels the same about seeing her momma, too."

"I'm pleased both of you are safe and adjusting to life at the seminary."

"Adjusting may be a bit of a stretch, Father, but we are coping, somehow." Looking upwards, Robert paused for a moment. He took a deep breath and exhaled. "What we'd really like is to be home with our families. What we'd really like is to bring our baby into the world in Conway."

"Hopefully all of this will be over by the time your baby arrives."

"I don't think I'm going to …"

Waiting for him to finish the thought, Father Donovan looked at him expectantly.

"You're not going to what?"

"I … I just don't know what may be in store for me in the near future."

"None of us do, Robert."

Robert opened his mouth to speak. He thought about what he was going to say and closed it again. He looked Father Donovan squarely in the eye. Without flinching, he said, "There is a woman who appears to me."

Father Donovan didn't answer.

"She's visited me several times now, trying to prepare me for something. I know you probably don't believe this, and think I'm delusional, but if I am, it's a hell of a delusion."

"Probably not from Hell …"

"Just what I need, comic relief."

"I do the best I can."

"She's told me I don't belong here and can't stay here much longer. You'll really think I'm crazy when I tell you that I know this woman from somewhere. I can't place her face, but she's very, very familiar. She plays an important part in my life. I don't know how and I don't know where, but in some way we're connected." He stopped talking. He looked away and mumbled, "Go ahead and tell me I'm disintegrating." He looked at Father Donovan. "Go ahead … Tell me."

"I've seen her."

"What?"

"I've seen her."

"That's not possible. She's not … She's not tangible."

"No, she's not. I don't really understand what she is, but her purpose is to guide your safe passage back to wherever you came from."

Robert made an effort to swallow. His throat was dry, and his heart was beating as if it were about to break through the chest wall any minute. "How do you know this? How could you possibly see an illusion in my head?"

"She's lovely, Robert. She was dressed in all in pink, had beautiful blonde hair, and a comforting soothe to her voice that I've never experienced before."

Father Donovan changed positions. He was now standing face to face with Robert. He was standing so close that Robert almost felt an invasion of his personal space.

Alive with passion and conviction, Father Donovan's eyes were dancing. *"I believe we saw a soul. Whoever is trying to reach you has sent the very essence of her being to find you."*

CHAPTER FORTY-FIVE

Eva looked around the small room. Located down the hall from the sheriff's office, the room held nothing but two wooden chairs situated in front of a narrow, rectangular glass window. Beyond the window was a stage of sorts. Several bright lights were focused on the platform. She walked to the front of the room and sat in one of the two wooden chairs. She'd wait for Luke to arrive.

She could not help but feel a little apprehensive; after all, she'd never been involved in a lineup before. This whole procedure was foreign to her, and she really didn't know what to expect. Lurking in the pit of her stomach was a feeling of dread. She could think of nothing that she wanted to do less than look into those cold, dead, blue eyes again. What if he recognized her? If he really did harm Beverly and knew she'd identified him, she'd surely be next.

"Looks deep to me."

Eva's train of thought was broken as Luke entered the room. He was smiling.

"Ready?"

"No, I'm not ready. Maybe you'd better explain how all of this works, first."

"It's simple. Four men will walk onto that stage. They can't see you because we've damn near blinded them with all of those bright spotlights. If you see the man we discussed earlier, we need a positive identification. No doubts, Eva ... No 'maybe' or 'I think.' You have to be certain we have the right man. We'll arrest him on suspicion of the kidnapping of Beverly Martin after a definitive identification. You'll be our star witness, and we'll build a case against him from there. Got it?"

"I got it."

Luke stepped from the room and yelled down the hallway. "Bring them in."

Four men walked onto the stage single file. Still not able to believe she was doing this, Eva felt as if she were sitting on thin air. Her heart was beating so fast that she could actually feel a pulse in her throat.

With much effort, she swallowed as the four formed a line facing the window. One by one, she mentally examined them. The man on the far left was short, blonde, and bearded. A fellow with shoulder length red hair stood next to him. Neither of these men remotely fit the criteria.

The third in line was a man too handsome to fit this scenario. He had soft, curly brown hair and dark blue eyes. His skin was porcelain-white and flawless. Obviously, there was no manual labor of any kind in his past. His family was rich and this must have been just for fun. Eva shook her head in bewilderment.

The last man was shorter. He had dark brown eyes and an unshaven face. Deep creases framed the eyes and the face was badly sunburned. Grey hair shown at his temples. *Too old ... .*

After what seemed an eternity, she said, "None of them."

"Are you sure?"

She turned to Luke. "Oh, I'm absolutely sure. He's not down there."

Luke stared at the window and shook his head a little. He let out a sigh that he didn't realize he was holding. "Well, OK then, I'll be right back."

Taking a left down the hallway, Luke left the room. She could hear him yelling to dismiss the men. None of these men were the person with whom she'd seen Beverly leave. This meant they still knew nothing, and her friend remained in possible grave danger. She walked out of the room.

"Luke?"

Luke was approaching from the back of the hallway. "I thought we had him, Eva."

"No, I'm sorry."

At that moment, Rupert rounded the corner. Luke felt someone walking behind him and turned to see Rupert approaching. He turned back to Eva. "I was sure this was the guy."

"Him?"

"Yeah, him."

Rupert by now had joined them. "Sorry to disappoint you and the other deputy, but looks like I wasn't lying after all."

"Best shut up and get your ass out of town, Rudolph."

"Rupert."

Eva's eyes darted between Luke and Rupert as the exchange took place. "I don't think I would have forgotten someone like this, Luke." She turned to Rupert. "What are you doing in Conway, anyway?" Suddenly, Eva seemed to have forgotten some of her apprehension. She was smiling at Rupert.

"Do you know the Davises?"

"Which Davises?"

"Ruby and Robert Davis."

"Very well, why?"

Luke interjected. "You just don't learn, do you stranger?"

"If you people aren't going to do your job, Deputy, looks like I'll have to do it for you." He turned back to Eva Nell. "I have some information for them which could be a matter of life or death."

Eva turned to Luke. "Am I missing something here? Why aren't you listening to this man?"

"We don't know this man, Eva. We don't know where he got his information or what his ulterior motives are. Furthermore, we'll get to know him a lot better if he doesn't heed my warning and get the hell out of here."

Rupert looked at them both, said nothing else and turned to leave. The door slammed behind him as he walked away from the sheriff's office.

Luke watched him exit. "Somebody better tell Valentino it's not a good idea to start butting into police business in a strange town. Things could get kind of sticky for him. Maybe you should tell him, Eva."

Eva didn't turn. She didn't move as she watched his silhouette begin to fade. After a moment she uttered, "Maybe I should." She took a breath and exhaled. "Maybe I will." She didn't look back; she simply walked forward from the office. She livened the pace in an attempt to catch Rupert. She'd listen to him, even if no one else did. He may shed some light on things, and at this point, some light was better than none.

* * *

"Rupert! Wait!" Eva Nell had begun to run in hopes of catching him.

Saying nothing, Rupert turned around.

Eva finally made her way to Rupert. By the time she'd reached him, she was out of breath. In between gasps she said, "I was running as fast as my short little legs would carry me."

"Sorry about that, but I wasn't aware you were trying to keep up. At last glance you and Luke were conferring in the sheriff's office."

Eva's breathing began to slow some. "Why do you want to know about the Davises?"

"Are you offering to help?"

Eva looked around. "Maybe ... we should go somewhere and talk."

In a half mocking effort, Rupert also looked around just as Eva had just done.

"Right here looks fine to me."

"Tell you what, why don't we go to Ben's pharmacy and have a soda. My treat."

"Oh no, that's how I got into trouble in the first place. 'Ole Ben' doesn't take kindly to strangers, especially strangers asking lots of questions."

As he said this, Eva put her thumb in her mouth and bit her fingernail. After a moment's contemplation, she said, "The café, then. We'll have coffee."

Rupert shook his head in resignation as they walked across the town square to the E &B Café.

Over two cups of coffee, Eva began.

"What business do you have with Robert and Ruby Davis?"

"They may be in grave danger."

"How do you know that?"

"It's a long story."

"I have all afternoon."

As she said this Rupert's expression turned to one of impatience. "You are sitting there playing private-detective, aren't you? Attempting to put all of the pieces together?"

"I have my own reasons, Rupert. This is no game."

"I don't even know your name."

Eva could feel heat emanating from her face. "Eva ... Eva Nell Alexander."

"Well, Eva, you may have all afternoon, but unfortunately I don't. Furthermore, this is really none of your business."

"Wrong on both accounts. This is my business, now."

"Judging from my first impressions of the people of Conway, I suspect you are not without a theory of your own about all of this."

"I have one, but it doesn't have a happy ending."

Rupert stared at her expectantly after she'd said this.

Eva said nothing else.

"So ... Are you going to tell me where the Davises live or not?"

She sighed and met his glance. "Luke told me what you explained to his partner about that woman. He told me you think she may have murdered Blanche." She paused for a moment and tucked a tendril of hair behind her ear. "Damn finger waves ..."

Saying nothing, Rupert continued to look at her.

"I have my reasons for asking these pointed questions, Rupert. Shortly after Blanche was killed and the Carraways returned to Conway, strange things began to happen around here."

"Strange? Like what?"

"This used to be a safe little place where everyone knew everybody. It was a good place to live and raise a family. Since Blanche's murder, something's different. I can't explain it, but it's a feeling that evil and corruption have emerged some kind of way. Think about it. There have been two horrible murders here. I can't ever remember something like that happening in Conway."

"There's evil everywhere, Eva. It didn't suddenly appear here in Conway. You just had a good, close look at it."

"You know what else? I've seen strangers in town lately ..." As if she could barely manage to drink it, Eva swallowed a sip of coffee in a long, hard gulp. She breathed deeply and continued. "My best friend has run off with a stranger, and I don't think she's coming back."

"You don't? Well, I'm sorry for you, but what does that have to do with any of this?"

"I don't think she'll be able to come back."

"As in something may have happened to her?"

"As in I've looked into the face of pure evil—the evil we were just talking about a few moments ago." She cocked her head to the right a little. "So that's why I'm so interested, Rupert. There have been too many horrible things happening in a short period of time. It's no coincidence, because they're related. My friend's fate, your friend Ruby's fate, Blanche Harrington's fate ... they are all tied by the same dreadful umbilical cord. We need to cut it before it's too late."

"I hope it's not too late."

"To answer your question, Rupert, the Davises are not at home. They've been gone for some time, now. They didn't say goodbye to anyone or tell where they were going; they just left. I suspect they are hiding out. Word has it Ruby's pregnant, so maybe they left to protect both her and that baby. That's all I know. If you want to know more, I can take you to see Lila and Ned Davis or Ruby's parents, Jed and Lorna. I can't promise they'll tell you anything, but it's the next logical step."

"So how is any of this going to help you find your friend, Eva?"

"Apparently, you weren't listening a moment ago. I just told you I think all of this is interrelated. My friend Beverly has been inadvertently sucked into this, and I don't think she's going to make it out."

"Well, if for whatever reason what you said might be true, there is no sense in wasting time. Let's try the Davis' household first. I'll tell you what I've heard on the streets of the Quarter on the way."

Which will probably help to convince me Beverly is doomed.

As they left the café and walked toward her automobile, Eva said, "I'll drive, and don't expect Ned Davis to greet you with open arms. He's not exactly the friendly sort."

"Is anybody around here?"

"Well, there was one … but she may be gone now." Eva said nothing else as she drove toward the Davis farm.

CHAPTER FORTY-SIX

Ned Davis was a man of few words. He wasn't particularly friendly to folks he knew, and was even less hospitable to strangers. A stranger in Conway usually stuck out like a sore thumb, and Rupert was worse than a sore thumb. Here was another man involved in his son's marriage. To have the audacity to show up at his house meant *gettin' shot if things got hot enough.* He didn't believe for one minute the impassioned plea on his son's behalf. All he believed was this fellow was either stupid, or well … He was just stupid. That was all there was to be said for him.

Rupert and Eva were just a few steps from the front door. Ned had not invited them in; he'd only taken a few steps back to allow them to say their peace and leave.

Eva smiled as he opened the door. "Hi, Ned."

"Eva. What can I do for you?"

"We need to talk."

"About what?"

"Robert and Ruby."

"I ain't got nothin' to say, Eva. Nothing to say at all. If that's what you came by for, you best be on your way. Good day." Ned started to usher them from the house by closing the door.

Eva put a hand up to stop the door from closing. "Wait, Ned, I have some news. There is something you need to know."

"I don't need to know anything from you, and I'm not discussing anything in front of this stranger."

Rupert extended his hand. "I'm Rupert Staten."

Ned did not return the handshake. He ignored Rupert and turned to Eva. "You need to leave now."

"Ned, there is someone after Robert and Ruby. Their lives are in danger. We need to know where they are so we can warn them."

"You don't need to know anything, and you don't need to be discussing our business with this strange man, either. We've got things taken care of, so leave our children be. Now both of you get out. I want you off my property."

"You don't understand, Ned ..."

Ned interrupted. "Lila, call the sheriff. Tell him he may need to send a truck if these two don't leave shortly."

Lila walked toward the front of the house. "What on earth are you talking about?" She looked and saw Eva standing there with Rupert. "Eva? What's going on here?"

"We need to find Robert, Lila. A lot of things have happened that we need to explain to you. We think they may be in great danger."

Rupert interrupted. "They are in great danger. It is in fact a matter of life and death. We need you to tell us where they are so we can warn them."

Ned looked at him in amazement. "You must be kidding. I've never met you in my entire life. You show up on my doorstep with some sort of news and expect me to let you waltz in and save the day? I don't think so. I might have been born at night, Boy, but it wasn't last night."

"Look, I will beg if I must."

"You ain't gonna beg, Boy. What you're gonna to do is leave. I'm going to tell you one more time this has nothing to do with you. And as for you, Eva Nell Alexander, in the future you can keep your strange bedfellows to yourself. Don't bother involving us in any of it."

"He's not my bedfellow, Ned, and maybe you'd better listen to him."

"I ain't listening to nothing. We got enough trouble already, and we don't need you bringing more."

Lila put a hand on Ned's shoulder. "Maybe we should hear them out, Ned."

"And maybe he's the one who killed Mabel, Lila. Maybe he's trying to find the whereabouts of our children so he can cover his tracks."

"Well then, Ned, I'd have to kill you and Mrs. Davis too, now wouldn't I? Then I'd better snuff out the pharmacist, the whole sheriff's department, as well as ole' Eva here. You have to understand that I have no tracks to cover, Mr. Davis. I know about Solange DeShotel. I know she is after your children, and I know she murdered someone because that person tipped off your son and daughter-in-law. Eva and I think the man Beverly left town with may be connected in some way as well. We don't have all of the pieces of the puzzle yet, but there are too many coincidences to overlook. I believe these people have somehow found where your son and his wife are hiding. If we can warn them before they find them, we may be able to save their lives. If we can't, well ... There may be three more murders."

Ned looked up at Rupert. "And who is number three?"

"My friend Beverly."

"Your friend Beverly? Your good whore-friend Beverly?"

"Ned! That's enough."

Ned continued. "Yeah, I heard her old car sat in front of the church house nearly a week before they pushed it away. Guess she's still laid up somewhere and not worried about it. Maybe she can give that young sheriff a little somethin' extra and get her car back without too much trouble."

"There is no somethin' extra. I was there when they left the church, Ned, and I saw the man she left with. I'm telling you she's in trouble, more trouble than I think she'll be able to get out of."

"That's what you get when you act like trash."

"Look, I really don't have the time or patience for any of your crap today. I'm not worried about how trashy you think Beverly Martin is. I'm worried about saving her life as well the lives of your children."

Ned walked past them to the steps and spit out what seemed to be a well-chewed plug of tobacco. "Maybe you better watch your tone of voice."

"Regardless of what you think of Beverly, she's in danger. She may already be dead. Morals aren't the issue here."

Lila stood up. "I'll handle this Ned."

"No, you won't ..."

"I said I'd take care of it." Lila glared at Ned as she said this. He didn't answer. Leaving the room, he just turned and walked past her. She turned her glare back to Eva. "As for you, Missy, you need to learn to control your temper—especially in someone else's home. I really didn't appreciate that outburst."

"As I told Ned, Lila, I ..."

Lila interrupted. "I heard very well what you said. I don't need you to repeat anything. Now you close your mouth and listen to me. I don't know this fellow and don't feel comfortable telling him anything. He's a stranger who's probably feeding you a line and knows too much already. You people have no place here, for this is none of your business. Leave it for the police, Eva."

"I'm only trying to help."

"Why? Why are you trying to help? Some good-looking man from ... from ..." Lila stammered a moment.

"New Orleans."

Lila began again. "Some good-looking man from New Orleans just shows up to lead the cavalry to our children's defense? It makes no sense." She turned to Rupert. "I can't believe you'd involve yourself in the lives of total strangers just for the sake of goodness. You don't strike me as that type. You have a motive."

"Inadvertently I became involved in this, Ma'am, and yes, you're right. I do know too much already. But let me ask you something. If you knew what I knew, could you bury your head in the sand and let three people die?"

Lila turned away as he'd said this. "It would be a difficult position to be in."

"Then tell us. Let us help."

"We're running out of time, Lila. Beverly, Ruby and Robert are in grave danger."

"Then call the damn police, Eva. If you won't, I will."

"And why haven't you called them already, Lila? I'll tell you why. You know there's not a thing they can do at this point to help us."

"Look, you two, we're going in circles now. The police will find those people and God is going to help us through this." Lila walked to the door and further opened it giving them passage out the doorway.

"Lila ... Please!"

"You two have put me in an impossible situation. There is no right answer. Now, for the last time, I'm not telling you anything. That's what I was told to do, and that's what I was warned I'd better do."

Eva began to cry. "You'll be sorry, Lila. When they're dead, their blood will be on your hands. You could have helped, but you chose not to."

"I'm only protecting my son, Eva. You're asking too much."

"Go to Hell, Lila. Go straight to Hell and rot there!"

Eva turned and walked out of the Davis' front doorway. Rupert and Lila looked at each other for a moment before he turned to follow her. "Is there any way we can change your mind?"

"Take what you have and go to the police, Son."

"I already did that. They handcuffed me and threw me in jail."

"Then take that as an omen. Leave this place, and leave this town. You don't belong. You know, Sir, I cannot for the life of me figure out why is all of this happening to such simple folk as us." Lila let out a heavy sigh. "We'll deal with it, but we don't need you to help us."

"There is a reason this is happening, Lila. Believe me, Robert and Ruby know what it is and that's why they're in hiding. It must be pretty serious for them to have run." Rupert paused for a moment. He ran a hand through his hair and gathered his thoughts. "Why is not important right now, Lila, but where they are could save their lives. If you can't tell us, then come with us. Come with us and bring Ned. Just let us get to them and warn them."

"I think I can warn them without the two of you."

"Where are they Lila?"

"Sir, you know nothing about Memphis. How could you help them if ..." After she'd said this she realized she'd revealed their whereabouts. Lila covered her mouth.

"Oh my God ..."

"Memphis. Where in Memphis?"

"Get out! Get out of here. I hope you're satisfied. You've badgered me until I've put my children's lives on the line. Get out! Get the hell out of here before I shoot you myself." Tears had come to her eyes as she covered her mouth again. She was crying, but there was no sound. Not saying a word, she stood at the door and watched them leave. Ned, who had apparently heard Lila, approached from behind to see what had happened.

Almost running toward the car, Rupert turned to leave.

"What happened? What did you say to her?"

"Let's get out of here before we get shot …"

CHAPTER FORTY-SEVEN

"Well, that narrows it down to a city, but that's about it. What on earth are they doing in Memphis?"

"Do you think they're staying in a hotel?"

"If they were, it would be under an assumed name."

"So, how do we find them in Memphis?"

"First, we talk to Jed and Lorna. Let's act like we know what's going on."

"Eva, don't you think Lila has called them by now?"

"Probably, but it's really our only option at the moment. Suddenly Eva looked at Rupert. "Or maybe not ... maybe there is another option."

"I'm open for ideas."

"Lera Helmquist ..."

"Who?"

"Lera Helmquist. She's the operator who's taken over Mabel's shift."

"Your point being?"

"She's a friend of mine. Maybe she knows something."

"As in she's done her fair share of eavesdropping, too. Tell me something, Eva, is illegal eavesdropping a prerequisite for the job of operator here in Conway?"

"I didn't say she listened in on anything. But what do you care? Do you want to find them or not?"

"We have to get out of here fast, Eva." Rupert thought for a moment. "Tell me again about this man you saw with Beverly."

"He had the most evil sneer."

"Physical characteristics, Eva. Tall, short? Blonde, blue eyes?"

"No, no he had dark hair. Much like yours but a little more gray. Blue eyes, ruggedly handsome ... Looked like he hadn't shaved for a day or so."

"You really looked him over, didn't you?"

"I did, but not for the reasons you're thinking. I didn't have a good feeling about him, Rupert, and he scared me. Maybe that's why I paid such close attention."

"Black hair and blue eyes describe a lot of people, Eva. Anything about him stands out? Something you might recognize again?"

"Yeah, now that you mention it, there is something. He had a big scar across his right cheek; it looked as if he'd been cut with a knife or something. The scar was smooth, straight, and kind of indented. It didn't detract from his looks, though. Actually, it looked rather sexy."

"I thought you were so scared?"

She ignored the sarcasm. "He was a physical type, like a laborer or lumberjack."

I don't think an artist such as myself is fit to take on the lumberjack sort ... "Wait a minute. He had a scar on his right cheek? Big, burly guy?"

"That's right."

"It couldn't be."

"What?"

"I spilled my feelings, my innermost thoughts to ... Oh God. Oh God! It couldn't be."

"Rupert, what's going on here? What are you going on about? I've missed something between lumberjack and big, burly guy."

... My insanely jealous lover is making his way back to us as we speak. Now is no time for a row. "It was her!"

"Who?"

"Son of a bitch! She was sitting right beside me."

"Who, Rupert? Who was sitting right beside you?"

"There is a speakeasy behind an abandoned warehouse downtown."

"I know ... so?"

"I've been there. It's been a few days, but I've been there."

"So have I. What's the speakeasy have to do with this?"

"I think the Sheriff knows about it, although he wouldn't admit it."

"I live here, remember? That is not exactly a secret."

"I saw a man who matches your description there."

"You did?"

"He wasn't really close to me, but he was everything you described. I was sitting next to this beautiful woman, talking about ..." Rupert paused mid-sentence.

Eyebrows raised, Eva waited for him to pick up the conversation. "Sitting next to this beautiful woman talking about?"

He breathed in deeply and exhaled. "Memories and cerebral ghosts. You wouldn't understand. It's out of context now."

"Get back to the man."

"I'll just bet that was the man Beverly left town with, and he's somehow intertwined with Solange and this whole nightmare."

"So, when does Solange come into the picture?"

"I'm not sure, but I think she was the beautiful woman I was sitting there talking to."

"You're kidding."

"No, Eva, I'm not kidding. The pieces are falling together. Her accent, her saying she was from far away ... I had a feeling we'd met before, but she said 'no.' I've seen her in the Quarter, Eva. I remember now. Somewhere, I've seen her in the French Quarter."

"Shit. Well, at least now we know 'who' to look for in Memphis."

"Get us over to the Carraways."

"And let's hope Lila hasn't already called."

"If she has, we might better duck."

Eva laughed. "Jed's a pretty good shot, Rupert. Ducking's not going to help."

* * *

"Evening, Jed."

"Eva. What can I do for you?"

"This is Rupert Staten."

"Nice to meet you. Have we met somewhere before?"

"In New Orleans, Sir."

"New Orleans ... so, what brings you to Conway? You have business here?"

Eva interrupted. "Jed, we have a story. We have to talk to you. Is Lorna here?"

"No, she's not."

"When will she be back?"

"I'm not exactly sure."

"Well, you'll have to tell her yourself. We really need to talk."

"By all means, come in. It sounds important."

Yeah, it's important. If you don't listen to me, half of your family is going to die. Let's just hope you're not as stupid as Ned Davis.

CHAPTER FORTY-EIGHT

"Where is she?"

"Mmmm baby, you look good enough to eat."

Wearing emerald-green satin, Solange stood in front of him. Accentuating her hair and eyes, she looked beautiful in green. "Where is she, Tom?"

"Gone. She went out."

"Will she return?"

"She'll be back. She can't resist my talents … Like someone else I know." Tom smiled as he said this.

"What is that?"

"I got her to get me a big suitcase. I'm going to stuff her body in it after I kill her; I figure I'd throw it into the Mississippi River. Packed with a few stones it ought to sink right down."

"Have you found the Davises?"

"They're holed up in a seminary across town."

"We may need this woman after all."

"For what?"

"She can help us get to the Davises. I assume they know her?"

"Hell," Tom snickered, "everyone knows her. She's real easy to get to know."

Solange thought for a moment. "Maybe we can use this woman as a front and gain access to the seminary." She stopped suddenly and turned to face him. "Or maybe instead of our trying to gain entrance, perhaps they should have no access as well. Lose their precious sanctuary? It would be devastating … Yes, that's what we'll do, have them thrown out of their safe, secure refuge."

"How?"

Solange ignored the question. "Go ahead and kill the girl. We don't need her after all. Give me a day or so, and I'll have a plan for you."

"What are you going to do?"

"Climb the chain of command, of course." She laughed aloud. "You know, Tom, no matter how clean and sanctimonious it may appear, every closet has dirty little skeletons."

"If you say so, baby."

"And we wouldn't want any of those skeletons brought to light now, would we? It could be very … damaging?"

"What the hell are you talking about?"

"Getting out of it, Tom. I'm getting out of Hell this time and leaving those Davises to rot where I left off."

As he watched Solange pace about the room, he said nothing else. Something evil loomed on the horizon and it filled him with fear. Trouble was he was too far into this to bail out now. He'd created his own special road to Hell. There were no options, none for him, anyway. He'd kill the woman and hope Solange really could get them out of here. He'd inadvertently made a deal with the Devil and damnation would be calling soon.

* * *

Signaling bad weather, the night brought blackness. No stars were shining, and the wind had begun to gust. The atmosphere was heavy and humid, as the temperature was unseasonably warm.

Solange looked around the room. Beautifully furnished, with English pine furniture, rich wood flooring and lush window treatments, the room exuded an air of wealth.

Things were so different. She walked into the kitchen. Polished to a lustrous gleam, the heavy stone counter tops were like none she'd seen. The refrigerator, along with all of the other appliances, donned a satin, metallic finish. The air in the house was cool. Obviously, much the same way air is cooled in movie theatres, some mechanism was in place to condition it.

This was another time and another place. There was a sense of freedom here—a freedom from the bondage she'd been forced to endure time and again.

I'll be damned if he gets back here before I do. I deserve to be free of the matrix. It is because of him that I am trapped in this matrix of Hell.

Solange passed from the kitchen into the next room. It was dark. In front of her, illuminating all that was around her, was a brilliant, golden sphere. No longer inside a structure, she was standing in a vast, bleak wasteland. Void of trees, grass, or any living thing, the wasteland stretched before her in a semicircular fashion. On the edge of the circle was a rim of fire. Hopelessness hung in the atmosphere about her.

The sphere in front of her brightened in intensity until she could no longer gaze upon it. "Damn you!" She screamed. "Why must you be so relentless? Leave me be and stop your ruthless pursuit of my damnation."

"Stop what?"

"Spare me of your sanctity."

"What?"

Solange realized she'd spoken out of her subconscious. She laid there and simply opened her eyes. Propped on one elbow, his head resting on his hand, Tom was perched over her. She waited a moment. "Nothing, Tom, I was dreaming. That's all."

"Hey, baby, it must have been some dream."

She smirked. "Not a dream, but reality."

Not comprehending the implication, he continued to look at her.

As she closed her eyes and reentered sleep, the room reappeared. An apparition now stood in front of her. It was that of a blonde, fair-skinned woman. So beautiful, the presence was virtually transparent.

The woman spoke. "You are not welcome here."

"I don't care. You can't stop me."

"This is not your time or place, and you have no right to interfere. You are destroying lives."

"I shall break free and the woman will enable it."

"You don't think your punishment can be worse, do you? You should learn from experience and realize there are varying degrees of Hell. To be damned and at the worst of it is an existence feared by Satan himself. You're a fool. Learn from your mistakes."

"The time is coming soon when I'll take care of you as well. I may not yet be able to touch your soul, but beware. The body and soul are closely connected. When you reach one, the other follows quickly."

"Play out your role, Solange. Your place in Hell could be worse. If you manage to ruin these lives, you'll wish your very existence extinguished. You had your chance, and you chose your destiny. Fulfill it now. It was your choice."

"Soon, you'll be begging for mercy instead of giving advice. Keep this in mind."

"Awake in your paradox and be gone, Solange. I have no use for you."

Solange opened her eyes. Anger consumed her at this moment. *I am going to kill you … . But first, you will watch everyone you care about die right in front of you.* She arose from the bed and walked toward the door.

Trying to focus through a sleep induced haze, Tom awakened again. "Where are you going?"

"To finish this."

CHAPTER FORTY-NINE

The bishop's office would best be described as austere. Although there was color in the space, most of it originated from various religious icons and paintings hung about the room.

For some sixteen years or more, the office secretary position was held by Verlene Hamilton Ghoulston. An efficient sort, Verlene never ventured far without pen and notebook in hand.

She was scrupulous about detail and had mastered efficiency and organization. While outwardly her appearance was that of a spinster who lacked much in the way of demeanor, her attention to detail far outweighed her esthetic shortcomings.

"Good morning, Bishop."

"Good morning, Verlene. How do the books look today?"

"Full. Your 8:45 is a woman by the name of Solange. She promptly informed me you'd insist that I appoint her today. I think her words were something like, 'Believe me, he won't want you delay this appointment.' She then referred to me as 'Madame.' Except for the fact that she had a thick accent, I found that strange. Maybe that's how they refer to people where she comes from."

Bishop Araden's face paled.

"Are you alright, Bishop? What is it?"

"Make sure this woman doesn't wait a moment. Show her in when she arrives."

"As you wish." A furrow crossed her brow. Usually arrogant and removed from his appointments, for him to be so actively interested in this one was a bit strange.

"Cancel the rest of my morning, Verlene. I'll not be seeing anyone else."

"Yes, sir."

Verlene stood perplexed for a moment, and then shook her head a bit to clear it. To ask why was not part of her job description. If the Bishop wanted the rest of the morning canceled, so be it.

* * *

Tuesday, May 3, 1932, 8:45 A.M.

Solange entered the outer office and paused by the door. She smiled to herself as she looked about the room.

Consumed with paperwork at her desk, Verlene heard Solange enter but did not look up. After a moment, she arose, turned, and knocked on the Bishop's door. He answered, after which she opened the door slightly and replied, "She's here."

"Show her in."

Opening the door further, she turned to Solange. Gesturing for her to enter, she said, "The Bishop will see you now."

Solange laughed aloud. "But of course." Yards of satin whisked past Verlene as she entered the room.

Verlene closed the door as she approached the Bishop. Pondering Solange's attire, she paused for a moment. *What a curious style of dress … women stopped wearing floor-length dresses years ago.* Realizing that this train of thought had nothing to do with her tasks at hand, she returned to her desk and began writing furiously.

* * *

"Have a seat, Mrs. …"

"You know perfectly well who I am."

The Bishop shifted a bit uncomfortably. "Well, with that said, what can I do for you?"

"I have a paramount situation, Bishop. I need your help."

"What kind of situation?"

"What kind of situation … Where do I start once again?" Solange took a deep breath and began. "You have two people sequestered in Saint Dominic's Seminary. They have something I want … let me correct that—something I *need* desperately. I want them out of there."

"I have no idea what you're talking about."

"Oh don't you? You arranged for their sequestration, Sir."

"These matters don't concern you, Miss."

"Madame."

"Pardon me. I assume we're not in confession here, and perhaps your vested interests in these people you say are sequestered are a matter the police in Memphis should be aware of."

We both know you don't want to do that."

"We do?"

"An outward presentation is that of a pious Bishop. He's religious, but quiet and a bit aloof. Delve beneath the surface, Sir. You don't have to go far, just look for it."

"Look for what, Solange?"

Solange smiled. "You remember my name now, do you? Picture a student at St. Paul's Catholic church, Bishop. Still innocent, but approaching ... how do you say ... adolescence? He's been taught to trust the clergy with all of his heart. The priests and the nuns are virtually infallible. Next to God, they are his messengers here on earth. A bond of trust is formed, Bishop. A code of silence is established as well. The boy has learned much more than he should have but will never break the vow between you two."

The Bishop paled. He swallowed hard. "I don't follow."

"You follow. You follow exactly. How many of these young boys have you bedded, Bishop? How many of them have you actually sodomized? How have you convinced them this is part of their duty to you and to God? Let us face it, Bishop; you have a problem. You fuck young teenagers and make them think it is what they're supposed to do. Shall I go on?"

"You're crazy."

"I am. That was never the issue. The issue at hand is this: If you don't get those people—and you know exactly to whom I refer—out of that seminary, I will make sure the authorities as well as this whole damned town knows that some balding, hairy old Bishop is having his way with the local fare here in town."

The Bishop said nothing. His face was ashen, and he'd begun to shake.

"Your being here at St. Paul's is much like a child in a candy store. You have your various desserts whenever you wish, and the choices are endless. Now, if you wish to keep your jollies in some young buck's rear end, Mark, I suggest you do as I say. If I were you, I wouldn't dally." She turned toward the door. Turning back briefly, she said, "You have twenty-four hours."

Still, he said nothing.

Solange emerged into the outer office. Still at her desk, Verlene looked up.

"You may want to get the Bishop a cup of tea. He seems a bit shaken." She laughed as she said this. "Take care, Verlene."

"How did you know my name? I don't remember telling you."

Solange smiled. She pointed to the nameplate situated at the front of the desk.

Verlene said nothing else as yards of cascading satin gracefully left the room. The door closed behind them with a quiet hush.

＊＊

Eva looked about the room. "You know, Rupert, such opulence was not necessary. We barely know each other, and really, we're not even friends. A bed at the local flophouse would have sufficed."

"You're right. We're not friends. I don't give a damn about Beverly or Robert, either. Make sure you understand that, too."

"So why are we here? Starving people are standing in line to have a bowl of watery soup and stale bread, and you put us up at the Peabody Hotel? I don't get your logic on this one. Not only are you spending entirely too much money, but you're spending it on a stranger you don't even like."

Rupert let out a long, exaggerated sigh. "How I can explain this? At the risk of sounding crass, I'm from a rich, culturally diverse background. New Orleans, especially the French Quarter, is a complex entity encompassing many different factions of immigrant culture. Combine this with three languages and diverging racial parameters, and you can see how I'm exposed to countless facets of society. Some are rich and some are poor, but diversity is ever present where I'm from. Where you're from there's none of that. It's either fit the mould or you're an outcast."

"And just what is the mould?"

"Local, white and Baptist."

"Before I get offended at your ignorant, egotistical narrow-minded-ness, realize that all you've said still doesn't answer my question. Why this expensive hotel?"

"It offers a small comfort in its European architecture and gran-deur. Serving to make things bearable until I return home, it's almost like an isle of my existence."

Eva stared at Rupert for a moment before she replied. "Either you're pathologically self-centered, or just some whimsical dumb-ass. I don't know which."

"Of course, you wouldn't know which. You're some small-town wench who functions in your own little existence, never experiencing anything past your safe little routine. Your small-town, narrow-minded Arkansas culture has brainwashed you into thinking you're happy, and this is what life is supposed to offer you. Anyone who is different is an outsider. Hell, he may even be … Evil." To accentuate his last thought, Rupert gave a dramatic hand gesture worthy of a melodrama. "The good news is that once all of this is over, you can return to your 'world under glass.'"

As he continued, she became increasingly enraged. She let him finish, and finally said through gritted teeth, "Oh my God, you're a pompous ass."

The insult apparently did not faze Rupert, or if it did, he simply chose to ignore it.

"I'll awaken you at four. We'll figure out how to go about gaining passage into the seminary in the morning."

"You do that." Eva turned to face the wall. Tucked under her right cheek, both hands were together as if she were praying.

Deep in thought, Rupert lay in the other bed. *I hate these people. I've intruded into their lives and I hate them. I'm driven toward them and yet despise my association with the entire lot.* His face fell into his hands for a moment. He wiped his eyes and lay back against the headboard.

He turned to look at Eva. With her back facing him, she lay toward the wall. "This obsession has consumed my world."

She didn't answer him.

He looked back down and closed his eyes. "Those consumed by an obsession eventually burn like a moth to a flame. I feel the burn." He then smiled bitterly to himself.

Slowly, she turned over in bed and looked at him. "As you well should, Rupert, it's too late to feel much of anything else."

* * *

Close to the Mississippi River, Third Street is located in downtown Memphis. Built four blocks from the waterway in the early 1800's, St. Dominic's Seminary sits at one end of the street. Surrounded by general commerce and various office buildings, the big, imposing structure is design-striking, with saintly statues designating the architectural angles of the building.

It was already warm outside, humidity emanating from the river made the air seem even thicker. "God, it's so nasty out here; I'm having trouble catching my breath. Do you think we can actually get them to answer the door at this hour? Maybe they're not up yet."

"Eva, chances are these people have already been to Mass, had breakfast, and are working."

"Doing what?"

"Doing what? I have no idea. Stop asking all of these questions and concentrate on making our way past that door. We need to see the Monsignor."

"You seem to know an awful lot about the Catholic faith. Are you Catholic?"

Rupert uttered a low sound that resembled a growl. "I guess you've forgotten where I'm from. Maybe it's the fact you've never been there and know nothing about it. New Orleans is predominately Catholic. You can't live there and not know about the faith, the holidays, Lent, etc. Ever heard of Mardi Gras?"

"Maybe I've read of it?"

"Or maybe you're nervous. Maybe you're frightened out of your wits. Maybe it's the fact we've become familiar with each other and you jabber on incessantly about nothing with people you know. Whatever the reason is, maybe you need to shut up and focus on matters at hand."

"You bastard."

"Wrong again." Rupert reached for the doorbell. "Here it goes, so let's hope we're right about this."

At that moment, the air was filled with thunderously beautiful music. The sound resembled the bells at Westminster.

"My God! What a doorbell."

"It's five A.M., Eva. The bell tolls on the hour."

"Well then, do you think they heard the doorbell?"

"Yes, we heard it."

Realizing the door was ajar and a man was now standing in front of it, they both looked toward the entryway. Dressed in black and wearing the signature white collar of clergy, the priest stood patiently in the doorway. He waited for Rupert and Eva to speak.

Eva stepped forward. "Um, Hello. I ... I'm Eva Nell Alexander. We're looking for our friends."

The Monsignor said nothing. Sometimes, saying nothing is actually more intimidating than trying to be intimidating.

"I understand they're staying here and we have to talk to them. It's very important."

Eva paused for a moment. She turned to Rupert and whispered, "He's not saying anything." Offering little in the way of explanation, Rupert shrugged. She turned back to the Monsignor.

"We really need to talk to them. It's a matter of life and death."

Taking a breath, the Monsignor began. "I told your friend a moment ago, and now I'll tell you, that this is a seminary, not a refuge for the wayward. If that were the case, then I might know what happened to them. However, young lady, if that were the case, I'd not be at liberty to divulge their whereabouts now, would I?"

"What friend?"

"Excuse me?"

"You said you told my friend the same thing."

"The young lady that was here a moment ago. She was asking the same questions you are. I just assumed you were friends."

"We are! Oh, we are. That must mean she's OK. Where is she?"

"I'm afraid she left a few minutes ago. She was in a bit of a state, I might add."

"Where, Father? Which way did she go?"

For the first time, compassion arose in the Monsignor's eyes. He pointed to the corner. "She walked to the corner. She was crying, I'm sad to say. She took a left and started up the block. I'm sorry, but that's all I know."

Rupert interjected. "What about Ruby?"

Replaced by one of cold indifference, the look of compassion vanished. "Who?"

"Ruby Davis, the lady that is staying here. Can we see her? Have you seen her?"

"I must go now."

The Monsignor began to close the heavy door. Rupert sprang forward and blocked him. "Wait! You can't go! I need to know. I need to know where she is and if she's OK."

"Son, I must go now. Consequently, I must close this entryway to the seminary. I wish I could be of help to you, but I cannot."

"Do you know where she is?"

"I'm afraid if you don't leave, I'll have to call the police. I don't want to do that, but if you insist on blocking my way, I will. Please, please go in peace."

"Rupert," Eva began, "please come on. Beverly can't be too far, and maybe she can help us. Maybe she can tell us something. Let's go. Let's try to find her before she gets away from us."

Watching the Monsignor close the heavy door, Rupert took a few steps back. "Is she OK? Tell me! I have to know! Is she alright?"

The Monsignor did not acknowledge him. He simply brought the large, heavy, wooden door to a close.

Damn him! "I thought men of the cloth were supposed to have compassion. Guess I thought wrong, even though I haven't been impressed with too many of them, so far."

"Beverly is our link, Rupert. We have to find her. Come on!"

"You don't know that. You have no idea if she's our link or not."

"What?"

"Let's go."

Leaving the seminary, they hurried down the street. Taking a left at the next block, they began to run.

"Rupert, I don't see her."

"Tell me something I don't already know."

"Not now, Rupert, please! Just help me find her. She knows something. I know she can help."

"On your left! There's an alley up ahead." They began to run toward the alley. On her right, Eva caught a glance of a woman standing in a darkened doorway. She stopped.

"C'mon, Eva, Let's go."

"I saw someone back there, hang on."

His breathing heavy and labored, Rupert stopped running. The warm morning air was hard to breathe as the high humidity made for difficult air uptake. After a moment he turned back to follow Eva.

Cautiously, Eva approached the doorway. Slowly, she peered around it in order to get a look at the face sequestered under the stoop. She then realized that she recognized the dress.

"Beverly?"

The figure said nothing.

Eva stopped.

"Beverly? Is that you?"

Still nothing.

"Bev? It's me, Eva." She realized she was speaking barely above a whisper. She began to raise her voice. "It's me, Bev. It's Eva. Answer me."

Rupert was standing about three paces behind Eva. It was difficult for him to have a good look at the stranger's face, as she was standing under a small, cantilevered stoop. The structure sheltered a back entrance to a building, with two wooden steps in front of the entrance leading to a white screen door. Pressed against the screen, the woman stood in front of the doorway.

The woman waited several moments before she answered. Finally, she began. "Did she send you here to find me? She knows where I am?"

"No one sent us here, Bev. It's me, Eva. We found you by accident … Or maybe it was divine intervention. I don't know, but we've found you." Eva exhaled loudly. By now, her voice sounded weary and haggard. "We've found you, thank God."

"God didn't lead you here. He doesn't come here."

"Yes, he does, honey. Come with me and let's get you out of here. We have a nice hotel. …"

"You want to leave here?" For the first time, there was a spark of light in her eyes. Her eyebrows raised in anticipation.

"Of course I do, and I want to take you with us." She gently reached for Beverly's arm.

"We can start over. We can't leave, but we can start over. It was better at the beginning …" Her voice trailed off, "and then it gets worse again."

Rupert looked toward Eva. "What is she talking about?"

Also mystified by the conversation, Eva chose to humor her rather than attempt to make sense of her remarks. "It was better then. Let's go, honey. We'll take care of you."

"No, Eva, you don't remember?"

"Remember?"

"I'm supposed to do this. I'm supposed to get us out of here. Don't you remember?"

"Maybe I can help this time."

Beverly looked down to the ground. She paused for a moment. "No. … It has to be me. It's always me."

"OK, OK, sweetie, it's you. Just like all the other times. Let's walk this way." She began to usher Beverly in the direction of the hotel. Beverly remained steadfast.

"She knows we're here, you know. She knows everything."

"Who? Who knows everything?"

Rupert looked at Eva. "I think she's talking about Solange."

Beverly screamed aloud. "Don't! "Don't say her name. You'll clear her vision. We'll never be able to hide then. We'll never have time to go back, to start again. She can make it worse, you know. She can send us deeper into Hell. She's very powerful."

"Honey, she doesn't know we're even here. You're safe now. You're with us." In a reassuring embrace, Eva put one hand on each of Beverly's arms. "I'm here now, Beverly, and you're safe. We're going to help you."

Beverly began to cry. "I always hate this part."

"What? What part?"

"Are you ready to leave? Are you?"

"Yes, honey, I'm ready. Let's go now. We'll draw you a nice hot bath and I'll wash and set your hair ..."

Beverly turned to Rupert. "I hope you can save them, but I think it's already too late. Evil ... Evil knows where they are. Evil knows it will take them." Her hands trembling uncontrollably, she began to cry again. Her face contorted into a peculiar mix of self-pity and amazement. "I have to do this; I have to help my friend. I have to do this."

"You can help me, Beverly. You can help me by coming with us now. We have to hurry."

Beverly extended one arm to Eva as an invitation to hug her. She was crying. The other arm remained under her jacket.

Rupert saw the two embrace. Maybe once they reached the hotel room they could help her regain her wits. Maybe she could help them find these cold-blooded killers and put this nightmare to rest.

He was deep in thought when he heard the explosion.

With a sickening thud, Eva hit the pavement beside him. As if somehow still confused by the murder, her eyes maintained a trace of disbelief in them. Thick, red blood spilled from the front of her dress, since the blast from the gunshot had destroyed most of her sternum. Facing upward, her head lay unnaturally cocked against the building. Her feet splayed ungracefully across the pavement in front of her.

Rupert began to hyperventilate and shake his head *no*. As he stood there trying to grasp the reality of the situation, he grabbed a handful of his hair. His head began to nod *no, no, no*, nodding more furiously with each passing moment.

"What have you done? What have you done?" He then screamed at her as loudly as his eruption of rage could bring forth, "WHAT THE

FUCK HAVE YOU DONE? WHY DID YOU DO THIS? WHY?"
Attempting to grab the gun from her, he then lunged at Beverly.

Aiming the next round at his head, she fired again.

Narrowly missing the side of his face, the bullet whizzed past him. Fired at close range, the blast was loud. The explosion subsequently deafened his left ear. He froze once more in hopes that she would not shoot a second time.

Beverly held the gun in place and began to speak. "I've already told you. I have to get us out of here. We're going back ... back to the beginning. It's nicer there. It's still safe for us there."

"You killed her. You bitch! You killed her! They told you to kill us didn't they? You're in with them. They let us find you." Rupert's rage had begun to reach maniacal proportions. "I'm going to kill you for this! That'll send a message to them. I'm going to kill their little messenger."

"I must leave now."

"You're not going anywhere. Someone heard you. They've called the cops. They'll get you. You'll hang for this ... YOU'LL HANG FOR THIS!"

The gun was still pointed at Rupert. Her grasp firm, she was holding it with both hands, but her hands were shaking badly.

Rupert did not move. "Put the gun down, Beverly. Put it down, NOW!"

She raised the gun in a peculiar fashion as if she were pointing it skyward. In a swift, simultaneous motion, she brought the gun up in such a way it was pointed at her face. The gun was now upside down with the trigger pointed upwards. As soon as it reached this position, she fired, blowing most of her head and face away.

Rupert put his hand to his mouth and remained where he stood as the corpse slumped onto the steps of the doorway. In front of him, bathed in a sea of hot, sticky blood, were two mangled, dead women. Too thick, too hot ... suddenly, there was no more air. He couldn't breathe; his senses were overloaded. He began to vomit. Evoking a loud wheeze with each one, the contractions were fierce. Dry heaving, he had vomited until there was nothing left. *Where was everyone? There were two gunshot blasts, for Christ's sake. Someone must have heard them ... Someone had to call the police. Oh God, he needed help! Where was God?* He prayed, "Please help me." At that moment, as if in answer to his prayers, his ears began to ring. There was a gray swirl, the ground came rushing up and then nothing.

CHAPTER FIFTY

The police in Memphis hadn't detained him but asked that he not leave the city until the matter was resolved. The evidence at the crime scene clearly pointed to a murder on Beverly's part followed by suicide.

Finally, as Rupert regained consciousness, he realized a mix of neighbors and local Memphis police had surrounded him. Hitting the pavement had left a significant bump on the back of his head. While unconscious, he'd also apparently vomited again. His clothing was heavily soiled, with remains of regurgitate still clinging to the left lapel of his shirt. He awoke to a kind-faced, older woman wiping a cool rag across his forehead. His head lay in her lap.

The proper authorities had been called. Apparently, the coroner arrived while he was unconscious. The two women were pronounced dead at the scene, after which a local funeral home began the gruesome task of body removal.

Relatives and next of kin were notified at once. Rupert was also escorted to the Memphis Police Station whereupon his statement was immediately recorded in detail.

While giving this statement, Rupert vehemently tried to warn police of Solange DeShotel's presence in Memphis. The Memphis Police made it clear they were aware of the situation and were indeed on the lookout for her. Until now, there was no trace of her or alleged accomplice Tom Banks. They went on to tell Rupert that Arkansas authorities had recently informed them of the murder of Mabel Agnew, and they had obtained detailed information from the United

States Bureau of Investigation on the murder of Angelique Gravois. Wanted for questioning in conjunction with both of these murders, Solange DeShotel was a prime suspect. The police knew nothing of the whereabouts of the Davises, for apparently their sequestration in the seminary had been kept secret from the very people who may have been able to help them.

Rupert returned to The Peabody Hotel around 9:00 that morning.

* * *

A phone booth was something to which Rupert was accustomed, as several hotels in the French Quarter had them. Although a rather upscale invention, they were useful for both privacy and shelter from a barrage of noises that were ever present.

"This is the operator, your room number please."

"Operator, I need to make a long distance call."

"I'll have to connect you with long distance. One moment, please."

Rupert waited in the booth to place the call. Numb was the best way to describe him at the moment. Deep in thought, he had no concept how much time had passed before the long distance operator came online.

"This is the operator, number please."

"I need to make a call to New Orleans, Louisiana. The number is Esplanade3, 8758."

"Hold the line, Sir, and I'll place the call. This will take a few moments."

"I'll wait."

"If you'll hang up the receiver, I'll call as soon as the connections are made."

"Thank you."

Staring into the hotel lobby, Rupert sat in the phone booth. He watched as people walked past. He hadn't been to bed, and there was no possibility of sleep for him any time soon. As he looked about, he thought to himself, *what could people be rushing to do at 9:30 in the morning?* Not an early riser by nature, life in the French Quarter tended to sleep the mornings away and awaken in late afternoon. Nighttime was the real source of life there.

The brash ring of the telephone brought him to reality. "Hello?"

"I have your call, Sir. You're connected."

"Caris?"

"My God, man, where are you?"

"Memphis, Tennessee."

"When that operator called, I didn't know what in the hell to think. Rupert, what are you doing there? You didn't tell anyone you were leaving. You just closed the gallery and disappeared. A lot of folks down here think you're dead. They think you've been murdered."

Rupert put his hand to his left ear. "You don't know how close to being right they really are. Caris, I've landed in a nightmare. I'm in this thing so deep that I don't know how to fix it."

"What thing? Fix what?"

"She's going to kill them."

"Solange?"

"Yes, I ..." Rupert paused with his mouth open. *He had to think for a moment how to phrase the next statement.* "I'm not sure I'll be able to stop them."

"Them? Who's them?"

"She has an accomplice, Caris. It's a long story I can't afford to tell right now. This is costing a fortune."

"I realize that, Rupert, but you called me, remember? What do you want?"

"I need some help. Can you come up here?"

"You're kidding. You want me to come to Memphis?"

Rupert exhaled loudly. "Why in God's name do you think I'm calling?"

"Leave this to the police, Rupert. Get out of there and come home. I've already told you that you're intruding in a world you don't belong. This doesn't concern you. If you save these people, then what? Then what, Rupert? You get a pat on the back? An 'attaboy'? What's your motive in this? Crazy is what all of this is."

"You know the police won't find Solange, Caris. They can't reach her. She will kill two innocent people in the very near future, and I for one cannot live with that on my conscience. We can help, Caris, because we were meant to help. This isn't all happening by chance. I know that now."

Trying to digest the notion, Caris stared ahead. "OK, I'll come. I don't know why I'm doing this, but I'll come. You realize it will take a day or so to get there."

"I realize. I'm staying at the Peabody Hotel, room 320."

"I'll make the necessary arrangements today. I'll send a telegram to the hotel with all of the information concerning my arrival." Caris mumbled something else and said, "I must be insane to do this."

"This whole thing is insane, Caris. I'll look for your telegram and hopefully see you soon." Staring at the phone, Rupert replaced the receiver. *Things were about to become a whole lot worse before they got better. The real question was, were they indeed going to be any better?*

* * *

Friday, May 6, 1932

Ned Davis was sitting with Jed in the Carraway living room. The stress of the entire affair, as well as the news of Eva and Beverly's untimely deaths had finally taken their toll on Lorna. Dr. Belton had given Lorna medication to help her sleep, while Lila sat in vigil beside her. Both of their children were in trouble, bringing the four of them together for comfort and strength.

There was a knock on the door. Jed arose to answer it.

"Good Evening, Mr. Carraway."

"Father, what can I do for you?"

"May I come in?"

When he saw the priest enter the room, Ned arose as well.

"I've come to check on the kids. Have you heard from them?"

"Heard from them? No. Thanks to you, nobody has heard from them." Ned glared at Father Donovan.

"Easy, Ned." Jed turned to Father Donovan. "I'm afraid things are a bit of a mess. We haven't heard anything from them. Lorna tried to reach them with no luck at all. We called to tell them about Eva Alexander. Have you heard?"

"I've heard."

"I guess the news is all around Conway by now. Beverly Martin killed her and then killed herself. Sounds like it was a grisly ordeal, and from what I understand, the bodies were in pretty bad shape."

Ned sat back down. "Beats anything I ever saw."

"Jed, I have something to tell you."

"Don't give me any more bad news, Father."

"I'm afraid it's something you must know. I received a call from one of the priests of St. Dominic's Seminary. He asked that I keep this information confidential, but I would not give my word not to tell you."

"Tell us what?"

"Your children are no longer sequestered there."

Ned arose. "Where are they?"

"I don't know. I asked the same question, but all he knew was that they had been ordered to leave. The orders came directly from the Bishop."

Ned became enraged. "What kind of Church do you come from? Who throws someone in danger of being murdered out in the streets? Is that some commandment I didn't learn in school?"

As he spoke, Lila walked into the room. "What on earth are you yelling about, Ned? Lorna is trying to sleep."

"It seems the Catholic Church has thrown our kids out onto the streets, Lila. Nobody knows where they are. We don't even know if they are alive or not."

"I assure you it wasn't the Church, Ned. I don't know …"

Ned interrupted. "That's right. You don't know. You don't know a damn thing about anything."

Lila's face paled. "We have to call the Memphis Police. We have to go to Memphis."

Jed turned to Lila. "Lila, who told you about Eva's and Beverly's murders?"

"Oh gosh, Jed, there was a gathering of ladies down at Pringle's. Several of them rushed up to me and began talking all at once."

"Who found them? Who found Eva Nell and Beverly?"

"I don't know. They didn't say. I just heard they found three people passed out on the street and the two women had been shot. They found a gun in Beverly's hand, surmising that she'd shot Eva and blown her own head off."

Lila turned away after she'd said this.

Jed turned to Ned who was standing beside Father Donovan. "They found three people. One guess who the third person was."

"That man from New Orleans. He has a hand in all of this."

"Oh my God!" Lila sat down as she said this. "I'm the one who told that man our children are in Memphis. I didn't mean to … it just slipped out."

Ned sat down beside her. "It ain't your fault, Lila. That man badgered you until he had you all flustered. If I get my hands on him, I don't know what I'll do."

"Jed," Father Donovan began, "do you have any idea where your children might have gone? Any idea at all?"

"None. I know nothing about Memphis. Most all of this was kept secret from me as well."

"We'd better start with a call to the police in Conway. We'll tell them all we know and then call the Memphis Police." Father Donovan paused for a moment. "I'll take a train to Memphis. Being of Clergy, an audience with the Bishop shouldn't be too difficult. I'll find some answers. I'll also pay the seminary a visit as well."

"We have to find our kids. Their running away was nonsense in the first place. We never should have listened to them."

"We didn't listen to them," Lila interjected, "they left. This priest here arranged for their departure. We had nothing to do with any of this."

"I now regret my decision. At the time, it seemed the right thing to do. I was honestly trying to help those kids. I had no idea things would end up like this."

Jed put an arm on Father Donovan's shoulder. "We know that, Father. None of this is your fault or anyone else's."

"I just want my son back." With that, Lila walked from the room. Ned followed shortly afterwards.

"I can drive us up to Memphis, Father. We'd probably get there a lot sooner."

"I know the way. I can help you drive as well."

"When do you want to leave?"

"It would be cooler if we left tonight."

"I'll see if Lorna can stay with the Davises while we're gone. I don't think we need to include Ned's hot temper if we can avoid it."

"We'll do the best we can." Father Donovan smiled. "I'm leaving. I'll be back around five, packed and ready."

"Take care, Father Donovan." Jed walked Father Donovan to the door and saw him out. He closed the screen door behind him and secured the latch.

They'd find some answers tomorrow. They'd get them one way or another ... he'd make sure of it.

CHAPTER FIFTY-ONE

Everything was lackluster gray. There was no color. Although the wind seemed to gust forcefully, there was no apparent movement of any kind. Across the vast expanse of pasture in front of her, remnants of fall randomly swirled and scattered. Their presence contributed to an atmosphere of loneliness and desolation. Further contributing to a forlorn, abandoned ambience, the landscaped seemed unkempt. Standing on her front porch, Lorna gazed across the family farm. All was quiet ... Too quiet.

She turned to walk inside the house. As it slammed shut behind her, the screen door made no sound. Ruby was sitting at the breakfast table. Lorna entered the room and smiled, but there was no reply. "Ruby?" The sound seemed to echo as she uttered her name. "Ruby!" The reverberation made her dizzy. She had to sit down. As she sat at the table, she noticed Robert seated beside Ruby. She had her children back, and they were home. Ruby and Robert moved their chairs away from the table. Lorna again noticed no sounds as they scooted their chairs across the kitchen floor. Saying nothing, they both arose.

"Wait," Lorna said, "don't leave! I've only just found you." Still, they said nothing. They turned away and began to leave the room. Lorna had to stop them. Now that she'd finally found them, she couldn't let them leave again. Suddenly, there was a blinding flash there was a loud explosion of some kind. Lorna realized an electrical storm was quickly approaching. As if he'd been struck, Robert's knees buckled with the boom. He managed to right himself and continue walking. "Wait! You have to wait! Don't leave me. I can't take it!" *Another boom.*

This time Robert was transparent. Everything was transparent. Lorna stood and grabbed for her daughter, but her hand went through her. "No! Don't do this! I can't take it, Ruby! I can't take it!" Slowly, Ruby turned her head toward her mother. Her words echoing as she said them, she spoke. "It's OK, honey; it's going to be OK."

Lorna opened her eyes. Wiping her forehead with a wet rag, Lila sat beside her. "It's OK, honey. You've just had a bad dream."

Lorna swallowed hard. Her throat was so dry. "Oh, God, Lila, I can't take much more of this."

"Try to rest."

"I want my children back."

We all do, Lorna. We all do."

"Do you think it's too late to save them, Lila?"

"No, I don't."

"They'll be back." Lorna gritted her teeth in protest. "By God, they have to come back. I've lost Blanche and I will not lose the rest of my family."

"No, honey, you're not going to lose anyone."

"Lila, with all of the tragedies that have befallen us lately, have you noticed a common thread?"

"Tell me."

"Who was in New Orleans comforting Ruby when Blanche was killed? Who was in Conway when Mabel was murdered? Who was in Memphis when Beverly supposedly murdered Eva and committed suicide?"

"The men were talking about that awhile ago, Lorna."

"Now you tell me why the police are letting him run free. Three cities, four murders ..."

"Five if you count that housekeeper in New Orleans."

"And he's out looking for our children. He wants to help. You think he wants to help? I think he's the killer. I think he murdered my niece and now he's trying to murder my child."

Lila said nothing. She simply looked at the floor. *Lorna made a lot of sense.* A streak of terror ran through her. *They may indeed never see their children again.* As Jed walked into the room, her train of thought was broken.

She arose and met him at the door. "She's had a nightmare, Jed. I think all of this is getting to her. I don't know how much more she'll be able to stand."

"Let me have a moment alone with her if you don't mind, Lila."

Lila said nothing else and left the room.

Jed walked over to the bed and sat down beside her. "Father Donovan and I are leaving for Memphis tonight. We're going to find our children and bring them home. It's time to take matters into our own hands."

"That Rupert, Jed ... that Rupert is the cause of all of this. He's trying to kill our daughter. He has some sick fixation with her. Think about it. Every time there has been a murder, he's been lurking. Take care of this, Jed. Take care of this situation before he kills our Ruby."

Jed stared at Lorna for a moment in silence. "I'll do whatever I have to do to protect my daughter and grandchild, Lorna. Whatever it takes. Get some rest. You're not well."

"When are you leaving?"

"I'll try to sleep a couple of hours and then head out."

"Ned is going with you?"

"No. We don't need his big mouth and hot head along on this one."

"How in heaven's name can you keep him from going?"

"If he wants to go, he can go. He'll just have to do it by himself. Father and I aren't mentioning anything to him. When we get to Memphis, we're heading to that seminary for some answers. Father Donovan can get us in. Meanwhile, if you hear from Ruby, tell her the plans. Decide on a meeting place for us. I'll be in touch as well. Maybe this might work."

"Be careful of that Rupert, Jed. He's a cold-blooded killer. I know he killed Blanche, and he's in with that Solange. They're in this to-gether, He means to do my daughter and grandchild harm."

"And he may end up in a wooden box, Lorna. If I have to spend the rest of my days in jail to protect my family, so be it."

"So be it, Jed."

CHAPTER FIFTY-TWO

Saturday, May 7, 1932

The trip was long and arduous. Caris really didn't have the financial means to make this trip to Memphis, but for the love of his friend, he did so.

As he looked around his hotel room, he shook his head at the extravagance of his surroundings. One chance meeting, one unremarkable perusal into Rupert's gallery had involved him in all of this. He resented the hell out of that fact. He resented the very existence of a woman, who through no fault of her own denied him what was rightfully his. He hated her for it, and more than that, he hated himself for feeling this way.

He had begun to unpack his belongings when he heard a knock at the door. He walked over to the door and answered it.

"Caris Delcambre."

"As I live and breathe."

"For now, anyway."

He gestured for her to enter.

"I trust your trip was uneventful?"

"You trusted wrong. This whole thing is wrong. I don't have any business being here."

"Oh but you do. And you'll do exactly as I say if you want your long, tall, lover back in your arms where he belongs."

"And that's exactly where he belongs, Madame DeShotel."

"Oh, it makes no difference to me where he lands, Caris." She smiled. "I've had occasion to talk to him. He's a fool. He's a love-struck, impulsive fool."

"I don't care what you think of him. I really don't care what you think about anything, Madame. In reality, you want something and so do I. For reasons beyond me, they both involve Rupert. That's the only relationship we share, and that's the only relationship I want to have with you."

"And I thought your boyfriend was the fool." She smiled and turned to him. "You have no idea the magnitude of whom you're dealing with here, Mr. Delcambre. I don't have time to dwell on such trivial matters at the moment, but for future reference, you may want to keep your mouth shut—if you value your life, that is."

She walked away from him a bit and turned to face him. "Now, as I've just said, you'll do exactly as I say. If you do, in the process you may get what you desire. If that does not happen, however, it makes no difference to me. Your life makes no difference to me. I hope you understand."

"Why don't we dispense with the 'war of words' and get on with it? What do you want me to do?"

"Your lover has access to something I need. It's in the possession of two people who've eluded me thus far, but this man, this Rupert Staten, will soon find them."

"How do you know?"

"That is none of your concern."

"Rupert has asked me to help rescue these people you speak of. I told him I would."

"Then do it. As long as I have what I want, their survival is really not of concern." She laughed aloud. "It really doesn't matter how hard you try to help them anyway. It really doesn't."

"I'm going to see Rupert tonight."

"Find those people, Caris. Come to me after you've done so. If you fulfill this, I'll reward you richly. You can live with your artist happily ever after. If you don't, well … Maybe you'd better just concentrate on finding them. Hell lasts a long time, and it's really quite hot."

"It's where you belong."

Solange laughed again. "You're right. But that doesn't necessarily mean I want to stay here."

"How do I get in touch with you?"

She handed him a card. "When you've found them, come to this address. Tell the man who answers what you know."

"And that's it?"

Solange walked over to the mirror and removed her hair comb. Falling about her face as if she'd planned the entire event, tresses of auburn hair cascaded downward toward her shoulders. She took her handkerchief, dabbed at the corner of her mouth, and removed a smear of lip pomade. Never looking at him, she turned away from the mirror and walked toward the door. "You have twenty-four hours." She then opened the door and disappeared into the hallway.

* * *

"*This is the hotel operator, room number please.*"

"Room 320."

"*Thank you, please hold.*"

The phone rang. Rupert rushed over to it and grabbed the receiver from its cradle.

"Hello?"

"I'm here. I'm in room 217."

"For God's sake, man, come up here."

"Can you spare a few minutes? I have to bathe."

"As fast as you can, get up here, Caris. Hurry!" Rupert put the receiver back in its holder. *Caris was here … he was here. Things were going to work out after all.*

CHAPTER FIFTY-THREE

Shortly thereafter, there was a knock on the door. *He must bathe awfully fast* ... Without first asking, he opened the door to his hotel room. Standing in front of him was a man and a woman. Rupert froze. He swallowed hard and tried to speak.

"Oh God. I ... I don't understand."

The man spoke first. "Neither do I. I don't understand what you're doing here. Bad luck seems to follow you around, Rupert. That's something we don't need more of."

"Maybe I'm following bad luck."

"We're going to find out now, aren't we?"

At this moment, Rupert realized they were still standing in the hallway. "Do you want to come in?"

The woman, who had said nothing until this moment, finally spoke. "That would be nice, if you don't mind."

"Come in and have a seat, both of you. Are you thirsty? I have bootleg whiskey." He blushed when he realized what he'd said. "Of course not, I'm so sorry. You're pregnant."

Robert spoke. "What are you doing here?"

"I've come to help you."

"We don't need your help. We don't want your help. You have no bearing on our lives, so I'll ask again. Why are you here?"

Rupert swallowed again. "I don't know how much you know, but Solange DeShotel may be here in Memphis. Mabel Agnew was murdered, and in a manner of sorts, Beverly Martin may have been kidnapped. At first I had to warn Ruby ..." He stopped himself. "At first I felt I had to warn you two of Solange's possible whereabouts."

"You talk as if you know these people. Why didn't you leave it to the police?"

"They didn't seem to want to believe me. They wanted to believe I murdered Mabel."

"And did you?"

"Of course not. That's how I met up with Eva Alexander. She had to identify the suspect in a lineup."

Ruby arose. "Suspect? I assume you mean the man suspected of murdering Mabel Agnew."

"Ruby, Solange has someone working with her on this. Inadvertently, I met up with Solange in a speakeasy."

Robert lunged forward. "Wait a minute. You what?"

Instinctively, Rupert stepped away from him. "Neither of us knew who the other was—at least I don't think so—but I did get a look at her 'insanely jealous lover.' That's how she describes him. Eva and I put two and two together. This lover of hers may be the person who murdered Mabel Agnew. Mabel must have known something."

Robert stopped. He thought for a moment. "Beverly worked for the telephone company. She had to tell this guy something, something she'd heard Mabel say. That has to be the connection among the three of them. Maybe Mabel's eavesdropping finally got the best of her. Maybe her nosiness got her killed."

Rupert looked at Robert for a moment and then at Ruby. "How on earth did you find me? The reason I'm here in Memphis is to find both of you."

Ruby spoke up. "The police. Without reason we were asked to leave ..."

Robert interrupted. "We were thrown out."

Ruby paused a moment and continued. "We were ordered to leave the seminary without reason. The Monsignor walked into our room and sadly announced he had orders from the Bishop that we were no longer to be housed there."

"Effective immediately," Robert added. "We didn't know where else to go but to the police."

"The Sergeant on duty took us into his office and explained all that had transpired. He told us of Eva's murder and Beverly's suicide. He also told us of your whereabouts."

"I wanted to kill you."

Rupert turned to Robert. "Why would you want to kill me when all I'm trying to do is save your lives?"

"Everywhere you go people die. Think about that Rupert. Still want us to think you're the good guy?"

"It's not my fault ..." He was interrupted by a knock at the door. The room fell silent.

"Are you expecting anyone?" Robert asked.

"I am. My friend Caris has come from New Orleans to help me find you."

Robert put his hand in his pocket.

Rupert saw the motion. "I swear he's come to help."

"And I swear I'll shoot him if what you say isn't true. Try something, Rupert, and I'll shoot both of you."

Rupert stood by the door.

"It's Caris, Rupert. Let me in."

Rupert didn't move. Staring at Robert, he remained standing by the door.

Finally, Robert spoke. "You can open it, Rupert, but remember what I said. I will kill both of you. I mean it."

Slowly, Rupert opened the door. Caris smiled when he saw him and then realized there were two other people in the room.

"Come in, come in." He gestured Caris into the room and closed the door behind him.

"Caris Delcambre, this is Mr. and Mrs. Robert Davis."

Caris felt the blood drain from his face. He swallowed. "Pleased to meet you."

Robert noticed the sudden pallor. His finger tensed on the trigger. "Is something wrong?"

"The whole reason I came to Memphis, Mr. Davis, was to help Rupert find you."

"Which I still don't understand, but understand this: from here on out, it ends. You people are out of our lives. One way or the other, I'll make sure that happens."

Caris turned toward Rupert. "It sounds as if our work is done. We're through before we've started."

"I had no idea. They've just arrived, Caris. I'm as surprised as you are."

Again, Caris looked across the room. After a moment, he gave a gesture of resignation.

"It seems that I have no further business here. There is nothing left for me to do but leave for New Orleans in the morning."

"And I shall leave as well. It appears all of our business is finished here."

Robert and Ruby said nothing.

Not knowing quite what to say or do next, Caris turned and walked toward the door. He opened it, walked through the doorway, and paused. Turning toward them once again he said, "I'll be off, then. I've a long day ahead of me tomorrow, and sleep, such as it is, will be most welcome." In a gesture of farewell, he brought his hand to his forehead. "Good luck to you, Mr. and Mrs. Davis. Hopefully, there will be no more dealings with Madame DeShotel. Rupert, might you stop by my hotel room before morning?"

"I doubt it, Caris."

"A pity ... then this is goodbye until I see you back home?"

"Until then."

Still not knowing quite what to say or to do, Caris paused for another awkward moment. The situation had obviously thrown him. Finally, he turned to leave.

Rupert followed him into the hall. "I'm sorry you have come all of this way for nothing. You'll never know how much it means to me, Caris. I'll reimburse you. I'll make it up to you somehow. I promise you that."

"I know."

"Take care on your journey home. I'll see you soon. Check on my gallery in the meantime, won't you?"

"I will."

Caris began to walk away and then stopped. He turned around. "You know I'd never do anything to harm our friendship, don't you?"

"I know that, Caris. You know I know that. Why would you say such a thing?"

Caris took a deep breath and exhaled. He opened his mouth to answer this and then closed it once again. "Forgive me. I'm not thinking clearly, but sleep will help. Goodnight, Rupert."

"Sleep well." Watching Caris make his way to the lift, he continued to stand in the hallway. As the elevator doors closed behind him, Rupert turned and re-entered the hotel room.

"Is he gone?"

"He's gone."

"Back to us, Mr. Staten. The reason for our little visit tonight is to give you one last warning. You can push people only so far and then they'll push back. We're leaving here and going home. We'll fight this Solange demon on our own grounds in our own town. You, on the other hand, are leaving us alone. I really don't care where you go, what you do or even with whom you do it, but we are not part of it. My next words will be with this." Robert removed the pistol from his pocket.

"Sounds like a threat to me."

"It is."

"Well save your threats, Mr. Davis. I've done what I've come here to do, maybe not in the order that I had anticipated, but nevertheless it worked out."

"Then we're leaving. Get your things, Ruby."

"Do you have a place to stay?"

"None of your concern."

"I understand that, but if by chance you don't, you're welcome to this room until morning."

Robert smirked in amazement. "Fat chance of that happening. When will you realize we don't need you or anything you have to offer?"

Ruby put her hand on his arm. "With all due respect, we really don't have anywhere to go."

"We'll get a room here."

"There are none," Rupert said. "The hotel is full, and you may have a hard time finding a place to stay in Memphis tonight. Use the room. I'll stay with Caris."

Robert stared at him a long time. Finally, he said, "She makes the call."

"If you wouldn't mind, Rupert."

Rupert smiled. "I'll call housekeeping and request fresh sheets and towels for you. Give me a few minutes to get my things together and I'll be out of here."

CHAPTER FIFTY-FOUR

Much of his work had been done for him. He didn't feel right about what he was about to do, but he had to protect his friend. Rupert did not belong here or in this situation. He removed the card from his wallet. Meticulously detailed in brilliant gold ink, the calligraphy was perfection. Such an extravagance to have one's number hand painted on cards, but then again, nothing pertaining to Solange DeShotel was ordinary. He'd gathered his things in order to leave when he heard a knock on the door. He froze. How had they known? How could they possibly have known? Somchow, they knew the Davises had made their way to Rupert's room. A feeling of dread overcame him. He walked to the door. "Who is it?"

"Got an extra bed for an old friend?"

It was Rupert. He took the key and opened the door. With a duffel bag of sorts slung over his shoulder, he continued to stand in the hallway. "Not so old ... long time friend would be a better choice of words."

"And one who's homeless at the moment."

"I can remedy that." Caris stood aside and gestured for him to enter.

"I gave the Davises my room. They had nowhere to go. I hope you don't mind if I intrude."

Caris smiled. "I'll get over it. Let's have some whiskey; I know you have a bottle in that bag."

"As a matter of fact, I do." Rupert removed his duffel bag and set it on the floor. "Bootleg at its finest."

Caris took the bottle, opened it, and took a long drink. The whiskey burned his throat like fire. "Damn, Rupert, this stuff is kind of green."

"It is. I like a little bite."

"Well, a toast then. A toast to a job well done."

"You asshole, we didn't do anything. They came to us."

"Nevertheless, it's worthy of an acknowledgment of satisfaction."

"Well, you go ahead and acknowledge. I need a bath."

"This room has a shower as well."

"That's even better. I'm exhausted and ready for some sleep. I'll sleep better if I'm clean." Rupert looked up to meet Caris' unflinching stare.

"Nice to have you back."

Rupert met his glance. "You know I'm in love with her. You know that, don't you?"

"I know."

"Then you understand?"

"I understand you're a self-destructing son of a bitch, Rupert Staten. You never did know what was good for you."

"I can't help the way I feel."

"Nor can I."

"Then I guess we understand each other …" Rupert paused for a moment.

He began again. "That being said, I'll take my shower now."

Caris said nothing else. He took another drink of the whiskey and walked over to the radio. He turned it on, adjusting the dial for a clear tone. Rupert waited a moment. Realizing that Caris had no intentions of pursuing the subject any further, he went into the bathroom. As Caris watched the door close, he drank again. *He'd wait for Rupert to fall asleep and then leave. As luck would have it, things had fallen into place. This would be much easier than he'd anticipated. Soon Solange would be gone with her caveman, and he'd be there to pick up the pieces of his lover's broken life. He'd mend his spirit and right things as they should be. It would be hard at first, but Rupert would soon realize what he truly needed. They were what Rupert really needed, together in the Quarter forever.*

Before he made any kind of movement, Caris made sure that Rupert was sound asleep. His head propped on one elbow, he laid there and watched him sleep. His breathing was rhythmic; so peaceful, it was hard to believe that so much tragedy had recently befallen him. Caris eased out of bed and dressed. Dressing quietly was a bit of a chore, as he was a little drunk from all the whiskey he'd imbibed. He removed the card Solange had given him from his wallet. Staring at it for a moment, he decided to make the call from the lobby. He hoped to God that he was doing the right thing. He also hoped he wasn't about to get everyone killed in trying to do so.

*   *   *

Several blocks behind the Peabody Hotel, an old, abandoned warehouse on South Second Street wasn't much to look at, and it certainly was not the caliber of accommodations Solange would choose for a stay in Memphis. His train of thought was broken with the realization he really didn't care how comfortable she was. *This wasn't odd. She was a murderer, and murderers usually hid from plain view. An old, abandoned warehouse was perfect housing for a bloodthirsty monster.*

Looking about the place, he made his way into the immense, dark structure. He couldn't see much, but he was able to make out a small stairway in the back, right corner of the room. Complete with railing and spindles, the bank of stairs lead up to a balcony. In this building's heyday, there may have been workspace up there; however, judging from the condition of the structure, those days were long gone. In an attempt to assure himself that no one lurked at the top of the stairs, he paused for a moment. Caris did not shut the door behind him, but he hovered close to it in case a quick escape was necessary. He felt for the gun holstered securely beneath his jacket.

Suddenly, a figure emerged from the second story walkway. Above him stood a woman dressed entirely in white. A rich, auburn chignon, tucked neatly at the nape of her neck, provided beautiful contrast to her flawless attire. Caris stared for a moment in wonder. *How could something so small, petite, and beautiful be so malevolent?*

"Welcome."

"I think my accommodations are a little nicer than yours."

She laughed. "No matter, they're both temporary, Caris. A gilded cage is still a cage, so why bother?"

Deciding on what to say, Caris looked around for a moment. Finally, he spoke.

"So ... you're the man who answers? The one I'm supposed to tell what I know?"

"Oh, he'll be along shortly." Smiling at him expectantly, she said nothing else.

"They're at the Peabody hotel. They're staying in Rupert Staten's room."

"Dropped into our lap just like that? What irony!" She laughed and began to descend the stairs.

Caris shifted his weight from one leg to the other. Her walking toward him made him uncomfortable. "Well, Madame, I've done what I came to do. I'm leaving now as I have no interest in the outcome."

"Oh, don't you?"

Knowingly, he looked at her. "You know what I want."

"Then perhaps you should wait a moment longer."

"For what?"

"I want you to bring me the coin."

"You what? I'm not getting you anything else. You want the coin? That's what your subservient ape is for, Solange. Have him do it."

Solange lost no composure. "Caris, my darling, I can have my 'subservient ape,' as you so deftly put it, kill you as we speak. Turn around."

Caris turned to see Tom Banks appear in the doorway behind him. Slowly he began to remove his hand from his right pocket.

Solange continued her descent down the stairway. "My poor darling, you may wish to consider putting that hand of yours back into your pocket. Otherwise, I'll shoot you with this."

He turned back around to discover that Solange had removed a small revolver from the folds of her gown. She now took aim at him.

"You insolent bitch! What more do you want from me?"

"For starters, perhaps a better memory. You forget I can kill you and your tall, handsome lover in a matter of moments. It would be wise for you to realize that if you don't watch what you say, I'll have Tom cut out your tongue, and, well … Use your imagination as to what he might do with it. It makes no difference to me what happens to any of you, Caris; none of this matters to me anymore. I'll be free of all of it in a short while."

"If you get the coin."

"Oh, I'll get it. The question at hand is do you still want to be alive after I have it? I assume the answer is yes?"

Staring straight ahead, he paused for an instant. Still not making eye contact with her, he began again. "You assumed correctly."

"Get me the coin."

"How am I supposed to do that, Solange?"

"Well, let's see. 'Madame' was spoken with a greater deal of humility than 'Solange.' I think 'Solange' sounds a bit too familiar. We're not friends, you know. I don't even particularly like you." Her left arm still pointing the revolver at him, she put her right hand on the balcony railing. "You know, Caris, in Spanish one speaks to his mere acquaintances in third person. It shows formality and respect. I like that."

"As Madame wishes."

"Yes, yes that's right; I do like that much better. Now go to the hotel, take the coin from them, and bring it to me. In that way, everyone lives, and I'm free of this bondage forever. We all win, Caris, except …"

"Except what?"

"Your handsome lover still pines for the unattainable love. How bittersweet."

Mockingly, he replied, "Yes, how bittersweet, Madame." He then turned to Tom. "Get out of my way."

Tom said nothing and smashed his gun across the side of Caris' face. The blow knocked him to the floor.

"Now, now darling, there will be plenty of time for that later. Don't scar that pretty face too much. It'll attract attention."

Tom looked down at Caris. The sneer across his face meant unfinished business between them. "Then I guess you're ready to go, Caris." He spit out the name, as if its mere utterance were disgusting.

Wiping blood from the side of his face, Caris said nothing and left.

As he made his way up the street, Solange and Tom watched his silhouette disappear. After a moment, Tom said, "How do we know the bastard will do what you say?"

"Because you will do what I say. Therefore, nothing can stop us now, darling, nothing at all."

CHAPTER FIFTY-FIVE

Sunday, May 8, 1932

Damn her! Damn them! He didn't know these people, and he didn't care about some godforsaken coin. He made his way back to the Peabody Hotel. It was now late into the night. *How would he get it? How would he coax the Davises into answering the door at this hour without suspicion?*

Caris stopped for a moment. *There was a way ... there was a way, but the price was high ...*

Was he prepared to pay it? Time would tell soon enough ...

* * *

It wasn't so much noise or movement that awakened Rupert, but the lack thereof. Rupert opened his eyes and arose in bed. The room was dark and there was no light in the bathroom. He was in bed alone. "Caris?" There was no answer. "Caris, where are you?"

At that moment, he heard a fumbling movement at the door. His gun was on the nightstand beside the bed. The door opened just as Rupert grabbed the gun and took aim.

"Whoa, ole boy! It's me, Caris ... don't shoot!"

"You scared the hell out of me!" Rupert's chest heaved. As if grabbing great gulps of air from the room, he was gasping. "Where were you? Why did you go out?" He was still pointing the gun at Caris.

Caris stammered for a moment. "I ... I had to go out."

Still breathing heavy, he looked at Caris expectantly. He waited for him to elaborate, but Caris said nothing. "I gathered you went out, Caris, but where did you go?"

"I went to see Solange DeShotel."

There was a moment of stunned silence. "What are you talking about?"

"I found Solange."

Still staring at him, Rupert shook his head in disbelief. "That doesn't make any sense. You don't even know who she is. You didn't find Solange, you lying son of a bitch! Where were you?" Rupert had become enraged. His face red with anger, he'd gotten out of bed now. The gun was still pointed at Caris, and Caris wasn't sure if he meant to do this or not.

"I did find her ... I really did." Caris swallowed hard. "I think we may be able to save your friends from certain death."

"Oh you think so?" Rupert took a step forward, putting the gun about twelve inches from his face.

In an attempt to reestablish the distance between them, Caris instinctively stepped backwards. "All she wants is that coin, Rupert. She doesn't care about killing anyone. She just wants the coin."

"Of course she wants the coin ..." Glaring at Caris, his face was red and he'd begun to shake. He dropped his hand to his side.

Caris exhaled in relief.

"You say she doesn't care about killing anyone? Then you're a fool. You're a stupid fool. She's a liar, Caris. She'll kill all of us if she has the opportunity." Rupert began to get dressed. He set the gun back on the nightstand. "You can't believe anything she says. I know she wants that coin ... everyone knows that. Everyone except you, I guess. I thought you were smarter than this." Rupert brushed his hair from his face and walked to the mirror. "I also know she has to be stopped. She's a psychopathic killer who cares for no one. She's totally devoid of emotion. Evil, anger, and hatred are all that reside in her soul." He began to button his shirt. He said nothing for a moment and began again. "You know what happens if we help her get away? You really want to know?"

Caris said nothing.

"We put countless other lives in jeopardy. Live with that, Caris."

"I don't care about other lives, Rupert. I only care about ours—yours and mine."

"It makes me sad to hear you say things like that. I thought of you as a better person."

Caris walked over to the mirror beside him. They were both looking into it at their reflections. "Well, that being said, I guess the next step is to tell those people what we know. Who knows? That may bring my character some redemption in your eyes ..."

"Perhaps ... and maybe you're tired. It's the wee hours of the morning and you really didn't mean what you just said."

"Perhaps."

Rupert walked over to the phone. "I'd better call and tell them we're coming up so as not to alarm them."

"Where's that bottle?"

"I don't think you need that right now, Caris."

"Where is it?"

"In my nightstand."

Caris walked around the bed to the nightstand. He took the bottle and drank heavily, gasping as he took the bottle from his lips. He took another drink, after which he said, "I'm ready when you are."

"I've just called them. Let's go."

Caris slammed the bottle down onto the nightstand. He retrieved Rupert's gun and walked toward the door. He handed it to him. "Here, we might need this."

Rupert took the gun. "Yeah, we might at that. I have a small pistol tucked into the front of my pants as well. Can you see it?"

"I can't. That makes three guns between us." Caris pointed to the lapel of his coat.

Rupert turned to leave. "Good." As if a thought suddenly struck him, he paused for a moment. "Caris?"

"Yeah, Rupert."

Standing in the doorway, with the hotel door open for him, he said, "How exactly did you find Solange, anyway? I don't get the connection here."

"I've known Solange for a long time, Rupert. I knew her in the Quarter. She did several readings for me."

"You never told me that."

"There's a lot I haven't told you. An audience with Solange is not an easy thing to arrange. If you manage to do so, you'd better keep your mouth shut. People who don't tend to disappear."

"Or die, right?"

"Yeah, or die. So you see why I haven't said anything?"

"Understand this. If I find out you're conspiring with Solange, your ass will rot in jail. I'll see to that. I'll make it my life's mission. If you've helped her, Caris, for whatever reason, then you're no better than she is. In fact, you're worse, because you know the difference between right and wrong."

Feeling no compulsion to answer the last statement, Caris said nothing else. Its meaning was self-explanatory. He left the room, walking down the hallway several paces ahead of Rupert.

* * *

As they walked off the lift onto the third floor, Rupert looked at Caris' face. "What happened to you, anyway?"

Caris instinctively put his hand to his cheek. "I ... Uh ... fell down."

"You fell down? What were you walking on, a wrought iron fence? That's a gash, Caris, and it looks pretty bad."

They were approaching room 320.

"It could have been a lot worse."

At that moment, they heard the sound of footsteps behind them. Grabbing for their guns, both men wheeled around.

"Oh I wouldn't, ladies. I have a silencer on here and it doesn't make a single, little sound. Great little gadget, you know. I can blow you away, drag you inside and no one will ever know the difference."

Rupert and Caris stood frozen. Rupert spoke. "Insanely jealous lover, I presume. I recognize the scar."

"Subservient ape," Caris added.

"Little girl, you must want another slash across that pretty face, and I can sure help you with that. Now gals, I'd love to stay and talk, but I have a reason for being here. If you don't feel like lying face down with a bullet in your brain—ruining this pretty rug I might add—I suggest you drop those guns, walk over to that door, and get us inside."

"You're crazy."

"You know, hon, I've been told that a lot lately. Now I'm going to kill both of you, and then I'm going to break into that room and kill both of them. I'd be glad to drag your bodies in there so you can all rot together, happily ever after." His face turned mean. "I'm not kidding. This is it. Either drop the guns and get me into that room or I start shooting."

"Then kill us. You're going to anyway. I will not help you murder two other innocent people."

Tom pointed and cocked the gun.

"Wait! WAIT!" Caris extended his arm toward Tom in earnest. "Please don't shoot!" He threw his gun onto the carpet, turned to the door and began to knock furiously.

Rupert was looking at Tom as Caris said this. His face exemplifying a mixture of disbelief and disgust, he then turned to Caris. "You coward! I ought to kill you myself."

Still pointing the gun at both of them, Tom shrugged with indifference. "Makes no difference to me, but first things first. Put your gun down, lover-boy."

Rupert reached into his coat, removed the revolver, and dropped it onto the rug in front of him.

At that moment, the door opened. Tom moved quickly to hide himself against the wall beside the door. Caris was standing in front of it as Robert peered out to see who was there. "Oh, it's you." He opened the door further to accommodate their entrance. It's hard to describe what accurately transpired in the next few moments. In order to let the two men inside of the room, Robert had begun to open the door. As it opened, Tom moved away from the wall and positioned himself behind the two men.

Looking slightly to his right, Rupert's peripheral vision perceived Tom making the move. "IT'S A TRAP!" Rupert yelled. "CLOSE THE DOOR!" He attempted to grab the back of Caris' coat in order to yank him from the doorway. In this way he'd hoped that Robert would close the door in time to keep them out and call for help. It was too late. Before he could grip Caris' jacket, Tom had turned sideways and forcefully slammed himself into Rupert. Rupert involuntarily lurched forward, subsequently knocking Caris into Robert. The result was a pileup, with Rupert and Caris falling onto the floor just inside the doorway. Robert had stumbled backwards a few steps into the room. Tom, with his revolver pointed at the men, stood over them and laughed. "Hey, that went better than I thought."

Ruby screamed.

He squatted, somewhat, reaching behind him to retrieve Rupert's gun. "Shutup, Bitch. I'll fill all of you full of lead if you don't shut your fucking mouth!"

Ruby said nothing else. By this time, the men—still on the floor—had turned onto their backs in order to see him.

He stood up and shoved Rupert's gun into his belt. "Get up. Get up off of the floor and get in there."

They managed to untangle themselves and rise to their feet.

Robert spoke first. "There are three of us and only one of you. We might not all make it, but you might not either. You can't hold all of us with only one gun."

He laughed. "I have more than one gun now, gentlemen," he said as he pointed to his belt. "None of you had better move or I'll shoot her first." He paused for a moment. "Hey, look at her." He made a face of enlightenment. "I could get two for one shooting her."

No one moved. Tom began again. "Besides, Ladies, I have backup."

Rupert looked at him. "Where?"

"Well … Right here." Tom extended his left arm behind him toward the doorway. The three men looked past him and saw Solange make an entrance into the room. She smiled and brandished a gun. Pointing it at them, she spoke. "Good evening."

No one replied.

"I guess this is the epiphany of our long journey."

Robert, Ruby, Caris and Rupert all stood staring in silence.

Solange took a deep breath and exhaled. "I trust you have the coin? After all, we all know that's what I'm here for."

Robert took a small step forward. "We have it. How do we know you won't kill us all after we give it to you?"

Patiently standing by the doorway, Solange remained smiling. "I don't plan on killing anyone, Mr. Davis. It really wouldn't make any difference at this point. All I need is that twenty-dollar gold piece. Give it to me and I'll be on my way."

"You're a liar."

Still pointing the gun, Solange took a couple of steps forward. She quietly closed the door behind her. "There, that's much better. There's just no telling who might walk by and we still have business here." The smile vanished from her face. "I'm done with cordiality. Give me the coin or we both start shooting. There is no more time for discussion. This room is not large so it shouldn't be hard to find. It's your choice, so make it now."

Ruby stepped forward to stand beside Robert. "If you won't shoot me, I'll get it for you." Her hand instinctively went to her belly. "Please ..."

"Get the coin." Solange said nothing else. The gun still pointed directly toward them, her aim did not falter."

Ruby turned and went to her suitcase. She opened it and pulled a small black box from an inner compartment. Clad in leather, gold inlay adorned the edges of the box. An emblem had been embossed atop the lid. "Here. Here it is. Take it. We don't want it anymore. Just leave us in peace."

Solange walked over to her and took the box. Eyes glistening with anticipation, she opened it. "Finally ... Finally I shall escape this Hell."

Tom grinned. "Why don't you go on and get ready, baby. I have a few loose ends to tie up here."

Rupert looked at him. "What loose ends?"

"Well, let's see. First, I'm going to tie you big boys up. That is, if I can get hold of any rope. If not I guess I can just shoot your fucking legs off." He laughed. "Next, I'm going to see what it's like to fuck a pregnant lady. Oh sure I've fucked some pregnant women in my time, but this one has class—a real lady she is."

The three men did not move. Robert's fists were clenched. He'd begun to sweat. Through gritted teeth he muttered, "You'll have to kill us first."

"No problem. I'll start with him." He pointed his gun at Caris and pulled the trigger. Shooting him between the eyes, Caris' body convulsed as the bullet made impact. The eyes didn't bother to close, and the look of bewilderment remained in them as he fell to the floor. His mouth open, gurgling noises emanated from it as he lay there dying. In small rivulets, blood began to flow from the wound in his forehead. A raspy, exhale rattle emerged from his lips, and then nothing. He was still.

Ruby screamed but there was no sound. She put her hands to her mouth in horror. This man ... No, this monster had just murdered a human being in front of her. Heloise's murdered image then came to mind. She could see the corpse slumped in the corner of her dining room, surrounded by a pool of dark, red blood. No one deserved such an indignant death. With no regrets and no remorse, this is who killed her. She was looking at him. She was looking at the murderous, psychotic maniac who would kill them all.

Tom pointed the gun at Ruby. "Now get some rope, boys. Find me a belt, suspenders, or whatever you can find. Let's get this show on the road ... I don't have all day."

Ruby looked about the room. She suddenly realized she was alone in the hotel room with the three men.

Rupert's head turned ever so slightly to the side. He was standing on the left side of Robert In an effort to conceal his left hand easing behind the waistband of his pants, he turned his right shoulder toward Tom. He had only once chance. If he were to save them, he had to get hold of the gun and shoot in one fluid, simultaneous motion. If not, they were all as good as dead.

Robert looked at Tom as if he were looking straight through him. "We're not getting anything, you mother-fucking son of a bitch."

"Ok, I can fuck a corpse. Makes no difference to me. She'll still be warm … just a little more willing." He laughed again. He raised the gun higher toward her face and cocked the hammer.

Although only an instant, the next few moments seemed like eternity. Rupert furiously grabbed at his pants in an attempt to free the hidden gun, while Robert simultaneously screamed "NOOOOOO!" and lunged at Tom. A shot was fired and then another. Rupert looked on as two bodies fell to the floor. Tom Banks and Robert Davis both lie dying on the hotel room floor.

Rupert began to hyperventilate. This wasn't happening … This couldn't be happening again.

A gun and two dead bodies. Clenching his fists, he shook his head as he stared at yet another crime scene. *If history is repeating itself, then fuck history … fuck fucking history! I want to erase the memory.*

CHAPTER FIFTY-SIX

The bullet had entered his sternum. Sounding much like a fire-cracker, there was a loud popping crack as it made its way through muscle, bone and finally the heart. Tom lay on the floor at a right angle to Caris. Staring straight ahead, he was lying on his side with the gun still in his right hand. Ready to pull the trigger and shoot, his arm pointed upward. Forming a rapidly expanding reservoir beside him, blood poured from the wound in his chest. His left arm, neatly positioned beside him, provided a dry island in the ever-increasing lake. There was no life in him. Tom Banks was gone.

Rupert looked toward Ruby. "Oh God, Ruby. I'm so sorry."

She was kneeling over Robert. She'd unbuttoned his shirt and unsnapped his pants. Exposing the gunshot wound, she looked up. Her voice was shaking. "He's bleeding, Rupert. He's bleeding badly, please help me."

Rupert ran to the bathroom and grabbed all of the available towels. He made his way back to them and knelt beside her. "Does he have a pulse?"

"He does, but there's so much blood." Tears began flowing as she realized the situation was becoming grave.

"We have to stop the bleeding or we'll lose him. Call the front desk and get help up here."

Ruby ran to the phone.

Rupert packed the wound in Robert's lower abdomen with a towel. In pulsating torrents, blood streamed profusely from his bowels. The towel became saturated. He packed another one on top of it. "Did you reach them?"

"They're coming." She became hysterical. "Oh God, Rupert, save him!" She ran back to them and once again knelt beside Robert.

Robert could hear the voices. As if just beyond vocal range, their sound was distant. He tried his best to reach them ... He tried to communicate to no avail. He felt no pain, however, only an overwhelming desire to sleep. He fought hard to stay awake, but the voices continued to fade.

"Get me another towel."

"There are no more."

"THEN GET ME A DAMN SHEET! I DON'T CARE WHAT IT IS, BUT GET IT NOW!" Rupert began to talk to himself. "He's bleeding too badly ... I can't stop the blood."

Ruby cried out. "Oh God, Rupert ..." She handed him the sheet. Tears were streaming down her face, and her nose had begun to run. Her face was a contorted mask of grief-stricken agony.

Rupert felt for a pulse. "WHERE ARE THEY? WHERE IN THE HELL IS THE DOCTOR, RUBY? WE'RE LOSING HIM!" He tried to regain composure. "Let's get the wound clear, Ruby. Get some water from the bathroom."

She grabbed the pitcher and filled it. She returned to Rupert and Robert on the floor.

Rupert removed the towels and sheet. "Get it clear so we can see, pour the water."

Ruby stood frozen. "There's ... There's ... Too much blood."

Rupert clenched his teeth. "Clear, Ruby, we're losing him."

Still she couldn't move.

Finally, he screamed at her. "CLEAR DAMMIT, HE'S DYING!"

This broke the catatonic state. She poured the water.

Suddenly he grasped his breath. The floating sensation was gone, and air returned to his lungs like stinging, hot nettles. He couldn't breathe fast enough. Gasping for air as if his lungs would burst, he couldn't breathe deep enough.

"We've got him."

He opened his eyes and saw someone with a stethoscope leaning over him.

He was going to live, he thought to himself. *He didn't have to fight anymore. They would save him.* He lay back and relaxed as consciousness slipped away. *He would rest now. It was over, and everything was all right. He would be OK.*

* * *

He didn't know how long he'd been asleep, but regaining consciousness had been a struggle. His first awareness was that of odd sounds and disembodied voices discussing his condition. As he began to recover his senses, the sound proximity became more distinct. Finally, becoming lucid enough to open his eyes, he looked around the room.

He was in a hospital of some sort. The wall to his left was all glass with a door on the right-hand side. His room and several others opened onto a circular nurse's station which lay beyond the door. The layout resembled a wagon wheel configuration.

Apparently monitoring his blood pressure, a nurse stood over him in the room.

"Blood pressure is 120/85. He's stable."

"Blood gases?"

"Within normal range."

He turned his head and looked at the attending nurse. A man who seemed to be a physician was standing beside her.

She smiled at him. "Welcome back. We thought we may have lost you."

He tried to sit up but was too weak. As he managed to prop up on his elbows, his head began to spin.

"Easy now, your body's been through a lot. You were in an accident. Lay back and try to relax."

He managed to utter, "Where am I?"

"You're in St. Christopher's Hospital. You're in CCU."

"What?"

"You were in an accident, Dr. Creighton. You apparently fell asleep at the wheel on your way home from work, and there was a rear end collision." Smoothing his sheet and blanket, the nurse straightened his covers. "It was touch and go there for awhile. We thought we were going to lose you. You coded several times en route to the hospital."

"NO!"

"It's OK," she whispered. "The other driver is fine. Try to relax …"

"NO!" Brad said again as he managed to sit up in bed. The pace of the monitor began to increase.

"Please, Dr. Creighton … please lie down. You're not well. You took a bad blow to the head and …"

"You don't understand. My wife …"

"She's fine." The nurse put a hand on each shoulder and tried gently to guide him back down. "She was just here."

He resisted. "My wife … She's in danger. He'll kill her. I HAVE TO GET TO HER … OUR BABY! WE'RE GOING TO HAVE A BABY!"

The attending physician turned to the nurse. "I wasn't aware Mrs. Creighton was pregnant."

"I don't think she is …" The nurse began again. "Please calm down, Dr. Creighton. We can get your wife in here if you like. I'll have someone call her right away and let her know you're conscious."

"What day is this?"

"It's Friday."

"What year?"

The doctor and nurse looked at each other as he said this. She answered. "Two Thousand Three"

"Oh God. OH GOD! I have to go back. I have to get back there. She's all alone … She needs me …" He began to climb out of bed.

"No, Dr. Creighton, you can't do this. You have to lie down." She began to subdue him.

"Get off of me! They'll kill her! Get your fucking hands off of me!" He began forcefully to push her away.

The doctor turned to the doorway. "We need help in here! Get an orderly, STAT!"

While urging him to lie down, they both tried to subdue him. "I NEED A SEDATIVE, NOW!"

With syringe and vial in hand, a nurse ran from the station. She drew up the medicine and inserted the needle into his I.V.

"NO! DON'T! YOU DON'T UNDERSTAND, PLEASE!"

Missing the "first pass" effect of the liver, medicines injected from an I.V. take effect immediately. Becoming awkward and lethargic, his movements slowed.

"Let me go. … I have to get to her." The words were slurred, and he was crying. The doctor and nurse gently coerced him to lie down. Finally, he did so, quietly moaning and crying. After a few moments, he was silent.

As he fell asleep, the doctor looked over him. "That should do it for now."

The nurse turned to him. "What about when he awakens? We may have the same problem."

"Get his wife in here and call a psychiatrist. I have a feeling he'll need one."

CHAPTER FIFTY-SEVEN

Dr. Raymond Salter had been on staff at St. Christopher's for some twenty-odd years. Well respected among his peers, he was usually the authoritative word on psychiatric matters at hand. More times right than wrong, his guesses were often better educated than diagnoses straight from the textbook. He'd been called to consult on the Creighton case, and was asked to piece together a plausible diagnosis for Brad's bizarre behavior. After examining the chart entries at length, and consulting with the staff on what had transpired, he'd agreed to meet with Jennifer Creighton to discuss Brad's condition and possible treatment modalities. Included in this examination was careful attention to the various drug therapies instituted since he'd been admitted.

His office was stark but tasteful. Although the walls were painted beige, the effect was softened somewhat with a tasteful splattering of abstract watercolors displayed in just the right spaces. Brown leather furniture provided seating, and also managed to warm the atmosphere a little. Jennifer had been asked to wait there until Dr. Salter finished his rounds. She'd been waiting about forty minutes when he finally appeared in the doorway.

He smiled. "I'm Raymond Salter. Sorry you had to wait."

She stood up. "I'm Jennifer Creighton, Brad's wife."

He had a stack of papers in the hand that extended toward her. "Please sit down ... keep your seat."

She sat back down. "Dr. Salter, I'd like to get right to the point."

"Please do."

"The hospital called about an hour ago and informed me that my husband has regained consciousness."

"That's correct."

"I understand there was an altercation."

"There was an altercation, and I believe your husband became anxious."

Jennifer was quiet for a moment. "I wish I had been there."

"They have him heavily sedated, Mrs. Creighton. He'll probably sleep through the night."

"I went ahead and brought my things. I plan to sleep here tonight as well."

"I'm sure he'll be glad to see you when he awakens."

As if in thought, she paused another moment and then began again. "Have you had a chance to review my husband's case?"

Dr. Salter took a seat at his desk. "Mrs. Creighton,"

"Please call me Jennifer."

He continued. "I've studied your husband's case thoroughly. I've consulted with the attending neurologist on this case, as well as the cardiologist, Dr. William Blaughton. As you know, his heart stopped for a brief period en route to the hospital. However, we've gone over his MRI, his MRA, and his X-rays carefully. All of his vitals are good, and his reflexes are fine. He seems to be improving daily. He's pretty banged up, but we're in agreement that chances are there is no permanent neurological damage. His heart is strong. The only reason we can fathom he coded is due to severe emotional trauma sustained as a result of the accident. In other words, that accident literally scared him to death. I feel the effects of this trauma are still manifesting themselves."

He paused for a moment, swallowed and began again. "Your husband is suffering from a condition we refer to as Post Traumatic Stress Syndrome."

Jennifer took a deep breath and repeated what Dr. Salter had said. "Post Traumatic Stress Syndrome ..."

Dr. Blaughton and Dr. McKey have also asked to consult with you on his heart and neurological findings, and they'll give you a more detailed analysis of his actual physical condition. I'm mainly here to deal with the emotional crisis at hand."

"Brought on by the accident, I presume."

"It was definitely the triggering factor." His eyes fixed as if deep in thought, he was looking straight ahead. Something broke the deep contemplation, after which he returned his glance toward her. "His body has been though a great deal of physical as well as emotional stress. Unfortunately, this can take a toll on many different biological processes. There is good news, however. The condition is treatable, and with time and therapy, the patient will usually recover."

"I'm willing to do whatever it takes."

"You'll need patience, Jennifer. He may never emerge exactly the same person he was, so you may have some adjusting to do as well."

"So … Where do we start?"

Dr. Salter smiled. "At the beginning. Be loving, understanding and try not to get your feelings hurt too easily. As a result of his own frustrations, he'll probably lash out at you from time to time. It will pass. Just give him some time and hang in there."

Jennifer smiled. "I plan to. I have to … he's my husband. I'm in this to the end, Dr. Salter, and I'm ready to put our life back on track."

"And you shall."

Jennifer turned to leave. "Well, it was nice meeting you, and thank you for consulting with me on this."

"It was my pleasure."

Headed toward the elevator, Jennifer left his office. As she left, Dr. Salter closed the door behind her.

* * *

She had packed her things before leaving for the hospital. Visitation was at six A.M., therefore, she planned to spend the night in the CCU waiting room. Wrapped in a blanket, she settled—with book in hand—into a chair in front of the television.

The slightest touch upon her shoulder awakened her. A bit disoriented, she stirred as the CCU nurse approached. "He's coming to. I thought you may want to be there."

"Is it six o'clock already?"

"No, Mrs. Creighton, it's only four-thirty. As I said, he's coming to. Would you like to go into the room?"

"Thank you. Thank you so much." She quickly gathered her things and followed the nurse into the unit. After passing the double doors, Brad's room was the second in the circle on the right. As she approached the room, she could see him lying awake. Lying on his left side, he was facing the window, but didn't bother to acknowledge her as she walked past the window into the room. She smiled and waved.

"Good morning, sleepyhead!" She walked over to him and kissed his forehead.

He looked at her as she approached. After she'd kissed him, he turned over onto his back. He winced in pain. "Good Morning. How long have I been out?"

"Since sometime last night, Brad. You've been unconscious for a few days now. The doctor said you were extremely upset when you awakened, and they had to sedate you."

"I remember."

"You do?"

"I remember everything."

Jennifer began to stroke his forehead with her fingertips. "Well, I for one am glad you decided to rejoin the 'land of the living.'"

"I didn't decide. It was decided for me. I had no choice in the matter." Brad had returned his gaze to the glass window once again.

She did her best to hold back the tears. It was a good try, but somehow the effort was lost. "I don't know what I would have done if you hadn't made it."

Showing no emotion, he continued to stare at the glass.

"I prayed for you, Brad. I prayed for this ... that you would recover. I dreamed about you ... sometimes it seemed so real."

He turned his face toward her. "I know. I was there."

Jennifer did not answer the knowing look. Her hand now resting atop his chest, she simply smiled again.

He winced in pain. "Ouch." He then tried to sit up but managed only to prop up on his pillow.

"Oh, honey, I'm sorry." Realizing that his chest felt hot, she gently rubbed her fingertips across his skin. Freeing the first two buttons of his gown, she discovered the smooth skin of his chest was fiery red in color. Two circumscribed lesions marked the spots on which the doctor had placed the defibrillator paddles. "It looks like they burned you with those paddles. We need to put some cream on these."

"So I did get shocked in the front yard. I knew I wasn't crazy."

"No, darling, they used those paddles in the ambulance. Your heart stopped en route to the hospital."

"I wish it had stayed that way."

Her expression hardened as he said this. It was a sharp, jagged comment and she'd had enough. "Look at me, Brad."

He turned his gaze back to the glass window.

She began anyway. "I don't regret that you're going to be OK. I begged God. I bargained with him and promised him everything I could think of for your life. I'd have sold my soul to get you back."

"No, you wouldn't have. You don't have that option."

Lowering her voice as she spoke, she bent down closer to him. "This doesn't affect only you. How do you think it feels suddenly to be faced with the reality that you're a single parent? To have a daughter who will never know her father? I would have to be mother and father to her, making all of the decisions for her future by myself. Do you think that would have been easy? How about fair? Do you really think you have the right to make that wish now, Brad?"

He turned toward her. "You broke through, you know. I knew you were there. I knew you wanted me back."

Jennifer stared at him for a moment. "I didn't know how I was going to tell that little girl her daddy had died." Walking across the room toward the chair, she turned away from him. "You can tell her some day that you didn't want to come back."

He half smiled—not a happy smile but one of irony. "I have a bad habit of dying on my children, don't I?"

Before she spoke again, Jennifer wiped her eyes and cleared her throat. "Like it or not, you're still very much alive." She then gathered her things and began to walk toward the doorway.

Facing the window, Brad had turned back on his side once again. He looked over his right shoulder. "You're leaving?"

"It's still very early. I'm going home to check on Caroline. Try to get some sleep and I'll see you at noon visitation. If all goes well, they may put you in a room tomorrow."

Waiting for her to leave the room, Brad said nothing else. Sleep would bring some relief. He'd try to rest for now.

CHAPTER FIFTY-EIGHT

Wednesday, December 17, 2003

Recovery had been a slow, gradual process. Physically, he had recovered from most of the injuries sustained in the wreck. Emotionally, the healing process was an ongoing battle. He gained ground some days, and at times, he regressed. Patterning his day to day routines after a life he'd known before the accident, he managed to resume his practice of dentistry. The attempt was in good faith, but realistically was just a facade concealing an empty, forlorn individual. Of course, he loved his wife and daughter; that was never the issue. The issue was in fact a lack of closure, resulting from an experience, which had traumatized and changed his existence forever. If he had awakened with no memory of it, maybe he could have resumed his ordinary life. Perhaps he would have been happy as before, but having to live without knowledge of the outcome of so much, left him riddled with anxiety. Fate had dealt him a hand he did not deserve, and as a result, he felt angry and cheated

"Dr. Creighton?"

His train of thought was broken. His assistant was standing at the doorway of his office. Raising his eyebrows in anticipation of her pending statement, he looked at her.

"Your patient is ready."

"How does my book look Friday?"

"Last time I checked, it was full. Why do you ask?"

"Ask Megan to clear it, and clear Monday as well. I will be out of town."

"OK ..." Processing the instructions he'd just given her, she stood there for a moment. "I'll get right on that." She turned to walk toward the front of the office. "If it's all right with you, I may just take a vacation day Friday."

"I don't care."

"By the way, you know that your patient is ready?"

"I heard you the first time."

She didn't answer. She simply left and made her way to the front office.

As a rule, he'd been rather short with the staff since the accident. His wife had asked that they please be patient while he recovered. It was difficult at times, but they managed.

He arose from his desk and walked toward the operatory. As he entered the room, he realized that taking this trip might be therapeutic. *The psychiatrist had not been of any help so far. Hell, more than anything, he aggravated him with all of those stupid questions. Maybe this weekend would bring some closure. Maybe it would be a small step toward recovery. He hoped so, anyway, as it was time for him to move on.*

* * *

Usually, the evening meal was prepared by the time he arrived home. They ate early in order to give him a chance to exercise before bed. As he walked through the doorway, he saw Jennifer was putting the last of the food on the table. She smiled when he entered the room.

"How was your day?"

"It was a day."

"Were you busy?"

"Always." He walked over to the kitchen sink to wash his hands. "Jennifer?"

"Yeah, Brad?"

"I know what I want for Christmas this year."

She laughed. "You're waiting kind of late to tell me; it's next week. I've done all of my shopping, dear husband. What's on your mind?"

"I need to get away. Maybe the two of us could get away for a weekend."

"Sounds like a good Christmas gift for both of us. Perhaps we can do something in January."

"This weekend. I've taken Friday off of work. I've marked Monday off as well."

"Brad, be reasonable. Next week is Christmas. Who will keep Caroline?"

"Your parents."

"How do you know that? We haven't even asked them yet. They may have plans."

"If you don't go with me, I'll go by myself."

"Well, I don't know if I can go or not. You suddenly decide we have to leave town and that's that—the plans are made. It doesn't work that way."

"I'm going."

"I haven't packed … you haven't packed. I have to get food for the baby …"

"Whatever."

"Well then go. If all I get is *whatever*, then *whatever* you have to do, do it. I'll stay here with Caroline. We'll be fine by ourselves."

"I didn't mean that how it sounded."

"Yes, you did."

"No, I didn't. Please come with me. I want you to come with me."

She let out a long, exasperated sigh. "Let me call Mother to see if she'll keep Caroline. I'll have to line up a babysitter as well." She walked over to the refrigerator and opened it. "I'll also have to do some grocery shopping so my parents will have food here." She closed the refrigerator door and walked from the room.

* * *

After a bit, she returned to the kitchen. "It just occurred to me that I don't even know where we're going. How am I supposed to know what to pack?"

"Conway, Arkansas."

"Conway, Arkansas? That's where we're going?" She was silent for a moment.

"When you said get away for the weekend, I was thinking more along the lines of New Orleans or Biloxi. We could even do Gulf Shores in a weekend. Where is Conway, Arkansas?"

"It's about four hours drive from here."

"And the reason we're going there?"

"Conway holds some answers for me, Jen. There are some things I need to know. If I'm to get better, I have some issues that need to be resolved."

"Well, if you feel this trip will help you, then by all means let's go. Do we have a place to stay?"

"No. I'll get on the Internet and make some reservations at the Rosalind."

"The Rosalind?"

"The Rosalind Hotel. It's down on Front Street."

"Since when do you know your way around Conway? Correct me if I'm wrong, but you've never been there before."

"I knew someone from Conway a long time ago, Jen, pretty well in fact."

"Who?"

"I ... It's ..." In an attempt to put this in context, he stammered for a moment. "It's someone I knew a long time ago."

She paused to see if there was more ... there wasn't. "And apparently you don't want to elaborate on this any further, do you?"

"You wouldn't understand. I'm not even sure if I do. I sure as hell didn't plan to, anyway. Why don't we drop this for now?"

"OK, then I guess the only thing left for me to do is to pack. I've talked to Mother, by the way. She said they did have plans, but they're coming to keep Caroline anyway."

"That's not necessary. Call them and tell them to go ahead with their plans. We'll take her with us."

"No, they just didn't want me here in town by myself. I have it all arranged." She turned to leave again. "Go ahead and eat your supper before it gets cold."

He walked over to the table. "Looks good."

"There's dessert in the refrigerator if you want it. Your mom sent Chess pie."

He stopped abruptly and turned around. "She sent what?"

"Chess pie."

"You're kidding me."

"No, I'm not. Why would I kid about a thing like that? It's your very favorite."

"Who told you that?"

"Oh my God ... Now we have issues with Chess pie?"

"No, no issues, I just don't know who dreamed up the fact that I like Chess pie. I mean, this whole fucking universe seems to think that."

"Well I, for one, didn't have to fuck the universe to find that out, Brad. Your mother was the one who told me. As for who dreamed up the fact that you like Chess pie, your shoveling it in that big mouth of yours like it's your last meal would lead one to believe that you actually liked it. Maybe that's why your mother bakes them for you."

"I guess I'll never get away from that shit."

"Then why don't you call your Mom and tell her that; I'm sure that it'll make her feel good. Now if we're done with Chess pie, I'm off to pack."

She said nothing else and walked from the room.

Brad watched her leave. *There she goes again. She just has to have that last smart-ass word followed by a big, dramatic exit ...*

CHAPTER FIFTY-NINE

Seventy-one years ... In a matter of a few weeks and two lifetimes, he'd been away from Conway, Arkansas for seventy-one years. He smiled. Let Dr. Salter analyze that one. Seventy-one years away from Conway may confirm the doctor's suspicions that he really had cracked up.

He was both anxious and apprehensive about returning to Conway. It wouldn't be comforting. Everything would be different. If still existing, familiar places would be old now. He was a stranger to Conway, a stranger to a place from which he was ripped against his will. How bizarre that he was a stranger in his own hometown and yet he'd never been there before!

"A penny for your thoughts."

"They're worth a lot more than that. Use a credit card."

"It's maxed out."

"Hmmmm. OK, write a hot check then. I'll cover it Tuesday."

"It had better be some serious thinking for all of that."

"I was thinking about Conway and what it would be like."

"From what I've read, it seems like a nice place ... Not too much of a vacation destination, though. However, it does have some interesting history. I bought a book. It's a pictorial with the history of the city interwoven."

"I'd love to read it when we reach the hotel."

"You have reservations at the Rosalind?"

"No, apparently the Rosalind burned some years ago. The Chamber of Commerce directed me to the Cambridge Inn. It's one of those chains—nothing fancy—but has the usual stuff."

"Ooh … Chocolate-covered almonds, microwave popcorn and diet cola … I can hardly wait."

"So sincere."

"Maybe they'll even have pay per view movies."

"Your darker side is emerging."

She laughed as she looked at her watch. "Well, you were right. Four hours and we're almost there. I don't think you're supposed to turn here, though. Stay on the interstate."

"We're taking a little detour."

"What detour?"

"You'll see."

* * *

Located southeast of Conway, Arkansas, Oak Grove Cemetery was old and rich in cultural history. The place was well maintained, with lush, rolling hills gleaming in the afternoon sun. Beautifully landscaped, a meditation chapel stood near the center of the graveyard. A glass atrium connected the chapel to the mausoleum. Vases—most of which contained fresh flowers—adorned each crypt in the structure.

Much of the history and genealogy of Conway could be found in the back of the cemetery. Remarkably, some of the granite monuments had remained intact throughout the years.

"A graveyard? This is the detour? A cemetery?"

"Maybe detour was the wrong word to use. This is our first stop."

"How romantic!"

"Now Jennifer, think back for just a moment. This isn't supposed to be a romantic getaway. This is a 'Brad has issues trip,' remember?"

"I know, Brad, but Mom has Caroline, and I was hoping we could make this a little getaway weekend for both of us. This is fine, though, the graveyard and all …"

Brad sighed. "Oh God … Let's just give me a break here …"

"It's fine, really. Let's just do what we need to do …" Focusing her gaze beyond the passenger's window, she turned her back to him.

He waited a few moments for her to turn back around. When it was obvious she had no intentions of doing so, he muttered, "Whatever …"

Ahead of them, he saw the main entrance to the cemetery. Slowly, he turned the car onto the main road. "It's so different now. The roads are all paved."

Her gaze still fixed beyond the window, she didn't answer.

"If I remember correctly, the plots are toward the back of the cemetery. There was a gravel road to the left ... it must be this road here." Brad maneuvered the SUV around the winding cemetery road. After a bit of frustration and several wrong turns, he managed to make his way to the rear of the graveyard.

"Here it is, I think." He left the car and began walking toward a large, granite monument lying on the rear border of the cemetery.

Jennifer lowered the window. "Where are you going?"

"To walk for a while."

"Do you want me to come with you?"

"No, probably not."

A small silence. "Well, I have a book, so go ahead. Take your time. I'll just sit here and read. I'll move the car if by chance someone needs to pass."

"I won't be long."

* * *

I guess this is my first taste of seventy-one years of change. The place looks nothing as it did before. Wandering about for several minutes, he began to walk in what he thought would be the general direction of the graves. Jennifer would occasionally drive by to check and see if he was OK.

Finally, he found his bearings. Much of the Davis family was interred in this part of the cemetery; he did remember that much. Here, he would find answers and resolution to a saga that began so long ago.

The shape of the tombstone caught his attention. Over the years, time has a way of weathering stone, but somehow, more than one-half century later, the engraving had remained legible. "My father's grave," he mumbled aloud. Before him was a large, granite monument. Rectangular in shape, an eternal flame was etched into the center of the stone. Two names were inscribed upon it. "Ned Davis," he said to himself. He looked to the right of the stone. "Lila Davis … So it was real. I didn't imagine anything." His heart began to pound. "I bought two plots about a half acre from here." He turned to his left and began searching for them.

Reading various headstones, he walked a bit. Some of them looked familiar, and many of them did not. As he climbed a small hill, he spied a woman pulling weeds. Working around the grave, she'd evidently just arranged a beautiful basket of silk flowers. He watched her place the bouquet before the tombstone.

Probably approaching seventy years of age, she was an older lady. Obviously, she was once beautiful, for she had smooth, ivory-colored skin with few—if any—wrinkles.

Cut above her ears in a fashionable bob, her hair was white. She must have grayed prematurely, as her hair was that lovely shade of platinum, which only comes with untimely gray. Perhaps it's some recompense from Mother Nature for the early demise of youth.

There was something very natural about this woman. She didn't wear much makeup or fussy jewelry. She was simply dressed—not to say her tastes were not stylish by any means, they were fashionably plain.

As he walked by, she smiled. "Hello."

He froze. Behind her, the tombstone read,

Ruby Davis Staten
Born: December 19, 1907
Died: January 28, 1988
Beloved wife and mother
You are gone but never forgotten
The Remnant is done

"Oh God."

The woman turned around. "Excuse me?"

Not knowing what to say, Brad stood there a moment. Finally, he managed a smile.

"I'm sorry."

A little weaker than before, she returned the smile. "I'm tending my mother's grave. It's her birthday. I'm trying to freshen it with some flowers and a bit of weed removal."

"I was ..." He paused, as the words he needed to express his thoughts had left him. Standing here, in front of a former existence, felt much like standing in front of a glass house. The abode was once his home, and yet, now he was forced from it. He could only observe the conclusions of this previous lifetime from afar. Brad had an empty, bizarre feeling that no individual should endure. None of this could have been planned. He had to have been a victim of circumstance. His distant gaze was broken as his thoughts returned to him.

He decided to try again. "I was searching for some of my family here ... some of my ancestors I guess I should say."

"Well, I've lived here all of my life. Maybe I can help."

"That's very kind of you, but I think I've found them." He pointed in the direction in which he'd come. "Lila and Ned Davis, they're over there."

She straightened and stood up after he'd said this. "Whom did you say?"

"Lila and Ned Davis."

"Well then, we must be related. Those were my grandparents. I don't guess I caught your name."

"Forgive me. I'm Brad Creighton."

"I'm Roberta Staten, Brad. I don't recall my mother mentioning any Creightons in our family tree. What was your mother's maiden name?"

"Spillman."

She stood for a moment in thought. "Doesn't ring a bell, either. You're sure you have the right family tree?"

"Yes, I'm sure."

Not really knowing what to say or do next, he stood there nonplused. Finally, he uttered, "Your mother was a beautiful woman."

Staring at him as he spoke, she stood quiet. After a bit, she answered him. "Yes, she was."

More silence.

"May I ask you a question?"

"I guess that would be alright."

"That's a strange epitaph on her tombstone."

"That sounds more like a statement than a question, Brad."

"Or a roundabout way of asking about it."

"Not so round about, there's enough there to read between the lines."

Brad and Roberta stared at each other knowingly. "You came to Conway for a reason, didn't you?"

"I did come for a reason."

"And I suspect your reason for being here lies in that question about the epitaph."

His eyes widened.

"No one ever understood that epitaph, Brad. Many years ago, long before I came into this world, the story of that epitaph began. My Grandmother Lorna—my mother's mother—told me of an incident which allegedly happened at a monument place here in town. The owner of the place, I think his name was Cecil something or other ..."

"Ullman."

She stopped in amazement. "Yes, that's right, Cecil Ullman. One day, right out of the blue, Cecil Ullman warned my grandmother that my father would soon die. He said this epitaph—the one you see on my mother's grave—his birthday and the date of his death appeared on a blank headstone. He swore no one put it there, that it just appeared from nowhere. Gams dismissed it as hogwash until my father was indeed killed the very day Cecil had predicted. Gams never quite got over that."

Brad breathed deeply and sighed.

"Mother never really did, either. She grieved for my father in a small private way until she died. She insisted on having this epitaph on her headstone. It's a pity that none of us has ever known what it meant. We've only had the history behind its appearance."

Brad said nothing. Tears were streaming down his cheeks.

Roberta set down the spade and took off her gardening gloves. She walked over to him. "She said you'd come, you know. She said our paths might cross one day."

"That means she believed me. She believed what I told her."

Roberta pointed to the epitaph. "You know what this means, don't you."

He shook his head yes.

"You'll tell me?"

"I don't know, Roberta. I could try, but it's a long, difficult story that even I have trouble processing. I cannot fully deal with it, and I'm an emotional mess. That's why I'm here. I'm trying to get well." Brad wiped his face with his hands.

"Here," she said as she reached into her purse. "Have a tissue. Have two."

Clearing his throat in an attempt to compose himself, he took them. "Roberta?"

She looked at him expectantly.

"You've had a good life?"

"I've had a good life."

"You never married, I guess."

She smiled. "My husband and I just celebrated our fiftieth anniversary this year."

"I thought you said your name was Staten ..."

"I did say that, didn't I? I practiced medicine for more than forty years as a pediatrician. I've now since retired, but I guess Dr. Roberta Staten is a hard habit to break."

Brad smiled at this. "So ... your father was a Staten?"

"Rupert Staten. He was actually my stepfather. He reared me as his own, though. He was a wonderful father. I was four-years-old before my parents married. Mother used to tell me 'after four years he finally wore her down.'" Roberta laughed aloud. Actually, it was a bit of a chuckle of remembrance. "She said he just wouldn't go away."

"God ... you got that right." Brad swallowed hard after he'd said this. "So, apparently he found work here in Conway?"

"He was an artist by trade, and had a little New Orleans gallery that his family managed for him. He also taught art at the University here in Conway. My dad was fabulously talented, Brad. He painted my brother and I every year of our lives until we were grown."

"A brother ..."

"James Rupert Staten. We're five years apart. James is a chemical engineer in Detroit."

"Maybe just one more question, Roberta?"

She smiled sympathetically. "I suppose it wouldn't hurt anything."

"Do you have any children?"

"I do. I have two girls and a boy. I also have five beautiful grand-children as well."

Brad's eyes were drawn back to the grave. The name Robert Davis was inscribed on the same headstone as Ruby Davis Staten. "Your father's not buried here, I see."

"Heavens no! Daddy never felt he really belonged in Conway. Mother's love was the only thing that kept him here. He died three years before my mother did. Most of the Statens are buried in St. Louis Cemetery in New Orleans, and Daddy asked that we bury him there as well. He knew Mother's wishes for burial and never intruded upon them."

Brad continued to look at the tombstone. He didn't say much. As tears continued to stream down his face, he just looked on. "I guess this is the end of the story, then."

"Not quite. Perhaps you could join us for dinner tonight? Maybe you can solve a lifelong mystery I've resigned myself to never knowing. I lie in bed sometimes creating scenarios for the epitaph, wondering how close I may really come to the truth."

"If not tonight, maybe tomorrow night. I'll ask my wife Jennifer. I'll shed some light on your mystery, Roberta, but be warned it's not a good story."

She took a pad from her purse and wrote her phone number. "Here is my number, Brad. Please call."

CHAPTER SIXTY

Thursday, December 25, 2003

The leaves were now falling, giving the holiday season an autumn feel more than that of winter.

Christmas this year was unseasonably warm, which wasn't much of a late December oddity anymore. Jennifer could well remember many past Christmases in shorts, and judging from recent winter weather trends, the days of frigid holiday weather seemed uncertain at best.

The house was decorated beautifully. Christmas trees, complete with white lights and color-coordinated ornaments, adorned each room. Both dining tables were elegantly set with red glassware and festive Christmas china, while the bookshelves provided a fine backdrop for the fifties era Christmas Village. Christmas CDs, along with strategically placed scented candles, ensured the sounds and smells of Christmas were everywhere.

From Santa this year, Caroline was the clear winner. Presents for her abounded across the living room. Both sets of parents were due to arrive around noon, as Jennifer had invited everyone to enjoy a fabulous Christmas feast.

The doorbell rang. Her parents had arrived.

"Merry Christmas!"

Jennifer held the baby in her arms as she attempted a hug from them both.

Her daddy smiled. "Let me have my baby."

Caroline held her arms toward him. Conversing with her about all the goodies Santa had brought, he walked into the house.

As they stood in the doorway, her mother said, "How are you doing, honey?"

Jennifer closed the door behind them.

"We're doing OK, Mom. Things are much better, and life finally seems to be moving on."

"And Brad? How is he?"

"I think the trip did him some good. He ran into some old friends—I guess that's what you'd call them—in Conway. We spent most of our weekend with them."

"Them?"

"An older couple from Conway. The lady was a pediatrician and the husband owned some sort of business there. I can't remember what exactly he did for a living, but they were very nice. She and Brad managed to talk for hours."

"How odd."

"Yes, odd because I don't think before this trip they'd ever met. To see them together, you'd think they were long, lost friends. I don't try to understand anymore, Mother. I quit doing that a long time ago. My life is almost normal now, and I want to keep it that way. I don't rock the boat … I just go with it." Jennifer took her mother's hand and led her through the dining room. "Here, come into the kitchen. I have some Wassail warming for you on the stove."

"Sounds delicious."

Most of the guests arrived shortly after twelve. After they had eaten, the ladies congregated in the kitchen to put away the leftover food. The men, plus Caroline, huddled in the den to digest the feast and male-bond while watching the football game. With Caroline plopped on Pa Paw's belly, the end result was an afternoon nap.

Around three o'clock, all awakened for the opening of gifts. As presents were distributed, wrapping paper accumulated in heaps upon the floor. Clearing the boxes, tissue, and torn paper, Jennifer policed the room with a trash bag. The gift ceremony usually signaled an end to the Christmas celebration; as kisses and hugs were passed, the family left to return home. Exhausted, Jennifer and Brad flopped on the couch.

"Another Christmas."

"Another Christmas, Brad. Next year, Santa will be part of this celebration as well. If you think you're tired now ..."

"Well, I have a whole year to recuperate."

"Good. I have a feeling you'll need it. That little firecracker is a bundle of energy. She's going to enjoy Santa."

"Well, now I think I'll grab a shower."

"Oh, Brad ..."

"Yeah?"

"You have one more gift."

He smiled. "You sneaky little thing. What do you have there?" He walked over to her and held out his hand.

She handed him a small square box wrapped in shiny gold foil. A luscious, silken, green bow enveloped the tiny package. "So fancy ..."

"This one is not from me. There is a story behind this gift."

As she spoke, he tore the paper away from the gift. Inside was a leather box. Aged and worn, a faded gold emblem adorned the lid. As he realized he well recognized the box, a streak of panic ran through him.

He interrupted her. "Where did you get this?"

"I was going to tell you. You know my friend Karen Belle, don't you?"

"Yeah, I know her. Her husband is the CPA ..."

"Right. She and I were at the mall Tuesday doing some last minute shopping. I think it was around seven in the evening. Anyway, before heading home, we stopped for a drink at Esmerelda's."

"And ... ?" He raised his eyebrows as if to say, "Hurry up!"

"This woman walks over to our table and asks me if I were Mrs. Bradley Creighton. I had never seen her before in my life."

"What did she look like?"

"She was beautiful. Short, and very thin, she had shoulder-length auburn hair. Decked to the nines, Brad. We're talking five thousand-dollar silk-tweed suit. Trust me, I know. I've been to the clothing shows."

It couldn't be ... That old familiar feeling of dread returned. "What did she say to you, Jen?"

"She handed me this gift and said, 'This is for your husband. Tell him I said thank-you, and that I'm returning it to him. I don't need it anymore.'"

"God, help us all."

"God help us all? Why do we need God to help us with this? What's the deal?"

He said nothing as he opened the box. In it was a small Lucite case encircling a 1907 twenty-dollar gold piece.

"It's a coin. 1907 ... almost a hundred years of age. I'll bet it's valuable, Brad."

He turned to look at her. "It was invaluable at one time, but not anymore ... not to me, anyway."

CHAPTER SIXTY-ONE

Dear Roberta:

Enclosed, find the final piece of the puzzle that you and I have spent the better part of seventy years solving. You heard me describe it in detail, and now, through an incredible sequence of events, it has made its way back to me. I personally consider it an icon of Hell, for it has brought nothing but pain and despair into my life from the moment it entered my existence.

Being that it was a wedding gift from your mother to your father, I feel this piece is rightfully yours. I also feel it is my duty to make you aware of the powers associated with this piece, but to do that, and to convey the magnitude of its possible impact on our lives, we must visit face to face. I hope there is no impact, but the experiences of both my recent and distant pasts will not allow me to assure you of that fact. I ask that you put this away in a safe place and tell no one that you have it. There are those who would recognize its signature, thus perpetuating the havoc it has wreaked throughout the ages.

Take care, Roberta. Our paths will cross again soon.

Sincerely yours:
Brad Creighton

✳ ✳ ✳

"What is that, Roberta?"

"It's a package from that young fellow we met at the cemetery."

"Hmmm. A twenty-dollar gold-piece … Looks valuable. Why on earth would he send it to you?"

Feeling it was unnecessary to elaborate further, she merely replied, "It's a gift."

"Maybe we ought to have it appraised. Might be worth something?"

She shook her head. "No … I think it's going into my safe deposit box with my father's journal. This one's value is better left untold."